TRUTHFINDER'S PROMISE

AN ASPECT SOCIETY NOVEL

MICHELLE MANUS

Truthfinder's Promise Copyright © June 2022 by Michelle Manus
ebook ISBN: 978-1-954400-16-0
Paperback ISBN: 978-1-954400-24-5
Publisher: Seclusion Publishing
Interior Design: Seclusion Publishing

CHAPTER

ONE

Why did every important man in Meredith Townsend's life have to have a name that started with *J*?

Jared Townsend, loving father, deceased. Jace Savage, ex-boyfriend, now married to one of her two best friends. Julian Astor, generally terrible person, currently the scourge of her existence. Jensen King, hotter-than-hell one-month fling who'd dropped her without so much as a farewell text.

Couldn't she have one, just *one*, loving family member, arch-nemesis, or ex-lover whose name started with a nice *S* or *T* or something? Admittedly, Julian Astor wasn't an arch-nemesis so much as he was the creepy thorn in her side, but the distinction didn't make her any happier to see his name flash across her phone screen.

She silenced the call and let her head drop back on the marble sarcophagus beneath her. It was three-thirty in the morning and her insomniac ass was awake and hanging out in her dead mother's mausoleum.

The space was an opulent affair of white marble, complete with modern-style sarcophagus. Meredith liked to come here because the empty tomb reminded her that once, just once, she'd successfully denied one of Savannah Townsend's wishes and not paid a price for it.

The woman was dead, had been for over a year now, and Meredith had cremated her instead of laying her to rest in this monument she'd built to herself.

Laying to rest. It sounded so peaceful when put in those terms. If ghosts or spirits or any kind of afterlife did exist, Meredith sincerely hoped her mother's wasn't peaceful. Goddess knew she didn't deserve it.

On nights like tonight, when the little sleep Meredith had managed had been filled with dreams of her father's dying screams, she came here to remember. Not all of the terrible things her mother had done, but that she had lived through them. She had survived, and she'd managed one final defiance.

It wasn't the pain of old memories that called her here, but how here, in this barren tomb, she felt a hollow emptiness that approximated peace. That...and something about the place itself kept drawing her back. The feeling was an itch beneath her skin that wouldn't subside. She'd thought at first that the pull was magical in nature, but every time she swept the small chamber the only magic she found was her own.

Maybe she was growing morbid, all this time spent in graveyards. Any day now she might don a black dress and a cape and demand people start calling her "Mistress." She snorted at the thought. Her friends were already worried she was losing it, if the number of times Siren and Valkyrie called her "just to check in" were any indication.

Her phone rang again, flashing Julian's name.

Maybe she should do something about him. One word to her best friends, Siren and Valkyrie, and Meredith had no doubt the Council's security would make Julian's life so unpleasant he ceased to function as a normal human being.

She silenced the call, knowing she would never say anything

to Siren or Val. She didn't want other people solving her problems. Wasn't one of the glories of sobriety supposed to be feeling like you were in control of your own life? Except she'd started drinking at fifteen *because* she hadn't had any control. That, and because passing out was how she'd gotten to sleep.

So far all sobriety had done for her was remind her that she was useless, knock her down to an average of three fitful hours of non-consecutive sleep a night, and make her painfully aware that she needed to gain some weight back and maybe take up running for the sake of her cardiovascular health.

Her heels clicked on the marble floor as she swung her legs down. Couldn't take up running in heels. Not even in the two-inch ones she'd worked her way down to. Any day now she might swallow her pride and let Siren's Life Aspect fix the fact that if she stood flat-footed it felt like every shortened tendon and muscle in her calves was about to snap.

Sure. Any day now she might also sprout angel wings and go for a nice flight around town.

Her phone's ringtone started up, echoing off the walls.

Seriously? It was three-thirty in the freaking morning. She hadn't answered a phone call from Julian since the old Council, of which Julian had been a temporary member, had been disbanded and put on trial for illegal blood magic use. He'd gotten off with easy sentencing on account of not being a full-fledged councilor. He was free to live his life so long as he didn't leave Seclusion's town borders, and apparently living that life involved stalking her.

She climbed into her car and pointed it toward home.

Julian had been her mother's favorite lapdog, so Meredith had been forced to play nice with him when Savannah was alive. She'd continued to play nice after because it had become a habit, one she hadn't identified until she'd made actual friends again.

When she finally dropped him it only made Julian's attention increase, until he exhibited textbook stalker behavior. But she'd known there was something wrong with him long before then. It was in his eyes. You knew when he looked at someone he didn't see *them*. He saw a thing. An obstacle or tool or prize to be won.

She pulled into her drive and found the gate to her property blocked by a black BMW X5. A sliver of fear kicked her heart into a higher gear, the subsequent flood of adrenaline turning her hands shaky where they rested on the wheel and shifter.

The BMW's door opened and Julian stepped out. Meredith made sure her own doors were locked, popped the shifter in neutral, and rolled the window down a single inch. Julian stopped next to the driver's door, a line of displeasure creasing his face.

"Why aren't you answering your phone?" He was blandly handsome in that way wealth could make almost anyone, burying otherwise unremarkable brown hair and average features under a two-hundred dollar haircut and clothes tailored to accentuate a physique honed by hours in the gym. At first glance he could be any harmless businessman, doctor, or politician. But one look in those eyes, and anyone with a lick of sense would run for the hills.

"Because it's almost four in the morning."

"You're awake. Your phone is on."

"Do you know who I answer calls from at four in the morning? My friends or my lovers. You're neither."

"I could be."

Not bloody likely.

"May I come in? I was hoping we could talk."

"I have nothing to talk with you about."

"That isn't exactly true. I think we have a great deal to discuss. I also think you'll find it more pleasant if we have this conversation voluntarily."

So they had moved on to coercion via implied threats. Wonderful. "Go home, Julian. Before I decide to call Siren and have the Council's security remove you."

He smiled. "Ah, yes. Your new pocket politician. I couldn't

help but notice you quit taking my calls after she ascended the ranks. How long do you think she'll stand by you once she realizes you simply traded one friend in a high place for another?"

Meredith's fingers clenched on the steering wheel. "Is there a reason you're still here?"

Julian ignored the question, musing aloud. "And if she doesn't put that together, there's still the inevitable question of how long she'll be comfortable having you around. A woman can get so touchy about her husband's exes, and you weren't subtle when you failed to win Jace back."

And now he'd moved on to telling her she was soon to have no one left, and was a failure. She ignored the small voice whispering that he was probably right. "Siren isn't so insecure that she's threatened by me."

Julian *tsked*. He put his arm on the roof of the car and leaned in. "When your happy little pretend family comes crumbling down around you, when they realize that you're not worth it and you have no one else to turn to, I'll still be here. And when you find things tapping at your defenses and you wonder what I wanted to talk to you about, I'll answer the phone when you call."

He patted the hood of her car and walked away. She didn't take a full breath until he drove off, didn't open her gate until he'd been gone for over five minutes. She pulled just inside and waited until they closed behind her before driving on.

When you find things tapping at your defenses... His words followed her into the house, where the white walls and white furniture made everything feel cold and sterile. Everything in Savannah Townsend's house was white, and the woman might be dead but this was still her house.

Things *had* been tapping at Meredith's defenses. Little testing scritches and scratches at her wards over the last few months. Careful, always *so* careful, so as not to draw attention. But she'd noticed anyway. Because some part of her had always expected her mother's sins to come back to haunt her.

Which was why, even in the grips of her alcoholism, she'd sunk every spare drop of her Aspect into her property wards. They hummed along the perimeter, sure and steady, so strong it would take a double team of Breakers to crack them open. That, or a lot of people willing to die.

The knowledge did nothing to make her feel safe. Had it been Julian poking at her wards all these months? Or did he simply know who was doing it and want to trade information? Or maybe no one was testing her wards and she was just a paranoid woman, living alone in a too-big house that gave her the creeps.

If Julian had tested her defenses at all he would have felt how much power was in them and realized she was worried about something breaking in. He probably didn't know anything. He'd guessed at her fears and was using them to get what he wanted. That was all.

She dropped onto the couch and kicked her heels off, pulling one of her feet onto the opposite thigh so she could rub at the sore arch. Of all the things she hated her mother for, high heels probably shouldn't rank near the top of the list, but they did.

She'd been forced into her first pair at twelve. They'd gotten progressively higher year after year, and she'd been allowed so little time out of them that her muscles and tendons had shortened. Meredith was working to stretch them back out, but she didn't know if the lifelong damage was something she could undo on her own. She did know that if she tried to walk flat-footed right now, she'd end up on crutches for a couple of weeks. She'd tried, she'd failed, she had the crutches in the hall closet to prove it.

The white walls glared at her. Maybe she should paint them. Some color her mother would think entirely inappropriate for a living room. Like red or neon green or black. She had the notion that if she could somehow make this house *hers*—this house, where she'd grown up, where her father had died, where her mother had controlled her—she would somehow mend the broken parts of herself.

She just didn't know how to *make* it hers. Every time she thought of doing something like painting or buying new furniture, she saw her mother's superior sneer, heard her cold, condescending voice tell her that she could paint the walls like a rebellious teenager, but it wouldn't change anything. Because Meredith could alter the house but *she* would still be the same. And she was nothing.

Feeling maudlin, she slipped her heels back on and walked down to the basement. It was outfitted like a separate apartment within the home, complete with kitchen, laundry, and private entrance via a cellar-like door. Most of her admittedly few fond childhood memories were in this basement. Where her father had lived. Where he'd died.

"I miss you, Dad."

The house didn't answer. It never did.

Her phone rang. She picked it up, fully intending to turn the damn thing off, when she saw Valkyrie's name on the screen.

She answered. "Hey."

"Hey," Valkyrie's smooth voice rolled across the line. "What are you doing?"

"Standing in my basement, staring at the spot where my dad died." It occurred to her that if Valkyrie chose to go back to *her* childhood home, she too could stare at the spot where her dad died. The difference was, Valkyrie's father had been the monster in her family unit and she'd killed him herself.

"You need to move out of that house," Val said. It was a testament to their recently-renewed friendship—and how much Valkyrie understood her—that her best friend didn't tell her she needed a therapist.

Meredith undoubtedly *did* need one, but she'd tried it once and couldn't bring herself to go back. Her Aspect—Truthfinding —meant she could spot a lie from a mile away. And everything about therapy had felt like a lie. The practiced spiel of a person whose job it was to listen to her, to nod understandingly and say all the right things meant to urge her toward emotional recovery.

But the woman hadn't *meant* any of it. Underneath the veneer of kindness had been a bone-deep apathy, a tired ennui born from years of listening to people's problems and insecurities. Meredith didn't want to be anyone's problem. And she certainly didn't want to pay someone to listen to hers.

"Mer?" Val prompted.

"I'm not moving out."

"Why the fuck not? Getting out of my house was the best thing that ever happened to me."

Yes, well, you got out of your house and into the loving arms of your new husband, Meredith thought.

"I'm just not." Moving out felt too much like losing, like letting her mother win.

"Are you drinking?" Val asked.

"No." Meredith didn't take the question personally. "But while I appreciate you asking, I'm assuming you didn't call me at four in the morning to find out if I'm having a gin and tonic."

"I've got a lead on the last one. Enough for you to Track, I think."

The last one. Valkyrie's deceased father, Elijah Winters, had spent years secretly performing illegal experimentation on people's Aspect. Mostly children, because the power that ran in an Aspecter's veins was more malleable the younger they were, and because they were easier to control.

He'd gone undetected for most of his life, but his work had crashed into the public eye when Siren Savage had stumbled into Aspect Society. She'd been one of Elijah's first experiments, her power trapped inside her for most of her life, building up until she contained more power than anyone in the history of the Society. It was Siren who had made them aware that someone was performing illegal experiments, but it had been Valkyrie who'd discovered it was her own father. Discovered it, and taken care of the problem.

In the six months since Elijah's death, Siren, Valkyrie, and Meredith had spent practically every waking moment combing through his files, trying to find all of his victims. He'd fancied himself a scientist, and they'd eventually found a file buried deep in his cloud storage that held a dossier of every experiment he'd ever performed.

After sorting the dossiers into two piles—one for those that ended with the conclusion *deceased*, and one for all the others— they'd known how many kids they were looking for. Diligent cross-comparison of the facts within those files had led them to several of the locations where he'd worked and kept his subjects.

While a few of the victims had been placed in individual settings, most had been in group homes run like prison-style boarding schools. To date, they had tracked down eight locations and liberated fifty-eight children who varied in age between three and eighteen, most of whom now resided at The Refuge. It was a home and school Siren had founded for them, overrun with teachers, caretakers, and the therapists Meredith herself refused to see.

There were thirteen remaining dossiers. Thirteen kids they hadn't found yet. Based on similarities in the file notes, they were relatively certain only one facility remained.

"What did you find?" Meredith asked.

"A kid at The Refuge was apparently shuffled around to a few different locations before Elijah settled him long-term. His therapist realized one of the places he was describing wasn't any of the locations we'd already found."

"The therapist broke confidentiality?" That was a massive breach of trust, even for something as important as this.

"No. She told the kid what she thought and asked if he'd be willing to talk to us. He agreed."

"At four in the morning?"

"He had a nightmare and he's an empath with projection capabilities. He woke the whole damn house up, the therapist went to talk to him, out came her realization, and now I'm on the phone with you. So what do you say? Think you can Track a memory?"

Meredith shrugged, even though Val couldn't see the movement over the phone. She'd Tracked stranger things lately. "Anything's better than sitting here."

TWO

Valkyrie's Jeep Wrangler bounced over yet another bump in the alternately rutted and lumpy dirt road. In the passenger seat, Meredith's teeth clacked together. She needed one of those mouth guards boxers wore, so she could come out of this drive without cracking a tooth.

"Are you sure we're headed in the right direction?" Valkyrie asked.

Meredith didn't open her eyes to even confirm what direction they were traveling in. Tracking long-distance was most easily done with her eyes closed, following the steady tug of her Aspect without regular sight clouding her magical sight.

"Would I have driven halfway across the state in this hulking behemoth you call a vehicle if I wasn't sure?" Meredith missed the gorgeous purr of her Porsche Spyder's engine, the smooth shift of gears and the way it hugged the road's curves.

"I'm not questioning your superior Tracking prowess, Mer, no need to get in a snit."

"All I'm saying, *Val*," Meredith replied, a smile tugging at her lips, "is that if you drag someone out of bed with the excuse that they're the only person who could possibly Track the shit you need Tracked, maybe don't insultingly question their results."

"You were already awake, and it's the lack of results I'm questioning."

"Do I need to separate you two?" Siren asked from the backseat.

"No, *Mom*," Val shot back.

At twenty-three, red-headed Siren was the youngest—and shortest—of the three women. She was also inarguably the most mature, and therefore got stuck with the mom jokes. Well, maturity, and the fact she was probably the only one of the three of them capable of raising a child and not completely screwing it up. Meredith herself was certainly never procreating.

Valkyrie sighed. "How much longer do you think—"

"Stop the Jeep."

Val stood on the brakes hard enough to make the seatbelt catch. Meredith opened her eyes and glared at her. "Really?"

Valkyrie grinned. "You know you're having fun."

She *might* be having fun, but damn if she was going to admit to it. "It's up ahead on the left." She could just make out the start of a black metal fence behind the thick layer of trees and the ubiquitous kudzu that covered so much of Arkansas.

The Jeep ambled down the road, the kind of slow meandering one might do if lost on a backroad. The trees cleared for a ten foot stretch to reveal a set of Victorian-era style wrought iron gates, behind which she could just make out a building that could double as a gothic cathedral. Or an insane asylum. The name worked into the gate—Blackthorn Manor—did little to sway Meredith much in one direction or the other.

"See signs of anyone?" Valkyrie asked once they'd driven down the road, past both the gate and the end of the fencing.

Meredith shook her head. "Siren?"

"No." Siren sounded bothered by the fact, and Meredith couldn't blame her. Every other one of Elijah's compounds had been well-guarded. "Pull off the road up ahead and I'll call the backup team."

Valkyrie huffed out a breath. "We left them back a town. It'll take them half an hour to get here. Besides, I'm insulted you think I need backup."

Siren smiled sweetly. "Need I remind you that the last time you tried to do everything without backup you would have died if it weren't for my awesome healing powers? We don't know what's waiting for us in there. It's a large building. Given who it belonged to, we're waiting for a full backup team."

Valkyrie didn't argue further. Her blue eyes turned dark at the mention of her father. Siren caught the change in mood and hastened to lighten it. "Besides, if you would just get your husband to figure out how to teleport on command, maybe he could, say, teach the backup teams to do it."

Meredith snorted and did her best friend duty of helping to drag Valkyrie back from the memories of her sadistically psychotic dead dad. "Oh please, Random can only summon the powers of teleportation when his One Twue Wuv Kyrie is in mortal danger."

"Shove off," Valkyrie grumbled without heat, the tension in her shoulders relaxing. "And only Random gets to call me Kyrie."

"Whatever. Between you and Random, and Siren and Jace, there's so much nauseating happiness in the air all the time I'm constantly on the verge of vomiting."

"Clearly, the solution is for *you* to be nauseatingly happy too." Siren turned to Val. "Should we start husband hunting for her?"

"I do *not* need a husband," Meredith said flatly, even as Jensen King's annoyingly handsome face surfaced in her memory.

She'd met him seven months ago in Fayetteville and he'd been everything she hadn't realized she was looking for. Handsome, funny, sweet. Normal. Absolutely scorching in bed.

Their one-night stand had turned into multiple nights, and then pretty much every night for the better part of a month. Rationally, she'd known it would never turn into anything more.

Sometimes, when he'd looked at her, she'd seen guilt mingled in with the desire. Like he thought he shouldn't want her.

He'd probably had a pretty little wife waiting for him at home, and she'd just been the available distraction while he was traveling. She'd never asked. She hadn't wanted to know. He was a Null, and she'd wanted to pretend she was too, so she'd shoved her Aspect so far down inside her when they were together that even she couldn't feel it.

But she'd been on the verge of asking about the potential wife because she'd gotten to that point in a fling she was supposed to know better than to get to—the part where she wanted more. So the cosmic hammer of fate had decided to descend upon her for her own benefit, and Jensen had just been gone one day.

They'd both agreed at the outset that the affair was temporary, but she'd thought he would at least say goodbye when it was done. Or text it. Or answer at least one of *her* texts. She'd allowed herself one phone call and one voicemail. When a week had gone by and he hadn't called back, she'd deleted his number and tried to forget about him. Obviously, she hadn't succeeded.

"Are you even listening to us?" Siren asked. She was possibly the only person in the world who could ask that and not sound passive aggressive.

What were they talking about? Oh, yes, her non-existent love life. "I would have been listening," Meredith answered, "but I was too busy figuring out how to avoid the many horrible blind dates the two of you would set me up on if I let you."

"Hey, I would make sure they're your type, if you would ever tell me what that type is."

Relax, my type isn't your husband. The words were on the tip of her tongue, but she bit them back. Clearly, Julian had really gotten under her skin last night. Of course, there was also that *look* in Siren's eyes. And in Valkyrie's. What was going on with the two of them?

Meredith had dated Jace—Valkyrie's brother, Siren's husband

—in her Academy days. They'd been over long before Siren ever entered the picture. Meredith had broken up with him for his own good—literally, as in, she was worried her mother might do him irreparable harm—and she'd lost her friendship with Valkyrie when she'd dumped him.

It was actually because of Siren that Meredith and Val were friends again—that Val had finally let Meredith explain *why* she'd broken Jace's heart at the lowest point in his life. Once Valkyrie had listened, she'd understood, because she and Meredith were the same in many ways. They'd been through a lot of the same shit and they'd both hurt people they cared about in the name of protecting them. But Valkyrie was the one who'd gotten the fairytale ending. She'd crushed Random Tremayne's heart and he'd still come back to her. That was what stupid in love did to a person.

Which was how Meredith knew she'd never been stupid in love with Jace. Loved him, yes, but not in that all-consuming way she read about in books. Because though she'd gone through a rough time when they'd broken up, it had had more to do with losing the one person who was kind to her than it had had to do with losing her boyfriend. The abrupt loss of contact from one-month-fling Jensen hurt more than her breakup with Jace had.

For the love of the goddess, get your mind off Jensen. Thoughts of him kept creeping in at the most inconvenient of moments. *Figure out why your best friends are so convinced you're still in love with Jace, and convince them otherwise.* Maybe then she could have some peace.

Meredith's history with Jace was something Siren had known practically since the day the two of them met. And Siren had been confident and fine with that knowledge up until recently. Oh, she never said anything about it directly, but the little redhead had suddenly become obsessed with the belief that Meredith needed a man to be happy. If Meredith could just figure out what had triggered this behavioral shift, maybe she could put Siren's fears to rest. But she had just enough pride to not want to discuss the matter directly.

Siren wanted to know Meredith's taste in men? "My type is six-foot three, dark brown hair, bluest eyes you've ever seen, and dresses like a lumberjack. He enjoys long afternoons spent in hotel rooms, watching bad action movies, and doesn't bitch about my driving. Think you can find me that, little matchmaker?"

"Umm," Siren said. "That's oddly specific."

"You're saying a woman shouldn't know what she wants?"

"I'm saying you described a person, not a type." Siren brightened. "Do you have a secret boyfriend?"

Meredith sighed. She didn't feel like baring her sad abandonment story to the world, but maybe it would be worth it if it got Siren off her back. Really, their friendship had sailed smoothly up until now. Zero concerns about the former Jace/Meredith relationship. And since Meredith had no interest in sniffing around those waters again, she couldn't for the life of her figure out what had made Siren get all weird in the last couple months.

"Look, it's a tragic tale, okay? I had a man, and I lost him. Now I've come to the conclusion that I am very, very happy being alone."

"Really? You look fucking miserable," Valkyrie said, with all of her usual tact.

"Maybe if you'd given me more than five seconds to throw on clothes before leaving the house, I wouldn't look 'fucking miserable.' "

"Nah, you still would. It's in your eyes."

"You know, I think I liked you better when you didn't pay attention to anyone's emotions but your own."

Valkyrie shrugged. "You were the one who wanted to be friends again."

"You were the one who *agreed* to be friends again."

"Because you wouldn't stop pestering me about it."

Siren's phone jingled. "Oh, thank God, the backup's early. You two bicker worse than an old married couple."

Two black SUVs pulled up behind the Jeep.

Meredith frowned. "I know martial endeavors aren't my forte, but shouldn't we be trying to be a little more discreet or something?"

"We're on a dirt road in the middle of nowhere. Discreet went out the window the second we drove by. If anyone is on watch, they've already seen us. Stealth isn't our goal."

"Then what is our goal?"

Valkyrie's lips drew back in what could more properly be called a baring of teeth than a smile. "Intimidation."

"On that note, let's go greet the troops," Siren said cheerfully, hopping out of the Jeep. Meredith and Valkyrie followed.

"She has entirely too much pep," Meredith muttered.

"Yep," Val agreed.

Men and women poured from the SUVs. Each vehicle could carry eight and they were both fully loaded, which meant sixteen people clad in black combat gear gathered around them in a semi-circle off the side of the road. Instead of guns, they carried bladed weapons. Guns had an alarming tendency to blow up in an Aspecter's hand, taking the hand with it. Gunpowder and magic didn't mix.

The unit leader, a tall woman in her early thirties, nodded at Siren. "Councilor Savage."

"It's just Siren, Nova," the redhead said wearily. Siren had been failing for a while now to get her underlings to call her by her first name. Meredith knew she was made intensely uncomfortable by the fact she even *had* underlings.

"Of course, Mrs. Savage."

Siren let out a world-weary sigh. She'd been thrust into leadership six months ago when Valkyrie had exposed that the council that had always led Aspect Society had gained and maintained that power through illegal means. Siren had been shocked at being elected, in Aspect Society's first ever democratic venture, as the interim leader.

Since she was the magical powerhouse that had contained the previous council so they could be brought to trial, Meredith thought Siren *shouldn't* have been surprised. But she had been, and now she found herself responsible for the first major revision of Aspect Society's political structure since its founding.

The five-person council that had always ruled was currently suspended. Siren had still been given the title of Head Councilor, because otherwise no one knew what to call her, but until a permanent decision was made about whether to keep the Council or go with something else, she had an eleven-person advisory committee. She made the decisions, the committee advised, and if they thought she was about to make a gargantuan mistake, they could overrule her if they could get a unanimous vote against her course of action.

Nova turned to Valkyrie. "Orders?"

Given the extent of corruption within the old council, Siren had needed people she trusted in key positions. To that end, she'd restructured the Council's security forces and placed Valkyrie at their head. Gaining the respect of those teams had been an uphill battle for Val. Her father had spent years painting his daughter as a ticking time bomb one wrong word shy of going off, and he'd done a thorough job of it.

Long-held opinions were hard to change, and Valkyrie hadn't bothered to pander to anyone to help change them. Nova and her team had come around to Valkyrie sooner than others, and they were Val's go-to backup when she needed people she could absolutely trust. They were the team she'd brought to the last five of Elijah's holdings.

"You all know the drill by now. No lethal force on the kids under any circumstances. Subdue if you are attacked, but do not initiate confrontation. Any adults in the building may be handled with all necessary force. Clear?"

"Clear," they affirmed.

She nodded to Nova. "Alright everyone, shields up. We have no visible threat or active defense on the property so we're going Code Blue. Ms. Townsend, Mrs. Savage, you're behind Mrs. Tremayne. Everyone else, positions."

Meredith dutifully brought her shield up along with everyone else and fell in next to Siren as they approached the massive gates. She didn't precisely feel like a fish out of water—she had an intellectual grasp on what they were doing and why—but she always felt useless after she'd found the location they were looking for and brought everyone to it.

Her dual affinities—Truthfinding and Tracking—weren't martially inclined and neither was she. Even Siren's presence didn't help her feel less out of place. The redhead might not have combat training either, but she had enough raw power rattling around inside her to survive a nuclear detonation. Meredith's only value was in finding the place and dragging the truth out of anyone inside, if necessary.

Valkyrie mashed the call button on the gate's speaker box. It rang, and rang, and rang. Eventually a soft crackle hissed across the speaker, indicating that someone listened, though no one spoke.

"This is Valkyrie Tremayne. These grounds and the people within them are now under the jurisdiction of the New Aspect Society Council. Surrender immediately, and you will be given a fair trial. You have thirty seconds to decide."

Meredith counted the seconds in her head. Keeping time was something she was good at, and she ticked her way second by second, almost like a meditation. Ten. Fifteen. Twenty-five. No one answered Valkyrie's ultimatum, but on the twenty-ninth second the iron gates swung inward.

Sure, that wasn't strange at all. Black, wrought-iron gates opening at some unseen commander's hand, inviting them all to enter the seemingly-empty, definitely creepy grounds surrounding the insane asylum-esque establishment? Who *wouldn't* fall for that?

Nova took a step forward, motioning to the others to follow. Unease hit Meredith's spine and she knew, by the tenseness rippling through the group around her, that they felt it too. Typically, Elijah's holdings still had *some* line of visible defense. The emptiness felt more frightening than a greeting party of kill-happy mercenaries would have.

Nova issued a series of hand signals Meredith knew well enough by now to interpret. *Proceed with caution. Forward, then split into teams. Surround the building.*

Bad feeling firmly in place, Meredith followed Val and Siren through the front gates.

CHAPTER

THREE

S urrounding the building turned out to be impossible, because something else already had.

"Is that an actual moat?" Siren asked.

"Yep." Meredith took out her phone and snapped a picture.

"Really, Mer?" Valkyrie said.

"What? It's not every day you see an honest-to-goddess moat." The moat in question stretched an impressive fifteen feet across in width. The surface of the water was about a ten foot drop, but the water itself was murky, making the depth impossible to guess.

"Marco, could we get a bridge?" Valkyrie prompted.

Marco, a tall man with light brown skin and short-cropped black hair, stepped up to the edge of the moat. Combat units typically came equipped with at least one Elemental, and Marco was Nova's.

Two Battle Aspecters flanked him, taking over shielding for him as he sank his magic into the ground. Nothing happened. Seconds passed and sweat broke out along Marco's forehead, far more Aspect pouring out of him than it should have taken an Elemental with a high earth affinity to build a dirt bridge.

"Marco?" Valkyrie asked.

"Encountering resistance," he said through a mostly locked jaw.

Resistance? The only resistance that could stop him was another high earth user. And while Elementals *could* work from inside a building, it greatly reduced their range and capabilities. For one to combat Marco this effectively, they should need to be out here.

"Pull back," Valkyrie ordered.

"I can. Take them," he gritted out.

"Pull back, that's an order."

Marco's Aspect vanished and he dropped to one knee, panting. The rest of their unit who weren't shielding Marco were furiously scanning the landscape.

"Siren?" Meredith asked.

A soft wash of power swirled around the redhead, and she shook her head. "We're the only ones out here. Everyone else is inside the building."

On the other side of the moat, the home's front door opened. No one emerged, but Meredith could just make out a shadowy figure within. They called out in a deep voice that sounded a little strained. "Leave now."

"Come out so we can talk," Valkyrie said.

"Leave," the figure called back. "You have thirty seconds to decide." After throwing Valkyrie's earlier ultimatum back at her, the figure slammed the door shut.

Meredith started counting elapsed seconds again.

"So they've got a fancy Elemental," Nova said. "They can't have more than one. We can jump the moat, get in fast and take them out." With a glance at Siren and Meredith Nova added, "Well, most of us can jump it." She flashed them an apologetic grin. As the only two in the group who didn't bear a Battle Aspect affinity, they were also the only two who couldn't amp up their strength so they could somersault over a fifteen foot divide.

Ten seconds elapsed.

Valkyrie considered it and then shook her head. "I don't like it. Something goes wrong mid-air we're sitting ducks. We wait their thirty seconds. I want to call their bluff and see what happens."

Twenty seconds.

"Come on," Valkyrie murmured. "Show me what you got."

Twenty-five seconds. The air shifted, teasing at the edges of Meredith's hair.

Twenty-nine seconds.

The air shifted again and Meredith dropped flat to the ground, pulling Siren down with her a second before a gust of wind slammed into their party.

Six of Nova's team closest to the moat tumbled over the side. Valkyrie dropped to her knees, Aspect saturating the air as her fist punched into the earth. She sank her arm up to her elbow, using enhanced strength to anchor herself. Valkyrie grabbed Meredith with her free hand and Nova did the same with Siren.

Meredith rode it out, eyes closed against the stinging winds and clutching to Val's arm with everything she had. She *really* didn't want to find out firsthand if anything lived in the moat.

The winds died off as quickly as they'd come, but Meredith didn't trust the reprieve enough to stand up yet.

"There's no one out here," Nova growled. "Elementals can't *do* this shit from indoors."

Correction, Meredith thought, *normal Elementals can't do this shit from indoors.* It all came together and she started laughing, at which point everyone understandably looked at her like she'd lost it.

"It's the kids," she managed in between wheezes of laughter. "There isn't any security here. The only ones left are the kids."

Adults, much as some of them might geek out over the idea of a moat, were unlikely to actually build one. Furthermore, adults who had been met by a Council Battle Aspect crew would not have offered them the option to simply leave. They would know that anyone under the authority of the Aspect Council would simply return with a larger group if necessary.

But a bunch of scared kids who maybe didn't even know what the Aspect Society was, depending on what Elijah had told them? Oh, yeah, those kids would build a moat. And try to knock people into it.

Speaking of people in the moat... Panicked thrashing sounded below and then Siren called, "I've got it!" Her eyes went a little dreamy and out of focus and the thrashing stopped.

Meredith wanted to see what manner of creatures Siren had subdued, but she also didn't want to find out what else the kids had in their bag of tricks, since they clearly had at least one Elemental who could summon high-force winds without needing to step foot outside of the house.

Meredith rose up on her knees, keeping hold of Valkyrie's arm.

"What are you doing?" Valkyrie hissed.

"Testing a theory," Meredith murmured. She took a deep breath and yelled. "Elijah Winters is dead. She—" Meredith pointed at Valkyrie "—killed him. We know what he was doing here and we can guarantee nothing like that will happen to you again."

The wind swirled ominously around her, shoving her hair into her face until all she could see was a blonde cloud. Getting the tangles out of it later was going to be an absolute delight.

She tried again. "If you don't want to spend the rest of your lives running from shadows, let's talk."

"I don't think—" Valkyrie cut off when the front door opened.

"We can talk," a new voice called—or maybe the same voice, just less concerned with trying to sound like an adult. "But you try anything and we've got worse things than the alligators in the moat."

There were alligators in the moat? Sweet.

CHAPTER

FOUR

N o one emerged from the building, but an earthen bridge formed across the moat. Marco's face took on a pained expression.

The bridge completed itself and a staircase branched off, descending into the moat for the fallen members of their party to climb. They did so, waterlogged and pissed off. As soon as the last one reached the bridge, Siren let go of her hold on the alligators, looking paler than usual.

"Are you okay?" Meredith asked Siren. Holding a few alligators in place should have been a cakewalk for a Life Aspecter. Especially since Siren housed enough of that raw Life Aspect inside her to obliterate everyone present with a snap of her fingers. The obliterating tended to come with intoxicating kill-happy side-effects, which was why they'd brought the backup team instead of relying on Siren alone to handle everything.

At least, Meredith *thought* that was why they'd waited. Looking at Siren now, she wasn't so sure.

"I'm fine," Siren said.

"You look sick."

"No, I just—" Siren clapped one hand to her stomach and one to her mouth, like she was about to throw up. Which should be impossible. Siren *was* Life. She didn't get sick. Siren swallowed, hard, shook her head and repeated, "I'm fine."

Meredith didn't buy it for a hot minute, but now wasn't the time to argue.

They crossed the earthen bridge, which mercifully did not dissolve while they were on it, but did disappear once they reached land, removing any quick means of escape.

"Nova, you and five others with me, the rest of you cover the perimeter," Valkyrie ordered.

The front door opened onto an expansive, rectangular foyer that did nothing to diminish the insane asylum vibes Meredith picked up from the place. She was beginning to strongly suspect the building had, at one point in its history, *been* an insane asylum.

The Truthfinder affinity, while most widely known for giving its bearer the ability to tell if someone was lying, did have other facets. They were ones Meredith had suppressed while her mother lived, not wanting to give the bitch another tool to use. But her mother had been dead long enough that those secondary abilities were more and more often refusing to be ignored.

Lately, Meredith had been feeling the truth of places and things. It wasn't like she could view an object and tell you its entire history, but she frequently got a sense of whether it agreed or disagreed with certain thoughts she had. And her thoughts that this place felt like an asylum were ringing firmly true according to her talent.

"Is Elijah really dead?" The voice was soft—young—but it echoed off the foyer walls. Echoed, and demanded an answer with a power kin to Meredith's own.

Weak Truthfinders required straight yes or no answers to differentiate truth from lies. Stronger Truthfinders could handle more complex statements, but most required an initial physical connection to a speaker to use their ability. Meredith didn't, though in her years of playing dumb and useless, she'd intentionally tested low enough that people believed she did.

The strongest Truthfinders could compel an individual to answer a question. Meredith had done it twice. Both times, it had required the whole of her Aspect to force the answer. Whoever this Truthfinder was, not only did they not require physical connection, but they'd cast the compulsion out in a wide net with enough raw power to demand an answer from anyone caught beneath it. Meredith had never seen anything like it.

She called her own Aspect, tossed it up to meet the net and braced herself as the two clashed. The other Truthfinder added more power, expecting a brute force conflict. But Meredith simply tugged on her rope of Aspect, drawing the net away from the others, collapsing the shape of it until it coiled into a ball in her hands.

More power poured into the ball and the urge to answer the asked question burned like acid in Meredith's veins. Holy shit, this kid was strong. But Meredith was too, and she had more experience. The easiest way to beat this much raw talent was to sidestep the question altogether. If you could work up the will to say something other than the answer to the asked question, you could break the original compulsion.

"You don't need to compel us, little Truthfinder. We'll answer your questions, but we don't take kindly to being forced."

The ball of Aspect in her hands twitched, shuddered, and winked out.

"To answer your question, yes. Elijah is really dead. Perhaps introductions are in order?"

Time stretched out, the silence broken by the soft murmurings of a discussion Meredith couldn't quite make out. Then two figures stepped into view on the mezzanine floor above them, a boy and a girl. The girl was around twelve. The boy looked about sixteen, maybe seventeen, and Meredith guessed he was in charge, if the protective hand he had on the younger girl's shoulder was any indication.

"Hi," Meredith said, when it appeared no one else in either

group was going to talk. "I'm Meredith. I'm a Truthfinder too." She spoke the last to the girl.

"I'm Veritas," the girl said, and Meredith wondered if she'd chosen her own name. "I'm stronger than you." She said it with absolute certainty. No condescension, no question, just simple declaration of fact.

Meredith laughed. "Probably. But strength isn't everything."

Veritas frowned, like she thought there was something deeply flawed with what Meredith had said, but her Aspect couldn't find the lie in it.

"And you?" Meredith asked the boy.

"You can call me Rath."

Meredith could feel the shape of the name on her tongue like a living thing. Rath without a *W*. A nickname?

His gaze fixed on Valkyrie. "You look like him. Why do you look like him?"

"Because I was my father's first experiment," Valkyrie answered. "Fitting that I ended him. Don't you think?"

Rath glanced to Veritas for confirmation. The girl nodded with complete confidence, and *that* was something. Any ordinary Truthfinder would have needed a clearer statement from Valkyrie to confirm that she had indeed killed Elijah. Saying that it was fitting that she had ended him was a shaky statement that didn't directly say she *had*.

"So he's dead. What do you want from us?"

Siren stepped forward. "Do you know what the Aspect Society Council is?"

Rath kept his mouth stubbornly shut, obviously not wanting to admit to any ignorance. But Veritas shook her head.

"Everyone with Aspect in the United States falls under the jurisdiction of the Aspect Society Council. It's meant to govern our kind and make sure no one is taken advantage of simply because others are stronger than us.

"I won't lie to you—when I first found out what I was and fell under that jurisdiction, I did not receive a warm welcome.

You see, I was Elijah's second experiment. And I didn't even know I had power until I was sixteen. He trapped my Aspect inside me and stored it up like a bomb, because that's how he intended to use me.

"And when I stumbled into this world, the Council was very afraid of me. I think they would have killed me if they'd been given the chance. They were too focused on me, on what I could do, to bother trying to find the person who'd done this to me.

"It took Valkyrie to prove what her father had done. To kill him, and to remove the previous council. Since they've been gone, we've been working to find all of the people Elijah has harmed. You're the last."

"So why should we trust you?"

"Because that council is no longer in charge. I am. And I don't hold people accountable for things they haven't done."

"What happens if we come with you?" Veritas asked. "Will you separate us?"

How many of "us" were there? Rath and Veritas were the only two who had shown themselves. Were the rest of the kids here, or had some of them left?

"You won't be separated," Siren assured them. "There are others like you. They live at a school together."

After Elijah's death, Valkyrie had wanted nothing to do with the home she'd grown up in. She'd ended up donating it to the Savage Foundation, which was the organization Siren had founded to help others like her and Valkyrie. Valkyrie's old home was now called The Refuge, and it was both school and home to all the kids they'd found so far.

"Should you decide to go there your education, both the Null and the Aspect sides, will be finished. You will have time and space to plan for the future, and you'll have a home at the school for as long as you need one, even after you turn eighteen."

Rath was quiet for a moment, and the distant expression on Meredith's face made her think he was talking to someone. In his head. Which was not a thing. Telepathy was definitely *not* a thing. Then again, they'd all thought teleporting wasn't a thing either, and Random had finally proved that wrong so…

"And if we don't want to go with you?"

"Then you don't. I'm not here to control you. I'm here to try and fix what Elijah broke. I'm here because I understand how it feels to be on your own in a situation you don't understand and feel you have no control over.

"By the time someone offered to help me I didn't know how to take it. I didn't know how to trust them. And they didn't try to force me to. They just offered. So that's what I'm doing for you. Offering.

"If you want to stay here without oversight, that's your choice. We ask that you allow us to supply you with food and medical care, and station some of our people nearby in the event you need assistance."

"That's it?" Rath asked. "We don't want to come with you and we don't have to?"

Siren shrugged. "I told you, I'm not into force."

Rath nodded. "Good. Then get out."

"Alright," Siren agreed easily. "We'll have a couple people stationed off the property. Big RV, can't miss it. They have medical and trauma training, if anyone needs it. We'll drop off food and hygiene supplies as well. We can leave them outside the gate if you don't want to let anyone inside again. If you have any immediate, critical needs, let us know and we'll take care of them.

"And Rath? I have no doubt that you're doing a good job of taking care of everyone. But I also know you have multiple kids here. Most adults wouldn't be prepared to be a parent to all of them, and expecting it from yourself is a lot to ask. If you change your mind, my offer stands at any time."

Siren headed for the door without hesitation. Meredith had seen so many of these interactions by now that none of it surprised her. And Rath wouldn't be the first to turn down Siren's offer. Meredith knew some people would say Siren was making the wrong decision. That since some of the kids here were as young as six or seven, adults had the responsibility to make a decision for them regardless of whether they wanted it or not.

And maybe that was true. But Meredith also saw the wisdom in how Siren handled things. If she dragged them all out of here kicking and screaming, it could take years to ever earn their trust, and she might never get it. They would feel like they had no choice in anything that happened to them.

By giving them the option, Siren could ensure their needs were met while giving the older kids time to realize that they did not, in fact, want to be parents. To realize they'd already been forced to shoulder too much responsibility and it would be nice to have someone else help them out.

The longest any of the groups had held out before accepting Siren's offer was thirteen days.

They were almost to the front doors when a strong, clear voice called, "Wait!" A black-haired girl emerged on another side of the mezzanine. She was maybe sixteen, her skin a deep copper. "I want to go with you."

"*Ruin.*" Rath's voice was a tumultuous mixture of censure, hurt, and shock.

Rath and Ruin, Meredith thought. Oh, the kids had definitely named themselves. And when Rath got the same look on his face he'd had earlier, one now mirrored on Ruin's, Meredith was willing to bet money that telepathy was now a thing.

Watching people argue silently was…interesting. Ruin's face became smoother and more unreadable while Rath's expression became something more befitting his name.

Ruin ended the argument by speaking aloud. "I'm going. And Aerith and the others are coming with me." She didn't beg him to come too. At least, not aloud. But it was written all over her face.

Meredith was afraid she was going to have to watch teen heartbreak play out right in front of her. Then Rath's shoulders sagged, and he looked at Siren with the kind of mutinous glare only teenagers could manage. "You'd better not be lying."

Veritas looked affronted. Meredith was affronted on her behalf. Truthfinders really didn't get enough appreciation.

It took a mere half an hour for thirteen kids to load up all of their possessions, probably because not a single kid had more than two bags worth of stuff. They were heading for the doors when a boy who couldn't have been more than five said, "What about Monster?"

"Monster?" Meredith asked.

"The monster in the basement. We can't leave him."

"It's probably dead by now," Rath told the kid.

"No, he's not. I've been feeding him."

Rath cursed. "*You've* been stealing the food?"

"It's not stealing," the kid defended. "He's one of us. I wasn't going to let him starve. And I won't leave him."

"No one's leaving anyone," Meredith decided. "Show me to the basement."

CHAPTER

FIVE

Valkyrie gave Meredith an odd look she shrugged off. She *felt* like a monster most days. Maybe a real one was what her life needed.

After a brief discussion, Meredith, Valkyrie, Rath, and the kid —Merlin—headed for the basement with Nova and three of her team. Siren stayed above with Ruin and the others. The redhead wasn't happy about it, but Val and Meredith both refused to budge. After seeing how Siren had looked after holding back the alligators, Meredith didn't want to put the woman in the same room as an alleged monster. Something was clearly going on with the little spitfire, and Meredith had every intention of figuring out what it was at the earliest available opportunity.

But for now…

She followed Merlin to an enclosed stairwell equipped with low, flickering lights straight out of a horror film. Her heels made loud, decisive clicks on the concrete steps, echoing off the bare walls.

Rath looked at her footwear with something approaching actual horror. "Why do you wear those?"

Because I am an invalid without them. "You might say I'm made to wear them," she replied breezily.

"I like the clack they make," Merlin said seriously.

Valkyrie rolled her eyes. "Don't encourage her."

"You're just irritated by them because walking in heels is like the one thing in the universe you can't do." Meredith had put Valkyrie in heels once, and desperately wished she'd recorded it. Her best friend had looked like she was trying to walk on stilts.

A loud, rumbling growl emanated from below. It was low and deep and did not sound like it belonged to any sane creature. They hit the bottom of the stairs and Meredith found herself on a landing facing a steel door. The metal was battered and dented from the inside. Two thick bars on the outside were reinforcement for six deadbolts.

"Monster, it's me," Merlin called. The growling ceased, which proved that whatever lived behind that door at least had enough intelligence to know who fed it. Merlin skipped forward and rolled an apple through the four-inch-by-four-inch slot at the bottom of the door.

An apple for the creature, Meredith thought.

"Monster, I brought some people with me."

Another growl.

"They're nice," Merlin insisted. "They're going to get you out, so you can't eat them." Another noise that might or might not be an agreement.

"Does anyone actually know what's behind there?" Meredith asked. There were no windows on the door, no way to see inside.

Rath shook his head. "They brought it here in a cage, all covered up. Took six people to carry. Elijah used to come down here all the time, after he came back different."

Came back different. Meredith juggled the timeline of events in her head. A few months before Valkyrie killed Elijah, Siren had nearly accomplished the feat. Elijah hadn't looked so pretty after the fact.

"Then he stopped showing up and we heard the guards saying he wasn't coming back. They were thinking about jumping ship. We decided to help them along in making that decision. After, we didn't really know what to do about this." He gestured at the door.

Great. "Keys?"

Rath shook his head.

"I tried to pick the locks," Merlin said. "But it's easier on YouTube than real life."

"You tried to—" Rath cut off, which was probably a good thing, because he looked like he might have an apoplexy if he finished the sentence. Clearly, being a dad to twelve kids barely younger than him was wearing on him. She was surprised there wasn't any gray in his hair.

Meredith studied the door. If *she* had a set of lock picks she could see if her skills were still up to snuff. But she didn't. "Val?"

"I can open it."

"And whatever's behind it?"

"Is likely half-starved. I can handle it."

"You won't hurt my monster, right?" Merlin did not sound very trusting in that moment, and she had an absurd image of them opening the door for the five-year-old to heroically throw himself in between them and a twelve-foot tall, tentacled monstrosity.

"I might have to knock it out," Valkyrie said honestly. "But I won't kill it."

Merlin looked to Meredith for confirmation, and she was a little touched he seemed to trust her more than Val. Then again, she did have the superior footwear. She nodded at Merlin. "Your monster's safe with us. But I think it might be best if you and Rath waited at the top of the stairs."

"Okay." But he walked up to the door first. "Monster? My friends are gonna get you out. Please don't eat them. They said they'll have to knock you out if you try to eat them and I don't want them to knock you out." Then he obediently trotted up the stairs. Rath's only concession was to climb six steps, positioning himself as the last line of defense between the monster and Merlin.

Meredith was interested to know what he thought he was going to do against something that, if it made it to him, would have taken out Valkyrie, Meredith, and four members of an elite combat unit. She gave him a pointed look. "You do realize if whatever this is gets past all of us, you should be running, right?"

Rath gave her a contemptuous look. "Want to take your own advice, Truthfinder?"

Ugh, had she been that bratty as a teenager? Probably. On the surface, he had a point. Truthfinders were not combat Aspecters by any stretch of the imagination. The only true weapon a Truthfinder possessed was their Telling—the ability to force an individual to confront every truth about themselves they'd ever tried to hide from. It didn't work on everyone—there was always the rare individual who had fully accepted who they were and weren't bothered by it—but it left most people sobbing on the floor.

"Oh, if it comes to that," she told Rath, "I guess we'll find out if monsters are afraid of monsters too."

Val lifted the heavy metal bars like they were toothpicks. She didn't try to wrench the door open—likely the handle would give before the deadbolts in that scenario. Instead, her Aspect coated her fist in a protective layer of armor, lending temporary strength to the bones and muscles in her arm and fist. She proceeded to knock every single deadbolt out of the door, each punch equaling one hole through the steel.

"Show off," Meredith muttered.

Valkyrie had a dagger in her left hand as she grabbed the handle and pulled the door open. No terrifying, tentacled creature came charging out to drag them through a portal to another realm. Instead of the earlier growl, a low, soft whine issued forth.

Ignoring the common sense that dictated Meredith stay behind Val, the person actually capable of fending off a physical attack, Meredith stepped up beside her, feeling along the inside of the room's wall for a light switch. She found one, and the same horror-esque yellow lights that illuminated the stairwell flooded the room.

Valkyrie blinked in surprise. "It's just a dog."

A dirty creature covered in matted white fur hunched pitifully in the middle of the room. It looked like a dog. It had a tail and four paws and cute little ears just like a dog, and when she looked at it, everything emanating from it said *dog, dog, dog.*

It was definitely not a dog. Because when Meredith looked at it and thought dog, her power screamed *lie, lie, lie.*

"Monster's a puppy?" Merlin tried to dash down the stairs, but Rath caught him and held him back.

"Why would Elijah bring a dog here?" Rath craned his neck, trying to peer around the people in front of him. "It doesn't make any sense."

"I don't know," Valkyrie said, her voice lacking any real concern. "But that's all it is."

Meredith stared at her. "You seriously think that's just a dog?"

Valkyrie Tremayne, formerly Valkyrie Winters, who had grown up with the calculating evil that had been Elijah Winters, who knew better than anyone that Elijah never did anything without a purpose, and that Elijah certainly wouldn't have been interested in a mere dog, shrugged. "Anyone else see anything besides a dog?"

Nova answered Valkyrie's shrug with one of her own. "Maybe Elijah needed someone to listen to him bitch."

Rath, who had been the only skeptical one at the outset, relaxed the longer he looked at the white mutt.

Meredith narrowed her eyes at the not-dog. He whined even more piteously and crawled a couple inches toward her.

She softened. She was overreacting. It *was* just a dog. A sad, miserable dog that needed care and proper food and—

Lie. Her Aspect roared awake and for the briefest second, she caught the strands of *something* woven around the not-dog. It wasn't Aspect—they'd all have felt it if the creature had Aspect —but it *was* magic.

Not all kinds of power were Aspect—some abilities, like those the Oracles possessed, were something different. This was one of those different things.

Meredith focused, trying to penetrate the shroud that surrounded the creature. It wasn't illusion. It almost felt like... belief? But when she pressed, the shroud wove together more tightly, leaving no cracks or crevices for her power to slip through.

"What are you doing?" Valkyrie asked.

Meredith's concentration slipped. Everyone was looking at her like she was nuts. "Nothing." She glared at the dog. It crept forward on its belly, close enough to rest its wet nose on the toes peeking through the open toe of her boots.

"Looks like it likes you."

It didn't like her. It recognized that she was the one person present its concealing magic didn't entirely work on, so it was cozying up to her.

What kind of power could not only make Valkyrie see a dog, but also override all of the logic that should be convincing her that even if she *thought* she saw a dog, it didn't make any sense?

"Can I keep him?" Merlin asked. "Do you think the nice lady will let me?"

Oh, no. If an adorable kid asked Siren if he could keep his monster dog, she would absolutely move heaven and earth to make that happen. And since Meredith was the only one who could tell the dog wasn't a dog, she needed to nip this in the bud.

"He's really sick," Meredith said. "He's going to need constant care. I think it's best if he comes with me and maybe when he's better Siren will let you keep him." The not-dog was never getting anywhere near Siren's home for wayward orphans. Meredith was going to figure out what the hell it actually was.

"*You're* going to keep him?" Valkyrie asked.

Meredith had never been terribly fond of anything that sprouted fur. Animals shed everywhere, they required daily attention, and they tended not to like her anyways.

"Why not? Maybe if I have a dog, you and Siren will finally stop trying to find me a husband." She rested her hands on her knees and bent down, put on her most obnoxious baby voice, and dared the creature to not act like a dog. "What do you say wittle woofy-woof? You wanna come home with me?"

It gave another heart-rending whine and licked at her fingers, all sloppy and dog-like.

Eww, gross. Was that actually a dog tongue licking her? What if it was some alien-like tentacled thing? She carefully wiped her hand on her pants.

"Well, come on then," she told it. "Let's get you out of here." The not-dog struggled to his feet, letting out soft whimpers of pain. It took two steps and fell over. No matter how convinced Meredith was that it was *not* a dog, that didn't change the fact that whatever it was, it had been starved and beaten and locked in a dark room. For months.

"I can carry him." Valkyrie started forward.

"No," Meredith said quickly. Better if everyone thought she was already attached. Less likelihood of Siren deciding to add him to her growing family of furballs that way. "I've got him."

Valkyrie did not question Meredith's ability to carry the dog up a flight of stairs, and Meredith took that as a sign that the last two months of working out were finally starting to show. She leaned down, gently placed her hands under the creature's belly, and whispered softly enough the words wouldn't carry, "I don't know what you are, but if you bite me I will smack the hell out of you."

The not-dog licked her face. "Dear goddess, your breath is disgusting." It smelled like something had crawled in between his teeth, died, rotted, and then sprouted mold.

She hefted him up, straightened, and clutched the not-dog to her chest. It looked and felt like a starved medium-sized dog.

She could feel too many bones beneath the fur and flesh, and she was fearful that the wrong move might cause those bones to snap like twigs.

The not-dog relaxed, as if there was nowhere else in the world he'd rather be than in her arms. If that wasn't weird as hell, she didn't know what was.

CHAPTER

SIX

J ensen King was hallucinating. It was the only thing that explained how Meredith Townsend was carrying him out of the torture basement. He'd never pictured himself as the type to have a rescue fantasy but here he was, obviously having one.

When he'd heard the kid outside his door, the one that brought him food, he'd ignored the apple that rolled into the cell. Shifter magic and its ability to speed or slow his metabolism had kept him alive far longer than a regular human would have managed in these conditions, but he'd known death would come in a matter of time. The apple would only prolong his suffering.

Then he'd heard more voices. Part of him wanted to ignore the apple anyway, and get the process of dying over with, because logic told him whoever was on the other side was Aspect Society, and Aspecters meant more pain. Then Natalie's face had flashed into his mind and he'd shoved down the selfish part of him that wanted to die. His sister needed him to live, so he could find her.

He'd eaten the apple. Maybe it had been laced with something, and that's why he was having Meredith fantasies? Drugged or not, the apple had given him the boost he needed to fuel the glamour that made him look like an ordinary mutt. He almost hadn't bothered, assuming the Aspecters would already know what the cell contained. Would know that even if they saw a dog, that wasn't what he was.

But while they were definitely Aspect Society, they didn't question finding a dog in the cell. None of them except Meredith, who seemed to recognize he wasn't what he appeared, but also couldn't see past the glamour to his true form.

It *couldn't* be her. This woman walked like her, talked like her, but it couldn't be her. Because if it was, that would mean that the woman who had kept him from sliding off the cliff into absolute despair when he'd been unable to find Natalie, was an Aspecter.

The meager energy he'd gained from the apple was already failing, and he let his exhausted head drop onto her shoulder.

"Your fur smells worse than your breath," she muttered. That was her voice, her cadence. She gripped him firmly but gently, and the touch felt so good he stopped thinking about what it meant that she was Aspect.

If he lived, if this wasn't a hallucination, he would care about it then. For now he buried his nose in the thick fall of her hair and inhaled the light, fruity scent of her shampoo. He remembered that scent, and after months of smelling nothing but dank concrete, steel, and his own filth, she smelled like heaven.

"Oh goddess, it *is* fur I'm touching, right?" Her voice was soft and low but mildly panicked. "You don't have tentacles, right? Please, goddess, don't let me be holding a slimy, tentacled creature."

He grunted. Tentacles? What did she think he was, Cthulhu?

By the time they reached the top of the stairs, Meredith had started breathing hard. "I have been working out," she muttered to herself, "and goddess knows quitting the booze helped, but you weigh like forty pounds."

Forty pounds? That was alarming. He'd known he didn't weigh anything close to what he should, but forty? A Shifter's second form was typically larger than that of its ordinary animal counterpart. In cases of starvation their magic could shrink their form, so his frame probably wasn't much larger than a dog's right now, but forty pounds meant he was even closer to death than he'd thought. And that he would require a lot of food before he could manage to shift back to human.

They emerged into a foyer he'd never seen before—his cage had been covered when they'd brought him to wherever this was—and it was packed mostly with children.

Meredith shifted sideways, giving him an unobstructed view of the room. A redhead saw them and locked onto him, concern filling her eyes. "Oh my god, is he okay?"

She rushed toward them and the power spinning around her reached for him. He bared his teeth and gave a low warning growl. She stopped in her tracks, looking hurt.

"Hey, stop that," Meredith scolded. He had a feeling she would have popped him on the nose if she'd had a free hand, and just for that he licked her ear. She shuddered, no doubt fearing she'd just been scraped by a tentacle.

"It's okay, buddy," the redhead tried in a soothing voice. "I'm here to help."

He growled again and snapped at her. He didn't care what she was trying to do, he wasn't risking it. Wasn't risking that if she touched him with her power, she might figure out what he was.

"Maybe if Valkyrie holds him for me?" the redhead said.

Meredith's hand came protectively over his face and she stepped back. "I think I should just take him home."

"He's in bad shape, Meredith."

"I know. But he's also upset and needs time to adjust. He's made it this long, he'll make it a few hours back to Seclusion."

Jensen had no idea why Meredith was invested in keeping her suspicions about his nature to herself, but he chose to be grateful their goals aligned. Even if she *had* just said she was taking him into Seclusion, the heart of Aspect territory.

"I only need a few minutes to fix him."

"Do you?" Meredith challenged. "I saw you after the alligators. You looked like you were going to pass out."

Alligators?

"I'm fine."

"I don't even need to Truthfinder you to know you're lying."

A Truthfinder. Meredith was a Truthfinder. If he'd had the energy, he would have laughed. Shifters had a basic working understanding of Aspect and its affinities, and he'd grown up being warned that a strong Truthfinder wouldn't be completely fooled by a Shifter's glamour.

He'd gone to bed with the one woman who could see right through him. How had she hidden her Aspect? He'd never gotten the slightest hint of it when they were together.

"And while this isn't the place for the conversation about why you are not fine," Meredith continued, "which we are definitely going to have later, I'm not letting you pour power into a —" she clearly hesitated over what to call him before settling on "—dog in this bad a condition."

"But—" The redhead broke off as her face turned a sickly shade. She whirled around and called to the group of kids at large. "Bathroom?" Fingers pointed, and she turned and ran.

One of the kids—a young girl—narrowed her eyes at him. Meredith turned abruptly, hiding him from the girl's view, and trailed after the redhead. Outside the closed bathroom door, Meredith took the opportunity to put him down, careful to keep her body between him and any onlookers.

The tall, black-haired woman who had opened his prison came to stand next to them. A frown creased her brow as she stared at the closed door. "What is going on with her? She looked like she was going to hurl after holding back the alligators earlier."

Why did everyone keep talking about alligators? Were there native alligators in Arkansas?

"I have no idea. I think she *is* hurling now. She shouldn't be sick. It's impossible for a Life Aspecter to get sick, isn't it?"

The two of them really couldn't figure it out? He'd smelled it on the woman as soon as she'd come within six feet of him.

"Unless there's something wrong with her Aspect?" Meredith suggested. "Should we call Jace?"

In between the sounds of dry-heaving coming from within the bathroom, the redhead managed to yell, "Do *not* call my husband. I am fine."

"You're throwing up," the black-haired woman said.

"No shit, Val." A toilet flushed, water ran, and the redhead emerged. "Look, I know why this is happening, and it's not life-threatening, okay?"

Meredith frowned, like her magic was calling bullshit on that assertion.

"Does Jace know you're unwell?" Val asked.

"No. I'm going to tell him, and I swear to your stupid goddess if either of you say *anything* to him before I do, I will make both of you break out in acne."

"Can she do that?" Meredith asked in a stage whisper.

Val shrugged. "Probably."

Jensen bumped his head against Meredith's side. He was exhausted and he wanted to be gone from this place.

Meredith glanced down at him. Her brow was still furrowed in an adorable frown, clearly irritated by her inability to figure out what he was, but he must have looked pathetic enough to garner some sympathy anyway. "I think my rescue dog needs to get home ASAP. Are the kids ready to go?"

Why he'd been in a cell below a house filled with children was another question for another time.

"Yeah," the redhead said. "the bus from The Refuge just arrived. I'm going to ride back with them and get them settled in." She looked at Jensen again. "Are you sure I can't—"

He growled, but it was drowned out by Meredith's firm, "No. Absolutely not. I will nurse his ugly hide back to health, but you are not touching him in your condition. Whatever that condition is."

"Do you even know how to take care of a dog?"

"I'm not an idiot. And there's the Internet."

The redhead sighed. "Don't let him eat or drink too much at first or he'll just vomit, and he should definitely be seen by a vet."

"Noted." She picked him up and mercifully hauled him outdoors. The bright sunshine hurt his eyes after months of darkness, and he squeezed them shut. But he could still *feel* the sun on his fur, smell the fresh air, feel the blissful lack of walls closing him in.

He opened his eyes against the sun just long enough to see Meredith drop him on the back seat of a Jeep and climb in next to him. He was so desperate for contact after months of isolation that he used the last of his energy to crawl forward and place his head in Meredith's lap. Then he gave in to the inexplicable sense of safety her presence brought and let sleep drag him under.

CHAPTER

SEVEN

Meredith thought the not-dog might be dead. It had fallen asleep during the four hour drive back to Seclusion and hadn't woken when Val parked the Jeep in front of Meredith's house. Since he was still out and presumably not dangerous, she let Valkyrie haul him inside for her.

"Where do you want him?"

"Kitchen, I guess?" It was tiled, so if he made a mess it would clean easier, and it had a conveniently located sliding glass door to the backyard. Since she had no idea if its true form was capable of using a modern bathroom, she had every intention of dragging him outside for those necessities.

"Shouldn't he have some pillows or something to sleep on?" Val asked.

"Got you covered," a new voice called. Random Tremayne, Valkyrie's husband, strolled into the kitchen with a giant dog bed in his hands. He put it on the floor against the kitchen island and his wife deposited the not-dog on it.

Meredith considered the dog bed, the sleeping creature on it, and then Random. "Was this one of your intuitions or did Siren think I couldn't be trusted to provide for a dog?"

"Both?" Random flashed her a grin. "I had an urge to duck into Paws and Tails for some reason and then Siren called to say you'd heroically agreed to take on a dungeon mutt and could I please buy you things for it."

Dungeon mutt. It had a nice ring to it.

"I'll just be back with the rest of the things." Random darted outside.

Meredith looked at the creature passed out on the fluffy gray bed. It *looked* like a poor, pathetic starved dog. Was she crazy for thinking it wasn't? Had she not given up the gin in time to stop it from addling her brain?

Random came back in, both arms weighed down with canvas shopping bags. He hefted the bags onto the island and headed back to the car again.

"There can't possibly be more." Meredith stared at the counter. There were already four giant bags. How many things did a not-dog need?

"You know how he is." Valkyrie unpacked a bag full of dog food containers that looked like they could be gourmet meals for humans. She frowned at them, then shoved the stack at Meredith. "I think these have to be refrigerated."

Meredith rolled her eyes. "He would buy the hippie-dippy fancy shit."

"I was conned into it by the sales lady," Random defended himself, walking back in with a large dog crate he placed on the floor next to the kitchen island. "She heavily implied that I was a terrible human being if I bought a dog anything besides expensive, organic, grain-free superfood."

"You're such an easy mark." Valkyrie's lips pulled up in a half-grin that Random returned, and Meredith wanted to barf. Couldn't someone—anyone—in her general vicinity be miserable alongside her?

She eyed the not-dog. It was unconscious, but it did look pretty miserable. Maybe they were a good match.

Valkyrie and Random were still making puppy eyes at each

other. "Can you two take all that disgusting happiness somewhere else? I have a mostly-dead dog to hover over and ten years worth of dog supplies to put somewhere."

In short order, Valkyrie and Random took their leave. Meredith left the dog supplies on the counter because, for one, she had absolutely no one to impress with her skills of maintaining a tidy home, and two, the damn thing sleeping on the dog bed wasn't a dog.

It wasn't. So whenever it woke up, it wouldn't want to play with a squeaky hamburger toy or lick peanut butter out of something that looked like a plastic beehive. And it might never wake up. Its breathing was so shallow she might just be imagining the fractional rise and fall of its chest.

The faintest stirrings of worry pricked at her. Yes, the thing was lying about what it was, but…it had also been locked in a basement at one of Elijah's facilities. She wouldn't be very trusting after that experience either. And nothing deserved to go out like this.

Given the gaunt thinness of the creature's frame—if what she saw correlated in some way to its true form—then magic had to be tethering it to life, because it was far too gone otherwise. It had woken up briefly in the Jeep, drank a little water out of her hand, passed back out, and hadn't stirred since.

She would just check if it was still alive.

She crept forward, stopping about a foot away. When it didn't wake, she slowly reached for it, pressing her palm to its side. She felt a single rise and fall as it breathed. Then it lunged into wakefulness, snapping and snarling.

Meredith jerked her hand back, mere millimeters from sharp canines sinking into her flesh, and fell back, gracelessly scuttling away.

JENSEN CAME AWAKE to the feel of hands reaching for him.

Not again. He wouldn't go through it again. Not the poking, the prodding, the slicing into his flesh. Wouldn't let them rip him apart again just so they could watch his magic stitch him back together while they tried to figure out how it worked.

He'd given up thinking he could escape. But maybe he could force them to kill him this time. To finally end the torture.

He gathered his strength and lunged, snapping for the hand. His jaws clamped on empty air. Instead of the sharp hit of a fist to his head or a metal bar to his ribs, he heard a soft *oomph,* as if he'd knocked something off-kilter.

His eyes focused. The barren concrete walls and steel door were gone, replaced by white walls and shining white tile. Instead of dank concrete floor, something soft and comforting lay beneath his paws.

And in front of him, clearly having just fallen on her ass, was Meredith. It came back to him then. He'd been rescued by his former fling.

Which would be fine—wonderful even—if she was susceptible to the glamour that made the world see a dog instead of a wolf. Were that the case he could bide his time, regain his strength until he was healthy enough to shift again, and then simply leave. But Meredith suspected he wasn't what he appeared.

Even now she watched him warily, her eyes narrowed, studying him. He couldn't stop the growl that rose to his throat at that look. He was so tired of being studied. Of people trying to figure him out. She knew he wasn't a dog. So why had she brought him here? And where *was* here?

She tensed at his growl, then visibly forced herself to relax. "I don't trust you," she said. "Because you're lying about what you are. And you're doing it well enough that no one else even questioned why Elijah Winters would waste time having a dog locked in a basement."

Elijah Winters. The devil had a name, then.

"So I don't trust you. And because I don't know what you

really are, I don't even know if you can understand me. Can you?"

The viscerally human part of him that had been isolated and alone wanted to give her some indication that he could. This was the first time anyone had spoken *to* him as opposed to about him since he'd been taken. Well, aside from the little boy who'd been bringing him food.

But the voice of reason urged him to be cautious. Maybe he had liked her a lot. Maybe she had liked him a lot when they'd both thought the other was just an ordinary person. But he didn't really know her. He didn't know why she'd taken him in. So while she might not believe he was a dog right now, if he looked like one and acted enough like one…

He settled onto his stomach, laid his head between his paws, and whined.

Her expression softened. Then she looked irritated with herself for her lapse in wariness. "Goddess." She ran her hands over her face and he noticed, for the first time, how exhausted she looked. Like she'd been running on fumes for years. "Either you're a hell of an actor or I'm fucking insane."

He whined again and she shook her head. "Can you eat dog food?"

A Shifter metabolism meant he could eat pretty much anything without getting sick, and it had been so long since he'd had anything besides the scraps the kid had slid through his prison door that he didn't even care what it would taste like.

She sighed in frustration when he didn't give her any response. "You're getting dog food because that's what Random bought. Because everyone thinks you're a dog."

Who was Random? Her boyfriend? He had to quash a wave of jealousy. Women like Meredith—pretty, smart, funny—didn't stay single for long unless they wanted to. When he'd up and disappeared, she'd probably gone straight on to someone else.

And was he really jealous of the woman's theoretical boyfriend in the current situation?

While he'd been busy with irrational emotions, she'd been clanking bowls around somewhere behind him. She returned with a dish of water and another full of something that looked more like a Sunday dinner pot roast than it did dog food. Not that he was complaining.

"Siren said you probably need to take it slow, so this is all you're getting for now."

Siren? Must be the redhead who'd been radiating enough power to make his bones shiver. Meredith placed the bowls on the floor. Jensen's humanity was buried so far down he didn't have any self-respect left. He lunged at the food, the primal, starved part of him terrified that if he didn't eat it right this second, it would disappear.

Meredith sighed. "Try not to hork. If you don't hork you can have more in an hour."

MEREDITH THOUGHT MAYBE she *was* losing her mind after all. The day had almost entirely passed them by now, and so far the not-dog—okay, Monster, because she had to call him something—had been the epitome of an abused, starved dog. He hadn't done anything except eat, sleep, and whine at the door to go outside and do dog-like business.

Then she forced herself to focus past the belief magic wrapped around him and remembered that this morning he'd been a medium sized dog she could feel every rib on, and now he was a slightly larger, slightly less ribby dog. This morning, he'd been so weak he could barely manage the trek outdoors and back in, and he now managed a little bounce in his step.

None of which was normal. Starved creatures on the brink of death didn't just bounce back in the space of a day, even if he had eaten his way through all the dog food. But save the initial snapping incident when she'd woken him up —an obvious trauma response—he hadn't tried to hurt her.

In fact, if she had to put a label on his behavior, it would be "polite."

She was having a more and more difficult time imagining he grew tentacles. When he woke up from his eight billionth nap of the day, she decided he'd had enough rest and hydration to take care of another matter that sorely needed tending to.

She gathered a brush, a cup, and the dog shampoo Random had bought and took them to the first floor guest bathroom. She started the tub water, mixing and matching the hot and cold until she got an even warm temperature, and filled the tub halfway. Then she went back to the kitchen.

"Here's the thing," she told him. "You smell atrocious. Which I get isn't your fault, but you really, *really* need a bath. Are you going to follow me to the bathroom or do I need to carry you?"

He gave her a look of pure, doggy innocence. *Wonderful.*

She walked halfway to the bathroom. Monster stayed where he was. She walked back. *Carrying it is.*

"I'm going to pick you up. Please don't bite me. I have an extremely knee-jerk reaction to pain and I can't promise I won't drop you or throw you at a wall. We good?"

Monster whined.

She crouched, slipped her hands under his stomach, and lifted. She didn't even get all four paws off the ground. She dropped him and stared. "How much weight have you gained?" Thirty pounds, at least. Maybe more. She did a conversion calculation given the admittedly large amount of food he'd taken in today, and it still didn't make any sense.

"Okay, well, I can't carry you anymore. I get that you're sticking to your I'm-a-dog story, but the fact that this morning I could carry you up a flight of stairs and now I can't even pick you up kind of puts the lie to that. You're obviously intelligent. Don't make me go stand in the bathroom door and call *Here, boy,* just so you can maintain an illusion I'm not buying."

She stalked to the bathroom. After a moment of hesitation, Monster followed. He hopped onto the stone-tiled deck that surrounded the tub and carefully stepped down into the water. He sat down, his face frozen in what was either fear or a grimace, or both.

"I'll be as quick and careful as I can." She settled onto the deck, grabbed the cup she'd brought and dunked it into the water. She poured the water over his back, then repeated the process until she'd gotten all of his fur wet.

He sat frozen through all of it, shivering a little. Meredith squirted a large glob of shampoo onto her palm and decided this would be easiest if, for the duration of the bath, she just pretended he *was* a dog, instead of wondering what exactly she was running her hands all over.

Firmly acquiescing to the magical lie of *dog*, she lathered the shampoo in her hands and set to work.

JENSEN TENSED as Meredith worked the first squeeze of shampoo into his fur. He knew she wouldn't be going to this much trouble for him if she intended him harm, but every physical touch he'd experienced during his captivity had been harsh, clinical, or abusive.

And though she was none of those things, though she was kind and careful, he couldn't stop flinching every time she touched him. He hated that. Hated that though he knew a blow wasn't coming, he couldn't stop the reflexive flinch at each stroke of her hands. He endured it as she carefully lathered shampoo through his fur, as the water around him turned a muddy brown and then nearly black.

By the time she drained the water and started rinsing the soap off of him he was so on-edge his entire body was shivering, and he still didn't feel clean.

"I'm sorry," she said quietly, putting the stopper back in and letting the tub fill again, "but you need another round."

It was those two words—*I'm sorry*—spoken and obviously

meant, that clicked through to his brain and made him stop shaking. This time, when she started working shampoo into his fur, he didn't flinch. This time, he felt. Felt the near-ecstasy brought on by the feel of the suds working through his fur, onto his skin.

Being dirty—filthy—with no way to maintain basic hygiene, had a dehumanizing effect on a person. He hadn't realized just how much it had done so to him until he felt his humanity coming back to him with each gentle stroke of her fingers. She massaged his muscles as she worked, as if she knew just how stiff he was. As if, even though she didn't know what he was, didn't know *who* he was, she thought he deserved to be treated with care.

That was what broke him. The man—Elijah—had known exactly what Jensen was—a man capable of taking the form of a wolf—and he'd treated him like nothing. Meredith thought he could be some unknown tentacled creature that might or might not be sapient, and she still treated him with compassion.

Because of that, he gave in to what he'd wanted ever since he saw her again. He placed his front paws on the lip of the tub and buried his face in her side. He'd been alone too long. He needed comfort and familiarity, and she was here.

Meredith froze. He thought she would scramble away from him, and he wouldn't blame her. But then, seemingly perched on the edge of fight or flight, she did the unexpected. She slid into the tub, uncaring of her clothes, and held him to her, one hand gently stroking over his fur.

"I'm sorry," she whispered. "I don't know exactly what you've been through. But I know a thing or two about torture and pain, and I'd guess you've experienced both. I'd tell you it gets easier, that you get better, but…" She shrugged. "The more I try to get better, the worse I seem to get. All I know is we have to keep going, you know? Because otherwise, what the fuck was it all for?"

~

MEREDITH'S HEART wanted to break, which was a surprise, because she hadn't realized she still had one. She held Monster until his shaking from fear turned into a shiver because the water had gone cold.

"Come on," she said between chattering teeth, "or we're both going to get sick."

They got out and she toweled Monster off before shucking out of her wet clothes. He turned around, as if giving her privacy. Interesting.

She discovered Monster was amenable to being blow-dried, because after she found clothes and started drying her own hair, he padded into the bathroom and yipped at the blowdryer. Ten minutes later she had a not-dog with a blowout.

She was also exhausted, her eyelids heavy enough she thought she might actually manage some sleep if she got in bed that instant. As she drew the sheets back and climbed in, Monster sat beside the bed, a low whine in his throat. She hesitated, but screw it. She didn't want to be alone tonight either.

"Come on, then."

He hopped up, and when she shifted onto her side he settled in against her back. The steady rise and fall of his breathing against her was more comforting than it ought to have been, like a soporific dragging her under.

Maybe she just needed another person around to actually fall asleep. She'd slept well the few times she'd stayed the full night in Jensen's hotel room. With him, it had almost been like she was a normal person.

Her last thought as she drifted off was that she really had to stop thinking about Jensen King.

Bright, red-hot pain seared Meredith's chest, jolting her awake. Her wards. Something was trying to break through her wards. And they were succeeding.

She ran downstairs on the tips of her toes, barely aware that Monster followed, and grabbed the Aspect-imbued dagger hanging by the front door. Valkyrie had made it for her, and the runes etched into the hilt ensured accuracy of aim and strength. Two things Meredith couldn't manage much on her own.

Another spike of pain flared through her chest, another raw puncture in her warding. Tying the wards to her in the way she had—to her emotions, to her pain—might have been risky, but it was effective. She burst outside and jumped onto the dirt bike that was parked by the front drive for just such a need as this one. The engine growled to life. She toed the bike into gear and twisted the throttle, shooting off down the half-mile drive from the house to the front gate.

Monster tore after her, keeping pace with the bike. Impressive, considering yesterday he'd looked like he was at death's door. She didn't have much time to dwell on it. The intrusion into her wards was like a festering wound, unable to close over.

Which meant whatever had caused the breach was still there, doing damage.

That was fine. *Stay there, you asshole,* she thought. *Stay right there and let me see your face.*

But when she slid the bike to a stop just shy of the front gate, it wasn't a person she found.

The tip of a short sword bit into her wards, right between the bars of the front gates, like a knife plunged into a tree. No hand held the blade. To a Null, it would look as if the sword hung in midair of its own volition.

Aspect poured from the blade and the tip sank deeper, fully piercing the first layer of her protections. The blade and hilt were covered in dozens of runes, each one steeped in power. So much power. The weapon must have been years in the making. Six of the runes had gone dark breaking through her first ward layer and two more darkened as it sank halfway through the second.

Her wards had four layers, each successive one stronger than the last, shored up by daily additions of her Aspect. The setup was far more paranoid than even Valkyrie would bother with, because Valkyrie knew she could kill anything that got through to her.

Before this moment, Meredith would have said it'd take nothing shy of a dozen Breakers to get through her defenses. Certainly more than a single, unmanned, imbued weapon.

But the sword bled Aspect like the resource was cheap. Rune after rune went dark, until the blade pierced through the second layer and kissed the third.

Half of the runes on the blade were still unused, and there were all the ones on the hilt to go after that. Even if Meredith poured all the Aspect she had into bolstering her defenses, it wouldn't be enough.

Monster growled at the sword, muscles bunching like he was about to launch himself at it.

"*Don't,*" she ordered sharply. She didn't know how the wards would react to him. If they interpreted him as an animal they wouldn't harm him. But if they recognized him as something *other* they would grip and hold him, freezing him in the sword's path.

Mercifully, he obeyed her command, but he looked at her and gave another pointed bark at the sword.

"I know it needs to come out, I'm just not stupid enough to step on the other side of the magic line to do it." In addition to leaving her defenseless, if she tried to pull the sword free there was no telling what touching the hilt would do. Some imbued weapons defended themselves if anyone but their maker attempted to use them, and there often wasn't a way to find out if that was the case short of picking one up and seeing what happened.

She needed a way to remove the weapon without stepping across the ward line *or* physically touching it. The dagger in her hand vibrated, as if sensing her conundrum and offering its services.

She looked down, considering. The Aspect stored in it was in no way equal to what the sword possessed. But the sword had been set to the task of bringing down the wards, not fighting off another attack.

There was a chance, if she hit her target perfectly, that she could force the sword out. Ordinarily, she would put her chances of success in such a scenario somewhere downstream of ten percent. Ordinarily, she didn't have a dagger spelled for true aim by Valkyrie Tremayne.

She hefted the dagger in her hand. The magic in the runes perked up and she focused her objective, her intent, on it. Sincerely hoping she was better at giving an enchanted blade directions than she was at stabbing things with an ordinary blade, she trained her gaze on the tip of the sword and thrust the dagger at it.

The rune beneath her palm came to life, a steadying warmth burning soft against her skin, guiding her hand. Her wards, sensing her hand behind this movement, allowed the dagger to slip easily through them. Tip of steel hit tip of steel, and for a moment the two blades were perfectly balanced, point to point.

Then the remaining runes on the dagger woke, channeling strength and fury into her thrust. The sword, already battling the halting force of her wards, resisted her attempt to force it out.

But imbued weapons, for all that they were powerful, were not sentient. The sword could not make a decision to shift its power use from attacking the wards to defending against the dagger. Only its wielder could change that course for it, and no wielder appeared out of thin air to give it such instruction.

Prompted by the dagger's guidance, Meredith shoved forward. The sword popped free of the wards, clattering to the ground, its runes three-quarters dark.

Meredith considered leaving it before deciding the risk was too great. She flipped her grip on the dagger and reached across the ward line, catching the sword between the blade and the crossguard. The two weapons sparked with animosity, but Meredith managed to drag the sword through the boundary.

She examined the depleted runes. There were two types of runes in Aspect Society: standard and specified. Standard runes were the kind any Aspecter could use to imbue an item. Generic runes like that gave almost no indication of who had carved them, unless they still contained their maker's Aspect and you happened to be familiar enough with said Aspect to recognize the signature.

Most Aspecters never went past standard runes. Their use took a certain level of skill to master, and most people wasted more Aspect than they managed to imbue the rune with. Aspecters who found an affinity for rune work tended to move quickly from standard runes to specified. No dictionary of specified runes existed because they were created by, and unique to, the Aspecter who made them.

Looking at the markings on the sword, Meredith carefully placed the dagger next to it. The weapons sparked again, like two cats hissing over territory. Looking between them the similarities were obvious. The runes weren't identical but they had much in common, as if one style had been learned from the other and then modified.

"Well, fuck," Meredith said to the night air. Monster growled, seemingly in agreement with her sentiments. "What are my chances of you bringing me my phone while I guard this thing?"

He took off at a run and returned a few minutes later with her cellphone clutched delicately in his mouth. He dropped it into her outstretched palm.

"Thank you." She wiped off the slobber and called Val.

"Why are you FaceTiming me? You know I hate this shit."

"You didn't have to accept the video part of the call Your Freaking Majesty. And I did it because I need to know if you've ever seen this before." Meredith flipped the camera so it showed the sword.

Valkyrie's sharp inhale was all the confirmation Meredith needed.

"Where did you get that?"

"Someone shoved it into my wards."

"Who?"

"I don't know. They didn't stick around to chat." *Please don't ask why, please don't ask why, please don't ask—*

"I'll delay asking why until I'm there. Get it inside and whatever you do, don't touch it with your bare hands."

"It's not my first time, Val." The call ended. She sighed and looked at Monster. "You do phones, I don't suppose you do blankets too?"

Monster did, in fact, do blankets. A few minutes later she wrapped the sword up, placed it carefully between the handlebars of the dirt bike, and drove back to the house.

CHAPTER

NINE

Valkyrie stalked into Meredith's living room looking every bit a mythical battlefield warrior. Unsurprisingly, Random was on her heels, looking concerned.

She glared at the length of steel laid across Meredith's coffee table, as if her will alone could make it cease existing. "It's Elijah's," she said flatly.

Monster growled and took a step forward, putting himself between Meredith and Valkyrie. Val narrowed her gaze at him. "Is he always this friendly?"

"How should I know? I've had him all of one day." Meredith put a restraining hand on Monster's neck, hoping he didn't decide to take it off at the wrist. "He clearly just recognized Elijah's name." And possibly Valkyrie's family resemblance to the man, but Meredith wasn't going to say that out loud.

Instead, she crouched down beside Monster, once again hoping her actions were not going to result in her getting bitten in the face. Or, you know, injured by whatever natural defenses Monster's true form possessed. He was practically vibrating under her palm with how he growled, and if he attacked Valkyrie it wasn't going to end well.

"I realize this looks bad," she told him, "but I promise you we didn't like the bastard any more than you did. She killed him, I helped, and that—" she pointed at the sword "—is just a relic. One Val's powerful enough to see doesn't cause any more damage to anyone. We good?"

Val rolled her eyes. "You know he can't understand you right?" She jerked her thumb over her shoulder at Random. "He's the only one who's managed animal communication and it was a one-bird thing."

Monster, who had ceased growling while Meredith spoke, turned a scathing look on Valkyrie. Then he bumped his head into Meredith's stomach and plopped down on the floor beside her, every inch the epitome of a well-behaved dog.

"I think he just told you to fuck off."

Valkyrie started to respond, then just shut her mouth in a grim line and turned back to the sword, dismissing Monster. "Elijah started working on this one right after my mother died." She touched her finger to a rune, then another and another, picking out over half the runes on the blade. Though the Aspect in the sword grumbled, it didn't bite at her. "These are all mine. It wasn't uncommon, when he was in a foul mood, for him to have me drain my power to the dregs into runes."

Random's hands settled on Valkyrie's hips, a casual, gentle reassurance that once again made Meredith hate happy couples everywhere.

"I made this last one—" she tapped a particularly complex rune "—at twenty-one. I never saw the sword again after that. How did it end up in your wards? And how did you get it out?"

Meredith pointed at the dagger Valkyrie had given her. "Technically, you got it out. And it was in my wards because someone stuck it there."

"No shit, smartass. Who and why?"

Meredith shrugged. "I don't know." Technically the truth, even if she had her suspicions. "Clearly someone who knew Elijah, if they had one of his most powerful imbued items in their possession. It's probably just someone who misses the good ol' days and is pissed off Elijah's gone, so they thought they'd take out a little frustration on me."

"So they wasted a weapon that was *fifteen years* in the making to get through a set of wards? I don't think so." Valkyrie frowned, looking at the sword again. "Meredith," she said slowly, "half the runes on this are used up. How exactly are your wards still standing?"

"I invested a little more in security after my dear mother died."

Valkyrie gave her a submit-or-die stare. Meredith stared back.

Random fanned himself, which made Valkyrie roll her eyes, and effectively cut the tension.

"Fine, keep your secrets about the wards. But if you expect me to buy that a random Elijah underling decided to waste this because they miss the big bad, you must think I'm an idiot. If that was their purpose, they'd come after me. I'm the one who killed him."

"I helped," Meredith said defensively. "Everyone always forgets that I helped. I was vitally important."

"You were knocked unconscious during the entire fight."

"Yeah, but you would literally be dead if I hadn't gotten him to tell you how the forbidden magic bond thingy worked."

"Fine, you were vitally important, and don't think I don't realize what you're doing."

"What am I doing?" Meredith asked innocently.

"That thing where you blabber on pretending to be flighty but really you're distracting people into either avoiding the things you don't want to talk about, or letting slip what you do want them to talk about." Valkyrie crossed her arms. "So spill. What's going on?"

"Nothing." At Valkyrie's disbelieving look, she added, "It's seriously nothing. Just, after Elijah died I kept getting these flutter-touches like someone was testing the wards."

Random looked like he had a migraine. "Elijah died six

months ago. Are you, Siren, and Valkyrie *all* incapable of asking for help?"

"Yes," Meredith and Valkyrie chorused in unison.

"And I don't need help," Meredith continued, "because nothing is actually happening." Aside from Julian. But Julian was her problem. Of the previous councilors, he had suffered the least fallout. He was generally well-liked in Aspect Society, and most popular opinion was behind the idea that he—being a temporary member of the previous council—hadn't known what all they were involved in. Julian had fostered that belief diligently.

If Meredith told Valkyrie she thought he was the hand behind the sword, she and Siren would use the Council's resources to hound him. He would notice, he would make sure other people noticed, and then everyone would say that Siren was on a personal, prejudiced vendetta, and it would hurt her position.

Meredith had no intention of jeopardizing the new, better direction Aspect Society oversight was headed in by opening her mouth where Julian Astor was concerned.

Valkyrie pointed at her father's sword. "That isn't nothing."

"It was an isolated event."

"Or the beginning of a pattern of escalation."

"If the fifteen-year-in-the-making sword is the *start* of the escalation, what's next? The Infinity Gauntlet?"

Valkyrie's brow furrowed. "I don't know what that is."

"You know, *Avengers*? Powerful glove of Thanos, embedded with infinity stones?" When this didn't erase Val's look of confusion, Meredith turned an accusatory look on Random. "Don't you ever take her to the movies? You're supposed to be teaching her to have fun."

"She doesn't like the ones with magic in them," he said defensively.

"I don't know if the infinity stones can be properly classified as magic. We don't fully understand what they are. They could just be advanced technology or something."

"For all intents and purposes of the viewer, they look like magic," Random argued. "If you consider—"

"She's doing the distracting thing to you again," Valkyrie said.

"Huh." Random gave Meredith an appraising look. "You're really good at that."

Meredith shrugged. "It's easy with lawyers. You like to argue and you're bad at letting things go."

"I'm putting a security detail on the house," Val said.

And, here we go. "No, you aren't. This isn't a matter for Council security."

"If someone is trying to break through someone's wards, it is absolutely a matter for Council security."

"If I weren't your friend and something of this nature occurred, Council security would take a report and look into the matter. And only then if the homeowner asked to file that report in the first place. I don't want to file a report and I don't want a security detail."

"You know, when I was hellbent on doing everything on my own, you literally stalked me until I accepted your help."

"I hung out outside Random's house *one* time waiting for you to sneak off on a suicide mission. It doesn't qualify as stalking. And this is different."

Monster shifted to rest his head on her thigh, as if resigning himself to being here for a very long time. In that moment, it was difficult to remember that he was not a dog, and this therefore wasn't cute. Ignoring the urge to stroke his fur, she glared at him.

"How is it different?" Valkyrie asked. "And why are you looking at that dog like it's going to eat you?"

Jensen was wholly confused about just what the hell he'd gotten himself into. The scene playing out before him was more like something out of a soap opera than ordinary life. Then again, he didn't know if anything involving Aspect or Shifters could reasonably be termed "ordinary."

He'd settled in for the long haul, which Meredith didn't seem to appreciate.

"We're in an uneasy truce," Meredith said.

"He's a dog, Meredith. All you have to do is feed him and he'll be happy. He's practically in your lap."

"I'm aware," Meredith muttered. Jensen grinned and licked her hand. She jerked it away. "Gross, Monster. Licking me is not the way to my heart. *Anyway*, are we done here?" she asked Val.

"Not until you agree I'm putting a security detail on the house."

"Are you *trying* to undo all the work we've done regarding the Council? How do you think people are going to take it if it looks like Siren's playing favorites where her friends are concerned? The security teams are understaffed as it is with all the people she's had to fire in the corruption investigations, and you want her to have to explain why she's wasting around-the-clock details on my house over *one* incident?"

"Kyrie," the man called Random said, "you know I hate to disagree with you, love, but she does have a point. Siren's handling her detractors well, but they'll latch on to any excuse they have to find a problem with her. Our little redhead's exhausted, which I know because Jace is driving me nuts worrying about how exhausted she is."

"So you think we should do nothing?" Her tone was so caustic it should have melted flesh off the bone. Random looked at her like she'd said something particularly sweet, and stroked a soothing hand up her arm.

"No, love, I think you should leave Meredith a few more imbued weapons, set some extra wards around the doors and other entry points to the house, and agree that if something happens again she's going to call us. Immediately."

"I am?" Meredith asked.

"Yes," Random answered, completely self-assured, "because if you don't, we're moving in."

"You can't just move into my house. It's *my* house."

"Have you met my wife, your best friend? You try stopping her from parking her ass here twenty-four hours a day to keep you safe."

Meredith let out an adorable frustrated growl. "Fine. I promise I'll call if something happens."

Valkyrie narrowed her eyes. "Immediately?"

"As soon as reasonably possible."

"Are your fingers crossed?"

"What are we, twelve?"

"Are they or not?"

Meredith grumbled and held her hands up. "I promise to call if something happens."

Valkyrie nodded, satisfied. "I'll go set up some backup wards. There's so many damn windows on this house I might as well just do a full perimeter ward directly around it, inside your main setup. I'll leave it un-keyed so you can take over adjustments. Random, if you want to take her out to the car, she can pick whatever she wants from the weapons in the trunk."

As soon as Valkyrie swept outside, Meredith said, "You let her take over your trunk with weapons? I guess it's true what they say about a man just wanting a woman to rearrange his furniture."

"Very funny. If you were married to her you'd let her put her damn weapons in every moving vehicle you owned, too. She's a trouble magnet. If that woman walked into a sunny spring meadow full of flowers and frolicking kittens a dragon would descend out of nowhere to challenge her, and don't think you're getting away with the distracting thing again." He pointed directly at Jensen. "I wasn't sure earlier, but I am now. That's not a dog. Why does Kyrie think it is? More importantly, why haven't you told her it's *not*?"

Jensen refrained from growling at Random because acknowledging he understood what the guy said would make him seem less dog-like.

Meredith settled what felt very much like a possessive hand on his back. He didn't hate it. "What makes you think I think he's not a dog?"

"For one, because if you actually thought he was a dog, your response would have been, 'What the hell, Random, why are you acting weird?' For another, the part of my Aspect telling me it's *not* a dog feels suspiciously like truth."

"You are such a weird freak of nature."

"I'm going to take that in the loving, friendly spirit I'm sure it was intended in. What is he?"

"I don't know," Meredith answered. "I'm just hoping his true form doesn't have tentacles."

What was with her obsession with tentacles? Did she have an extreme fear of sea creatures?

"But I would appreciate it if you didn't mention this to Val. Or anyone else for that matter."

"If anything happens to you and she finds out I failed to tell her your dungeon mutt was not in fact a dog, she's going to kill me."

Jensen almost rose to the bait of being called a *dungeon mutt,* but the challenge in Random's eyes when he spoke the words told him the man was hoping to get a rise out of him. The worst thing he could do right now was look dangerous. He scooted closer to Meredith and pressed his head into her stomach.

"Yes, he's quite vicious, as you can see," Meredith said wryly.

"He's certainly smart, as he's cozying up to the woman intent on keeping his dirty little secrets. *Why* are you keeping them?"

Meredith sighed, and Jensen was suddenly very interested in what she would say next. "Look, he hasn't tried to hurt me and I don't think he will. You didn't see him when we pulled him out of Elijah's basement. He was basically dead. And whatever the man did to him down there couldn't have been pleasant.

"If I went through that? I wouldn't exactly trust Aspecters either. And let's face it, our society has a history of elitism and bigotry and fearing everything it doesn't understand. You saw what they tried to do to Siren when Jace found her. You know what they would have done to you if they'd understood when you were younger just how powerful your screwball Aspect was going to be."

"Again, taking that in the loving spirit I'm sure it was intended."

"The point is, there are many different forms of power out there. It would be foolish to think we know what all of them are. But while we may not know about them, I'm pretty sure they all know about us. Aspect doesn't maintain a low profile in the magical world. So if Monster wants to keep what he is to himself, I'm fine with it so long as he doesn't hurt anyone."

A knot in Jensen's chest unwound, even as he told himself not to get too comfortable. Meredith saying she was fine with him being something *other* was one thing. Her seeing it and being okay with it was another.

Random looked at Monster. "Any magical being in Seclusion has two weeks to identify itself to the Council upon entering our borders."

Jensen felt Meredith bristle. "Are you *threatening* my not-dog?"

Random sighed. "Of course not. I'm merely letting him know that once he's recovered enough, he should go home before he hits his two week limit."

IT TOOK ANOTHER HALF AN HOUR, but Meredith finally convinced Random not to say anything to Valkyrie about Monster, and then convinced them both that she wouldn't be killed or kidnapped the second they left. She had dutifully promised to key herself in as the primary on the wards Val placed around the house, and now she was done. Exhausted. She figured she'd gotten maybe an hour of sleep before the attack had woken her up, as it was now past one in the morning.

Monster still sprawled across her lap—he had moved from resting his head on her leg to practically crawling on top of her—and she would swear the front half of his body alone now weighed fifty pounds.

"You can stop pretending to be asleep," she told him. "Everyone's gone."

He opened a bleary eye and looked at her, and she thought maybe he had actually fallen asleep after all. Clearly, however his magic worked, it required large doses of sleep and food to do its job. She wondered if running out after her had set his progress back, and she was oddly touched that he'd done it.

"You gonna get up?" she asked him. "You're not as light as you used to be and my legs are half asleep." He made a grumbling sound and gently picked himself off her, no paws digging in to soft flesh like a normal dog would do. He walked over to the food bowl she'd placed on the floor for him earlier and sat there, expectantly.

"I don't know how to tell you this," she said, "but that month's supply of dog food Random brought? You already ate all of it. Can you eat human food?"

In answer, he went to the fridge and pawed it open. Then looked back at her with a disappointed, mildly accusatory look. She thought there might be a carton of orange juice in there. Maybe.

"What? I'm not exactly Susie Homemaker. If you wanted a casserole, you'd have had better luck with Random. When I asked if you could eat human food I meant do you want to order takeout? We have a great twenty-four hour place that delivers."

He trotted over. She pulled the menu up on her phone. "Uh, I guess just bark or whatever when you see what you want."

She'd barely gone past the appetizers when he barked. And kept barking every time she scrolled. "Are you changing your mind about what you want or are you trying to tell me you want all of it?"

He barked again. It was starting to hurt her ears. "Was that a yes or a no? Paw my knee if you want to order literally every entree on the menu." He pawed her knee enthusiastically. Of course he did. "Fine, but only because I'm still feeling sympathetic towards you on account of the basement torture, and you heroically running out after me when my wards got attacked."

She went through the virtual checkout, muttering. "You'd better be glad you landed with a rich bitch, Monster, because no one else could afford to feed you."

The food arrived forty-five minutes later, delivered by a bleary-eyed twenty-something surprised to find one woman and one dog waiting for the order that required her to make three trips from the car to the kitchen island. Meredith opened the containers for Monster, set them on the floor, and left him to it. If he was actually capable of consuming that much food, she figured the activity was one best left unobserved.

She went upstairs, grimly determined to attempt sleep again. But it wasn't until Monster jumped up on the bed an hour later, his back pressed against hers again, the she finally fell asleep.

CHAPTER

TEN

Sunlight hit the backs of Meredith's closed eyes, dragging her into the land of the living. She never bothered to close the window curtains because she never managed to sleep past the dawn. Except this morning, she apparently had. She felt amazing. Rested. Not even the smell of dog fur in her face could ruin how glorious her body considered a full night's sleep.

Wait a second. Dog fur?

She cracked an eye open and realized, to her great mortification, that sometime in the middle of the night she had rolled over onto Monster's side of the bed. She was not, thank the goddess, cuddling him, but she was smooshed up next to him and her face was buried in his neck ruff.

She extricated herself with extreme care, so as not to wake him. Really, a lifetime of sleeping alone should have made her more likely to want to maintain her space in a bed, but the few nights she'd slept over in Jensen's hotel room had proved she was apparently a sleep snuggler. Every morning she'd woken up wound around him like a boa constrictor and worried it was going to annoy him. He'd never seemed to mind, though, and it was just another thing she'd liked about him.

"Oh, for fuck's sake," she muttered to herself, "stop thinking about him."

Monster, who had woken up despite her best efforts at stealth, gave her the canine version of an inquiring stare.

"Not you." He still looked curious. What the hell was he interested in her life for anyway? She sighed. "Just asshole men who disappear and then never bother to answer your texts." Weren't men supposed to outgrow that leave-and-dodge-responsibility behavior once they hit thirty? A simple, *Hey, it was fun but it's over*, could have done wonders for her peace of mind.

And she was still thinking about him. Clearly, she needed to occupy her mind. "You hungry?" Monster yipped. "Right. You're always hungry."

Jensen had been like that. The man had a metabolism that could rival a teenager's, and *what the hell was wrong with her?* She'd been doing an excellent job not thinking about him until Siren and her damn matchmaker plans dredged up his memory. At least, that was as good of an excuse as any for why the guy was suddenly taking up all her brain space.

She placed a grocery order on her phone, which was later delivered by the same young woman who'd brought their takeout the night before. Apparently she did the restaurant orders at night and grocery orders during the day. The lack of sleep had made her go from bleary-eyed to red-eyed, and she looked as confused as ever about the amount of food she was delivering to a household that still only contained one woman and one dog-like creature.

Meredith tipped her a ridiculous amount in the hopes she could afford to take a day off from work and get some sleep. Then she put her limited culinary skills to use—they were at least better than Val's—and cooked a breakfast suitable for a family of five. She gave four-fifths of it to Monster and picked at hers while she stared at her phone's contact list.

She would rather eat glass than call Julian Astor. Especially after he'd shown up at her house and told her she would do just that. Monster looked up from the food he'd mostly eaten through, as if sensing her dilemma.

"What do you think? Ignore the problem and hope it goes away, or call my creepy stalker and find out why this is happening?"

He whined.

"You're right. Ignoring problems never makes them go away." She made the call.

Julian's cultured voice drifted across the line. "Meredith, to what do I owe the pleasure?"

"You left one hell of a calling card last night."

Julian chuckled. "I'm quite certain I have no idea what you're talking about."

Of course. "You said you wanted to talk to me about something. I'm ready to listen."

"Shall I come over?"

Hell no, you shall not come over. "No. I'll meet you at The Poisoned Leaf in an hour."

"I would prefer a more private setting."

I'd just bet you would. "You aren't the kind of person best met in private. I'll see you in one hour."

She hung up, then stared at the phone for a moment before she rose and grabbed her keys, heading for the door that led to the garage. It would only take her fifteen minutes to get there, but she preferred to arrive early.

Monster jumped in between her and the door.

"I'm not having a good day," she told him, "and I need to leave."

He shook his head, a low growl emanating from his throat. "Look, I will be back in plenty of time to make sure you don't starve to death if that is the problem. Or if you want to leave now I can let you outside the house and the perimeter wards. But I need to go."

This time, he didn't answer her. He just gave her a stare she would swear was a little sad and a lot resigned. The magic that had surrounded him since she'd found him in Blackthorn Manor's basement, that had so successfully hidden him even to the sight of her Truth Aspect, shimmered, flickered, and dissipated.

Gone was the innocent-looking mutt. In its place stood a massive wolf, pure white, and so tall its shoulders were at Meredith's navel. She barely had a shocked second to think, *Well, at least he doesn't have tentacles,* before the wolf trembled and began to change.

IT HAD BEEN SO LONG since Jensen had worn the human form he'd been born to that he was afraid he'd forgotten the way back to it. It happened sometimes, Shifters driven by grief or necessity into their animal form for an extended period, until eventually they forgot they'd ever been human. But though his magic resisted him at first, he held tight to the memory of being human, of having two legs instead of four, and hands that did things. The once-familiar prickle of the shift danced through his paws.

The pins and needles grew from unpleasant to painful as his fur melted, giving way to skin. Then agony replaced pain as the crunch and grind of his bones breaking and regrowing swept through his body. Time ceased to have any meaning as his body reformed, but he suspected it took longer—far longer—than it should have for him to shift.

When it was finally done he was sweaty and panting, still hunched on all fours on the tile kitchen floor. He looked up. Meredith's eyes had gone wide, moving through the different stages of confusion, disbelief, shock, and finally fury.

Slowly and deliberately, as if afraid he might lunge for her, she backed away, her magic wrapping around her and growing dense, like a shield. She back up two feet, then four, then six.

Just as slowly, just as deliberately, he stood. She hadn't run away screaming or thrown anything at him. Based on his experiences with people confronted with the existence of Shifters for the first time, that was a good sign. But he didn't like the wariness in her eyes.

"Jensen?" She whispered his name, the two syllables laced with confusion and incredulity.

If he'd had more time, he would have prepared what to say to her. As it was, he didn't know what words would put her at ease, if any could. So he went with what he'd wanted to say since he'd found her again. "Hey, darlin'."

The strangled noise that came out of her mouth bore no resemblance to anything human or animal he'd ever heard. Considering he'd grown up in an enclave of Shifters, that was saying something. She spun to the right, grabbed the first thing within reach—a toaster, as chance would have it—and hurled it at him.

Fortunately for him, her throw was hampered by the fact that toasters were not particularly aerodynamic, and she'd neglected to pull the plug from the outlet before lodging it at his head. It was a testament to the energy she'd put into the throw that it still reached him.

He caught the toaster easily and placed it on the counter nearby. It would serve as a decent shield in the all-too-likely event she decided to throw something else at him.

He broke out his most soothing tone, the one he used on kids who had just come out of their first Shift and were wild-eyed and a little feral. "That's a reasonable reaction. I can understand why you'd be upset. But I think if we just—"

"You can *understand* why I'd be *upset*?" she shrieked. Yes, shrieked was definitely the right word for that tone of voice. And he was willing to wager that pretty, polished Meredith had never once shrieked in her life. "You've been living in my house and it didn't occur to you to try and communicate that you're a freaking werewolf?"

She stiffened, as if her own words had made her come to

some inner realization, and before he could muster a reply she said, softly, almost to herself, "Werewolves don't exist. Everyone knows that." She took another step back, away from him and closer to the butcher block of knives sitting on the counter. "And whatever you are, you can apparently look like anything you want. What game are you playing at? I haven't done anything to hurt you. I helped you. I don't fucking deserve this."

"I'm not playing a game, Meredith. And I'm just a Shifter. Nothing else."

She gave a low, dry laugh. "It's convenient, how you pulled on a human skin after I mentioned missing someone. Are you a Memory Reader?" She scanned his body, as if trying to find something that would indicate he was indeed a Memory Reader —whatever that was.

"I don't know what a Memory Reader is. I'm just Jensen."

ELEVEN

Meredith checked that her Aspect shield was firmly in place and inched closer to the kitchen knives. Whatever this thing was, it wasn't Jensen. So what if Memory Readers—beings who could pluck memories from a mind and make a person see them—had been extinct for over a hundred years? It was still a more plausible explanation than a werewolf.

"Jensen wasn't—isn't—part of the magical world. He owns a construction company for goddess' sake." She sounded like a bad actress in an action film where a woman discovered her husband was really a super spy. *No, you've got it wrong. Dan isn't a secret agent, he's a sales consultant.*

"I do own a construction company." Jensen's voice took on a distinct soothe-the-crazy-person tone. "I'm also a Shifter."

"I've never heard of Shifters."

He arched an eyebrow. "What happened to the pretty speech you gave Random about being certain that things existed you didn't know about?"

Oddly enough, that statement made things easier for her to understand. Everything he'd done so far—from how he'd acted to who he looked like now, to throwing her own words back at her—followed a pattern of being curated to her expectations, playing into things she'd foolishly told him when he'd looked like a dog and she'd been grateful for his company.

"Oh, I'm certain it's still true. I'm certain I don't actually know what you are. I'm also certain I can't trust a word you say, and I don't have the time or the inclination to get the truth out of you."

So what if her Aspect had stopped saying *lie* now that he'd taken human form?

"I have to go. I have no interest in harming you, but since you've clearly recovered, I also have no interest in leaving you in my house. You can follow me out and we'll go our separate ways."

She stepped forward. He didn't move.

"I can't let you go meet him," he said softly.

"You can't *let me*? *You* don't *let me* do anything. No one *lets me* do anything. *I* do things. *I* control my life. Not you and not anyone else." Not anymore. Never again. "Now get out of my way."

He winced, and in that moment he looked so much like Jensen she almost believed her Aspect telling her it *was* him. "I'm sorry, those weren't the right words. My human side's a little rusty. But I need you to talk to me. That guy on the phone? He gave me to Elijah. He kidnapped my sister. I have to find her if it's not too late and I need your help for that. So please, talk to me."

Meredith was pretty good at telling when people were lying, even without using her Aspect. It came part and parcel of living life as a Truthfinder, and all of her instincts, in addition to her magic, were telling her that Jensen wasn't lying. But instincts were fallible, and powerful magic could trick almost anyone. His ability to fool everyone around her except for her and Random was proof enough of that.

But if he *wasn't* lying... Jensen had looked haunted the entire time she'd been with him, as if some dark burden weighed on him and he only found brief moments of lightness when he was with her. She'd felt the same way about him. It was part of what had drawn her to him. Had that weight, that darkness, been a missing sister?

He must have marked the chink in her resolve because he said, "Your magic—it has something to do with truth, right? That's why my glamour didn't work on you? Can't you use it now? Tell I'm not lying?"

I already am, and I don't like what it's telling me. If she made the physical connection lesser Truthfinders needed to tell truth at all, there would be no doubt to what her power told her.

Wisdom dictated she send him on his way. But in the end, she didn't have it in her. If he really was Jensen, she couldn't just throw him out and tell him to deal with his problems on his own. Especially not if Julian had been responsible for those problems.

"Alright," she said, sounding steadier than she felt. "But first thing's first. You need pants."

Somehow, in the midst of this crazy, he found an amused smile. "It's nothing you haven't seen before."

"Which is why we're covering it up. I know exactly how distracting it is." The words just fell out of her mouth. *Dear goddess, what was wrong with her?* She fled the room for the basement. Walking through the apartment-like space hurt. She didn't usually go in. Lurking in the doorway and reliving painful memories was more her speed.

They clawed at her now, begging her to *remember, remember, remember.*

Remember leaping off the stairs, one-hundred percent certain her father would catch her. He had, even though he'd been on a business call. He hadn't been mad, and he hadn't made her leave, just held her on his hip and walked around with her as he talked.

Remember sneaking down here when she'd had bad dreams

and wondering why Daddy didn't live upstairs with her and Mom. Thinking how much nicer things would be if he did.

Remember—

Remember his screams the night he'd died, and how long they'd gone on before she'd had the courage to come down here, and by then it had been too late. Remember him smiling through the pain she was all too intimately familiar with. Remember him saying, "I love you, baby girl," before his heart gave out.

"Meredith?"

She jerked. Jensen stood at the top of the stairs. How long had she been standing lost in the middle of this room, if he'd come to check on her?

"Are you okay?"

"I'm fine." She strode into the closet. The clothes within were pristine, untouched by time, the result of preservation spells she diligently touched up every month. She'd cast them on the basement a few months after her father died, needing to hold on to what little she had left of him.

Her mother had never commented on Meredith's upkeep of the room, and she didn't know if Savannah had ever even noticed. For all Meredith knew, her father and everything associated with him had gone right out of Savannah's mind the second his heart stopped beating.

Meredith searched through the clothes for anything that might fit Jensen. Malnutrition had left him thinner than she remembered, but he was still a larger build than Jared Townsend had been. She found a pair of sweats and an old t-shirt that might work and tossed them at Jensen.

He dutifully donned them. The sweats were predictably a little snug around the waist and the t-shirt stretched tight across the shoulders, but at least he was clothed. They could go back to the kitchen and get this over with.

He reached out as she walked by, the lightest brush of his fingertips and a soft, "Hey," all it took to stop her in her tracks. She'd missed him and that…hurt.

"Whose room was this?"

She shook her head. "No one's. Come on. I need to leave, so we need to get through this." Back in the kitchen, she said, "I need a physical connection." She held out her hand. He didn't take it.

"You didn't need a physical connection to know something was off when you found me."

To lie or not to lie? "I don't typically require it. But since your magic has fooled me once already, this will guarantee foolproof results. Is that a problem?"

He placed his hand in hers. She pulled her Aspect up to the surface, let it flow through her into him. She heard his quick intake of breath, but he gave no other indication that her power bothered him.

"Tell me your name."

"Jensen Michael King."

She tested the feedback from her power, considering its reaction to his response. Most people begrudged her the truth of their answers, fighting the inevitable tug and pull of her power. Jensen didn't. Her Aspect tested his words easily, its conclusion clear: true.

"Are you the man I met at Savado's, and that I was involved with for almost a month?"

"Yes." Again, no hesitation on his part or her power's.

"Did you approach me at that bar because you knew I had a connection to Aspect Society and you wanted to exploit it?"

"I approached you because I was lonely and you looked like you were too."

Nice try. "Truth, but not all of it."

"You can recognize half-truths?"

"Yes. What else made you approach me?"

He gave her a look she didn't know how to interpret. "Why does anyone approach a stranger at a bar?"

"That isn't an answer." Was there something he didn't want

her to know? He hadn't give her a direct *no* to the Aspect question.

"You're hot," he clarified. "I also approached you because you're hot."

Right. Now she felt like an idiot. "Did you have *any* ulterior motives for approaching me other than the ones you've mentioned?"

"No."

"Did you at any point in the course of our—" she almost called it a relationship, but quickly shifted it to "—involvement become aware that I was a member of Aspect Society?"

"No. I liked you. Is that so difficult to believe?"

Yes. And it sucked that he was telling the truth because it meant they'd actually had something. Whether or not it could have lasted, she'd never know. That foundation had now been, if not obliterated, at least buried beneath the hefty baggage of two intersecting magical lives.

"And Julian abducted you?"

"That's the bastard's name?"

"He was the man on the phone, yes."

"Then yeah."

"And he took your sister?"

"Yes."

She could think of only one reason Julian would abduct anyone, much less give one of those abducted individuals to Elijah Winters. "Did Julian know that you're a—" what term had he used? "—Shifter?"

Jensen nodded, a movement her Aspect pinged as true.

"How?"

"I don't know. Believe me, I wish I did." True. "My kind does everything we can to stay hidden from yours. Aspect Society is the bogeyman we frighten our children with."

She frowned. "Why? I've never even heard it theorized that Shifters actually exist."

"That's because we've worked very hard to make it that way. Your kind and mine have an unpleasant history. If I'd known you were Aspect when I met you, I never would have come anywhere near you."

Ouch.

"Did Julian take you and your sister at the same time?"

"No. Natalie disappeared a couple months before that, and eleven more Shifters right after her. I had no idea *who* took her, but it stood to reason it was Aspect-related. So I came to Aspect Society's doorstep hoping to find some trace of her."

She'd met him in Fayetteville, on one of those times she'd made the twenty minute drive from Seclusion, hoping that acting like a normal person in a normal city would make her *feel* normal. It hadn't, but he had.

"I'd shift and glamour and search the city. Never found anything. I was about to admit I was never *going* to find anything when Julian grabbed me outside the hotel." His eyes turned cold. "This guy. How do you know him?"

"He used to work with my mother, and before you ask, no, she wasn't a nice person."

"You called him after you found the sword. You think he tried to break in here. Why?"

"If I knew why, I wouldn't be meeting with him. He has an unhealthy obsession with me, but even I can't see him spending Elijah Winters' sword on my wards just because he can't get into my pants. He wants onto this property and I'd bet ten to one it has something to do with my mother.

"As for you...don't take this the wrong way, because I hate the man, but are you sure he took your sister and the others? He gave you to Elijah. My friends and I have spent the last six months tracking down absolutely everything to do with Elijah, and there's nothing left of his to find. You are the first Shifter we've come across."

"I'm sure. The guy practically got off on telling me because he knew I was looking for the others. Because he wasn't sending me where he sent them. From what I gather, he owed Elijah some kind of debt and I was payment. The guy specifically wanted a wolf Shifter."

"So you aren't all wolves? Some of you become other animals?"

He hesitated. "The less you know, the better."

"Better for me, or better for *you*?"

"Both." There was something in the tone of his voice that set all of her alarm bells off.

"Why do I get the feeling you aren't supposed to be discussing any of this with me?"

He hesitated. "Because you have good instincts."

"Elaborate."

He ran a hand over his face. "Don't betray Shifter existence is the first edict Shifter kids learn to live by. Especially where Aspect Society is concerned."

Which begged the obvious question. "And what happens to those of us a Shifter *has* told?"

"If they're Null, most of the time they don't believe whoever told them. In the rare event they do, we convince them they were confused, or we discredit them. It's not hard to do these days with social media. If that doesn't work, more extreme measures are taken."

Uh-huh. "And if they *aren't* Null? If they are, for example, Aspect?"

He didn't answer, which was answer enough.

"I see." Her voice dropped several degrees. "Were you planning on getting rid of me once you were done with me?"

"No. I was planning on you staying here while I go handle Julian. I was planning on trusting that the kind of woman who would take care of what was, to her, an unknown magical creature, wouldn't turn around and betray my existence to the whole of Aspect Society. My people don't ever need to know you were involved."

She put all that together, making sure she had the pieces right. "So your brilliant plan is that you, barely back from the brink of death, are going to go off and, what, interrogate Julian until he tells you where your sister and the other Shifters are?

"Suppose you do manage to get the drop on him, avoid his Aspect, and miraculously get him to give you the answers you want. Let's be extra suppositional and suppose you even manage to recover the Shifters. What do you think happens then? Do you mean to tell me that, with absolute proof that Aspect Society was involved, your people aren't going to seek retribution?

"We'll be on the verge of a war and Aspect Society won't even know it's coming. You have every reason to dislike us, but there are good people here. If you think I'm going to stand by and let them be harmed, you're very mistaken."

"I have no intention of seeing our peoples go to war."

"*You* may not. Can you make decisions for the whole of your people?"

His jaw clenched. "No."

She hadn't thought so. "Then let's handle this together. I know Julian. If you think he is working alone, you're wrong." Julian had ambition, but he'd never had vision. He'd been her mother's lapdog, then Elijah's. He would have found a new master to serve after Elijah died. Someone else powerful enough to make him feel untouchable again. "He won't be an easy target. Even so, I'm not going to hold you prisoner. If you want me to let you walk out of here alone, I will. But if you take that route I don't think I'll ever see you again, and it won't be because you've found your sister and you're living happily ever after.

"This is my world, Jensen. And like it or not, you need me to navigate it. You need help."

He ran his hand over his face again, shoulders slumping. He looked as tired as she felt. "Why?"

"Why what?"

"Why help me? You think I'm going to die if I do this on my own, so why not let me? Nothing would get back to my people that way. No proof, no worries about Shifter retaliation against your people. It's the easy way out."

CHAPTER

TWELVE

Jensen could tell he'd hurt her by the way her head jerked back. Then her face went calm, so expressionless he couldn't read a thing.

"Whatever you may think of *my* kind, I'm not a monster. Even if I didn't know you, I would try to convince you not to do this on your own. But I do know you. I liked you, Jensen. I'd rather you weren't dead."

He blew out a breath. "Okay. If you want to help, I'd be an idiot to say no. But if we're doing this, the odds of my people not finding out your involvement are slim to none, and I don't want your death on my conscience." He threw out the possibility of her death casually, almost cruelly, because the alternative was to face the truth of just how hard her death would hit him. He was already having to face the possibility that he wouldn't find Nat alive. He didn't want to contemplate another person he cared about dying.

Why had he had to fall so hard for Meredith? He barely knew her. Why did she have to turn out to be Aspect Society? He'd gotten himself through some of the rougher points of his captivity by remembering her. By imagining that he could get out and find Natalie and, once his sister was safe, he could come back here and find Meredith.

Come up with some bullshit excuse to explain why he'd been gone, and see if they could pick up where they'd left off. If she'd been a Null, it would have been fine. Shifters didn't have a law against dating Nulls. It wasn't even unheard of for Shifters to marry Nulls. But if they did, most of the time they had to move out of their enclave and keep Shifter existence a secret, in which case they couldn't have children because Shifter blood always ran true.

There was a second option. One way in which it was acceptable for a Shifter to reveal their true existence. They could bring their Null significant other into the enclave and show them what Shifters were. The Null was given a week after that, during which they were under constant guard, to accept what they'd seen and agree to be bound by magical oath never to reveal it.

Few Shifters took that option because if at the end of the week the Null didn't agree, they didn't leave the enclave alive. Only one Shifter in Jensen's enclave, Keelie, had ever gone that route. Her Null fiancé had taken the oath to save his life. Then he'd left and never spoken to her again. That had been three years ago and she was still broken up over it.

If Meredith had been Null like he'd thought, Jensen would have taken the first option. But Meredith was Aspect. He didn't have the first option. The oath was the only thing that would protect her. The respect his people had for that bond would convince them to hold their claws long enough for him to make them understand she wasn't a threat. Now he just needed to get her to agree to it.

"There's one way my people will forgive you knowing what we are. I need your oath that you will never speak of Shifters to anyone who doesn't already know about us. That you will accept my people as you would your own. In return, I give you that same oath."

She hesitated. "You do understand that being a Truthfinder

doesn't mean I can't lie? If you think any promise I make is binding because of my Aspect, it isn't so."

"I don't want you to promise. I want you to make an oath." His words did nothing to alleviate her skepticism, so he added, "A magically binding oath."

Her voice turned harsh. "I don't engage in blood magic."

"I'm not suggesting we cut our palms and shake on it."

"Then how does this magic work?"

"It just…does. I make a promise. You make a promise. Magic seals the bargain."

She frowned. "How?"

"How what?"

"*How* does magic seal the bargain?"

"I…don't follow." Magic was magic. Shouldn't Aspecters know that better than anyone?

She groaned. "Please tell me you aren't proposing to use magic you don't understand the basic mechanics of."

"It's magic. Not science."

"In all ways that matter, magic is *exactly* like science."

"If you say so."

She rubbed at her temples, as if he was giving her a headache. "Is this particular magic used often among your people?"

"Yes."

"Are there ever any adverse side effects?"

"Only if someone breaks their oath."

"Have you ever personally used this magic before?"

"No."

"Why not?"

"I've never been tempted to tell any non-Shifters we exist before."

"Are the risks equal to both of us? Does one party have an advantage over the other?"

Did she hang out with lawyers or something? "The risks are equal, and no."

"What happens if one of us fails to uphold our end of the bargain?"

"The oath will physically prevent you from speaking about Shifters to anyone who doesn't already know about us. As to our mutual promise to accept each others' people as our own, as long as we never deny the connection, it's nothing to worry about."

"And if we do deny it for some reason?"

"I honestly don't know. I've never seen it broken."

He could see her dislike of that answer on her face. Honestly, he couldn't blame her. But she let it go and pressed forward.

"Can the magic be nullified in some way?"

"If we both agree to its undoing, or one of us dies."

Meredith wore a pained expression. "You understand that what you are describing sounds remarkably like a reciprocal curse?"

He laughed. "Curses aren't real."

She gave him a look. "Werewolves aren't real."

He pointed at himself. "Not a werewolf."

"Fine." Meredith threw up her hands. "Shifters aren't real."

She had him there. "Point taken. So, uh, curses? Those are a thing?"

"Yes. They are technically illegal within the bounds of my society, but they are a thing. In fact, Siren, the redhead who wanted to heal you? She was cursed when I first met her."

Jensen's eyebrows rose. "What kind of curse?"

"The kind that wouldn't let her tell us anything about the man who'd been hunting her for years. We worked around the issues it posed, and she eventually killed the man who cursed her, thereby ridding herself of said curse. *Now* do you understand why I'm seeing similarities between what you're proposing and a curse?"

Grudgingly, he had to admit she had a point. "Are all curses bad?"

"Of course they're all—" She broke off, considering. "I don't know. Can I see the spell structure?"

"Spell structure?" he echoed. What the hell was she talking about?

"How do Shifters describe your magic use if 'spell structure' isn't in your vocabulary?"

"We don't."

She gestured vaguely. "You know, *spell structure*. How you weave the magic together to make the spell form?" He shook his head and she gave a little huff of frustration. "How exactly do Shifters use magic if none of this is ringing a bell?"

"We just use it," he said. "I don't see you weaving spells every time you determine truth."

"Truth is an innate affinity for me, of course I don't need a spell to—" She broke off, her eyes narrowing. "Are you telling me that Shifters have an innate ability to use curses?"

"You're really hung up on the logistics of this, aren't you?" Which was good for him, since her obsession with understanding how it worked was distracting her from asking anything else about it.

"I dated an Aspect-theory-obsessed genius nerd for four years. It rubs off."

He tamped down on the jealousy that flared at that casual statement. "What happened to him?"

She waved a dismissive hand. "He married Siren."

"Your ex married one of your best friends?"

"Yes, though I fail to see how that's relevant to this conversation. Alright, so we're engaging in a mutual curse." She pursed her lips and he could see her thinking—no doubt running through all those genius nerd theories she'd learned from her ex. Then she gave a delicate little shrug. "I suppose there's no real harm in it."

Whatever had prompted her to agree, he was willing to bet it had absolutely nothing to do with her thinking there was "no real harm in it."

"Can the oath be modified?" she asked.

"What?"

"The oath, can it be modified? At the moment, I'm promising two things—my silence and accepting your people as my own. You're only doing the latter. It seems unevenly skewed in your favor."

"So your issue isn't with voluntarily engaging in a mutual curse, but that it's not an equal bargain?"

"What can I say? I believe in equality."

Alrighty then. "What do you want?"

"I want you to promise that you will do everything within your power to prevent bloodshed between Shifter and Aspect societies."

"You so sure that's a decent bargain? For all you know I'm wildly unpopular and no one takes my opinion seriously."

"You're extremely popular and everyone takes your opinion seriously."

He raised an eyebrow. "Did you divine that truth out of thin air?"

"I didn't have to. You're an easy man to like, Jensen."

Her words hit him right in the gut, almost as hard as the realization of what he was about to do. He never thought he'd make this oath. Never thought he'd care about any woman enough to make it, and the knowledge they planned on dissolving it didn't make it all that much easier to swallow.

It's a strategic alliance. Not a damn marriage. Sure. Tell that to his people.

He managed to unstick his throat. "You've got a deal."

You're an easy man to like? Where the hell had that come from? She was supposed to be a Truth*finder* not a Truth*spouter*.

Why don't you go wrap your arms around his neck and tell him you missed him and you really thought you might have had something special?

Goddess. She made a disgusted noise at herself, which made Jensen look at her weird. What had he said last? Oh, yes. They had a deal. "Great. How does this work?"

"Give me your left hand."

She dutifully held it out. For a minute she thought he was going to hold said hand. He sort of did, but instead of palm-to-palm he slid further, his hand closing gently around her wrist. She closed her own hand over his wrist in imitation and ignored the happy little thrum that went through her body at touching him. Clearly, she needed to get out more.

"Ready?" he murmured. Did he have to say it all bedroom voice, like touching her was affecting him as much as it was her? And was she imagining things, or had his thumb just stroked the inside of her wrist?

She glanced up at him and immediately knew looking at him had been a mistake. His eyes were hot, practically the definition of a smolder, exactly like he'd looked at her the first night in that bar when he'd asked if he could kiss her. This time, she knew it wasn't her imagination when his thumb swept over the pulse in her wrist.

Her breath hitched and he shifted closer. "I missed you," he said softly.

She wished her magic would pin the words for a lie, but it didn't. *I missed you too.* She didn't say the words. She knew better. She also knew if she didn't do something to freeze the heat sizzling between them his lips were going to end up on hers. Then they would forget all about society-bridging magical promises and the fact they had a very limited timetable to get this done before she had to go meet the devil.

"You were locked in a basement for six months," she said lightly. "I imagine you missed everyone under the sun. Let's get this over with, I need to leave in" —she glanced at the clock— "ten minutes." She saw in Jensen's eyes that he wanted to argue, so she pulled on the cold, empty society princess mask she'd worn for so much of her life, retreating behind poise and indifference until, as one person had memorably told her, it was difficult to discern if she was a person or an ice sculpture.

Confusion flickered across his face. She'd never been *this* person with him. She'd never had to be. "Jensen?" she prompted coolly.

He cleared his throat. "Yeah. Right." Magic sprang between them without warning, like the way a spark could send a room up in flames in a matter of seconds. Magic encircled their wrists and hands, twining over the back of her palm and then down between them to curve back over Jensen's, like an invisible ribbon binding them together.

Jensen locked her gaze. "I, Jensen Michael King, give my oath that I will treat your life as my own. That I will treat your people as my own. To the best of my abilities, I will do all I can to prevent bloodshed between our two societies."

The way he spoke the words, the phrasing and the intensity, made her think uncomfortably of wedding vows. But then, in the modern world, people didn't usually make vows outside of the marriage kind, so she shouldn't find the similarity that disturbing.

The magic curling between them grew hotter, more intense with every second she remained silent. It demanded she open her mouth and return the vow. "I, Meredith Dawn Townsend, give my oath that I will not speak of Shifters to anyone not already aware of their existence, and I will treat your people as my own."

The magic snapped taut, like a ribbon being tied tight, binding them together.

"So witnessed," Jensen said. He looked at her and she repeated the words.

The magic sank into her skin and vanished. She pulled her hand from Jensen's grip. A tattoo marked the underside of her wrist. An infinity loop stretched from one side to the other, drawn in silver and edged in a smoky black. In the right circle rested the Aspect symbols for her affinities. A lit torch, to symbolize how the light of truth reached into even the darkest of places, and an old stylized compass, meant to show that a Tracker always found her way. The left circle held an ornate stylized number one with a *J* layered over it, both of them stamped on top of a wolf's paw print.

She dragged her eyes from her tattoo to Jensen's. His was an inversion of hers, the infinity symbol black edged in silver.

"You failed to mention this vow came with permanent ink."

"To be fair, you didn't ask." He gave her an apologetic grin, dimples popping into existence. That smile was a weapon, meant to disarm. She had no doubt he knew it and exploited the effect ruthlessly. "Think of it like a protection mark. See a Shifter, wave tattoo. You look good with ink."

She stabbed a finger at the overlapping *one* and *J* in the lower loop of her tattoo. "This is you, I take it?"

He nodded.

"What's the *one* for?"

"It's my lineage symbol. There were six founding Shifter families that came to this part of the world. The Kings were the largest so we're considered the first. The *J* is obviously me."

That was when something absolutely horrible occurred to her. She had a *J* tattooed on her wrist. Next to a freaking number one. Inside a damn infinity loop. Julian would inevitably think it was about him. Siren and Valkyrie, weird as they were being lately, would undoubtedly think it was about Jace. It did have a sort of romantic look to it, what with the *J* in one half of the infinity loop and her Aspect affinities in the other.

What were the odds she could convince everyone it was some sort of memorial tattoo for her father? Why did she know so many men whose names started with *J?*

Ugh. "This is worse than getting married."

Jensen made a choked sound that he quickly turned into a hacking cough.

"Tell me it's not worse," Meredith demanded. "Your initial is on me like a freaking ownership brand."

He finally managed to stop coughing and replied, "If I own you, you own me in return." He waggled his own tattooed wrist at her. "I just had no idea your views on marriage were so strong."

She shrugged. "Marriage is great for people who want to do it. I just don't see the point of trying to chain someone to me with a legal agreement that makes it difficult for them to leave me. Someone signing their name on a piece of paper doesn't prove they love me, and I'd rather know someone's with me because they want to be, not because they feel like they have to be."

He stared at her. The expression on his face fell irrefutably under the definition of "dumbfounded." A creeping sense of horror overcame her. "Oh, goddess, don't tell me you're one of those men who thinks there's something wrong with a woman if she doesn't want to get married and have two-point five children."

"No," he said quickly. "I'm just usually the one being told something's wrong with him. Most Shifters are convinced they have a biological imperative to form happy little family units and produce at least one, but not more than four, little baby Shifters."

Relief hit her as his words rang true, before she reminded herself that it didn't matter if his relationship views lined up with hers. They weren't in a relationship. They were not *going* to be in a relationship. But she couldn't stop herself from asking, "Why not more than four?"

He grimaced. "No one's masochistic enough to want to run herd on more than that many small humans capable of sprouting fur and claws."

It was on the tip of her tongue to ask if all Shifters turned into predatory species and what determined it, when her gaze fell on the stove clock. "Shit. I need to leave."

He stood as she grabbed her keys and purse. "I think you mean *we* need to leave."

He had to be joking, right? "You said Julian was the one who took you."

"And?"

"So won't he recognize you in human *and* wolf form?"

"Yes," he acknowledged.

"Then how do you think you are going to come with me? *Oh, it's fine, Julian,*" she said, switching to an empty, air-headed voice, "*just ignore my Shifter friend. Yes, don't worry, I'm still totally willing to listen to anything you have to say. No, Jensen completely forgives you for kidnapping him.*"

"I'm suggesting you put me on a leash."

"What?"

"Elijah wanted two things out of me: to understand how Shifter healing worked, and to break me. He wanted the Shifter version of a trained German Shepard. I'm guessing Julian knows that you and your friends took down Elijah's compound. He's already going to be wondering what happened to me. How hard do you think it will be for him to learn you took a 'dog' home with you? The easiest thing to do is pretend Elijah succeeded in breaking me, and you're my new master."

"That's sick."

"It's practical."

"And you're okay with playing broken?"

"If it's my best chance of getting Natalie back? Yes."

She mulled it over. "There's one more thing you should take into consideration," she said. "When I told you Julian was obsessed with me, I meant it literally. There is every likelihood he found you in the first place because you were involved with me."

"I've already considered that. I don't blame you for it."

How generous of you. "Neither do I. But even if it's not the case, Julian's likely aware that I was involved with you, that you know me. If he knows I took you out of Blackthorn Manor, he isn't going to trust that you wouldn't have revealed who you are to me, hoping for support. I can get around that, but I'm going to have to say some unpleasant things."

"Like what?"

"Like pretending I knew exactly what you were all along. Like pretending maybe *I* was in the market for a Shifter from the beginning."

"You think you can make him believe that?"

"Please. I convinced the whole of Aspect Society, including my own mother, that I was an empty-headed idiot for most of my life. Convincing Julian I'm as ruthless as my mother was, as he *is*? He'd love nothing more than for that to be true."

CHAPTER

THIRTEEN

Meredith shifted and nudged the Porsche Spyder a little faster, but the smooth feel of her car hugging the asphalt as she sped around curves at inadvisable speeds wasn't having its usual soothing effect on her. She hadn't realized how nice it had been just being herself the past few months, until she was faced with the necessity of being something else again.

She parked outside The Poisoned Leaf tea house and touched up her lipstick in the rearview mirror. Jensen had shifted into his wolf form, his glamour on to show a big, friendly white dog.

Meredith dropped the lipstick into her purse and couldn't quite bring herself to meet Jensen's gaze. "Just remember that how I act in there, the things I say—that isn't me."

She got out and Jensen followed, the two of them walking inside. The tea house was a small affair, three storefronts down from Old Hank's Hand Me Down Sound and directly across the street from the Knitting Needle, owned by Old Hank's paramour, Betty Lou.

Despite the cafe's grim name, it was as colorfully decorated as the woman who sat behind the counter. Ella Tremayne was somewhere in her late sixties, with black hair and olive skin. She wore a dress that bore every color in the rainbow. It would have looked ridiculous on any other woman, but on her it seemed almost severe.

She was Random's great aunt, and Meredith had grown up calling her Aunt Ella. Meredith hadn't dared to use the familiar address since she'd broken up with Jace all those years ago. Aunt Ella viewed both Random *and* Jace as her sons, and Meredith had more or less ceased to exist to the woman—at least in any positive light—after the way Meredith had ended things.

So for the last few years, she'd been relegated back to the ranks of Aspecters who publicly called Ella *Ms. Tremayne*, and privately called her the Queen of Death. While Meredith and Jace were on good terms again, she still wasn't entirely sure where she stood with the Queen of Death, so she settled for a neutral, "Ella."

Aunt Ella inclined her head.

Meredith cast a glance around at the empty cafe. When Valkyrie had told Meredith her mother-in-law had decided a tea shop was the thing to do with her spare time now that she no longer had the Council to keep her busy, they'd both had a good laugh envisioning it. Now that the store was open, neither of them were laughing. Mainly because Random forced them all to patronize the shop on a rotating basis, because ninety-percent of Aspect Society was too afraid of Aunt Ella to go anywhere near it.

Today the cafe was empty, but every single table had a triangular sign resting on the top. "Reserved?"

"Betty Lou's having a knit-off across the street. They've reserved all the tables for the after-competition victory celebration." She gave Meredith an appraising once-over. "Isn't Monday your day to stop by? Or did Random think if he put you on a rotating schedule I wouldn't realize he's humoring my small-business plans?"

"No idea what you're talking about." Meredith smiled.

"I'm sure."

"I need outdoor seating anyway." She patted Jensen's head.

The Queen of Death fixated on him. Quicker than a blink, a slip of power streaked from her. Meredith snapped a shield around Jensen. Ella's Aspect bit into it. Meredith fed more power into the shield. "That's rude," she said mildly, "and you're on probation."

Aunt Ella sighed and her Aspect winked out. "What have you brought into my shop, child?"

"Nothing you need to concern yourself with. Can I get a poisoned earl and an arsenic brownie?"

Ella swiped Meredith's credit card and handed it back. Tying an apron over her dress, she set about pretending to be a normal woman who ran a death-themed tea house. A couple minutes later she set an Earl Grey tea and a double-fudge brownie on the counter.

"Thank you." To tell Aunt Ella she was bringing Julian Astor to her cafe, or not to tell her? Ugh. Never a bright idea to surprise the Queen of Death. "I'm meeting Julian. Would you send him outside when he arrives?"

Ella's eyes narrowed and she took on a gentle tone. "Dear, I know you had hoped things would go differently with Jace—"

For the love of the goddess, if *one more person* mentioned the fact she *used* to date Jace a hundred years ago, she was going to discover heretofore-unknown-to-her Elemental fire powers and explode into a volcano of molten rage.

"—but you shouldn't settle for someone like Julian. Oh, I know he was let off the Council business with a slap on the wrist like I was, but the difference between us is I was there to try to prevent worse harm from occurring. He was there to foster it. And besides, the man's a wet towel. Ruthless, to be sure, perhaps a bit of cunning in the mix, but no real brains to speak of."

Nice try, but I'm not going to tell you why I'm meeting him. "I'd be a fool to ignore advice from someone so old and knowledgeable."

The Queen of Death chuckled. "You always did know how to

play the game too well to be goaded into giving out information. I pray you know it well enough not to get yourself into waters too deep to swim out of."

You and me both. She took her tea—in a bright yellow mug shaped like a cat, complete with little kitty ears—and her brownie outside. A large white oak dominated the center of the courtyard, its branches spreading wide. Of the tables scattered beneath its canopy, Meredith chose the one nearest the tree. She took the seat that put her back to the wide trunk. Jensen settled onto the ground next to her and dropped his glamour.

Julian emerged into the courtyard ten minutes later. Ella had served his tea in a pastel pink owl mug, and it grievously offended him if the way he set it on the table was any indication. She supposed it didn't match his suit.

"Did you have to pick this place? That old hag is insufferable."

"That old hag could kill you without lifting her pinky."

"I doubt she remembers how. She hasn't done anything interesting in years. All that power and she opens a bloody tea shop."

Meredith took a sip of said tea. Say what you wanted about the Queen of Death, but she knew her tea. "Did you want to talk about entrepreneurship, Julian, or did you want to talk about why you put a sword through my wards last night?"

"At the moment, I'm more interested in where you got that." He pointed at Jensen.

"Monster? I picked him up in a charming little holding of Elijah's called Blackthorn Manor. Of course, I wouldn't have had to spend the last few months tracking them all down looking for him if you hadn't stolen him from me in the first place."

Julian's eyes narrowed. "So you *did* know what your little contractor was when you were fucking him."

"Was he actually a contractor?" Meredith gave a breezy laugh, to Julian's obvious annoyance. "How delightful. You know, I can't decide if I should be annoyed with you, or grateful. On the one hand, I wasted a month fucking him, as you so charmingly put it, only for him to be stolen out from under me right when I was getting somewhere with him.

"On the other hand, sometimes it is nice to just send a dog off to the trainer and not have to dirty your own hands with the work."

Julian appraised her. "I can't decide if I buy it," he said finally.

"Buy what?"

"This." He waved a hand at her. "I always suspected you weren't as empty-headed as you made out, but suddenly wanting to play on the dark side? You've spent all your time of late cozying up to the new Council."

She shrugged. "They have their uses. Like my little Monster does. The question is, Julian, are *you* useful to me?"

He leaned back in his seat. "I think we can be useful to each other. Especially if that—" he pointed at Jensen "—is as tame as you say. Unfortunately, given your association with Siren, we do have a trust issue."

"If anyone has a right to a trust issue, it's me. Why do you want onto my property?"

He didn't give her a direct answer. "Have you ever heard of the Oddities Auction?"

"No." But she had a very bad feeling she knew just what sort of "oddities" were up for bid.

"It takes place once every decade and deals in rare magics. Old magical items, mostly, and—" his eyes flicked to Jensen "—other things of interest."

"Things like Monster?" she asked casually.

"Perhaps. My employer runs the auction."

She'd known it wouldn't take him long to find a new master to serve.

"It's in two days. I want you to attend it with me."

"Flattered though I am by the invitation, magical artifacts aren't my thing. And what does any of this have to do with you shoving Elijah's sword into my wards? Wouldn't you have been better served selling that at your little auction?"

He smiled indulgently. "That wasn't me personally, for the same reason the sword wasn't worth selling. Elijah and Valkyrie were the only ones capable of handling it without causing themselves irreparable damage. I'm sure you've sent it back to her, but I am curious. How did you break it free? Once activated, it should have been unstoppable."

She'd gotten under his skin, then. Good. "If I tell you, will you finally answer my question?"

He inclined his head.

"Valkyrie sucks at birthday presents. She's obsessed with weaponry, so to her, the best possible gift is a throwing dagger personally imbued by her for strength and true aim. I had it lying around, so I gave it a go at pushing out the sword."

"I see." He almost looked disappointed. What had he been hoping she would say? "To your question, then. The items for the auction are often curated years in advance and delivered to various caretakers. Your mother was one such caretaker. We are missing the items that should have been in her repository, and Analisa has made me personally responsible for finding them."

Analisa. Meredith didn't think she knew anyone with that name, but she would double-check with Siren and Valkyrie. "And if you don't find them before the auction?"

"Analisa will be displeased." The tone of his voice left no doubt that Analisa's displeasure wasn't something to be taken lightly.

"And you've waited until two days before the auction to become serious about finding them?" That didn't make any sense.

"Oh, I'm quite serious about finding them. But they should have passed into Elijah's possession after her death. It wasn't until *he* died that Analisa realized he hadn't chosen a successor of his own, and the location of the items was lost."

Meredith decided to poke the hornet's nest. "Sounds like your mistress needs to keep a better watch on her underlings."

"She is my employer, not my master," he said sharply. "And people cross Analisa at their own peril. She is…a god, in her own way."

That boded well.

"Until now, my focus has been on searching Elijah's holdings for the repository. As you know, those holdings were many, and scattered. I saw no reason to interfere when you were doing such a marvelous job of tracking them all down for us."

He'd been watching them. Her, Siren, Valkyrie. The last six months while they worked to undo Elijah's misdeeds, Julian had been quietly watching.

"However, now that you've found the last one and we've scoured it, I'm certain Elijah never moved the repository from wherever your mother kept it." His nose wrinkled in distaste. "I never understood why she chose him as her backup. He cared for nothing except his experiments."

"Are your feelings hurt that she didn't choose you?"

He gave Meredith a sharp look. "I gave her ten years of my life. She owed me."

Meredith laughed. "My mother never cared about anyone but herself." She drummed her fingers on the table. "So you think this repository is somewhere on my property?"

"It stands to reason." He paused for a moment, then, "I have until tomorrow evening to work with you in finding the repository."

"Or?"

"Or Analisa's thralls will find it instead. I assure you, they will have no difficulty with your wards."

Meredith had never heard of a thrall, but she disliked the idea of a bunch of them storming her metaphorical castle. "And, having told me precisely when I can expect this attack, what is to stop me from having Council security prevent it?"

He leaned in. "What prevented you from calling Council

security when you wanted me away from your home? From calling them last night? From taking an actual job for the new Council? Maybe your new friends don't trust you as much as you claim. Maybe Siren wouldn't be too upset if something happened to you. Or maybe," he settle back in his chair, "you know that you don't belong with them.

"You're wasted on them. I've put a great deal of thought into how Valkyrie could have lived after she killed Elijah. No one but him could have told her how to survive the dissolution of the Council's adnexus, and that's a thing he would have had no reason to tell her."

Meredith's blood went cold.

"You're far stronger than you've let people believe. Tell me, do your little friends know you can compel truth?"

"No," she lied.

A smug smile teased his lips. "I didn't think so. They underestimate you. I don't. Work with me."

The man actually thought he had a temping offer. "For Analisa?" *Tell me something useful about your mysterious employer.*

"For now. Her influence extends far beyond Seclusion. Beyond Aspect Society. This place is…small, in the grand scheme of things. She's a stepping stone. One we'll use as long as it's convenient."

Meredith pretended to take the offer seriously. "I'll consider it. I'll find this repository for you. I'll attend the auction and meet Analisa. After that, we'll see." She stood. Julian's Aspect lashed out and froze her in place. As an Immobilizer, his Aspect had a paralytic effect. Though she'd seen it used often enough, she'd never been subject to it herself. Hadn't thought he would dare to use it here, in Ella Tremayne's cafe.

Her eyes, the only part of her body he'd left under her control, must have darted toward the door because Julian said, "I'm not afraid of her." He stepped into Meredith's space and lifted a hand to brush her hair from her face, his fingers lingering. "You are so beautiful."

Every inch of her fought to jerk away from him, but he had complete control of her body. Beside her, Jensen gave a low, warning growl.

"Tell him to shut up if you want him to live," Julian snarled, and he released her from the neck up.

"Everything's fine, Monster. Lie down." For a moment, she was afraid he wouldn't listen. She could break Julian's hold on her—but she didn't want him to know that. It was the ace up her sleeve, to be saved for a more desperate moment than him getting handsy with her. But if Jensen attacked him and Julian retaliated, she wouldn't have any choice. And any hope they had of getting to the auction, where Julian's sister was most likely going to be up for bid, would go down in flames.

Slowly, deliberately, Jensen dropped down at her side, but the damage was done. Julian had been toying with her before, letting her know he held the upper hand. Now he was pissed.

"Does it still have feelings for you?" Julian's fingers tightened in her hair, bringing unwilling tears to her eyes. "Do you have feelings for *it*?" He stepped closer, his breath hot in her face. "Do you let it turn into a man and fuck you at night?"

She didn't give an answer, because he didn't truly want one. There wasn't anything she could say that wouldn't enrage him. This was the side of Julian few people had been privy to. In public he was urbane, sophisticated, incapable of being rattled. But in private, *this* was Julian. He went from calm to fury faster than her car went from zero to sixty.

The fist in her hair tightened again, strands ripping from her scalp. "I don't like to be toyed with, Meredith. You know this partnership isn't just a working relationship. It's you and me, and you already know you'll take it, because you have nowhere else to go. You're mine." His free hand snaked out, crushing her against him, his Aspect releasing just enough to turn her body pliant. "No one else touches what's mine, am I clear?"

Every cell in her body rebelled at that statement. *Remember what's at stake.* She forced herself to nod.

"Then kiss me. Kiss me like you kissed *it* in that trashy hotel, like you couldn't wait for it to rip your clothes off."

Oh, goddess, had Julian watched them? The thought made her sick. The room had been on the fifth floor. They hadn't always bothered to close the curtains.

"Make me believe it, and if it doesn't lift a whisker to intervene, I'll let it live."

His Aspect released her fully. That made it worse, and he knew it. Because she had to choose to slide her arms around his neck. To pull his face down to hers and brush her lips to his. To close her eyes and take it further, until his hand fisted in her shirt and his body stiffened with a response she didn't want.

And then he shoved her off him, like she was somehow degraded, and wiped his mouth. His eyes glittered with something that might have been rage or lust or both. "Find the repository. Call me with its location by tomorrow evening."

He turned and walked out of the courtyard. She stood there, frozen, as he climbed into his car and drove away. Then her whole body started to shake, like a leaf in the wind, and wouldn't stop. Jensen whined low in his throat. He pressed up against her, but his warmth couldn't cut through the chill in her bones.

"It's fine," she managed. "Everything's fine."

She swiped her keys from the table, dropping them twice before she got a firm hold. The courtyard didn't have an exterior exit, so she walked back through the cafe. It was filled with cheerful knitters who all went silent as she walked through. That was when she realized she was crying.

She was almost to the door when Ella's disappointed voice said, "I thought you had more sense, girl."

She glanced over her shoulder, hands fisting at her sides. "Oh, fuck you."

Meredith was in her car doing ninety, going anywhere but home, before it occurred to her that she'd told the Queen of Death to go fuck herself.

FOURTEEN

Jensen watched Meredith drive, the rage boiling beneath his skin making shift magic itch in his bones. Her hands gripped the wheel and the gear shift so tightly her knuckles had bled white. She looked as sick as he felt. It had taken everything he had to lie still while Meredith wrapped herself around Julian. Everything he had not to rip out the man's throat.

There was a bone-deep insistence beneath his skin whispering that Meredith was *his*, even if she wasn't, and that made him even sicker. To remember the way Julian had said, *You're mine*, like she was property.

If he could shift maybe it would dispel some of his fury, the energy consumed by the transition enough to calm him. But every time he started to regain his human form Meredith snapped, *"Not yet,"* and he held off.

He had no idea where she was going. It wasn't back in the direction of her home and she was speeding so egregiously, the speedometer nudging past one-hundred miles-per-hour, that he couldn't even memorize the turns they were taking.

Aspect poured off her in soft waves, trailing out like a ribbon behind the car, and he scented the same type of magic that had made his sister's trail impossible to follow when she'd gone missing. Meredith was ensuring they weren't being followed, and she was spending a lot of power to do it.

By the time she finally slowed and pulled the car off the road, driving down a dirt path a vehicle this low to the ground had no business being on, he had no idea where they were. Because they weren't *anywhere*. The path swerved, ending in a small clearing hidden from the road by a thick shelter of trees.

Meredith turned the car off and just sat, staring out the window, her jaw clenched. When he started to shift, she didn't tell him not to. It went more quickly this time, his human form easier to find, a few minutes of pain and reshaping bones before he could open his mouth and demand, "Are you okay?"

"I'm sorry," she said without looking at him.

She was sorry? "For what?"

She shivered and refused look at him. "The things I said about you—the way I treated you."

"I'm the one who should be sorry." She'd told him Julian was obsessed with her. But she'd said it so flippantly, like it was nothing, that he hadn't taken it for the literal truth. He asked again, quietly, "Are you okay?"

When she still didn't answer he raised his fingers to her cheek, to the small bruises already forming where Julian had dug his fingers in. For a moment she was perfectly still. Then she shuddered and closed her eyes, pressing her face into the palm of his hand.

"It's okay," he said soothingly.

She gave a sharp, short laugh. "Liar."

Of course he was a liar. Nothing about what had happened was okay. "It'll *be* okay." He would make it okay. Somehow. Whatever he had to do, he wouldn't let Julian do anything worse to her than he'd already done.

"How?" she asked softly.

"Come here." The way she'd leaned into his hand told him she needed to be comforted, to feel a touch that wasn't Julian's.

He could give her that. He *needed* to give her that. He drew her across the console and she came willingly, maneuvering through the small space in the car like a master contortionist until she straddled his lap, the roughness of her jeans sliding against his naked thighs.

He'd meant only to hold her, to rub some warmth and feeling in her until the fire came back into her eyes. But she'd barely settled atop him before she leaned in and kissed him.

He froze. If he moved at all he was going to rip every stitch of clothing off her, and he wasn't going to do *that* until he was certain it was what she wanted.

She stilled at his lack of response and opened her eyes. There was need in them, tempered by confusion and hurt and the fear of rejection. "Is this not okay?"

"It's more than okay, darlin'. I just don't want you to regret it."

She relaxed, the hesitance in her eyes giving way to desire. "I won't. But it's just sex, Jensen. We're clear on that?"

"Just sex," he repeated, and if she heard the lie in those two words, she didn't call him on it. Sex with her wasn't *just sex*. It never had been. But he wasn't thinking about it anymore when she drew her shirt over her head and stripped off her bra, baring the lush curves of her breasts. He palmed them and flicked his thumbs across her nipples. She arched into him, her core pressing down against his hardness.

She adjusted the seat back as far as it would go and then her fingers fumbled at the clasp on her jeans, undoing the button and zipper, but that was as far as she got. The car was small, and he didn't see any way in hell she was getting her pants off inside its confines.

"We going anywhere after this that requires you to have pants?" he asked.

"I have spare clothes in the trunk."

"Perfect." He gripped her jeans to either side of the zipper and tore. The fabric split along the seam under the assault of

Shifter strength, a perk he hadn't truly appreciated since his teenage years, which was the last time he'd found himself so desperate to fuck a woman that he took her in a car off the side of a road.

He'd barely finished shoving jean material away before she took hold of his cock, shoved her panties to the side and slid down onto him.

He groaned as her tight heat wrapped around him like a fist. "Fuck, are you still on birth control?"

"Yes."

Maybe there was a god after all.

MEREDITH TOOK Jensen in to the hilt, and the aching emptiness that had plagued her since…well, since he'd left, finally abated. She was full of him, his shaft stretching her to her limits. She settled there, her hands on his chest, his gripping her waist, and let herself feel completed.

Just sex. It had never been *just sex* with him. But she needed to pretend it could be, needed to let herself have this, have something that felt right, after how wrong Julian had been. So she pushed the *what-ifs* and the fears away and just *felt*. Felt Jensen's hands as they skated up her sides to cup her breasts again, felt every movement of his shaft deep inside her as she drove herself forward, riding him.

There was no finesse to the coupling, no slowness, because that wasn't what either of them needed. She built a fast, hard rhythm, her fingers coming between her legs to work her own need, sending her skyrocketing up the slope of pleasure. She balanced there at its peak, listening as the sounds of Jensen's breathing quickened, feeling it as his muscles grew taut beneath her. Another swivel of her hips drove him deep inside her again and when he jerked, spilling into her, another circle of her fingers sent her hurtling off that edge of climax after him.

THERE WAS no small part of Jensen that wanted to stay in this moment forever, with Meredith cuddled against his chest, spent and satisfied, his arms around her. In this moment, stuck in that sense of limbo pleasure brought on, they could both pretend there weren't worlds and problems between them.

But those things *were* between them, and he knew she'd remembered it when she sat up, the easiness leaving her body as she slid off him. He wanted to pull her back to him, to kiss her, to tell her exactly how much he'd missed her. But her words, *Just sex*, whispered in his head.

He pulled on the clothes he'd brought and then darted out into the frigid December air to retrieve Meredith's clothes from her trunk. She cleaned herself off with her old shirt, put the new clothes on, and then pulled the car back onto the road. Neither of them spoke until they pulled up to her estate.

Everything was in place, the front gates closed, but as she punched in the code and they drove through, he couldn't shake the feeling that something was wrong.

"Could he have sent someone here while you were gone?"

Meredith shook her head. "You saw what it took to try and get through the wards. Exactly four people can pass through mine without alerting me, and I trust them all implicitly."

She pulled into the garage. As she shut the car down and got out, he sprinted to the door ahead of her. He still couldn't shake that feeling of wrongness. "Let me go in first."

She rolled her eyes. "You're not getting all protective on me, are you Jensen?"

It was so good to see her snappish and sarcastic again, instead of shaking and terrified, that he grinned at her. "And if I am?"

"Goddess, sex makes men stupid."

No sense in denying the truth to a Truthfinder. He went in ahead of her. The house felt wrong, too, but he couldn't put his finger on what. To his Shifter senses it smelled like home should: the lingering scent of breakfast, the smell of Meredith through-out, and Shifter.

Shifter. Shit. *Meredith's* home shouldn't smell like Shifter.

"Get out of here," he ordered.

A furry shape hit him like a freight train, knocked him down and sat on his chest. Claws pierced his throat, not quite breaching the carotid, but close, while a second heavy form landed on his legs. It was a submission hold. He was stronger than an average human, but not enough to throw off the combined weight of the two Shifters holding him down. With the claws on his throat, if he Shifted, he'd cut his own carotid. It wouldn't kill him, but it would knock him out of commission for a few minutes while magic sealed the artery and grew new blood cells.

Meredith didn't have a few minutes. Jensen strained, knowing it was futile. "Get off me, Hel."

The lynx snarled in his face, her claws inching a fraction deeper into his neck.

CHAPTER

FIFTEEN

Meredith had barely registered Jensen's order to get out when something large, furred, and snarling rammed into her. Her back hit the edge of the kitchen island, sharp and hard, the air fleeing her lungs in a rush. A jaguar latched onto her front, claws digging into her right shoulder to hold its position as its other paw raked down her chest, lines of acid-dipped pain ripping through her skin.

But Meredith and pain were old friends. She got her knee up between her and the cat's hind legs before it could make a cat's classic move to disembowel, and she snapped her arm in front of her neck, preventing its teeth from latching on to her throat. Sharp fangs bit through her forearm and clamped down.

She did the only thing she could think of. She shoved off the counter and bore the jaguar to the ground, landing on top of it. She thought it was surprise more than anything else that made it let go. Whatever the cause, it gave Meredith the split second she needed. She scrambled back and wove an Aspect shield in so short a time even Valkyrie might be impressed. The jaguar leapt to its feet, lunged for her, and hit hard against the protective bubble.

Physical shields, like this one, were rarely used in actual

combat, because while they prevented anything from getting to the person they protected, they also prevented the person inside them from interacting with anything outside. Using one was a last ditch, *I am so fucked I am going to hide in this bubble and hope someone rescues me*, kind of shield.

Meredith was *so* fucked. Her chest and ribs burned from the lacerations, and the amount of blood pouring down her arm suggested something important had been pierced by jaguar teeth. She clamped her hand over the wound. Fat lot of good it was going to do, considering she didn't have much strength to put into the effort.

The world went woozy. She was vaguely aware that Jensen was fighting two people—no, Shifters—across the room but her vision wouldn't focus enough for her to notice any more than that. She slumped against the kitchen island and pressed down harder on her arm. The problem was, she couldn't feel the fingers in her left hand anymore.

The jaguar flung itself at her shield again and again. When Meredith inevitably passed out, her shield would come down and those sharp fangs would close over her neck. If she didn't bleed to death first. She had never spent a great deal of time imagining her own death, but had she, she didn't think she'd have come up with death by jaguar. Certainly not death by jaguar Shifter.

She was thinking through fuzzy thoughts, trying to arrive at the conclusion that she should find something to use as a tourniquet, when a black-clad form hurtled into the jaguar.

Valkyrie. Either this was the luckiest day of Meredith's life, or Val hadn't been able to leave well enough alone. Not that Meredith was complaining. Jaguar claws swiped and tore at Val, trying and failing to pierce the Battle Aspect armor that coated the warrior like a second skin.

Meredith heard what sounded like every faucet in the house turn on and a rush of water spilled into the room, separating Valkyrie, Meredith, and the jaguar from Jensen and the two others. The two dropped Jensen and focused on coming to the jaguar's aid. But there was no crossing the wall of water before them because Jace stood in its center, the water subject to his every thought. Each time the shifters tried to navigate it, the water hurled them back.

A few feet away, Valkyrie bore the jaguar to the ground, her blade readying to strike a killing blow, and Meredith didn't need Jensen shouting her name in a plea for her to scream, "Val, stop!"

Val froze, the tip of her dagger just piercing the jaguar's chest. "It tried to kill you," she pointed out.

"This has just been a big mis—" Her vision hazed and she blinked hard, trying to focus. "Misunderstanding," she finished. She tried to move forward again but something held her back.

"Sorry, sorry, I should have been here sooner." Siren was at her side. She sounded tired and faintly ill again, and Meredith wanted to tell her not to fix her, that she wasn't worth it when something was obviously wrong with Siren herself. Unfortunately—or fortunately, she supposed, since the cool Aspect flooding into her body was literally saving her life—she never managed to form the words.

Her vision and thoughts cleared as her wounds knitted closed. An uncomfortable sensation, like IV fluids being pumped into her veins, spread through her.

"Are you regrowing my blood cells?" she asked.

"Yes," Siren said, sounding more tired and sick than ever. "Be grateful."

"Well, you've regrown enough of them," she snapped. "I'm not going to die, but you look like you might if you keep going."

Jace's head jerked toward his wife at those words, his grip on his Aspect faltering, and in the momentary opportunity provided by his lapse in attention, Jensen broke through the water wall. He made it all of two feet before Random cut him off with an upheld hand, his be-whatever-it-needs-to-be Aspect freezing Jensen in place.

"I really wouldn't," Random said casually. "I'm a reasonable man, but the women in this room are a little kill happy."

Great. Everyone was here. So much for secrecy. How in the hell was she going to explain this?

Siren finally stopped pouring Life Aspect into her, fingers trailing down one of her arms, then the other, as if she might find some wound in a physical inspection that she'd missed with a magical one. Her hand paused on Meredith's wrist.

"When did you get a tattoo? And why does it have a *J* inside an infinity symbol next to your Aspect Affinities?"

Every Shifter in the room went dead still, a change that wasn't missed by any of the Aspecters. The pinned jaguar let out a noise Meredith couldn't begin to guess the meaning of, and shifted. Gold and black spotted fur melted away, and after a minute or two of cracking and shifting—during which Valkyrie didn't so much as blink at what was happening beneath her— the jaguar was gone and a very beautiful, very naked woman lay in its place.

Her golden eyes sparked with fury, and she looked at Jensen like no one else was even in the room. "You *married her?*"

Meredith would have laughed at that obvious misunderstanding if Jensen hadn't immediately replied, "Yes."

Every gaze in the room swiveled to her. Meredith's went to Jensen. His eyes practically begged her not to say any of the things she instinctually wanted to say. Among them, *What the hell?* and *Are you fucking kidding me?* and, *Please tell me this tattoo is not a Shifter wedding band.*

Goddess, she'd even *thought* it felt like a wedding ceremony.

The naked woman threw Valkyrie off her. Val allowed it, probably because the whole of the woman's focus was on Jensen. She stalked to him, black hair spilling in a wavy curtain down her back, completely unconcerned with her nudity in a room full of strangers. She grabbed Jensen's left hand and flipped it over, baring the tattoo on the underside of his wrist.

"You're married," she whispered again, and there was no mistaking the hurt—or the betrayal—in her voice.

Something twin to those feelings stabbed through Meredith as it occurred to her that maybe her throwaway thought that Jensen—when she'd still thought he'd just been Jensen-the-traveling-contractor—was married, hadn't been so far off the mark.

"Yes," he repeated. His voice was soft, gentle even, as he pulled his arm out of her grip. "That's what I was trying to tell everyone before Hel and Dom decided to hold me down 'for my own good'." He actually did literal air quotes over the last part.

"Great," Valkyrie said. "Now that your *husband*—" she threw Meredith an accusatory look "—is free to talk, someone explain what is going on before I kill someone."

The naked woman—and Meredith really wished she was a little less naked, a little less beautiful, and lot less close to Jensen—tossed her hair and shot back, "You could *try*."

Valkyrie's eyes narrowed. "Pretty ballsy for a cat who would have taken a dagger to the heart if I hadn't stopped."

"We can go for round two any time."

"I think if we could all just calm down," Jace and Random started in tandem, at which point both women snarled at them and they wisely did not finish the sentence.

Valkyrie turned back to the jaguar woman. "What *are* you?"

"Are you really married?" Siren asked Meredith.

"Does everyone agree that this woman was just a jaguar five minutes ago?" Random asked, while Jace narrowed his eyes thoughtfully and said, "Holy hell, I think Dennigan's theory on the transmogrification of the human body *wasn't* batshit insane."

Siren gave him one of those, your-brilliant-mind-totally-turns-me-on looks.

"Maybe we could start with everyone agreeing to not kill each other for the next ten minutes so Jace can remove the ocean from my living room?" Meredith suggested. Everyone just stared at her. She rolled her eyes and stood, wildly happy when her legs held. She grabbed a robe lying on the back of the couch and tossed it at Jaguar Woman, who looked at it like the green silk personally offended her. Mercifully, she put it on anyway. Great. Now Jensen's ex-whatever was only *half*-naked in her living room.

Meredith peered over the top of the water wall at a lynx and what she thought might be a jackal. "Can you two be chill if we dispense with the waterworks?"

They shared a look. Then fur melted, bones shifted, and a man and a woman stood naked in their place. Meredith was all out of conveniently available robes. The woman shrugged and said, "Anything for Jensen's wife?"

Jaguar Woman snarled at the *W* word. Meredith wanted to snarl at it too, but she was neither a jaguar nor stupid. Well, maybe she was a little stupid, since she was apparently married and didn't even know it, but she wasn't stupid enough to claim she *wasn't* married in a room with four Shifters, three of whom were likely to try and kill her again if they thought she wasn't married into the—what had Jensen called it?—enclave.

One thing at a time. "Jace?" she prompted.

"Someone want to open a window?" he asked. Random obliged him. Jace stepped back until he stood protectively next to Siren's side before he sent the water in a stream out the window. He put a hand on the small of her back, a frown worrying his lips. Siren didn't look so great. But she also didn't look like she was about to die, so Meredith figured diffusing Shifter / Aspect tensions should be the priority of her focus.

Unfortunately, the entirety of her focus was on one specific person. So instead of coming up with something diplomatic to say, something that would ease tensions and smooth ruffled feathers, she jabbed a finger in Jensen's direction and said, "You. I need to talk to you. In private."

"You aren't taking him anywhere alone," Jaguar Woman said.

Jensen sighed. "It's fine, Serenity."

"*Fine?*" Serenity whirled on him, and all the fury and hurt washed back into her face. "Nothing is *fine*. You've been missing for seven months. You left without saying a word to anyone, just left some cryptic message that you were going to look for Natalie.

"I thought you were dead or worse, and then a Shifter passing through this area picks up your scent. I came down here expecting to find you in some Aspect dungeon and instead you've *married* one of them? Mister marriage-is-an-outdated-form-of-imprisonment married an *Aspecter* he's known for less than a *year*?"

"Less than two months, technically," Meredith offered.

"Excuse me?" Serenity's voice hit a pitch that definitely qualified as a shriek.

"I've known him approximately five weeks. He *has* been in a dungeon—well, basement—for the last six months. I rescued him. I believe *thank you* is the general response."

Serenity gaped at her. Meredith didn't care. She'd hit her limit of bizarre after dealing with Julian, having incredibly hot car sex, nearly bleeding to death by jaguar Shifter bite, and then finding out she was *married* by Shifter standards. Her system was overloaded and she was now saying whatever she wanted with zero tact involved.

"Is this some weird sort of Stockholm Syndrome?" Serenity asked Jensen. "Have you been brainwashed?"

"You married a guy you've known for five weeks?" Valkyrie asked Meredith. "Have *you* been brainwashed?"

"Wait, Jensen is Monster?" Siren broke in. "The dog in Elijah's basement was a—a werewolf?"

Serenity snorted at the term "werewolf." Meredith looked at Jensen. The urge to drag him off somewhere so he could explain, in excruciating detail, exactly how they were hitched and how to reverse it, was overpowering. He had the look of a man who understood full well that he was in deep shit, and for some reason that infuriated her further.

Forget diplomacy, she needed answers. She moved toward Jensen. Serenity blocked her.

"I don't know what you've done to him, but if you think for one second you're going to—"

"Has anyone ever told you that you're exceptionally tiresome?" Meredith asked. She said it in the bored, indifferent tone of voice that had an unparalleled ability to make people lose all rationality. Serenity's jaw clenched. The two other Shifters slid in closer at her back, and Meredith's people crowded nearer to hers.

Jensen stepped around from behind Serenity, likely trying to find some way to insert himself between them, but neither woman was having it.

"Release him from your vows and *maybe* I won't rip your throat out."

Oh good, the vows were reversible. "You know what they say," Meredith answered breezily, "if you have to kill the competition to hold on to a man—"

Serenity lunged at her—and crumpled immediately, though no one had touched her. Her knees hit the ground, as did Jensen's and the other two Shifters'.

CHAPTER

SIXTEEN

S iren appeared calm and serene as she held the Shifters immobile, if you didn't know where to look to see that she wasn't. Meredith did. Their fearless leader was on the verge of passing out.

The Shifters, caught under Siren's influence, squirmed. Fur broke out in patches, then melted back into skin.

"Meredith." Jensen's voice conveyed everything. She could only imagine how he felt, being held immobile now after what he'd been through.

"Can we all agree to a ceasefire for half a goddamn hour?" Meredith asked. "No one attacks anyone, Siren lets everyone go, and we figure this out like reasonable adults?"

"Agreed," Jensen said. No one else spoke.

"I need verbal agreements from everyone," Meredith said, sounding too much to her own ears like a kindergarten teacher.

"If everyone agrees, then yes, I'll let go." The strain in Siren's voice was audible.

The Aspect side agreed, followed by the two Shifters behind Jensen. Serenity remained mutely silent.

"Ren." Jensen didn't say please. He didn't have to. It was in his voice.

Meredith told herself she absolutely did not care that Jensen had a cute nickname for his stunning...ex-girlfriend?

"Fine," Serenity snarled out. "Yes, I agree. Thirty minutes."

Siren's power vanished. It wasn't the smooth reeling back in of her Aspect that usually occurred. It was as if her power had simply given out the second she stopped exerting her control over it. Jace studied her with a mix of concern and misery that told Meredith his wife's condition hadn't gone unnoticed by him, but she wasn't talking to him any more than she was to anyone else.

"Well?" Serenity demanded.

Meredith realized everyone was staring to her. Typically, Siren and Jace were the calm leader types everyone looked to for guidance. But since Siren looked like she'd throw up if she opened her mouth, and the whole of Jace's attention was on his wife, Meredith supposed that left her.

Deciding it was harder to be angry with people over comforting beverages, she turned to Random. "If you would please make coffee, I think we could all use it." What had Jensen called the two naked people? "Dom, Hel, if you go into the hall and take the stairway to the left down, you should find some clothes in that room that might fit you. If we could all then sit down, Jensen and I will explain everything. I don't think any rational human being will want to kill anyone else by the time we're done."

She didn't actually expect everyone to do what she said, but apparently if you gave reasonable orders most people would follow them. Hel and Dom disappeared, then reappeared a few minutes later, no longer naked. Her kitchen island had enough barstools for everyone and in short order they were all settled around it, the coffeemaker burbling on the counter.

Serenity folded her arms across her chest and looked at Jensen. "We saw you at the cafe. She treated you like a dog. She kissed another man. And you want me to believe she's your *wife*."

Jensen winced. "That was…necessary." He held up a hand to forestall protests. "But if you want to understand it, I'm going to have to start at the beginning." So he did. When it came to the point in the story where Julian came in, he handed it off to Meredith. Valkyrie shot her a glare worth a thousand daggers that said they were going to *talk about this* once they were alone.

No one knew any woman named Analisa.

"I'll double-check the reports from Julian's probation check-ins," Valkyrie said, "but it would have stood out to me if he was meeting with someone regularly. As for his mention of thralls, I've never heard the term used."

Jace's face took on the pinched expression reserved for dredging up some obscure passage he'd read a lifetime ago. "It sounds vaguely familiar but I can't think of where. I'll do some digging and see what I can come up with." He looked between her and Jensen. "So, uh, you never explained the whole married thing. Where does that come in?"

Siren shot him a look like it bothered her that he'd asked. Seriously, *what the hell* was going on with them?

Serenity rolled her eyes. "That part's obvious, really. Under enclave law, a Shifter's spouse who has taken our vows is considered a part of our enclave and therefore one of our people." She met Jensen's gaze. "You felt you owed her your protection for asking her to help you. I should have guessed a sense of *obligation* was the only thing that could tempt you into matrimony."

Serenity had wanted to marry him? That meant she wasn't just an ex, but a serious one. And that so wasn't the most important thing to be thinking about right now.

Meredith decided to cut short the whole matrimony discussion. "Since I am willing to overlook nearly being murdered in my own home—" because really, what was the alternative? "—can we all agree that no one here has any reason to attack anyone else?"

"No reason?" Serenity repeated slowly. "We've hidden our

existence for centuries so we don't end up enslaved to your kind or worse. A fact our missing people should make obvious."

"I can't imagine what it's like to live under that kind of fear," Meredith said. "And while it doesn't excuse what some of our people have done, most of Aspect Society *literally* had no idea you existed. We couldn't exactly fix what we didn't know about. So the way I see it, you have two choices. You can either stay in Seclusion and try to figure this out on your own, or—"

"They can't, actually," Siren said.

Every head swiveled to look at her.

"I'm sorry, I don't mean to be rude. But I've been performing a thorough analysis of our current laws, and Section Three Clause Fourteen states that any individual possessed of any magical persuasion must reveal themselves to the Society within two weeks of arrival. However, once revealed, they may not remain in Seclusion unless they petition to join Aspect Society. Only those who possess Aspect may join."

Wait a minute. "What about the Oracles?" Meredith asked. Charles came and went in Seclusion as he pleased. "Wouldn't that clause mean the Oracles aren't actually allowed to be in Seclusion?" They had their own town on the outskirts of the city limits, but Meredith had always assumed that was because they *wanted* to remain separate. Questions thrown at Oracles tended to knock them out of present reality and into future what-if reality, so being around non-Oracles was difficult for many of them. "Charles is on your advisory council."

"I am aware. The Oracles signed an agreement with us over a century ago that allows them to make their home at our borders, and they can come and go in Seclusion as long as they never spend more than a full day here, but I don't like the legal exclusion.

"Why do you think I'm so familiar with the terminology? Anyway—" she turned back to Jensen "—given the wording and how archaic the laws are, I'm thinking it makes sense that clause might have actually been meant for you."

"Can't you just not tell the law and order we're here?" Hel asked, speaking up for the first time.

"I sort of *am* the law and order."

Dom's mouth pressed into a thin line. "We might not want Aspect Society to know about us, but we *do* know about you. You're run by a council."

Siren nodded. "A council that has been indefinitely disbanded, leaving me as the elected interim head of Aspect Society."

"How did you manage that?" Serenity asked. "What are you, nineteen?"

"Four years off the mark," Siren fired back, "and I 'managed it' by exposing a long history of corruption, illegal magic use, and then holding the Council accountable for it. Ending up in charge was never my intention. It just sort of happened. And while I think this particular law is unreasonable, I won't break faith with my people by bending the laws to suit my own personal whims."

"No," Random agreed, "but since things don't have to go to a Council vote, seeing as how we don't have one, you could grant them temporary clemency under Section Eight."

Siren frowned. "The refugee section? I thought that was meant for people trying to leave Aspect establishments in other countries."

"Probably was. But the actual wording states that anyone of any magical persuasion who is facing persecution or physical harm, to either them or their family, which might be alleviated by remaining within Aspect territory, may make the appeal and have it granted. Since the law does not specify biological family, I believe the term could be interpreted in a broader sense to envelop Shifters in general as a family."

"And that section supersedes the other?"

"Yes."

Hel looked at Random. "What are you, a lawyer?"

"Among other things, yes. I can pull up the necessary forms, which would require the signatures of Siren, all Shifters involved, and two good faith witnesses, of which any of the Aspecters in the room could serve as."

"I'm willing to grant it, with stipulations." Siren turned back to Jensen. "I can't begin to imagine what you're feeling right now, and I have the utmost sympathy for you, but my first responsibility is to my people. If you stay, you will be bound by our laws for the duration of your time here. Should you break any of them or harm any of my people outside of defending yourself from a direct attack, you will face an Aspect trial."

"You have no authority over us," Serenity protested.

"If you sign this agreement," Random said, "you are agreeing to be held accountable by our laws."

"Do we have another choice?"

"Not if you want to remain in Seclusion," Siren said. "Random can provide you with a copy of the Aspect Charter, so you can review the laws. You may stay here tonight—" she looked to Meredith for approval. *Oh, what the hell?* Meredith nodded. "—and make your decision in the morning. Do not leave this house until a decision has been made.

"Should you opt not to sign, we can escort you out of Seclusion in the morning. Return, and you will be trespassing. With or without you, we will make every attempt to find those who were taken from your enclave and return them."

Serenity, Hel, and Dom shared a look. It was Hel who finally said, "Signing a legally binding agreement might be difficult for us."

Jensen groaned. "You don't have Grams' permission to be here, do you?"

Grams?

"She wouldn't have given it," Dom answered. "Better to ask for forgiveness, and all that."

Random frowned. "Do you need your grandmother's permission to sign a document as a legal adult?"

"Grams is our Siren," Jensen said, "and our laws don't allow any of us to reveal ourselves to non-Shifters who aren't married into our enclave." Here he had the decency to at least send Meredith an apologetic look. "They've shifted in front of Aspecters, and given your positions within Aspect Society the, ah, typical recourse in this situation is out of the question."

So if you're a Shifter and you reveal yourself to your enemy's leader, the enclave is not going to try and assassinate said leader on your behalf. Good to know.

"Even though the damage is likely irreversible at this point, putting the existence of Shifters on a signed legal document is not a decision they can afford to make."

An idea popped into Meredith's head. "What about a peace agreement?"

"What?" Serenity asked it, but all of the Shifters might as well have echoed it, what with the way they were looking at Meredith like she'd just suggested the Earth was actually made of marshmallow fluff or something.

"You know, a mutual agreement between two groups of people not to kill each other? If I'm not wrong, the entire point of the secrecy of Shifter existence is to keep you from being subjugated by other magic users. Clearly, that isn't working out for you. And whether you intended to or not, you just outed your entire people to the head of Aspect society.

"It can't be undone. So why don't we stop trying to go back and try to move forward? Would your—" she glanced at Jensen. "What is your grandmother's title?"

"She's the enclave protector."

"Would your protector let you sign the refugee agreement if a larger agreement between Aspecters and Shifters was on the table?"

"I...don't know." Jensen looked to Siren. "Would you be willing to make an agreement?"

"Yes, but—" Siren cut off, one hand going to her stomach like she was nauseous. She swallowed and shook her head. "Yes, but I may need the night—and my favorite lawyer—to make sure I have the authority to do that. Aspect Society has never had an interim leader. I'm ninety-percent certain this is a decision I can make, but I won't make you promises I can't keep."

Jensen ran his hand over his face. "Please find out and let me know. If a peace agreement is something you have the authority to do, we will contact Grams. Until then, provided we see no issues upon review of the Aspect Charter, I'll grant the authority to sign it."

He would grant authority? As in, he had some sort of authority to grant?

"You can't," Dom said.

"In an emergency, yes, I can."

"In an emergency where you can't contact the protector. All you have to do to contact her is pick up the phone. I'm sure she'd be overjoyed to hear from you."

Jensen gave Dom a flat stare. "If the enclave's secondary finds themselves in a situation where contacting the protector might put the lives of anyone in the enclave at risk, they may delay doing so. I feel Natalie *and* my wife's life would be endangered by contacting the protector at this time."

There went that *wife* word again. Ugh, she was going to murder him. If Dom didn't do it first, by the way the guy was looking at Jensen. After they did the manly staring thing for half a minute, it was Dom who looked away and said, "Fine."

Jensen turned to Meredith. "Are you sure you don't mind if they stay here?"

She shrugged. "It's an ugly, gigantic house full of terrible memories. What else am I going to do with it?" Besides, she could imagine few things that would have made Savannah Townsend *less* happy than her home being used to offer sanctuary to a group of Shifters. "The second floor has an abundance of bedrooms. You're welcome to any you want. I'd appreciate it if you stayed off the third floor, and kept the first floor wanderings to the kitchen and living room. Go wherever you want to outside."

"Right. Thanks." Hel tapped her fingers on the counter. Silence fell. If they weren't talking peace or legally binding agreements, no one seemed to have any idea what to say.

Meredith was going through her options—did she need to formally disperse them all or something?—when Siren, who'd been looking progressively worse as the minutes ticked by, clapped a hand over her mouth, jumped up, and ran for the first floor guest bathroom.

"Okay," Valkyrie rounded on Jace, "what is going on with her? She shouldn't be sick. She's *incapable* of being sick."

"Do you think I haven't asked her a hundred times?" Jace said tightly. "She isn't talking to me."

"Could it be some delayed side-effect of what Elijah did to her?" Random asked quietly.

Meredith shook her head. "I don't think any side-effects would be *that* delayed. And he didn't alter her Aspect just… bottled it up. Maybe—"

"Oh, for heaven's sake," Serenity burst out, looking at the Aspect half of the room like they were all absurd. "Have none of you been around a pregnant woman before?"

The room went completely still. Jace looked like he'd been hit by a semi and then shoved off the side of a cliff. He lost all color and, with a stiff, "Excuse me," went after Siren.

Meredith settled a cool gaze on Serenity, her voice tight. "Tell me, do you lack tact as a general rule, or do you simply enjoy being cruel?"

"How is it my problem his wife didn't tell him she was knocked up?"

"It *isn't* your problem. That's my point. Considering she chose not to tell anyone, it wasn't your place to do it."

Serenity opened her mouth but Hel cut her off, linking her arm through the other woman's. "Why don't we go pick out rooms. Maybe later you can apologize to the leader of Aspect Society for outing her secret pregnancy to all of her friends and, if you do it nicely enough, maybe she'll still want to sign a peace treaty with us." Hel steered Serenity toward the stairs, pausing long enough to look back at Dom. "You coming?"

"In a minute. I need to talk to Jensen."

From the tone of Dom's voice, Meredith didn't think it was going to be a happy talk.

Jensen had obviously picked up on the fact, because he answered with a resigned, "Yeah, okay." They exited through the patio doors and walked out of sight, leaving Meredith with Valkyrie and Random.

All three of them blew out a collective breath.

"I don't even know where to start," Random said.

Valkyrie did. "How about *what the hell*, Mer? You promised to call if anything else happened and then you went off to meet *Julian* without backup?"

"I agreed to call if anything happened with the wards, not Julian. How did you know to show up here?"

"I didn't, exactly. Aunt Ella called and said something about you meeting Julian. I called you half a dozen times but you didn't pick up, so I got worried and I dragged everyone over here to have an intervention."

Meredith sighed. Siren was the one who needed an intervention, not her. "Well, it's all out there now. How long are you going to be pissed at me?"

Valkyrie relented. "Probably just another hour or so. Since, you know, I don't really have room to speak where keeping secrets is concerned."

"Neither does our little redhead." Random nodded in the direction of the guest bathroom, where Jace and Siren's voices were rising and falling in volume as they argued, though never quite loud enough to make out what was being said. It spoke to the level of emotional distress they were in that neither of them had put a silencing spell on the room.

Valkyrie glanced down the hall. "Do you think they were trying?"

Speaking of silencing spells...Meredith didn't know how

acute Shifter hearing was, but on the off chance that it was above average she encased them all in a soundproof bubble of Aspect before she pointed out the obvious. "Siren would have to have been, at least. She *can't* get pregnant on accident." The benefits of Life Aspect and its full control over the human body's systems was that her Aspect could literally be her own birth control. "I can't see her deciding to get pregnant without Jace being on board, but she obviously hadn't told him she *was*, so…"

"She wouldn't keep it a secret without a reason," Random said. "And she wouldn't want to hurt Jace."

A reason. Of course. "There's something wrong with the pregnancy."

Valkyrie and Random swiveled to stare at her.

"Think about it. Siren shouldn't be sick. She should be the one woman capable of going through pregnancy without a single unpleasant symptom. But she *is* sick. And it's worse when she uses her Aspect. And if she thought she was going to lose the kid…"

"She wouldn't tell Jace she was pregnant," Valkyrie finished. "I'm going to murder her."

"Not if Jace does first," Random muttered. "Goddess, you three could drive any man to an early grave. Maybe Jace and I should form a support group and invite Jensen."

Meredith winced. "Look, Jensen and I aren't…I don't know what we are."

Valkyrie raised an eyebrow. "You're married."

"By Shifter standards and I didn't know that. It can't be a valid marriage if I didn't know I was getting hitched. As soon as he gets his ass back in here I'm asking for a divorce."

"And then?"

"And then *what*?"

"After you divorce him. Are you going to keep him?"

"Why would I?"

Valkyrie shrugged. "He looks about six-foot three. He has dark brown hair and very blue eyes and, when wearing your dad's old clothes isn't his only option, I'd bet he dresses like a lumberjack."

"So you *do* listen when I talk. I'm touched."

"All I'm saying is it seemed like you liked him."

Meredith pressed her fingers to her eyes. "It is very complicated. Besides, it's not like it's all up to me. There are two of us involved in this sham marriage."

"Okay, fine. Do you want to keep him?"

"No. Yes. Maybe. I don't know. We had a great affair and I wanted it to be something more and then he disappeared, and now it turns out he's a werewolf and our respective peoples are mortal enemies and he tricked me into matrimony for the sake of my safety, and I'm really hoping the stunning jaguar shifter on the second floor is his *ex*-girlfriend. How am I supposed to have logical thoughts about any of that?"

"Huh. Good point."

Random shook his head. "Definitely forming a support group."

CHAPTER

SEVENTEEN

J ensen was prepared for the punch. Dom had *that* look on his face, even if Jensen didn't know exactly what had put it there. He thought about taking the hit—sometimes it was better to just let Dom get it out—but he'd taken too much pain lately to take it from someone close to him.

He blocked, driving Dom's arm up and then lunging in to shove him back.

"Nice to see you, too," he bit out. He and his cousin's relationship had been a little rocky for the last couple years, for reasons Dom had never bothered to discuss with him. But whatever it was, Jensen didn't think he deserved a punch to the face after everything he'd just told them he'd been through. Granted, he'd glossed over the worst parts, but the subtext was readable.

"Well?" he prompted when Dom continued to stare at him, fists clenched.

"What is that in there?" Dom jerked his head at the house.

"You'll have to be more specific. The house? The interior decorating? The—"

"*Her.*"

"Meredith?"

Dom's lip wrinkled. "You throw Serenity away like she's

trash because she wanted a life with you, and then two months later you're gone. Nobody knows where you are. We don't hear from you again, and when Ren convinces us to come track you here because she still cares about you, for some dipshit reason, we find you married to an Aspecter?"

Jensen bit his lip on an instinctually rude response. There'd been a whole lot of Serenity in Dom's speech.

"You didn't hear from me because I was locked in a damn basement. I didn't have enough strength to shift human until this morning and no, I didn't call because I wasn't leaving without Natalie, and as long as it was just me here it was my risk to take."

"You weren't locked in a basement the first month you were down here. You toss Ren over and go screw the first thing you could find?"

It was official. This had absolutely nothing to do with him. And his cousin was still as fucking self-absorbed as ever. "You got a self-righteous stick up your ass or are you just in love with my ex?"

Dom's nostrils flared like a horse that had just run a three minute mile. "I don't know what you're talking about."

"Really? Half the damn words out of your mouth have been Ren this, Ren that. You think I did her so wrong? She and I are both adults, Cuz. We wanted different things. Not that it's any of your damn business, but she told me to either marry her and give her a couple kids, or get out of the way so someone else could.

"Not my fault if I couldn't make the choice she wanted. And I hate to break it to you, man, but your two years of pent-up aggression over a woman you never bothered to tell anyone you liked is about the least important thing on my mind right now.

"Take a walk and cool off. Don't come back until you can remember that what matters right now is the fact that my sister —who is just a kid—is still in the hands of some asshole who wants to sell her to the highest bidder, and all Meredith has to do with that is that she wants to stop it from happening."

The muscles in Dom's neck strained. "That an order?"

"Yeah, it's an order." For a tense moment, Jensen didn't know if Dom would follow it. Then he gave a jerky nod and headed down the path to the gardens. "And Dom?" His cousin paused. "You may all think I married Meredith to protect her, and it's true. But she *is* my wife. Touch her, disrespect her, and you answer to me."

As Dom resumed walking, the bushes to Jensen's right rustled and Hel popped out. He wished he could say he was surprised to see her, but Hel had been eavesdropping on everything and everyone since before she'd understood the meaning of the word.

She brushed dead leaves off her jeans. "It is *so* hot when you men do that whole, touch-my-woman-and-die spiel." Her nose wrinkled. "Or it would be hot, if I weren't related to you by all but blood." She grinned, launched herself forward, and caught him around the middle in a bear hug. "For the record, *I* am happy you're alive and not missing your teeth or eyes."

Hel always said the most random, weird shit. He hugged her tight. "I missed you too, kid. Why would I be missing teeth and eyes?"

"You can't keep calling me kid just because I'm younger than you. And everyone knows that's how you torture people. Pulling out teeth and stuff."

He grunted. He knew he should make himself make a joke in response, but he couldn't bring himself to do it.

"Shit," Hel said, "that was really insensitive. I always say the wrong thing, you *know* I always say the wrong thing."

"Don't worry about it, *kid*."

She pushed back and looked at him, her brown eyes worried. "You okay? I mean, I know you're not *okay*, but like..." She trailed off.

"I'm okay for now. I'll figure the rest of it out later." He turned to the house. "I need to go explain to Meredith about the whole married thing."

Hel looked at him, horrified. "You didn't tell her she was marrying you?" She smacked him on the chest. "Jensen! You can't go around marrying women without their consent. It's wrong. And damn it, I'm sorry I hit you."

"I'm not physically fragile, and I'll divorce her as soon as this mess is over with. Happy?"

"I'm not certain the promise of a speedy divorce will make this any better."

"To her, it will. That's the only woman I've ever met as opposed to marriage as I am."

Hel's eyes sharpened. "Wait a minute. You *like her* like her, don't you?"

He rubbed at the back of his neck. "Is that such a bad thing?"

"No. Just saying if you like her, maybe you shouldn't be so quick to divorce her."

He looked at her warily. "So you aren't coming down on Serenity's side in all this?"

"It's not like either of you did something wrong, so I don't feel like I need to take sides. Admittedly, finding out you're married had to hit like a sucker punch, but again, it's not like you ever intended for her to find out, so I can't blame you for it."

"Have I ever told you you're my favorite almost-cousin?"

She snorted. "It's not hard to come out ahead of Dom. We all know I love him like a brother, but he needs to work on his people skills. So are you going to think about it?"

"About what?"

"Keeping the marriage?"

"Marriage isn't a stray cat. It doesn't just show up one day and you decide to keep it. It's a commitment between two people. One neither I nor the pissed-off woman inside wants to make."

Hel sighed. "If you say so." She linked her arm through his and walked him back into the house.

JACE AND SIREN still hadn't come out by the time Jensen walked back in. He was down Dom and up Hel, though she broke away and trotted upstairs with a wave at the rest of them. How had she gotten outside in the first place? Last Meredith had seen Hel, she'd been walking upstairs with Serenity.

Meredith killed the silencing spell she'd conjured, and Jensen held up a motel keycard. "Any chance you want to take me for a drive? Hel says all their stuff's at the Convenience Inn off the highway into town. Plus, she brought some of my clothes and, uh..." He looked down to where the waistband of her dad's old sweatpants was threatening to give way. They hadn't been *that* small on him this morning. "I think I'm going to need them."

"They had the foresight to know you'd need clothing?" Valkyrie asked.

Jensen grinned. It was a good grin, easy and charming, and brought out the dimples that never failed to make Meredith's heart beat faster. "Shifters are always losing clothes."

Considering the alternative to the hotel field trip was Serenity living in the robe Meredith had lent her, or—heaven forbid— Meredith loaning her actual clothing, the answer was obvious. She snatched the keycard. "Let's go."

"You sure you should go by yourself?" Valkyrie asked.

"Julian isn't going to touch me until I bring him my evil mother's stash of magical artifacts. I'm more worried about making sure things are okay here. You two are staying, right?"

"Consider us your new roommates," Random said.

As if she didn't have enough of those already. But truthfully, she would be happy to have them all under one roof until this mess was over. "If Siren and Jace come up for air, you think you can convince them to stay, too?"

"The more difficult path would be convincing them *not* to stay."

Meredith felt marginally better once she was behind the

wheel of her car and tipping the speedometer up past eighty. It was half an hour to the Convenience Inn, and she used the stretch of mostly-empty highway to work out her aggression.

Jensen was quiet and tense in the passenger seat beside her. Quiet wasn't unusual for him. Tense was.

They were maybe ten minutes into the drive when he said, "Can you pull over?"

"Why?"

"Can you just do it? Please?"

She was a sucker for *please*. Probably because it wasn't a word she'd heard much. She was more accustomed to being ordered around. There wasn't an exit for another fifteen miles, but it wasn't a popular stretch of highway. She pulled off the road and slipped the gear shift into neutral, hitting the parking break.

"Okay, we're pulled over. What was so impor—"

Jensen opened his door, stalked over, pulled hers open, hit the release on her seatbelt, and hauled her out. He pulled her in tight, buried his face in her hair, and inhaled.

"I thought you were dead. I thought you were dead because of me."

She gave in to what she wanted and hugged him back. "I've sort of been trying to pretend that didn't happen." Unlike Val, Meredith wasn't practically on a first-name basis with death. Pain? Yes. Death? Not so much.

"Fuck, I'm so sorry." He squeezed her tighter and the warmth and solidity of him made the memory of teeth and claws sinking into her skin less visceral. He leaned back, his fingers trailing down her arm to the tattoo on her inner wrist. "The whole point of this was to stop that from happening. And it didn't."

Meredith sighed. "It stopped the living room of my house from turning into an all-out war zone, so it did something, but...*married*, Jensen?"

He winced. "For what it's worth, that tattoo *does* just represent an oath. It doesn't intrinsically mean marriage."

"But I am assuming that is what your people use it for?"

"Yeah."

"You didn't lie when you said we could undo it. So that means we can get divorced, right?"

"Yes, but—and I would understand if you told me to go fuck myself on this—I think it would be best if we held off on that."

Meredith tilted her head. "Why? Is your girlfriend likely to try and kill me again if my magical marriage tattoo disappears?"

He winced. "*Ex*-girlfriend. And no. At least, I don't think so. It's completely selfish, but I'd just…feel better if we waited until this was all over."

It was in her nature to demand to be done with it now. Understanding what the tattoo meant, what people would see it as, made it feel like another cage. She'd been in too many of them—maybe not literal cages, but those born of familial bonds and societal expectations, and she was done with all of them.

The look in Jensen's eyes—the fear hiding behind the blue irises—kept her from outright refusing. She drew her Aspect forth, let it hum along her skin where he could feel it. She didn't *need* to do that to know if he told her the truth, but she wanted him to know what she was doing.

"If I asked you to dissolve it right now, would you?"

"Yes." No hesitation, no lie. "I'm not trying to trap you. The truth is, I don't want to be married. Ever. It's one of the reasons Ren and I broke up. It's why she's so pissed about this." He tapped the tattoo.

Meredith thought about it, weighing what she felt she needed against the situation. They were trying to get the Aspect and Shifter societies to agree to coexist peacefully. It stood to reason that having an Aspect/Shifter marriage to display might be advantageous. It certainly wasn't going to hurt. One way or another, she had a feeling it would all be done by the time the auction was finished. A couple days. It wouldn't kill her to stay "married" a couple days.

"We can wait, for now."

He blew out a breath. "Thank you."

What was she supposed to say to that? *Sure, no problem?*

"Sure, no problem. Can we go now? It's freezing." He moved past her and she blurted out, "Were you with her when we were together?"

He stopped abruptly. "No. We broke up a couple months before that."

Relief hit her like an avalanche, then yielded to anxiety again. "I know it's none of my business. We didn't—don't—have that kind of relationship, but..." But if they were all going to be living under the same roof, even for a short amount of time, she didn't need to be second-guessing everything every second of the day.

"But?" Jensen prompted.

"Do you still want to be with her? If she's changed her mind about the marriage pre-requisite?"

His gaze softened and he shook his head. "We broke up for a lot of reasons. That was just the final one. You don't need to be worried."

"I'm not *worried*," she said, sounding defensive even to herself. "This—" she pointed a finger back and forth between them "—isn't anything, this is just..."

"Sex?" he offered, stepping closer and pulling her to him.

"Exactly. Just sex."

"Like this is just a kiss?" He leaned in and took her mouth with his. The heat of him was a sharp contrast to the cold air. His lips glided against hers, and his tongue delved inside when her mouth parted to grant him access.

It wasn't just a kiss. Nothing with him was *just* anything.

When they broke apart, both breathing hard, his hands cupping her face, she knew they weren't fooling each other. But maybe they could pretend for a little while longer.

CHAPTER

EIGHTEEN

Meredith staggered into the kitchen under the weight of far more groceries than she'd ever before purchased. Jensen followed with the remainder, minus the staggering.

Random's eyebrows raised as she plunked them down. "Did you buy the entire store?"

"Yes. I was told Shifters get cranky when they're hungry."

Jensen slung his bags down next to hers. "Actually, what I said was that while Shifter metabolisms can slow to conserve caloric intake if necessary, irritability is a side effect."

"Which means you get cranky if you need a snack."

Jensen grumbled something under his breath.

"How did you fit all of this in that tiny car?" Random asked.

"I am an efficient packer, and I packed on top of Jensen." She'd snapped a photo of him covered in grocery bags because, well, it had been cute. "Have you not left my kitchen? Where is your wife?"

"The kitchen is the heart of any home, and yours needs a defibrillator restart." He eyed the groceries. "Which I guess I can now give it."

"If you haven't been cooking, what have you been doing in here this whole time?"

"Organizing."

Great. She already couldn't find anything in her cabinets and now he'd likely gone and rearranged everything on her. "And Val?"

"She went to grab clothes and stuff from our place and Jace's."

Meredith assumed "and stuff" encompassed a large array of weaponry. She glanced down the hall where Jace and Siren had disappeared earlier. "Have they come out?"

Random shook his head. "They moved to the guest room an hour ago but..."

"Do you think they're okay?" She'd thought they would have worked things out by now. The thought they might *not* work things out had never occurred to her. "They can't break up." It would destroy the whole of her faith in human relationships.

Jensen cleared his throat. "If it's any help, I'm pretty sure they're not breaking up."

"How do you know?"

"Let's just say they didn't move to the guest bedroom to continue talking."

"What do you—" His meaning dawned on her and her eyebrows crept up.

"You can't *know* that's what they're doing."

"Shifters have a great sense of smell."

"You can *smell* that? Do Shifters have any privacy?"

He shrugged. "It's kind of just normal to us."

She pinched the bridge of her nose. That was one gesture she'd picked up from Jace and never managed to drop. "Do me a favor. Don't you—or any of the Shifters in this house—let my friends know you can smell them having sex."

He gave her a mock salute. "And just so you know, they're done having sex and coming out. I'll make myself scarce so you guys can talk."

He trotted up the stairs as Jace and Siren walked into the kitchen. Siren's eyes were still tinged with pink from a large amount of crying, but since Meredith knew what to look for she could also peg the attempt to finger-comb bedhead back into submission, and the flush in Siren's cheeks that wasn't crying-related.

As for Jace… "Your shirt is on backwards."

He looked down. "Damn it." He walked out and returned a few seconds later with his shirt on in the right direction. Siren's cheeks went a little redder. No one said anything.

"Do you guys want to talk about it?" Meredith finally asked.

"Yeah. But can we wait till Val's back? I'd rather just do this once."

Val returned thirty minutes later, by which time the double batch of blueberry muffins Random had whipped up were almost out of the oven. She dropped two tactical duffel bags inside the door, her gaze zeroing in on Jace and Siren, who were holding hands on top of the kitchen island.

"We're good," Jace said, no doubt noting the over-protective older sister look in Valkyrie's eyes. She didn't look wholly convinced, but she relaxed a little and sat down.

"So you're pregnant?" Valkyrie said it in what was—for her —a gentle prompt.

"Yeah." Siren's smile wobbled, her eyes tearing up. "Stupid hormones," she muttered.

Jace squeezed her hand. "We talked about having kids a while back. I was ready but—"

"—I wasn't quite there yet," Siren finished. "When I decided I was, I sort of thought I'd just surprise him, you know? But I've been off since I realized I was pregnant. I thought—" Her voice cracked, and she swallowed and started over. "I thought I was going to lose it the first day. So I didn't say anything. And every day after that, I thought I was going to lose it. So I kept not saying anything, and by the time I realized it wasn't going to get any better I'd been *not* saying something for so long I didn't know how to start."

"Don't take this the wrong way, but how can you not know what's wrong?" Meredith asked. Siren was Life Aspect. She was literally growing new life. Her Aspect should be all about that.

"I don't know." Siren got the words out and promptly burst into tears again. Jace pulled her onto his lap while the rest of them looked at random points around the room to give her time to collect herself. Meredith had never actually seen Siren cry. Not in public.

"Stupid. Fucking. Hormones," she gritted out. She sucked in a deep breath and blew it out slowly. "I have to admit, I thought Life Aspect meant I could breeze through pregnancy blissfully mitigating all the shit normal women have to go through. I *should* be able to. I tracked down some journals from the last Life Aspecter on record, and *she* had the world's most perfect pregnancy. I know because she documented every boring damn day of it."

Meredith looked to Jace. "And you don't have any ideas either?"

He shook his head. "If the baby had a physical birth defect, something that would cause problems, her Aspect should fix it. Aspect itself doesn't manifest in the womb, so there shouldn't be a problem with the baby's Aspect."

"That's...not entirely true."

Every head in the room whipped to Random.

"Not the part about her Aspect being unable to fix a health problem" he said hastily, "but about Aspect not manifesting at this stage."

Jace's face promptly drained of what little color it had possessed. "Life and Death manifest at conception," he said softly.

Random nodded. "And I don't think she'd have any issues with Life."

Siren looked at her stomach, then back up. "You think I'm growing a Death kid?"

"I know one person who could tell you."

Siren pulled out her phone and tapped the screen a couple times before putting it to her ear. "Aunt Ella, hi. Can Jace and I stop by for tea later? Your house, not the cafe." Siren paused to listen and frowned. "No, we do not need marriage counseling. And last time I checked you were not a marriage counselor. Why would you think we needed that?"

Siren listened. "Hold on a minute." She hit the phone's mute button and wiggled around on Jace's lap to glare at him. "You told her I was being *distant* over white jasmine?"

Aunt Ella did practically everything over tea.

"She said it was a 'bolstering tea', and you were," he muttered, pulling her in a little tighter. "I couldn't talk to our friends about it because I didn't want to be unfair to you, so I drank a lot of tea in the last two months."

"Wait a minute, so *that's* where you've been sneaking off to all the time? Aunt Ella's?"

"Yes," he said, drawing the word out. "Where did you think I was going?"

"Nowhere," Siren said quickly. *Too* quickly. And just like that Siren's sudden interest in Meredith's love life made sense.

"You did *not* think we were having an affair," Meredith accused. "*Please* tell me you didn't think that."

"No!"

"This is why you were so obsessed with finding me a boyfriend."

"You thought I was sneaking out to see Meredith?" Jace asked.

"Well, yes, but not because I thought you were having an affair, just because you guys *are* friends. You've known each other a long time and you have history and shit. You and I weren't really talking, which was totally my fault, and if I lost the baby everyone says losing a kid kills a marriage, so I was afraid we'd break up.

"Then you, being alone and bereft, could fall back into old patterns with Meredith, but if she had a boyfriend that option wouldn't be on the table, and after enough time had passed you would realize you missed me and come back to me and we could save our marriage."

Siren sucked in a lungful of air, because that was the longest sentence in the history of ever. Jace stared at her. "I can't decide whether I should be pissed off again, or concerned that all of that was going through your head. You vision-planned our tragic child-death breakup, complete with me falling into the understanding arms of my ex?"

"I read somewhere it helps to live through your fears so it doesn't hurt so much if it happens."

Jace pinched the bridge of his nose and looked like he was counting to ten in his head.

"Maybe you should pick the phone back up?" Random suggested.

"Oh, shit." Siren un-muted the call. "Yes, Aunt Ella, I'm still here. I—what? No, I'm not having an affair. Neither of us is having an affair. I think I'm—think *Jace and I* are—pregnant with a Death kid." Siren drummed her fingers on the counter. "Half an hour? Perfect."

Siren slid off Jace's lap and faced Meredith. "I owe you an apology. I promise I never thought you would do anything while we were together. Either of you."

While they were together. Good goddess. Meredith looked over Siren's shoulder at Jace. "Do you want to tell her, or should I?"

Siren's eyes widened. "Tell me what?"

An amused smile tugged at Jace's lips. "Tell you that even if we lived in an alternate universe where you didn't exist, Meredith and I would not be getting back together."

"Do you want me to change his ringtone to Taylor Swift's *We Are Never Ever Getting Back Together?*"

Siren winced. "Okay, I deserved that."

"What happened to the woman who took me to a bar and told me I didn't want Jace back even when I actually thought I did?"

Siren crossed her arms, hugging herself. "That woman almost died a lot, got married, got thrust into a leadership role, got pregnant, is afraid her kid is going to die, and is slowly crumbling under a mountain of stress."

Random picked up a muffin and thrust it at her. Siren took it. "Thank you."

"Everything is going to be fine." Jace came up behind Siren and wrapped his arms around her. "Let's go talk to Aunt Ella so we can prove that everything is going to be fine. And for goddess' sake, the next time you think I'm having an affair, try asking. Or, better yet, consider whether I would ever cheat on you and realize the answer is no."

"I *didn't* think you were having an affair. Can we all be very clear on the fact I did not think an actual affair was occurring? I am just scared and stressed up to my eyeballs and I think I'm going to cry again."

"Eat your muffin," Valkyrie advised. "It won't make you stop crying, but it tastes good. And get on the road before you're late and you make my mother-in-law cranky."

Siren squeezed her eyes shut. "I shouldn't even be leaving with all of this going on."

"Don't be ridiculous," Meredith said, "making sure your kid is fine is absolutely a qualifying reason to leave."

"But…" Siren looked up the stairs, at what Meredith had decided to refer to as the Shifter floor.

"In fact, I need you to go because I sort of told Aunt Ella to fuck off earlier and I'd really appreciate it if you could smooth that over."

"You told her to *what*?"

"Julian riled me up. And frankly, she was being rude. So go on, we'll be fine."

"Yes." Valkyrie slapped a dagger on the counter. "Just fine."

Siren pointed a finger at Val. "We're working towards a peace agreement. No stabbing anyone."

Valkyrie saluted her with the dagger, and Jace dragged Siren out the door. No one relaxed until they heard Jace's ancient truck rumble to life and drive off.

CHAPTER

NINETEEN

J ensen was relieved when Meredith asked if he and the others felt like combing over every inch of her estate to look for the repository of magical items. Bored Shifters were bad enough. Bored Shifters in fragile emotional states in hostile territory were worse.

They were all gathered in the kitchen, ready to do a scavenger hunt for who-knew-what, located who-knew-where. The kitchen island held a wide array of homemade food items— okay, fine, *snacks*—and Hel and Dom looked a lot less irritable— fine, *cranky*—as they tore through them. Ren looked *more* irritated, probably because she was resolutely ignoring the banquet of said snacks. It included a tower of blueberry muffins, which were her favorite.

He was grateful when Hel shoved a muffin in her hand and said, "Just eat it." Serenity grumbled but finally did.

He needed to talk to her. Clear the air. But when he'd tried, she'd refused to come out from behind the locked door of the bedroom she'd chosen, so short of breaking down a door in Meredith's house, he hadn't been able to force the conversation.

Meredith slapped a piece of paper down on the counter. It bore a hand-drawn map of the property on a piece of paper, complete with landmarks such as *House*, *The Old Barn*, and *Greenhouse*, all represented by little rectangles. "The total property is twenty-one acres. There's an electric fence around the property line. It is functional, so touch at your own risk."

"Any idea what we're looking for?" Hel asked.

Meredith shrugged. "Forgotten cellar, invisible outbuilding, hidden inter-dimensional storage shed?"

"Is that last one actually a thing?" Hel asked.

"Probably not, but I wouldn't put it past my mother to have found a demon and made a deal with it for something like that."

"You expect us to believe you have no idea where it is?" Serenity said. "Haven't you lived here your entire life?"

Meredith smiled sweetly. Jensen knew that smile. It was the one that preceded some awful tidbit about her life.

"Have you ever experienced pain so intense you thought your brain would melt down and ooze out of your ears?" She didn't wait for a response. "Has that pain ever continued for so long that you couldn't distinguish between what you were actually seeing and hearing, and visual and auditory hallucinations? Because that was my life any time I was home and my mother didn't want me paying even accidental attention to something. So, no. I have no idea where it is." She tapped her index finger on the map. "House, eastern half of the property, and western half. Who wants to start where?"

"Me, Dom, and Ren can take the east half." Bless Hel and her chipper, if occasionally chaotic, nature.

"We'll take the west," Val said, indicating her and Random.

"Which leaves me and Jensen with the house," Meredith said flatly. He wasn't sure if she was unhappy about being stuck with the house, him, or both. "If anyone finds anything remotely interesting, radio the rest of us."

She waggled her cell phone, where the walkie-talkie app she'd made them all download on their own phones was open. He'd picked up a burner cell at the store they'd ducked into earlier, and he was surprised by how much more human and normal the over-priced, sleek chunk of metal, glass, and plastic made him feel.

"If no one finds anything, we'll all swap sectors and look again."

"And if we don't find it at all? What are you going to do then?" Serenity asked.

"Vacate the premises and let Julian ransack the place, I guess."

No one had anything to say to that, so the outdoor teams left.

"Split up or go together?" Jensen asked.

"Together," she said finally. "I don't have any objectivity when it comes to this house. I've seen it all a million times, and I hate all of it."

They started on the top level, working their way through room by room. Some of it obviously hadn't been touched in years, if the outdated furniture and thick layering of dust were any indication. He'd developed a permanent sneeze by the fourth room, and his finger pads had a coating of grime from running them along baseboards and walls, looking for hidden doorways or levers or anything else unusual.

The longer they looked, the more he wondered why she stayed here. She had more than enough money to have a cleaning crew that regularly took care of the house, but if she hired anyone it looked like they only did the common areas and her room. She could have emptied the unused rooms and shut them up, if she just didn't want to deal with them. She could sell the house.

Instead, she'd done this. Left everything the way it was and let it settle, like each room was a museum she didn't want to take care of but couldn't let go. By the time they'd worked their way down to the bottom floor, his curiosity had hit its peak. "Can I ask you something?"

She looked at him warily. "In my experience, when people ask that what they mean is they want you to not get your feelings hurt about whatever they say."

"I don't want to tell you how to feel. I just want to ask you something but I don't want you to feel like you have to answer me."

"Okay." She blew a strand of hair out of her face. "Ask."

"Why do you live here?"

She shrugged. "This is my home."

He looked at her. "You're rich, right?"

Another shrug.

"So you could sell this place and get anything you wanted. You're not doing upkeep on anything but the common spaces, and you've already said it's nothing but bad memories. So why do you do it?"

Her attention turned back to the wall she'd been inspecting, and he thought she wouldn't answer. He didn't push. He'd meant it when he said he didn't want her to feel obligated. She came to the end of the wall, dusted her hands off on her jeans, and walked over to him.

"Why do you want to know?"

"Because this place makes you unhappy."

She took a step closer. He was barely taller than her when she had heels on, but she tilted her head to look up at him. "So why do you care?"

He knew two things with that single question. One, that she wasn't going to answer him, and two, that she was asking a question that could take them somewhere he wasn't sure either of them was ready to go.

It's just sex, she'd told him in the car. They were never supposed to have been anything more. Not months ago, not now. Their chemistry was phenomenal, but chemistry could fade. Meredith was young and beautiful and rich. She didn't need him. He had no idea if she wanted him.

Why did he care if she was unhappy? "Because I care about you, darlin'."

Her eyes narrowed. "You don't have to pretend this is more to you than it is."

Interesting choice of words. More to *him*. "You're the Truthfinder. Was I lying?"

"You can care about someone for any number of reasons. Because your ex-girlfriend nearly killed them and you feel guilty. Because they are your best chance of finding your sister. Because—"

"Because you like them. Because you want nice things for them. Because before you ended up in a basement, you wondered if there was any chance at all that a woman that smart and that beautiful would ever be interested in you for anything more than a good time."

"You don't know I'm smart." Meredith latched onto that as the safest part of everything he'd said to respond to.

"You do calculus for fun at breakfast."

So he'd noticed that. Apparently it had been so long since she'd had a man actually pay attention to her, she'd forgotten that some of them did. "It's meditative," she mumbled, staring at his chest.

He made a noncommittal sound and tilted her chin up to meet his gaze. His fingers stroked along the edge of her jaw. "So would you be? Interested?"

Dear goddess, having this conversation was such a bad idea. "If things…hadn't happened the way they did, if we were just two people and you hadn't been taken, what would you have done?"

"I would have asked you to be mine. Would you have said yes?"

She closed her eyes. "Yes." He caught her waist and pulled her in. She opened her eyes. "But we aren't just two people. There's everything between us and it's complicated. We can't promise each other anything."

"Then we don't make promises. I just want to know if you're

willing to see where it goes, or if I need to put that to rest right now."

Of course she wanted to see where it went. But every instinct honed from early childhood was screaming at her to say no. To stop this before it started. Because it *was* complicated, and the likelihood of them being anything when this was over was next to nothing. She'd end up hurt.

I would have asked you to be mine. "I don't know how to do this," she whispered.

"Do what?"

"Trust."

"I'm not sure anyone really does. People screw up relationships all the time. I think that's pretty normal. Most people have to fail at something a few times before they get it right."

She didn't want to screw this up. She wanted to be fixed. To not be so broken she couldn't go into something with the actual hope that it could work out. She didn't want to be having this conversation, making these decisions.

She smoothed the worry from her face. She boxed the hope and the fear away, shoved them down, and looked up at him with a playful smile. "You sound so wise. Is it because you're so very, very old?"

He frowned at her sudden change in tempo. A second later actual concern marred his features and she knew her redirection had worked when he said, carefully, "And exactly how old would you be?"

She laughed—he had the look of a man suddenly afraid he was robbing the cradle. She batted her eyelashes at him dramatically. "Does it matter? I am smart and beautiful, after all. What's age except a number?"

"Meredith."

He looked so serious, she burst out laughing. "Relax. I'm twenty-six."

He blew out a breath. "Good. That's good. And for the

record, I am not very, very old. I'm thirty-four, not on my death bed."

He didn't look thirty-four, and the age difference couldn't have mattered less to her. Except he looked so bothered by it, she couldn't help but tease him. "Not your death bed, but tragically on the other side of thirty."

"If you think that's old, I have bad news for you about how many years typically come after that." He walked her back until she hit the wall, caging her in with his hands. "And I don't remember hearing any complaints about my age when I do this."

He kissed her, his tongue parting her lips and brushing against hers in a long, languorous stroke. She moaned into his mouth, and when his hand slipped under her shirt she arched into him. His fingers paused just beneath her breast and he drew back, looking her in the eye.

"This isn't just sex."

In or out, Meredith. "No. It isn't just sex. But no promises."

"No promises."

She steadied her hands on his shoulders and jumped, locking her legs around his waist. His hands slid under her thighs to hold and steady her, and she leaned in to brush her nose against his.

"I guess all that Shifter strength must make up for the old age part."

He held her up with one arm and used the free one to slap her lightly on the ass. "Watch it, woman."

She opened her mouth to tell him that she didn't *actually* think he was old, when he dove in and kissed her again. She rapidly reversed her decision and decided that maybe she would reserve teasing him about their age difference for special occasions. Because he claimed her mouth like he had something to prove—hot and hungry and thorough—and she was more than willing to keep her mouth shut and let him prove it.

CHAPTER

TWENTY

"There isn't anywhere else to look." Meredith's voice was just short of a growl, which she considered ironic since, of the two of them, Jensen was the one capable of *actually* growling.

Dusk was falling, and each team had been through every "sector" of the property. She and Jensen were finishing the final sweep of the eastern half of the acreage, but it was obvious they weren't going to find anything.

Everyone was in the predictably sour mood that could be expected from searching for an entire day with such diligence that they were all now cross-eyed, and having nothing to show for it. Nothing that was going to help them get Jensen's sister back.

The worst part was, Meredith couldn't even say she was surprised. It was just like Savannah Townsend to stifle her daughter even after death.

"Are you sure it's on the property?" Jensen sounded as tired as she felt.

"No, I'm not sure," she snapped. "If I were sure, I'd have some kind of clue as to where it was."

Jensen raised his hands in the universal sorry-I-asked gesture.

Meredith blew out a breath. "Sorry. But my mother wasn't the type to leave something this important to chance. The repository would be on a property she owned. *This* is the only property she owned."

"Any chance the lawyer who handled the estate lied to you?"

Meredith shook her head and started trudging back to the four-wheeler parked by the outer wall. "No. I hired Random to double-check everything. He doesn't miss things." And he was honest. It had been a tense working relationship, seeing as how at the time she'd still been on the outs with the Jace/Valkyrie/Random friendship team, but if he hadn't been willing to do his due diligence, he would have simply turned her down. She'd always been surprised he hadn't.

"She didn't have any businesses that could have owned properties?"

"No." Meredith swung her leg over the four-wheeler. Jensen had earned major points for never once suggesting that she let him drive. "Savannah Townsend didn't do businesses. Social scheming and power plays? Yes. But actual businesses require actual work. *Work* was what my father was for."

She had her fingers on the keys when Jensen's hand covered hers, stopping her from turning the engine. "What happened to him? Your father?"

Meredith's throat closed up. But she wanted to tell him, to tell everyone, because it felt like her father's life had been erased the way her mother had covered everything up. "She killed him. Once he'd made her enough money that he was more trouble than he was worth. He knew something wasn't right in the house. With me and her. He was going to take me away, so she killed him."

She twisted the key in the ignition, the loud roar of the engine cutting off any response as she opened the throttle and sped back toward the house. On the bad days, she let herself wonder what her life would have been like if her father simply hadn't confronted Savannah.

If he'd just told Meredith to pack a bag and they'd run away in the middle of the night. If she'd grown up with him teaching her how to drive the cars they both loved and taking her to the baseball games he'd always told her she'd like, but they never went to because her mother wouldn't let her.

Meredith liked to think maybe she would have been someone nice in this alternate life. Sweet and happy, the kind of woman who would never date a man because her mother told her to, and never break his heart because she didn't know how else to save him. The kind of woman who wouldn't have developed a drinking problem so she could sleep at night, who had mostly pretty memories with a small dark spot in the past she could pretend was nothing more than an old nightmare. The kind of woman who would have been useful to society.

Maybe it was the bright sunshiny day. Maybe it was Jensen's hands on her waist, or the way he never acted like she was a waste of space, even when she was being difficult. Maybe it was all the people in her house, making noise and waking her up from her year-long bout of self pity, but for the first time, it struck her that she could still become that woman.

She would never have her father back. She would never have the happy childhood she'd so desperately wanted. But she could take the ragged edges of herself and mold them into something different. Something better.

Some*one* better.

As MEREDITH and Jensen walked back into the kitchen, she quickly surmised that no one's mood was any better than had been conveyed via walkie-talkie phone interactions. She highly suspected the array of readily available snack foods was the only reason no one's temper had snapped. Thank the goddess for Random. She was getting him the world's best birthday present this year, just as soon as she found out when his birthday was and what the perfect gift was for a motorcycle-riding lawyer married to Valkyrie.

He'd had to leave two hours ago to meet with a client for his actual job, and Siren and Jace still hadn't returned from Aunt Ella's, which left her, Valkyrie, and the Shifters.

Jensen had barely dropped onto a barstool when his phone rang. Which was odd because he'd just bought that phone. Who outside this room would have his number?

He looked at the display and stilled. Then he turned the screen around at the Shifters, and they all went quiet. "Who wants to explain this?" Silence. "Dom?"

"It wasn't him." Serenity straightened, brushing invisible dust off her jeans. "Rebekah had a right to know her grandson was alive. She had a right to know what's going on."

Jensen fixed the woman with a look Meredith herself hoped to never be on the receiving end of. "We'll discuss this later."

The defiant lift to Serenity's chin told Meredith nothing good would come from the two of them having that conversation. Jensen answered the phone with a terse, "Grams," and stepped outside.

Suddenly, all the Shifters had pressing business that demanded they go upstairs, leaving her and Valkyrie alone.

"Given everything that's happened," Val began, "you should rethink my offer to school you on the basics of self-defense."

This again. It wasn't that Meredith didn't want to. Maybe she'd even looked up a few self-defense basics on YouTube before realizing it was hard to practice them without a partner. But with Val it always came down to one thing. "Are you going to let me keep my shoes on?"

"No. Heels compromise your balance."

"I'm perfectly balanced. I've spent a lifetime in heels. Besides, if I find myself in a situation where I need to defend myself, I am going to be in heels, so shouldn't I train in them?"

"It's just going to make you more likely to injure yourself while you're learning. Take them off, we'll upgrade to heels later."

Just suck it up and spit it out. "I can't."

"What do you mean you can't?"

"I mean I can't. You remember a few months ago when I took that spur-of-the-moment trip to Rome?"

"Of course I remember. You bailed on movie night for a random vacation."

"I didn't go to Rome. I hobbled around on crutches for two weeks because I'd decided I was finally going to take up jogging."

"I don't follow."

"When I was growing up, I was allowed to take my heels off in two situations: when I was asleep or in the shower. Adults who wear heels a lot can have their muscles and tendons shorten. I started wearing heels when I was twelve. I don't think I even developed normally.

"I've been working on stretching everything out. Anyway, that week I got tired of it all and decided fuck it, I didn't care if it hurt, I was going to put on some tennis shoes and go for a run."

"What happened?"

"Let's just say I didn't get very far before it felt like every part of me from the knee down snapped and contracted. So if you want to teach me self-defense, fine, but I'm keeping my heels on."

"Why didn't you just have Siren fix it? I'm sure she could."

"Because I wanted to do something on my own. I wanted one thing in my life to not be another sob story about my mother. By the time I would have asked for help, Siren was being all weird, and now that that's sorted out, she's probably not going to be doing significant Aspect work until that kid comes out. I'll ask her later."

Valkyrie nodded. "Okay, keep the heels on and show me to your gym."

Meredith groaned. "Another time, Val? We both know if I get in a fight, an Aspect Shield will always be my better line of self-defense."

"I'm just trying to help you work through your issues. Physical activity will get you out of your head."

"I appreciate the intention. But I don't think physical aggression is the method that's going to best help me through my issues."

"Then what will?"

"If I knew that, I wouldn't have so many problems. Speaking of issues, can I assume you've noted the giant security vulnerability glaring us in the face?"

Valkyrie got a pinched expression, looked up to the second floor, and snapped a silencing spell around them.

"You mean the fact that Serenity, Dom, and Hel apparently walked right through your wards?"

"Yeah. I didn't even know they came through." Wards could be set to different levels of alertness. Almost without fail, people set them up to let them know if anyone not allowed access attempted to force entry. Others, like Meredith, also set them up to alert them any time an allowed individual passed through— no point in being surprised by a visit if your wards could give you a heads up. The exception being that, since wards allowed animals to come and go freely so as not to screw with the environment, most people did not opt to be alerted every time a bird or fox or mouse crossed their property line.

Animals. That was it. "They were all shifted when we came in. I'd wager anything they were shifted when they crossed the property line. The ward didn't react because it thought they *were* animals." And that presented a host of new problems. "Do you have any idea how many Aspect spells are built *specifically* around a human component?"

It wasn't something the average Aspecter would have cause to think about. Most people cared that spells worked and, once they passed their Academy Intro to Aspect Theory class, didn't give too much thought afterwards to *how* they worked. However, if you had dated Jace when he was working on his Academy thesis you had, by nature of his intense enthusiasm on the subject, absorbed a great deal of that information practically by osmosis.

"How many?" Valkyrie asked.

"Every single spell designed to work on the physical body as a generic concept, as opposed to a specific target. So every widespread combat, protective, or mind-based spell."

"Shit." Meredith could practically see the gears turning in Valkyrie's security-obsessed brain. "How long would it take to design new spells that include a Shifter physique?"

"Given a Shifter willing to let someone like Jace poke and prod at their magical makeup? Jace could probably design some basic revisions in a week. But teaching Aspecters to rely on them in a pinch when they're unproven and they've been snapping out the other versions by rote instinct their entire lives? Give that a few years."

"We are so fucked if we go to war."

"Yep."

Out of nowhere, a smile curled the corners of Valkyrie's lips. "You want me to drop the silencing spell before your husband has an apoplexy?"

Meredith startled, swiveling on her seat. Sure enough, Jensen stood just inside the doorway, staring at them with the most adorable mix of consternation and intensity on his face, like he was convinced if he just listened hard enough, he could hear them.

Valkyrie killed the spell and Meredith waved at Jensen.

"Silencing spells. A must for having private conversations in a house full of Shifters."

He shook off his confused expression and focused on Meredith. "Can I talk to you in private?"

Valkyrie glanced at the watch she wasn't wearing. "Oh, look at the time. Must go work out. So busy." She slid off her chair and disappeared in the direction of Meredith's gym.

"I think I liked her better before she developed a sense of humor."

"That qualifies as humor?" Jensen asked.

"For her it does." She lifted her fingers, Aspect sparking at her fingertips. "You wanted a private conversation?"

"You're going to do the silencing thing?"

"Unless you would prefer to get on the four-wheeler and drive however far is necessary for this private conversation to be private."

His face took on a martyred expression. "Go ahead."

JENSEN COULDN'T SEE the bounds of Meredith's silencing spell. "How do I know I'm inside your magic circle?"

Meredith frowned. "You can't feel it?"

"I feel…something. Like an itch under my skin, but I don't exactly know where it's coming from."

"Interesting." The floor beneath them burst into brilliant blue light. It extended in a circle about six feet in diameter, then rose up around them in shimmering translucent walls that closed in a dome above their heads.

"Why doesn't it look like that all the time?"

"Because Aspect isn't naturally visible. No point in telegraphing to everyone else what you're doing with it. You have to add a witchlight spell to make it seen. It's something we do for small children. If they're having difficulty feeling their way through spell construction, sometimes they do better if they can see it." She straightened her shoulders, as if bracing for bad news. "What did your grandmother have to say?"

He grimaced. "First, she interrogated me about the state of my health. Then she told me how disappointed she was that I didn't call her immediately, and went on in great detail for a solid ten minutes about what a difficult child I was to raise, and did I have no respect for how few nerves she has left. Then she asked about you. Despite explaining the truth of our 'marriage,' she would like me to offer you her congratulations on, and this is a direct quote, 'finally tying me down.'"

If Meredith had been drinking anything, she probably would have choked on it, by the look on her face. She swallowed. "And with regards to the whole Shifters, Aspecters, potential peace agreement thing?"

"That's the worrisome part. She took it well. Too well. She is, and I'm quoting again, 'excited to move our enclave into a new era of magical acceptance.'"

"That's...good, right?"

He'd like to think so. "Grams raised me. Rebekah King wasn't exactly a warm, knit-you-a-sweater-for-Christmas kind of parent. Don't get me wrong, she loves me, and she was never unfair, and technically she does knit, but she raised me in the same way she rules the enclave—with an iron fist.

"When I came down here, I did it without telling anyone where I was going. She would have ordered me not to go within a hundred miles of Seclusion. Then I got taken. Then I told you about Shifters. Then my ex and my crazy cousins decided they needed to rescue me, so I am now responsible for getting them involved in this mess and outing our entire species to our most-feared nemesis.

"She didn't have a single reproachful word for any of that. She just commented on how lovely it was that the Aspect leader sounded like such a reasonable person to negotiate with, and does Meredith like beef jerky, because she just finished a new batch and she would *love* to bring her new daughter-in-law some, and why did I not know that answer about my own wife?"

"I like beef jerky."

"Great." He texted Grams that information and ignored the four other texts from her asking various questions about Meredith's preferences. No, he didn't know what her favorite color was, if she would wear a hand-knitted shawl, if she liked homemade apple butter, or when her birthday was. "She's flying in. She'll be here in twelve hours to 'assess the situation.' I suggest you cherish those hours and take them to mentally prepare yourself."

Meredith gave him an amused smile. "I think I can handle your grandmother."

"That's because you haven't met her yet. Strong Shifters have crumbled under the weight of her disapproving stare."

"I eat disapproving stares for breakfast. Besides, I do come with the notable recommendation of having tied you down."

He shook his head. "Don't say I didn't warn you. I'm going to go fill in Hel and the others."

Meredith stopped him. "Jensen? About Serenity. I know you're pissed about her calling your grandmother, and that's your right, but we both know she only called her because of me."

"What's your point?" he asked, guarded.

"My point is, I don't think you talking to her about us is going to make her any friendlier toward me. I think you should let me do it."

"How is you talking to her going to make it better? She hates you."

"Maybe. But again, you aren't going to change that. Trust me. I've been where she is right now. I can handle it."

He blew out a breath. He didn't see how she was going to bring Serenity around, but he also didn't see how *he* was. If Meredith wanted to dive into those waters... "She's all yours." His phone buzzed again.

Grams: *What kind of music does she like?*

Oh, for heaven's sake.

He'd searched through the phone settings to turn off messaging notifications before he realized that he wasn't irritated that Grams was asking the questions, he was irritated he didn't know the answers.

Oh, hell. "Hey, when's your birthday?"

CHAPTER
TWENTY-ONE

It took Meredith until after dinner to get Serenity alone. The woman was so prickly right now that even asking to talk to her within hearing range of everyone else seemed like a guaranteed way to put her back up. Her pride was hurt and she was waiting to lash out at the slightest provocation.

Meredith knew the feeling. She'd felt that way when Jace had finally come back to Seclusion. He'd been the person she'd held on to when things with her mother were at their worst. She'd spent her teenage years thinking she would marry him, because that was what her mother wanted. Then Elijah Winters had disowned Jace, stripping him of the family name her mother wanted Meredith to marry him for.

Jace had asked her to run away with him. He hadn't known her mother was abusive, but he'd known she wasn't happy. It had been terribly romantic, and Meredith had wanted to say yes. But she'd also known she was one of her mother's most valuable assets, and Savannah Townsend wouldn't just let her go. If she'd married Jace, she would have ruined his life.

Not that she'd told him any of that at the time. He would have gone all white knight on her, because that was Jace to a *T*.

Instead, she'd told him he was worthless to her without his name, and dumped him.

So when he'd come home last year she'd thought it was her chance to rectify that past hurt. She'd been adrift and he'd seemed like the perfect life vest to cling to. But when she'd finally gone to see him, he'd had Siren wrapped around him. Literally. That was what she got for sneaking into the private quarters of a home at a ball.

She'd been truly awful to Siren for no other reason than Siren had what Meredith thought she wanted. And instead of being a bitch right back, Siren had reached out to her. Meredith hadn't appreciated it at the time, but it had quite literally changed the course of her life, for the better.

The least she could do was pay that forward where Serenity was concerned. So when the woman slipped out onto the back porch after dinner, Meredith followed. Serenity muttered something about the night air losing its freshness and turned back for the door.

"I wanted to talk to you." Meredith pitched the words low and soft. She'd asked Jensen for some pointers on Shifter hearing range, and she thought the words shouldn't carry to anyone else.

"Fine," Serenity said in a harsh whisper. "Let's get this over with." She walked off into the gardens. Meredith followed her into the moonlit labyrinth of mostly-dead winter foliage, reflecting on how nice it was that Aspect shields *did* work against Shifters, since they were designed to be a physical barrier impervious to *anything's* attempt to get past them.

If Serenity got cranky and decided to murder her, Meredith could hide behind her comfy shield and phone for help. It would be mortally embarrassing, but she could do it.

Serenity finally stopped beneath a barren arbor that would be overgrown with trumpet honeysuckle come spring. She faced Meredith, her arms crossed. "If you brought me out here to tell me to stay away from Jensen—"

"I didn't. I wanted to clear the air."

"So, what? You think because you're besties with your ex's wife that you and I are going to be friends?"

Well, that answered the question of whether Shifters on the second floor could hear conversations on the first if one forgot to put up a silencing spell. "No. If I'm being honest, I don't think you and I will ever be friends. I don't need you to like me. I do need you to be able to work with me. And if you can't do that, then I need you to go home."

"I can't go home. Rebekah ordered us all to stay here." She flashed Meredith a dark grin full of teeth. "I hear she's all excited about her new daughter-in-law. She never liked me much."

"I'm sorry."

Serenity snorted. "That she never liked me?"

"That he married me."

"You make it sound like a one-way decision."

"That's because it was. I'm not supposed to tell you this, since Jensen's worried his magical marriage tattoo won't have all its violence-repelling properties if I do, so keep this to yourself. We're not married in the way you think."

"Oh, please, do tell me how I think."

Challenge accepted. "You gave Jensen a marriage ultimatum. When he left, you told yourself it was because he wasn't the marrying type. Then suddenly he's married, and not just to anyone, but to an Aspecter. Now you feel hurt and betrayed. You think he must be so head-over-heels in love with me that he went to an extreme to protect me.

"But it wasn't like that. He's not in love with me. This wasn't some grand romantic gesture he made because if anything happens to me he'll never forgive himself. It was practical. He needs me to find Natalie. If I die, he might not get her back. Hence the marriage.

"Which he tricked me into, by the way. We're getting divorced as soon as this is over."

Serenity stared at her for a long moment. In retrospect, Meredith considered that maybe she should have left out the divorce bit, as it could come across as Meredith throwing away the very thing Serenity had desperately wanted.

Serenity let out a brittle laugh. "You actually believe all that don't you?" She took a step forward. "You think you know me so well? Well I know *him*. Let me tell you what you may not have learned about him in your *five weeks* of association.

"He's a good man. He is affectionate and attentive and it was easy to mistake that for love because he did more for me without trying than most men ever do. But Jensen King doesn't yield. He has too much of Rebekah in him for that. So if you think he married you because his back was up against the wall and he didn't see any other way out, you're an idiot." She laughed again. "You know, come to think of it, from what I've seen you're just as stubborn as he is. Put that way, you two are a match made in heaven.

"Congratulations." Serenity gave her a mocking bow and continued in a voice layered in sarcasm. "Your little heart-to-heart has warmed mine. Consider my interference in your marriage over. If you don't go through with the divorce, do send me an invitation to the belated bridal shower. I'm sure we'll be BFFs by that time, so I can give you all the pointers about what he likes in bed."

Deep breath in, don't respond to that, deep breath out.

Meredith stood under the arbor and watched Serenity walk away, somehow certain the woman had gotten the upper hand in what Meredith had not intended to be a contest. The next time she needed to extend a metaphorical olive branch to someone, she made a mental note to have Siren do it on her behalf.

Clearly, Meredith's forte was in playing roles and manipulating people, not winning them over with sincerity.

∼

Midnight came and went, followed by one a.m., then one-thirty. Jensen slept through every single time Meredith checked her phone, his arm slung over her waist. She stayed in bed longer than she ordinarily would have simply because she liked the feel of his weight on her, liked listening to the rhythmic rise and fall of his chest.

She'd wondered where he would go that night—her room, or an empty one on the second floor. They hadn't exactly been avoiding each other prior to turning in, but he'd been on the Shifter floor. She'd been on the first, checking in with Siren and Val.

Only once she'd walked into her room and found him waiting for her did she realize how much she'd wanted him to be there. The relief had hit her so hard she'd kissed him before either of them could screw anything up with words. A kiss had turned into more, and after they were both satisfied he'd pulled her against him, his warm body curled around hers, and he'd fallen asleep.

She wished she could do the same, but her brain wouldn't shut up. If Serenity's taunting words weren't running through it, Meredith's anxiety about everything else was. After the twentieth time she tried to count sheep or think of relaxing waterfalls, she gave up and slid carefully from underneath Jensen's arm. She grabbed her phone, slid on her bedside shoes, and crept downstairs.

She made a pot of coffee—decaf, because she and caffeine had been having racing heart problems of late—and took a cup down the hall to her mother's old office. Jensen's query about whether her mother had owned any other property kept nagging at her, so she dug out the file that contained the records concerning her mother's death.

Savannah hadn't made a will, which could have simply been lack of foresight, but which Meredith figured was more likely arrogant disbelief that she could ever die. The only final request her mother bothered to put in writing was to be buried in her mausoleum, but even that hadn't been done in a legally binding fashion. She'd just written it out, like she expected no one would dare contradict her wishes. Meredith had taken great joy in doing just that. Cremating Savannah Townsend was the most spitefully pleasant thing she'd ever done.

She flipped through the legal papers, looking for anything useful. But everything was as she remembered. Financial information mostly, the transfer of the bank and brokerage accounts, the deed to the house and the titles on the cars. A lengthy list of charitable organizations Meredith had ignored once she'd determined they weren't fronts for nefarious activities.

She still got letters from them all the time, reminding her of what a generous woman Savannah Townsend was, a true paragon of virtue and philanthropy, *blah, blah, blah*, and didn't Meredith want to follow in her mother's footsteps and put her fortune to good use?

She drummed her fingers on the desktop. She probably *should* do something with her mother's money. No, she decided, it was her *father's* money. He'd been the one to earn it and she felt less…wrong when she thought of it as his.

Money itself wasn't good or evil. She knew that. It was what people *did* with money that determined the morality, but it sure as hell felt a lot less tainted when she thought of it as her dad's. She opened her planning app and made a vague reminder for next month that read: *Do something useful with excessive wealth.*

There. Project Become a Better Human was at least in the planning stages. Now, if she could just pull something brilliant out of the mess of papers in front of her. She took a sip of coffee, made a face at the cold remnants, and went to get a fresh cup. She was three-quarters of the way through the hot coffee when she hit the last piece of paper in the stack and realized she was an idiot.

It was the deed for the funeral plot her mother's mausoleum rested on. She remembered finding it hilarious when Random had gone over that with her. That it was often cheap to die, and always expensive to be dead. Really, that you had to *buy* a plot of land for your corpse to decompose in was bizarre.

But you did. Which meant her mother *had* owned more than one property. The second one had just never been intended for the living.

CHAPTER

TWENTY-TWO

Meredith took a circuitous route to her mother's mausoleum, just in case Julian was having her watched. She hadn't been followed, which was a bloody miracle considering how many times Julian had texted her in the last day. Obsessive didn't begin to cover it. She'd responded just enough times to prevent him from actually calling.

Outside the mausoleum, she stopped long enough to lay a simple ward around the structure, tying it to her as the focal point instead of the actual building, so it would be easy enough to reabsorb upon her departure and not be a colossal waste of Aspect if she didn't need it. Out of an abundance of caution, she made it a fully impervious ward. Any insects or other living creatures who wanted to come this way tonight would have to wait an hour or two.

Precautions in place, she turned to face the center of the room. Unlike her house and grounds the mausoleum had only one potential location for a secret room: underground. The floor was smooth white marble of a seamless construction, not a grout line in sight, which spoke to the probable involvement of an elemental Aspecter in the building process. No part of the floor itself could move or slip aside to reveal a passageway. Which meant the entrance had to be through the stone coffin itself. Considering it was *supposed* to contain a body right now…

"I seriously hope the *entire* coffin moves," she muttered. It would be just like Savannah Townsend to make someone climb past her dead body to get to the things she'd hoarded in life.

Meredith dropped to her hands and knees beside the sarcophagus, inspecting where the base met the floor, running her fingers along the seam. Once she'd gone around it twice she had to admit there *wasn't* a seam. Definitely an Elemental Aspecter involved in the building process, and Savannah had had them fuse the marble base of the sarcophagus to the marble floor.

Which left her with the sarcophagus lid. Which would open to the place where a body was supposed to rest. Where her *mother's* body was supposed to have rested.

"You were a sick, sick woman, Savannah." Unsurprisingly, the empty coffin didn't answer.

The stone lid extended a couple inches past the sides. She ran her fingers underneath the lip, feeling where the two met. She felt the crack that proved it was indeed just a lid, but when she tried to shove it to the side, it didn't budge in the slightest.

Ancient Greek and Egyptian sarcophagus lids could weigh up to several tons and therefore be immovable by one woman without the aid of modern machinery. Since this one was a modern style, even though the lid appeared to be made of marble, she had been operating under the assumption that it was light enough to move. Because her mother would have to have moved it on her own every time she'd come here.

Certain spells could enhance strength, and Battle Aspecters like Valkyrie could do so as easily as breathing, but Savannah hadn't had Battle Aspect, and even that wouldn't move this thing if it weighed a few thousand pounds.

She lost track of time as she circled around and around the marble coffin, running her fingers over the intricate carvings, searching for any way it might open. Her hands took on a thick layer of stone dust, her skin drying and cracking.

She was crouched down, the fingertips of her left hand wedged in the space between two carvings, feeling for cracks or seams or hidden buttons, when something slammed into her wards. The force and surprise of the attack sent her shooting to her feet. One of her fingernails caught on the carving and ripped.

"Son of a *bitch*." The nail had torn almost clean off, blood streaming from the wound as whoever was outside continued to launch a barrage of assaults on her wards. They were physical assaults, not magical, almost as if whoever was outside was trying to beat through with brute force.

"Jensen?" she asked when she stepped into view of the mausoleum's doorway. He checked himself from where he'd been ramming the ward with his shoulder. His eyes were a little wild, something distinctly lupine in the irises.

"Let me in."

She decided to magnanimously ignore that he'd ordered rather than asked, and made a Jensen-sized hole in the ward that sealed up after him. He was extremely pissed off, if the expression on his face was any indication.

"What the hell is this?" He shoved something blue into her face.

Meredith looked down at the sticky note she'd left on the kitchen counter because she hadn't wanted to bother anyone before she headed out. Or, if she was being truthful, because she hadn't wanted anyone to come with her.

"That is a note I left for you."

"Precisely," he growled—and it was definitely an *actual* growl. Could he partially shift his vocal cords? How much control did that take? Or was it a lack of control that caused such a partial shift? "A note. A *fucking note*."

She took the piece of paper, because it seemed to be offending him, and tucked it into her pocket. "You have something against notes?"

MEREDITH ASKED the question with sugary sweetness, like he was being ridiculous. "I have something against being uninformed and purposefully left behind when you're going off on a hunch that could mean the life or death of my sister and could get *you* killed."

"I would have called if I'd found anything." Her tone was calm and measured. "I wasn't followed and, as you discovered, I took precautions."

Precautions. Maybe his shoulder would be sore later from trying to beat his way through her *precautions*, but he hadn't precisely been thinking. He'd just known that she was *gone*, and a dozen *what if* scenarios whirled through his head. What if Julian found her when she was alone? What if someone *else* connected to her mother found her? What if she got into a car crash driving like a speed demon? What if she got hurt?

He'd been gripped in the kind of fear he hadn't ever wanted to feel again after Natalie disappeared. The fear that something terrible had happened to someone he loved.

Shit. He couldn't love her. He *liked* her just fine. He liked her a lot. They'd had an instant, mutual attraction the moment they'd met. She was fun and sexy and easy to be with, and yes, he wanted to see where it might go.

But he couldn't love her. He wasn't ready to love her. Not when he could lose her. Not when he couldn't protect her because how *could* he protect her? He hadn't even been able to protect Natalie.

"Hello?" Meredith snapped her fingers a hairsbreadth from his eyes and he jerked back. "You look like you got hit by a battering ram."

He shook himself, and his gaze fell to the hand she had clutched to her chest. "You're bleeding."

"Yeah, well, *someone* scared the shit out of me banging into my wards like a one-man wrecking crew," she said sarcastically.

"I had really hoped to never experience the pain of having my nails ripped off again."

"*Again?*"

"Joking," she said unconvincingly.

He took her hand, careful to avoid touching the wound. It bled too much, though it still had roughly half the nail covering the nail bed.

"You have a first aid kid in your car?"

She sighed, as if severely put-upon to be asked such a reasonable question. "Yes, under the passenger seat."

"I'll get it. Stay right here."

She frowned. "How did you get here?"

He flashed her a grin as he walked out. "You have several cars, and the keys are meticulously labeled."

He grabbed the kit from her car and when he knocked on the invisible boundary of the ward, she opened a door for him.

He placed the kit on top of the coffin and uncapped the small bottle of hydrogen peroxide spray he found inside. Meredith laid her hand flat on the sarcophagus lid and he got to work. The impact of the spray on a wound that ragged had to hurt, but she didn't so much as flinch.

His anger—at her leaving him, coming out here alone—dimmed.

Placing a thick layer of antibiotic ointment onto a pad of gauze, he pressed it over the tip of her finger and wrapped it with medical tape. Again, she didn't even twitch, just breathed steadily in and out.

"Thank you."

She took her hand back while he swept everything into the kit and zipped it up. She hadn't made a single complaint about the pain, and the things she kept saying about her childhood...

"Don't take this the wrong way," he said slowly, abandoning the kit to draw her in. "But what did your mother do to you?"

He thought she would put on that fake cheerful mask she wore like a second skin and deflect. For a moment, that response flickered over her face. Then she sighed and pointed to a word written on the wall to his left.

"Agonia?" he asked. "That's…what? Latin?" Ancient languages weren't exactly in his wheelhouse. Normally, it wouldn't bother him or make him feel stupid, except he'd gotten the impression, from a few offhand things Jace had said, that her ex-boyfriend was genius-level smart. Which shouldn't matter, except that Meredith was genius-level smart, though she tried to hide it, and it occurred to Jensen she might get bored with him since he *wasn't*.

"Translated from Ancient Greek, actually. Everything is so much more mysterious and elitist if we say it in an ancient language. It more or less translates to anguish. Agony. Pain. That was my mother's gift. That was her Aspect."

"To…cause pain?"

Meredith nodded. "I'm sure it was quite useful in the less-civilized days of Aspect Society, back when we still went to war with other magical communities at the drop of a hat. One high level Agonian could drop two dozen Aspecters to their knees if they weren't prepared and properly warded. They wouldn't be able to hold so many for more than a few seconds, but a few seconds is plenty of time for the Battle Aspecters to sweep in and take everyone out. The problem is that there isn't any place for the talent in the modern world, but it still crops up from time to time. Aspect is meant to be used."

Jensen felt more than a little sick. "And she used it on you."

Meredith shrugged. "Aspect use is a compulsion. We *have* to let it out, or we go insane."

"Please tell me you're not making excuses for her."

"No. There are ways to manage Agonia. Ways my mother would have been taught from a very young age." Here, Meredith hesitated. "We don't blame a child for what they're born as. But a power like Agonia, one that can cause so much harm…those born with it have to prove that they can control it. It's an unbreakable tenet of our society that Aspect cannot be used to harm others." Here, her lips twisted into a wry smile. "Unless, of course, that harm is commanded by Council edict. But *all* Agonia does is harm.

"My mother was smart. She had iron control. She did what was necessary from a young age to prove to the Council that she was more than capable of being a harmless member of Aspect Society. But she didn't want to be harmless. I don't know if that was her Aspect, or just her nature. But once she had everyone fooled, she used her Aspect the way it called her to. She just happened to use it on me more than most."

"When did it start?"

She sighed. "Does it matter?"

"Yes."

"I don't honestly know. The first time I remember, I was four. It was my birthday, and my father had taken the day off to spend with me. They argued about something and she sent him away. I wouldn't stop crying. I think I told her it was her fault. She made it very clear to me that day that there were worse things than a ruined birthday." She straightened, brushing ineffectually at the dust on her jeans with her good hand. "And that is all the reminiscing I will be doing today. If you want to help, figure out how the lid comes off this tomb."

Jensen flinched. "I'll be the first to admit I have done some pretty questionable things at the request of a beautiful woman, but isn't your mother's corpse in there?"

"No. I cremated her and tossed the ashes in a dumpster."

"Isn't it illegal to dispose of human remains that way?"

"I have no idea. I didn't look it up. It gives me great joy to think of her ashes languishing in some landfill beneath old lasagna and rotting vegetables. The point is, I'm pretty sure that sarcophagus is the entrance to the repository but the damn lid won't budge."

Jensen glanced at it. "Not to be condescending, but have you tried shoving? It's already come off a little."

"Yes, I tried shoving. Shoving doesn't work."

The sarcophagus lid *had* moved, though, maybe a centimeter. Not straight to the side, like a person trying to shove it off would move it, but as if the center of the lid had a pin stuck through, and someone had started to rotate it on that pin, like the hand on a clock.

"Are you sure?" Jensen sounded skeptical.

"Would you like to roll up your sleeves and use your big, bad, manly werewolf strength to show me how it's done?"

He pointed at himself. "Still not a werewolf."

"You turn into a wolf at will. How does that *not* make you a werewolf?"

"Unlike fictional werewolves, I don't howl at the moon, am not allergic to silver, and I've never eaten the heart of anything, much less a man."

"Alright Mr. *Not* a Werewolf, do you want to use your manly Shifter strength to reveal how I, poor, merely human female that I am, simply lack the requisite strength to move the sarcophagus lid while you will manage it with ease?"

"Not when you put it like that." But he braced his hands on the lid, dug in and pushed. She felt the tingle of his magic—so different-feeling from Aspect—and his muscles bulged, thick veins popping out along his forearms as he strained.

Predictably, the lid didn't move.

Meredith popped her hip against the sarcophagus and dramatically fanned herself as he stopped pushing, breathing hard. "Oh, please don't stop on my account. I was just enjoying the view."

He straightened. The veins on his forearms had popped out, and it *was* a remarkably good view. He glared at her. "You could have told me it was magically sealed."

"Oh, but I don't know that it *is*. It could just be an extremely heavy piece of marble. I *do* suspect that magic achieved all of its current movement."

"Okay. What did you do to get it to move?"

"I don't know. It hadn't moved at all before you came. I was looking for a hint or some kind of hidden lever when you scared me and…" She trailed off, lifting up the hand with her damaged finger. "And I ripped off my fingernail." She laughed. "Fucking *of course*. We are talking about something my mother designed, after all."

"Of course *what?*"

Meredith nodded at the wall where Jensen had seen *Agonia*. Below the word were three short sentences inscribed in a looping scrawl. *The purpose of life is pain. The pain of life is death. But the cost of death is a life.*

"That means something to you?"

Now it did. "If the purpose of life is pain, and the cost of death is a life? Pain moves this door."

"Okay. How much pain do you think it takes to get us into the repository?"

"Given the inscription? I'd say the amount it would take to kill a person from pain alone."

Jensen looked at her with something that straddled the divide between trepidation and horror. "Are you telling me that your mother could quantify how much pain it takes to kill someone? Quantify it enough to tie it to a spell?"

To sugarcoat the truth or to just throw it out there? "Yep." The way he looked at her in response… She pasted on a fake smile. "Rapidly recalculating earlier expressed sentiments about trusting each other and seeing where this relationship goes?"

"Why would I be doing that?"

"Because you're looking at me like you just realized I issued forth from the womb of a monster. Which, fair, I kind of did. It's fine if I'm more than you bargained for. I assure you, my laundry list of baggage only has room to grow. In fact—"

He yanked her to him, his mouth covering hers with a kiss

that would have brought her to her toes, had her heels not already put her on them.

"You really do have trust issues," he said when he released her.

"Told you."

"Don't sound so satisfied. I can work them out of you."

She lifted an eyebrow. "I see humility ranks among your many amiable qualities."

"I can get you the list of the rest, if you want," he deadpanned, studying the sarcophagus lid. "So if it takes the pain of a death to fully open this thing...how does *that* work without killing someone?"

"Well, considering it took *this* pain as partial payment—" she lifted her bandaged hand "—I'd say the pain doesn't have to come all at one time or all from one source."

"Are you suggesting we line people up and rip off their fingernails one at a time until it opens up?"

Meredith tapped her nose in mock contemplation. "Well, between the two of us we have seven friends. If everyone donates a couple of fingernails, maybe a toenail or two, we could probably open this thing three inches by sundown tomorrow."

"Can't we just bring in a wrecking ball and crush the whole damn structure? Or bust through the floor?"

"Good suggestion. Well, not the wrecking ball part. It would draw entirely too much attention in a small town and lead Julian right to us before we're ready. As for busting through the floor..." She closed her eyes and felt for the edges of the spell without much hope of finding them. She'd searched for something like it when she'd first come in and found nothing. She didn't have any better luck this time, which meant the spell was only active and noticeable when drawing pain.

Her mother never could make *anything* easy. Meredith braced herself and jabbed her injured finger against the stone lid. A bright spark of pain ratcheted up her hand.

Since she was looking for it, this time she felt the spell as it activated and latched onto its structure, tracing the lines out. She'd gotten as far as the sarcophagus lid when it started fading. She jabbed her injured finger against her leg in a slow staccato pattern, just enough pain to keep the spell sitting up and taking notice.

After a minute of study, she stopped hitting her finger and let the spell fade. "I'm afraid a sledgehammer to the floor isn't going to help this situation. The room isn't impervious to physical destruction, but it would definitely require the kind of heavy machinery we can't use for the reasons I've already stated. If we want in, we're going to have to give it what it wants."

"And how do we do that? Even if we had a hundred people willing to come in here and sustain small injuries, wouldn't that also raise eyebrows in your small town?"

"Yes, and I don't think it would work, besides. It isn't the right *quality* of pain. The fingernail was, because it was violent and unexpected, and therefore I felt it more deeply. The kind of easy pain most people would volunteer for, and that we would be willing to dole out, isn't going to move the needle much." She held up a hand, forestalling whatever he would have said next. "I have an idea, just…give me a minute."

"Meredith," he said in a calm, reassuring voice. "Please hand over all sharp objects you might be in possession of."

She rolled her eyes before she closed them. "Relax, I'm not stabbing anyone, myself included. Now shut up and let me think."

She didn't need to think so much as she needed to remember. The spell's making was very specific. It required the *pain* of a *death*. While her mother could and had quantified the physical pain required to kill someone in that very specific manner, she had failed to put any further restraints on the interpretation of the requirement.

Pain didn't only come in a physical form. It could be emotional, too, and oftentimes Meredith thought emotional pain was worse than physical. As for death…the pain of a death could be interpreted as the pain caused to the living by their grief over that death.

Meredith hadn't thought she could hate her mother any more than she already did. But as she forced herself to recall the memory of the worst day of her life, her hatred for a dead woman grew a little bit more.

CHAPTER

TWENTY-THREE

J ensen didn't know what Meredith was doing, but he didn't like it. Her face went pale and he felt the unpleasant buzz of Aspect flood the room—the spell's Aspect, not *hers*. It was reacting to pain, as it had when she'd been stubbornly tapping her bandaged finger against her leg. Except she wasn't *doing* anything now. She wasn't moving, wasn't physically hurting herself.

The spell buzzed along and the sarcophagus lid began to move. Slowly at first, then it picked up speed. Centimeter by centimeter, the lid rotated on an invisible axis.

He didn't understand what she was doing until the tears slid silently down her cheeks, and he wanted to interrupt her but he didn't. Because they needed into this room—*he* needed into this room—and he hated himself a little for standing there and letting her continue to relive whatever memory she held that could cause her enough pain to fuel her mother's spell.

When he could no longer look at her, he looked down into the space revealed by the opening lid. It was...just like the interior of any coffin. Maybe three feet deep and covered in pristine white satin, but at least mercifully empty. The lid shuddered to a halt, the sound something makes when it hits a stop, but Meredith didn't open her eyes.

"Hey," he said softly. She didn't respond, didn't even seem to hear him. He rubbed his hands gently up her arms and she startled, her hands curling into fists before recognition lit her eyes and she relaxed. He lifted his hands and wiped the tears from her cheeks.

"Shit," she mumbled.

"You okay?"

She hesitated. "Not even close. Ask me again in a decade. Did it work?"

"Yeah, but..." He stepped aside to reveal the very normal-looking interior. Well, normal-looking for a final resting place, he supposed.

Meredith didn't seem surprised. "She *did* want to be buried in it." She stepped around him, feeling along the edges of the satin interior. Her fingers slid into the dip between two of the satin pillows and then she lifted out a three foot section of the interior.

The piece had a flat wooden base covered in white satin, cut precisely to rest on the one-inch-wide ledges that ran along the inside walls of the sarcophagus.

"I know you don't need me to tell you this, but your mother was one fucked up human being." He peered into the opening, shifting his eyes enough to make better use of the light that filtered down the stone staircase she'd revealed. He could see fairly well, but even wolf eyes couldn't see in the absolute darkness of enclosed spaces. He didn't relish the thought of climbing down in total darkness into a magical room created by a woman who'd been of arguably questionable sanity. "Wish we'd thought to bring a flashlight."

Brightness flared in his peripheral vision. A sphere of pure silver light the size of a baseball floated in the air at eye level. He grinned. "Nice parlor trick."

"Oh, you wanted tricks? You should have mentioned that

earlier." The globe of light shifted color, flashing from blue to yellow to green, then back to silver, picking up speed between transitions until it looked like a disco ball.

He laughed. "Do you do kids' birthday parties?"

"Goddess, no." She shuddered in mock horror and the sphere returned to a pure silver.

MEREDITH LED THE WAY, the steady silver of the witchlight illuminating a ten foot radius around them. She still had the slightest smile on her face. How was she *smiling* in this place? When was the last time she'd done Aspect just for fun? Spent it frivolously to make someone happy? Had she *ever* done that?

The stairs went down fifteen feet into the earth. A light hum buzzed along her skin, growing more intense the further they went, like she stood too close to a powerful electrical line.

She doubted her mother would have put electrical in this place, a belief confirmed when she reached the bottom of the stairs and the witchlight caught on the primary node of an illumination web. They'd fallen out of fashion in modern times, because it was easier to be on the city's electrical grid than it was to retrofit a house with illumination webs. And really, what was the point when they had to be constantly primed with Aspect that could be better spent on other things?

However, if someone needed light in a place they didn't want Null electricians barging in and out of, illumination webs were totally the way to go. She sank a chunk of Aspect into the primary node. The buzz she'd felt upon entering the stairwell grew stronger, as if responding to the use of her power.

The primary node lit and her Aspect traveled down the transmission lines carved into the wall, lighting the secondary nodes. Sphere after sphere sparked to life as her Aspect ran the course of the spell framework in much the same way electricity ran through wires.

Soft white light bathed the room. Meredith had privately been fearing a dank, dusty room with earthen walls and cobwebs everywhere, the place perhaps running rampant with spiders and the skitter of other things that liked to lurk beneath the ground. Layered into this unpleasant imagining had been a few rickety bookshelves or old chests holding items of a questionable nature.

She should have known better than to think her mother would ever lower herself to enter a space of that nature. No, the floors, walls, and ceiling were all of the same smooth marble stone as the floor in the mausoleum above, and she felt the preservation spells—fading now that no one had been by to renew them with Aspect—that kept away bugs and dust.

No rickety bookshelves or ancient chests disgraced the pristine atmosphere. Sleek podiums ran the room in neat rows, the glass display cases atop them holding items as if this were an exclusive, private museum.

"How did your mother build all this without anyone realizing it was here?"

"Elemental Aspecter with an earth affinity, most likely. A high-level Elemental could excavate it in a few hours. They would have handled the marble work too." After which Savannah had probably killed them to leave no trace of her super-secret room, but Meredith didn't mention that.

"Is it, uh, safe to walk around?"

Meredith smiled. "Yes. The room isn't booby-trapped, if that's what you're asking. As for what's inside the cases? That's going to be a little bit trickier."

"Do we need to open them? We have the location."

Meredith pursed her lips. Technically, they didn't. "I don't like the idea of handing this over without any idea what all these pieces do. More than that, I don't trust Julian, and he would be an idiot to trust me."

"So what are you thinking?"

"I'm thinking we split this room and take a picture of everything here. In theory, I'm supposed to be considering working with him, for Analisa. I'll bring him one item in good faith and he can have the location when I meet her."

Jensen took the left half of the room while she took the right. The buzz beneath her skin hadn't let up. As she moved from podium to podium, snapping pictures with her phone, it increased steadily.

"Do you feel anything weird?" she finally asked.

Jensen finished capturing a picture of a case that held an ordinary looking china cup. "Weird how?"

The nonchalance in his tone answered her question: he didn't. "Never mind. This place just creeps me out."

"I think that makes you normal."

Except she didn't feel normal. Her fingers were itching now, little needles pricking beneath the tips. It was the same sensation she'd felt each time she'd come to visit her mother's mausoleum, but far more powerful. The sensation intensified as she walked deeper into the room, becoming almost unbearable the further she went, until breathing became increasingly difficult.

She took a step forward and her chest constricted. She took two steps back and the pressure lessened. She found herself playing a bizarre game of hot-and-cold as she moved through the room. Move right—pressure. Left—less pressure.

"Meredith?"

She barely heard Jensen say her name. The push and pull consumed her, an itch that had to be scratched, a call that had to be answered. She followed the unseen guidance, rounded one of the pedestals, and saw it.

The circlet wasn't hidden, precisely, but it was on a podium in a back corner of the room, nestled on a bed of white velvet. As soon as her eyes locked on it, the hum in her body snapped into a taut line, drawing her forward.

Her hands closed on the edges of the glass case. Intricately woven white-gold wire formed the circlet, loops and whirls that conveyed elegance but also power. The design was neither masculine nor feminine, but somewhere in between. The strands of wire met in the front and tapered to a triangular point that would rest between the wearer's brows. Nestled in that *V* was a brilliant, pear cut yellow orange diamond.

She could practically feel the weight of the cool metal pressed against her brow, the way the circlet would fill out the hollow places inside her. If she put it on she wouldn't lack purpose or fulfillment, wouldn't need to prove herself to a dead mother or the friends she still felt like she didn't measure up to.

She would only need *this*. Her purpose was truth; it was the primary affinity that ran in her blood, and the circlet was made for truth. No more hiding from the full extent of her abilities, no more second-guessing herself. With the crown on her brow, she would become the embodiment of her affinity. She would finally see what her power had tried but so far failed to reveal: the world, as it truly was.

Glimpses of that truth had come her way lately—the feel of places and things—but not the entirety. And she wanted it all.

She lifted the glass cover, distantly aware of a nearby presence but unable to focus enough to know who it was. The cover didn't budge. She scrabbled at the edges before blindly beating at it, desperate to get through, to get—

Hands gripped her wrists, hauling her back against a hard, warm chest. She struggled futilely as the person dragged her away. The buzzing that had abated roared to life again, burning like the rasp of sandpaper beneath her skin, and she screamed.

TWENTY-FOUR

J ensen held on to Meredith while she fought him like a woman possessed. Her nails dug into his forearms. She kicked and clawed and screamed and didn't even seem to realize he was the one holding her.

At first, when he'd seen her strange weaving through the room, as if she was looking for something by feel rather than by sight, he'd thought maybe she was doing some weird Aspect thing. Then she'd stopped in front of that circlet and gone too still, too entranced, her power crackling in the air around her like lightning, so strong it had been uncomfortable to breathe. She hadn't heard him when he'd spoken, even when he'd shouted her name in her ear.

Now he held her a foot off the ground as he carried her toward the stairs, grateful for years of raising a baby sister who'd refused to come indoors at mealtimes. He'd always had to go pick her up kicking and screaming, at which point she inevitably shifted into her snow leopard form and proceeded to claw the shit out of him. Meredith's nails and stilettos had nothing on a snow leopard in the grips of a full-on temper tantrum.

At the bottom of the stairs he dropped one arm from Meredith's waist to dip and slide underneath her legs, hoisting her fully off the ground and taking an elbow to his right eye for the trouble.

He clamped her tight and bounded up the stairs. The opening at the top was too narrow for them to fit through together. He dropped her feet, gripped her waist, and tossed her up and out, leaping through after her. He caught her around the middle when she lunged for the sarcophagus, holding her until the lid slid back into place of its own accord.

Not until it had fully closed did she stop fighting him and straighten, her unfocused eyes regaining clarity.

She blinked. "Jensen? How did…" She trailed off, as if it was all coming back to her, and then she looked down at the blood under her fingernails and the scratches on his arms. "Shit."

She grabbed the first aid kit he'd left by the tomb and opened it hastily, items spilling everywhere. "Shit, sorry."

He wondered if she knew that the more flustered she got, the more she cussed. "You don't have to apologize, and you don't need to worry about it."

She grabbed a package of gauze, halted a rolling bottle of saline with her foot and bent to scoop it up, taking both back over to him.

"I clawed you bloody, what do you mean don't worry about it?" She pulled his left arm toward her.

"Trust me, you have nothing on baby snow leopard claws." He tried to take his arm back but she scowled at him and he figured it was better to just let her get on with it.

She practically drowned his arm in saline wash. "Baby snow leopard? Your little sister?"

He nodded.

"So you guys don't…I mean, you're a wolf. Your sister isn't?"

"It's the ability to Shift that's hereditary, not the animal we choose. We aren't born to a specific form, but we are bound to the first animal we shift into. Shifter lore claims that our animal matches our soul." He grinned at her. "Most people I know match their animal pretty well, but I figure that has less to do with the innate qualities of our soul, and more to do with being drawn to the kind of animal you already identify with.

"I really liked wolves as a kid. Didn't take a rocket scientist to figure out I'd end up shifting into one. Nat was the same way, always obsessed with feline furballs. Anyone could have guessed she'd go cat by the time she was three."

Meredith opened the gauze and wiped carefully at his arm. "She's a lot younger than you, right?"

He nodded. "Sixteen."

"So…your grandmother raised both of you?"

"Not exactly. Grams raised me. Mom dumped me on her when I was five and took off. I never thought I'd see her again.

"Then one day she showed up with a six-month-old Natalie. She shoved Nat into my arms, told me to take care of her, and took off. Grams was out of town, so I took care of Nat. When Grams got back I thought she'd take her, but she just looked at her and said she was done taking care of my mother's castoffs, and if I wanted to keep Nat so bad then I could, but she was my responsibility."

He could see her doing the math. "You would have been, what? Eighteen?"

He nodded.

Meredith frowned. "How did you change your grandmother's mind?"

He took a few beats to answer. He wasn't sure how she would feel about it. "I didn't," he said finally. "By Shifter law, Nat was mine the moment I took her. I'm her legal guardian." Meredith's hands froze for a second, then went back to cleaning off blood. He couldn't read what was on her face, she was so damn good at keeping her emotions closed off. "I'm the only father Nat's ever known. She called me Dad until she was old enough for me to make her understand I *wasn't* her dad." Pain welled up at the memory of that discussion. Nat had cried for days. "I still don't know if I shouldn't have just let her think I was. She's basically my kid. How the fuck did I let this happen to her?"

"This isn't your fault," she said softly.

He wanted to believe that. "Isn't it? She was so mad at me the day she disappeared. I don't even remember what about. So I wasn't worried when she didn't come home right after work. Figured she'd gone over to one of her friend's houses so I didn't start looking as soon as I should have. And then I couldn't find anything, and when I came down here I was still useless. I looked all through this town and found nothing. I didn't even know if I was looking in the right place." He swallowed. "And then I met you."

Her hands stilled. "You must have hated me."

"I wanted to." He'd hated himself. For wanting her, wanting anything, when Natalie was out there somewhere. For being rational enough to realize that the nights he'd spent with Meredith weren't even a betrayal, because he hadn't had enough leads to follow to do anything useful. Giving Meredith up wouldn't have helped him find Natalie, back then. But it had still felt wrong to be happy about anything, at the time. Even knowing that his time with her was the only thing that might let him find Natalie now didn't make him feel less guilty about the *then*, because he couldn't have known it would end up this way.

"So why didn't you? Hate me?"

"Because you're impossible to hate."

"I'm exceptionally easy to hate. Ask half of Aspect Society."

"They don't know you. I do. You kept me from drowning when I didn't know how to tread water anymore. You're doing it again right now."

Her breath caught. "Jensen, I—" She broke off as she cleaned the last of the blood off his arms, running her fingers over his skin. "You don't have a single mark on you."

"Perks of being a Shifter."

"You're telling me all the werewolf fiction that has you guys having super fast healing got that part right?"

"If I get *Not a Werewolf* tattooed on my chest will you stop calling me one?"

"Maybe, if you get it tattooed in flowery cursive. So, super fast healing? How does that work?"

He shrugged. "How does your fearless leader's super fast healing work?"

"She *is* Life," Meredith said, as if that explained everything.

"And we're Shifters. Going from human to animal and back isn't exactly fun. It hurts. It breaks your bones. What do you think Shifting is besides healing the body into a new form? It'd make *less* sense if we healed normal."

"Huh." She chewed on that for a minute. "I thought you said all the werewolf lore in fiction was wrong."

"No, I said I don't go around howling at the moon and eating human hearts." He shrugged. "We may have always kept a low profile from your kind, but extreme secrecy where ordinary humans are concerned wasn't as big a deal until cameras were invented. A Shifter kid makes a mistake and gets seen, you pick up and move your enclave before the angry mob shows up. It wasn't ideal, but it wasn't getting plastered all over the internet for everyone and their mother to track you down either. It's unsurprising that *some* actual Shifter abilities made it into the realm of public consumption."

She twisted the piece of gauze in her hand, rolling it into a smaller and smaller piece. "Anything else in the realm of public consumption that I should know about?"

She sounded nervous. Or worried.

"Like what?"

"Like..." She shoved her tattooed arm at him. "This *is* reversible? You said it was, and you weren't lying, and I don't *think* you were manipulating the truth, but you guys don't, like, *you know...*?"

Suddenly he did know. Nat had gone through a phase where she'd torn through shifter-based fiction and proceeded to tell him all the gritty details every night over dinner. A lot of them had one theme about Shifters in common. Jensen fixed a serious expression on his face when what he wanted to do was laugh. He met Meredith's gaze and held it, caught her around the waist and pulled her in.

He spoke deeply, his voice low and intense. "Like, do we all have one true mate? One we recognize instantly upon meeting them? One we would move mountains for, fight for, die for?"

Absolute horror filled her eyes, and he was sorely tempted to say yes out of sheer curiosity to see how fast and how far she would run for the hills before her Aspect clued her in that he'd been lying.

He leaned in and whispered, "No."

She exhaled in a rush, laughing, and punched him on the arm. "Asshole."

He laughed too, pulling her closer. "I'm the asshole you married."

"I prefer to think of you as the asshole I'm divorcing."

"But still sleeping with and seeing where it goes."

"Right now, the only place things with this asshole—" she jabbed a finger in his chest "—are going, are back down into the treasure room because we didn't get Julian a trinket before I got all hypnotized."

"*You* didn't." He reached into his pocket and pulled out the necklace he'd nicked before he'd gone and grabbed her. "I did."

Her nose wrinkled. "That thing smells like the magical equivalent of moral evil."

"Then Julian should love it." He shoved it back into his pocket, the laughter they'd shared fading from him altogether. "Do you want to call him now?"

She shook her head, heading back outside. "No, I'd rather do it from the house. Rationally, I know calling him won't summon him to my side, but…" She trailed off. She didn't have to say anything more. He got it. "Besides, I've been getting grief lately for not including others in everything I do. Which reminds me, I think you're invited to join a support group with Jace and Random."

"A support group?" he echoed. "For what?"

"Men involved with women who have issues asking for help."

Now that he might actually find useful. "What time are meetings?"

TWENTY-FIVE

Meredith was fifteen minutes from home when she felt Valkyrie open the house wards to let someone through. Given the number of people staying in her home, keying her best friend in as a secondary control had seemed like a good idea.

Three minutes later a text came through to her phone.

Rebekah King is here. You are not.

Shit. She mentally tried to calculate whether Rebekah's arrival coincided with the time frame Jensen had given her, but couldn't remember the exact time he'd said. She had expected a heads-up before his grandmother got here. Shouldn't he have had her flight number or something? Or shouldn't she have called him?

When she didn't answer the text immediately, Val sent another.

??? You can't disappear in the middle of the night at a time like this. If you haven't been kidnapped, I'll kill you myself.

Geez, she'd left a note—that Jensen had taken with him, she realized. She should have texted her friends instead of going with the archaic written form of communication, but she hadn't wanted to risk waking one of them up and having them insist on coming with her.

She was dictating a response text when another came through.

Jensen is gone too. He'd damn well better be with you. Do you have any idea how bad this looks?

And double shit. She sent back: *We'll be there in five minutes,* and punched the gas. In the rearview mirror she saw the Escalade Jensen was driving fall behind, then accelerate quickly and catch back up. Her phone rang.

"Where's the fire?" Jensen asked when she picked up.

"Your grandmother has arrived. We are both missing. Valkyrie is informing me it looks like a political nightmare."

"She's not supposed to be here for another three hours."

"Apparently no one informed her of that. See you at the house."

She parked by the front door instead of in the garage and Jensen slid to a stop behind her. She waited for him so they could walk in together. He threaded his fingers through hers, and she looked down at them before arching a questioning eyebrow at him.

He gave her an amused smile in return and brought their joined hands up to kiss her fingers. "To put to rest fears of political nightmares. A potential bonus is that my grandmother thinks you were so desperate to get your hands on me you dragged me out of the house so we could have some privacy. She will be thrilled we have such a healthy relationship."

Meredith shook her head at him, unable to form a response to that. He sounded genuinely affectionate when he talked about his grandmother. Which didn't mesh in Meredith's mind with the kind of woman who could tell an eighteen-year-old to raise his own sister.

She tried to tug her hand free but he wouldn't give, so that was how she walked into her house holding hands like a love-struck teenager. The kitchen was so thick with tension you could cut it with a knife. The Shifters were all sitting very straight, their eyes downcast. Basically, they'd done everything except roll over and expose their bellies.

Meredith couldn't figure out what was tension causing about the scene. Rebekah King sat at the end of the island, looking sweet and grandmotherly in a pair of cream slacks and a soft green sweater. She had one of Random's muffins in hand and was beaming at him.

"These are wonderful," she said. "You must try them with some of the apple butter I put in Meredith's gift basket. If you like it, I'll send you the recipe."

The gift basket in question sat in the middle of the island. Meredith could see the jar of apple butter through the clear cellophane wrapping, along with a package of what looked like the beef jerky Jensen had asked if she liked, and a bright green something that might be a scarf. Maybe a shawl.

All heads in the room turned to them as they walked in.

"There's my boy," Rebekah said to Jensen, smiling. She looked calm, collected, and beatific. Apparently, whatever emotions she might have had about her grandson's abduction and subsequent return had been gotten out over the phone, or were being reserved for private.

"Grams." Jensen inclined his head, then dropped Meredith's hand to move his to the small of her back, nudging her forward a step. "This is Meredith."

"A pleasure to meet you, my dear." Rebekah rose from her seat and strode over, holding both her hands out. Meredith took them and stood obligingly still for the air cheek kisses delivered next. Rebekah stepped back and gave her an appraising once-over. "Such a lovely young woman. It's a delight to welcome you to the family."

The part of her that was well-trained in etiquette answered on autopilot, giving the polite, "Thank you," in just the right tone and warmth that she would use if she had actually gotten married and was actually being welcomed into a family she was now a part of. The rest of her was trying to piece together what Rebekah King was up to.

Meredith couldn't question Jensen with her eyes, because that would involve actual eye movement his grandmother could see. Instead, she bestowed her questioning glance on the one person directly in her field of vision over Rebekah's left shoulder.

Serenity toasted her with a mug of coffee and mouthed what looked suspiciously like, "Good luck."

Comforting.

"Now," Rebekah was saying, "I need a few minutes with the two of you in private, and then we can get back around to rescuing my granddaughter and discussing alliance terms. Shall we move to the porch? I must see this silencing spell I've heard so much about."

Precisely when had she had time to hear about silencing spells? She'd been here all of, what, half an hour?

Meredith smiled agreeably and led the way.

"Delightful," Rebekah said when Meredith built the silencing spell, complete with witchlight glow for visibility. "You're quite certain no one can hear us?"

"Quite certain."

"Perfect." Her friendly smile didn't drop but it turned sharper, more calculating. She reminded Meredith of Aunt Ella. "Now, Jensen has informed me of the circumstances of your marriage and your intention to reverse it. I'm afraid that simply will not do."

Meredith matched Rebekah's easy, pleasant tone. "Oh? In what way?"

"I understand you weren't planning on a marriage, but the fact is that you're now in one. Shifters take commitments like this very seriously, you know, and it won't look good come negotiating time if Aspecters appear so fickle they can't even honor their matrimonial promises for more than a few days."

"Grams," Jensen started, but Rebekah shot him a look that could freeze lava and his mouth snapped shut with an audible click.

"You seem like a smart, capable woman," Rebekah continued, "so I'll be blunt. Our chances of getting the enclave protectors to sign a peace agreement are rocky. The first step will be successfully finding the Shifters who have been abducted. I won't contact the other protectors until we've done that much. The second step will be convincing them that Aspect Society is worth aligning with.

"A marriage between two young, vibrant individuals such as yourselves is the perfect story to bring us all together. But no one wants a story that doesn't end in happily-ever-after."

"I appreciate the thought you've put into this, Ms. King—"

"Oh, please, call me Rebekah."

"Very well, Rebekah. As I was saying, I appreciate the thought you've given the situation. I appreciate your bluntness, so allow me to be blunt in return. Jensen and I will be divorcing."

Rebekah sighed. "Ah, the stubbornness of youth. I do recall it. If you must, then you must, but the question is *when*? Think of the symbol you could present in these negotiations. Young, in love, married. Risking everything to rescue those who have been taken from us.

"All I need from you is to present that picture at negotiations. Is that so much to ask? A few weeks, at the most, then do as you will."

"Grams," Jensen said slowly, "why are you so interested in this agreement going through?"

Why indeed?

She waved off the question. "I've long thought this cloak-and-dagger routine between Shifters and Aspecters was outdated. All of this hiding in the shadows has gone on too long.

It's time for the Shifters to be respected in the magical communities again."

"It's easy to think something," Meredith said, "but people don't generally act on those passing thoughts, and certainly not with your enthusiasm. Why is this alliance so important to you?"

"Can't I simply be interested in my grandson's future? He obviously cares for you. Whatever will happen to the two of you if this alliance doesn't go through?"

"I'm standing right here," Jensen muttered.

"You're saying you want this alliance because Shifters have been in hiding too long, and because you want my and Jensen's relationship to succeed?"

"Yes, dear."

"You, Rebekah King, are a liar."

Rebekah sighed. "Truthfinding is such a bothersome talent. I'd hoped you weren't all that good at it."

"Oh, I'm exceptionally good at it. So maybe you could save us both the trouble and come out with the truth."

"I'm afraid I can't do that. But I can promise you that my reasons are not nefarious. They are simply personal."

True.

"Do you swear that your reasons—and my not knowing them—will cause no harm to either of our peoples?"

"I do."

True. She looked at Jensen. They couldn't very well sabotage a peace negotiation they'd asked for just because his grandmother wanted it to happen.

"Have you considered how it's going to look when she and I get divorced as soon as the ink is dry?"

"These things can be done quietly. As far as I'm concerned, no one need be the wiser if you revoke your oaths. So, what do you say?"

Jensen gave her a look that said, *I'm in if you're in.*

"Until the agreement is signed, then."

"Wonderful." Rebekah clapped her hands. "Now let's go in and see about rescuing my grandbaby."

"Rebekah?" Meredith called before the woman stepped out of the silencing spell. "If you knew we were going to get divorced, what's with the gift basket and the welcome-to-the-family spiel?"

"You don't have to be married to have a long and happy relationship. I have a good feeling about the two of you." She went inside.

Meredith lingered inside the silencing spell with Jensen. "She has a good feeling about us? She doesn't even know me."

"It's all part of her elder protector mystique. As long as she's always making grand predictions, half of them turn out to be right."

"She brought me a gift basket and welcomed me to the family."

"She's a giving person."

"It's a lot of pressure. I don't even know how to do whatever it is we're doing and I don't need other people putting labels on it." Putting expectations on it.

"Then it's not labeled." He stepped in, slid his arms around her waist and rested his forehead against hers.

She blew out a breath. Now wasn't the time to be having a non-relationship crisis. "Okay. Do you know why she wants this alliance so badly?"

"No. She raised me with the usual stay-away-from-Aspecters-at-all-costs line. I don't know where this is coming from. You ready to go in?"

She started to nod, then shook her head. "I need to call Julian first."

He tensed. "You don't want to do that inside?"

"Everyone will be listening, and watching, and worrying. Judging. I can't be who I need to be on that call in front of them." They'd worked out in advance what she would try to get from

Julian once they found the repository. Having her friends around would only distract her.

"Do you want me to stay?"

"Yes."

"Then I'm here."

"Thank you." She turned away, because she didn't think she could look at him either while she talked to Julian. But she was grateful when he pressed against her back, a strong, steady presence as she made the call.

CHAPTER

TWENTY-SIX

J ensen kept an arm around her as they walked back into the kitchen, and she didn't let herself worry over how much she liked it. Or whether he was just doing it because they had agreed to keep up appearances until this was all over.

"I found the repository," she said without preamble, "and I called Julian. He more or less agreed to what we discussed."

"We should have been present for the call," Dom objected.

"*I* was present." Jensen's words brooked no further comment.

"Julian's sending someone to pick up the proof item in an hour."

Jace's nose wrinkled. "Would that be what's in Jensen's pocket that smells so terrible?"

Shifter brows around the table furrowed. "I don't smell anything," Hel said.

"It's a magical smell," the Aspecters replied in near-perfect unison.

"I couldn't get anything out of him on the auction location," Meredith continued. "I refused to meet at his house—" she put a big *hell no* down for getting caught in Julian's home defenses and held as his personal pet Truthfinder "—and we compromised on Winter Forest Park. Lot three, six tomorrow night. I didn't even have to work to get Jensen in. Apparently, Analisa is excited to meet him because, 'none of the other ones are tame.' "

The words made the Shifters bristle, but also gave them hope. They were the first concrete proof they'd received that Analisa had the Shifters.

"Val, please tell me you have some idea where Julian's taking me."

Valkyrie's lips twisted in a grimace. "Yes, and no. As you know, Julian mostly got off with a slap on the wrist when the old council dissolved," she said, likely for the benefit of the Shifters in the room. "He can't leave Seclusion but we don't have the right to routinely monitor him."

"Am I to take it you've been *non*-routinely monitoring him?"

"Random city-wide security sweeps," she said with a straight face. "One thing those sweeps all have in common is a section on the northeast side of town. Or rather the lack of information on it in reports. It's always written off as 'nothing of interest' so it didn't raise any red flags until I cross-referenced it with the file on Julian. Sometimes he is logged as 'going for a drive' but the details on his route become vague around a certain northeast area.

"I sent a team to check it out. When I didn't hear from them after an hour I called for an update. They were back at base and hadn't remembered I'd sent them to check the area until I called. They're one of my best teams. I sent them back, along with a second team. The same thing happened again."

"Disorientation spell?" Meredith guessed.

Val nodded. "The largest and most complex I've ever seen. I haven't been able to fully map the perimeter because my teams keep getting too close to it and wandering back to headquarters, but I'd guestimate the area at roughly a square mile."

Hel raised her hand like she was in school. "What does that mean?"

"It means we have a square mile area that is completely unknown to us. Cross the threshold, and you will become confused and stumble around until the spell eventually spits you back out. You won't remember what you were doing or why you were there.

"County and Aspect records are useless. According to every map of Seclusion we have, the area doesn't exist. Which means the spell itself had its origin over two-hundred years ago. So a family or an organization has kept it running over the years."

Jace cleared his throat. "Or it could be the same person."

Val looked at her little brother like she thought maybe he'd been hit on the head recently with a blunt object. "Did you miss the over two-hundred years part?"

"No. When Meredith said Julian mentioned thralls, I thought I'd seen the term somewhere. It was a footnote in one of the books I read on Life Aspect. The note was short, about a Life Aspecter from the fourteen hundreds. I copied it." He pulled out his phone and read. " 'Shortly thereafter Gregory lost the path, and began to take of the life of others. The siphoning forged a bond between him and his victims, making them forever enthralled of him, completely obedient, even as their energy granted him unnaturally long life.' "

"That sounds creepy," Hel offered. "You have a really creepy storyteller's voice. You should write books."

That broke the tension as the Aspecters laughed.

"What?" Hel crossed her arms. "What did I say?"

"He *does* write books." Turning to Jace, Meredith said, "So you think Analisa's a good Life Aspecter gone bad?"

He spread his hands in an I-don't-know gesture.

"Siren? You're the Life Aspecter present. Is any of this ringing a bell? Have you ever thought you might be in danger of becoming an energy vampire and ascending to the ranks of the immortal?" *Immortal.* "Shit."

"What?"

"I hoped Jace was on an intellectual tangent that had nothing to do with reality but earlier...Julian said Analisa was a god in her own way. Gods live forever."

The table fell silent, digesting that. Siren broke the quiet. "I think it's possible. When Elijah had me, after I escaped the compound and killed several of my captors, there was a point before the kill where I feel like I could have done something different. Could have taken something into me instead of just ending them. But I sensed that if I did, I wouldn't be the same anymore. That my Aspect wouldn't be the same. If Analisa *was* a Life Aspecter, I don't think she is anymore. Not in the sense that I am, anyway."

"We may be getting ahead of ourselves," Rebekah said. "What this woman is or isn't must be dealt with regardless. Our focus remains the same. Rescuing my granddaughter. To do that, we don't need conjecture—we need to know what we're walking into. Can't you use some satellites or something to see what's on this land?"

Valkyrie looked like she'd just swallowed something particularly foul tasting. "I've tried. The disorientation spell has been upgraded over the years. Satellite images don't show it. The space isn't a blank spot on the image, mind you, it's as if it simply isn't there. And there's no point in flying a drone inside because it would immediately lose signal."

"Can we take the spell down?" Dom asked.

"It's not impossible," Val conceded, "though it does possess a dauntingly large amount of power, which means we'll have to spend a lot to get through it and exhaust some of our best resources right from the start. The real trouble is that the moment we start messing with it, whoever's tied in as the spell's anchor is going to know, and there's no way to avoid that. They'll see us coming—" Val looked at Meredith and Jensen "—and that will leave the two of you in a vulnerable place."

"You're still planning on sending them to the auction?" Serenity asked. "We know where to find Natalie and the others. Let's go get them and get this over with."

"Things are never that simple," Rebekah told her in a chiding tone. "You asked me once why I disapproved of you and Jensen.

This is a prime example. The future protector's wife must be capable of strategic thinking. Of assessing threats against the enclave and making plans of action. That has never been one of your skills."

Future protector? The whole *second* thing clicked for her. Jensen was Rebekah's second. Not just second-in-command, but second-in-line for leadership. Great. She'd accidentally married the Shifter crown prince.

Serenity's expression darkened. "I see. I don't have a single thought in my head, but you think Princess Barbie's a strategic thinker?"

And here we go.

Rebekah cocked her head at Meredith. "Well? Would you care to explain to Serenity why we aren't barging in guns blazing?"

"No. That would be rude."

"Your magnanimity is overwhelming," Serenity said. "See? I know big words too."

"But," Meredith said to Rebekah, "I'll explain it to you, since you seem to think we're in class and you'd like me to be well-behaved and take the pop quiz."

Rebekah's eyes sparkled. Meredith hadn't pissed her off, she'd amused her.

"In addition to giving Analisa advance notice that we are coming, taking down the disorientation spell will deplete a large number of our assets. We will be forced to go in blind, since delaying would allow Analisa time to ready any defenses she is capable of mustering.

"Given that the area has been right under our noses for so long, it is likely the defenses she can muster are impressive. We could be overpowered. If we aren't, and she is faced with a frontal assault she cannot win, every Shifter in her possession becomes a hostage. She will use them against us or kill them. Either way, it ends badly.

"Finding a way to sneak through the disorientation spell

undetected is a better option, giving us the advantage of surprise. However, since confrontation is the inevitable point of the exercise, the Shifters will still end up in the position of likely hostages. At which point having Jensen and I behind enemy lines gives us the chance to find and protect them."

Meredith waited, wanting to see if Jensen's grandmother had thought it through to the bonus question.

"And?" Rebekah prompted.

"And if we wait until the auction night, not only are Jensen and I inside to aid the Shifters, but the auction attendees will be there as well. While they likely do not encompass every Aspecter who would have an opposition to the Shifter and Aspect societies forming an alliance, they will be some of the most powerful who would do so. Their arrest and subsequently their very public trials will go a long way toward quelling dissent."

"Very good. I'll grade you at an even 'A.' I'd give you the plus, but your delivery lacked enthusiasm. The ability to give a rousing speech is also important in a leader."

I'll give you a rousing speech.

"Of course, so is the ability to surprise those closest to you."

The Aspect half of the room was gaping at Meredith. Well, all of them except Siren. Siren had that *I knew it* expression on her face.

"Is it really *that* surprising?" she snapped at the others.

"You do remember yourself in Academy, right?" Valkyrie asked. "I was in Mr. Struthers' Aspect History course with you junior year. It was an open-class oral final. Your answer to the question, 'How could the Aspect civil war of 683 been prevented?' was facials."

Hel choked on her coffee.

"You went on to explain in great detail how you read in a magazine that the bacteria on your face can affect your mood, and clearly everyone was cranky back in 683 because they didn't have facials to balance their microfauna out. You were very earnest about it, and when Mr. Struthers accused you of making a joke out of the final, you burst into tears and said that no one appreciated you."

"Because no one *did* appreciate me. Do you have any idea how smart you have to be to act that dumb? I even said micro*fauna* instead of micro*flora*." She crossed her arms. "Do you remember how I got Jace to date me? Mr. You Have to Hit Him With a Sledgehammer to Make Him Realize a Woman is Coming on to Him?"

"Umm…" Clearly, Valkyrie did not remember.

"You were failing math?" Random offered. "He tutored you."

"Exactly," Meredith said, "I was failing math." Jensen shot her an are-you-kidding-me look that she ignored as she turned to Jace. "Ask me a math question you can do in your head."

"Fifty-three times twelve?"

"Six-hundred and thirty six. Ask me something that's actually difficult."

He thought for a second. "Square root of 16,384?"

"One-hundred and twenty-eight."

Jace looked like a decades' old conundrum had finally been solved. "That explains why none of your mistakes working through a problem made any sense."

"If everyone is finished *oohing* and *ahing* over the fact that Meredith can do math, can we get back to the problem?" Serenity asked. "Like how we're getting in there if we aren't taking this disorientation thing down?"

Meredith shared a look with Valkyrie. "Unless Analisa has modified her version, it has the same vulnerability our wards do."

By the lack of expression on Valkyrie's face, Meredith could tell Valkyrie had already considered it. As the head of security, Meredith figured it was up to Val to decide if they wanted to reveal this particular gap in their defenses to the people capable of exploiting it.

"What vulnerability?" Dom asked.

Valkyrie came to a decision. "You. None of you should have

been able to get through Meredith's wards. Did you feel *anything* when you crossed the property line?"

The three of them shared a confused look. "No?" Hel said.

"Because the wards are set to allow animals entry and exit, and the magic thought that's what you all were."

"You think we can just waltz right through?" Dom asked.

Hel sprang up. "One way to find out." She looked at Val. "Send me in, coach."

"Absolutely not," Jensen and Rebekah said in unison.

"I can do it," Hel protested. "I'm the only one who can. Wolves, jackals, and jaguars are not native to this area. You'll all just raise suspicions."

"You have no impulse control," Jensen said.

"You have no attention span," Rebekah added. "What happens when a pretty butterfly crosses your path and you decide you want to chase it?"

"Or when you forget why you're there?" Dom added.

The crestfallen look on Hel's face was pissing Meredith off. She knew what it was like to stand there and have everyone tell you that you weren't good enough for something. "Don't you think you're being a little harsh?" she gritted out.

"Do you know why we call her Hel?" Rebekah said. "It isn't her birth name. Hel is short for Helter Skelter, a nickname she got at four when she set the enclave hall on fire because she liked watching the matches burn."

"Maybe you shouldn't have left a four-year-old with matches."

"Oh, we didn't. Her fascination with trouble was already well-noted at that point in her life, so I had all flammable items safely tucked away where a bobcat cub couldn't reach them. So she turned into a raven and flew up to find them."

Jace frowned. "The same Shifter can take multiple forms?"

"The rest of us?" Jensen said. "No."

"I'm a freak of nature," Hel said bitterly. "Too *helter skelter* to get tied down to one animal. I can be whatever I want." She turned to Rebekah. "Which is why I need to be the one to go. No one will notice one more bird flying around."

"No."

"Oh, for heaven's sake," Serenity said. "You want her to grow up but you won't stop treating her like a child. She's twenty-one, not four."

"Do you know what she did just last week? She put the kettle on for tea, then decided to go for a run and left it on. Six hours later she finally came home. Her apartment wasn't on fire but she sustained third-degree burns on her hand because she couldn't think to put on an oven mitt before she picked up the kettle."

"Maybe if someone gave her attention any time other than when she's screwing up, she wouldn't do it so much."

"And maybe she wishes you would all stop talking about her like she's not right fucking here." Hel's hands were planted on her hips. "I know you think I can't do anything right, but no one's ever let me try. *Every* time I've tried to do anything, you've stopped me. When I wanted to go to cheer camp you told me I'd get distracted mid-somersault and break my neck. When I wanted to join the volleyball team, I'd also get distracted, and then a coach would yell at me and I'd be too emotionally thin-skinned to handle that and I'd cry in public and embarrass myself. Should I go through your responses when I wanted to learn piano, sign up for track and field, or join the 4H club?"

Rebekah's lips pressed into a thin line. The anger in her eyes wasn't that of a leader outraged that she was being talked back to—it was the look of a woman realizing that maybe, somewhere along the way, she had messed up, and now she didn't know how to handle it. Certainly not publicly. She was going to respond with something critical that would shut down the conversation for good. It would hurt Hel, and Rebekah would regret it later.

"Hel?" The sinking expression on Hel's face told Meredith

she'd pretty much forgotten everyone else was in the room. "Can you do this?"

Hel's eyes hardened with resolve. "Yes."

True. She believed it.

"Can you memorize everything Valkyrie tells you, do exactly as she says, and come straight back here?"

"Yes."

"Then go with Val. She'll run you through everything you need to know."

Hel hesitated, looking to Rebekah. Rebekah didn't look back. Her gaze was focused on Meredith, something that looked almost like gratitude in her eyes. She nodded.

SEEING the look of hope and excitement in Hel's eyes as she followed Valkyrie out of the kitchen, Jensen pitted a lifetime of knowing his cousin against his hope that Meredith's belief in her wasn't unfounded. He'd never have put his objections in words as harsh as his grandmother's—which probably meant he'd make a shitty protector some day—and he'd never have laid it all out there so publicly, but he didn't disagree with Grams' assessment.

Not once in her life had Hel managed to stay on-task for longer than fifteen minutes. But...Serenity's comments had gotten to him, too. Hel *wasn't* a kid anymore. In his head she'd probably always be the teenage hellion who'd stolen Mike Carter's tractor and driven it into the local pond.

Hel was right. Somewhere along the way they'd given up on her. Everyone loved her—she was impossible not to love—but they'd stopped expecting anything out of her. Stopped letting her even expect anything out of herself.

Meredith had given her what no one who loved her seemed to be able to: trust.

He wanted to kick himself and kiss Meredith at the same

time. Except what he needed from his pretty wife right now was her absence, so he could talk to her ex. He caught Grams' eye and gave a slight nod at Meredith.

"Meredith, dear, take a turn about the gardens with me, won't you?"

Had his grandmother actually just said *take a turn about the gardens*? How many period dramas had she been watching without him around to rein her in?

Meredith took this in stride, even accepting the arm Grams held out to her. *Be nice,* he mouthed. His grandmother flashed him a large smile. Everything about it was polite and sweet, and yet the very sight of it could instill terror in the entirety of the enclave's members. He was certain that somewhere way back in the day, a wolf Shifter with that exact smile had inspired the Little Red Riding Hood folk tale. Fortunately, he'd developed an immunity to it somewhere around age fifteen.

He gave Dom a look and his cousin took the hint. "Come on, Ren, let's go make sure Hel understands what tactical instruction is."

Random cast a single glance from Jensen to Jace and said, "Jace, I'm borrowing your wife."

"What for?"

"Wouldn't you like to know?"

"Don't make me punch you on principle, man."

"As if."

Siren rolled her eyes, leaned in and kissed Jace. "Jensen wants to talk to you, so we're leaving."

"It's as good an excuse as any." Random swept Siren into his arms and carried her toward the back porch.

"Put my wife and my kid down!"

"Not a chance," Random called back. "Valkyrie is solid muscle. I have to dramatically sweep someone into my arms to feel manly and your wife is a more manageable size."

They disappeared outside, Jace shaking his head as he looked after them. "One day I'm going to have to remember why I thought it was a good idea to let my sister marry him."

Jensen laughed. "I get the feeling no one *lets* Valkyrie do anything."

"You're not wrong." Jace rubbed at the back of his neck and looked at Jensen warily. "You wanted to talk to me?"

"Yeah. You're the research person in this group, right?"

"Uh, I guess? You want me to research something?" It was the surprise—and the relief—on his face that made Jensen realize the guy had probably thought Jensen wanted to talk to him about Meredith.

"Any chance you recognize this?" Jensen showed him the picture he'd snapped of the crown before he'd hauled Meredith away from it.

Jace studied it, finally shaking his head. "Some reason you think I should?"

"More hoping you might. It drove Meredith ballistic."

"Define ballistic."

"She had no response to outside stimuli and was trying to claw the case open to get to it. I had to physically pull her off it, but she didn't come back to herself until we were out of the repository. None of the other objects did that to her. It seemed… specific to her. I want to know if it's going to be a problem at the auction."

"Text me the picture and I'll see what I can find." He hesitated. "She didn't mention this."

"Uh-huh. Because she's a woman who likes to broadcast what she would view as a personal failing."

Jace let out a tired sigh. "Right. That reminds me, Random tasked me with inviting you to the—hell, I forget what he called it." He scrolled through his phone. "Oh, right, the Support Group for Men with Brilliant but Exasperatingly Independent Wives. Geez, the guy's a lawyer, couldn't he come up with something that would acronym? Anyway, I think it's his excuse to make us throw darts and drink beer once a week. You in?"

"You do know Meredith's divorcing me, right? Pretty much as soon as it's politically feasible."

"Yeah, but she likes you, and you obviously like her. You'd be an idiot not to stick around. I'm sure we can adjust the membership rules to include ex-husbands."

Jensen blew out a breath. None of this was logical. Even if they got an agreement signed and Meredith decided she didn't mind putting up with a single parent who came with his metric ton of baggage, it was unlikely their lives would magically fit together. But he'd be a dick to turn down the offer. He liked Jace and Random.

"I can't do Wednesdays," he said finally.

CHAPTER

TWENTY-SEVEN

A black sedan idled outside the estate gates. Meredith brought the dirt bike to a stop and swung her leg over, Jensen a solid presence at her side, two-hundred pounds of claws and teeth and white fur.

Not that she should need him. She had precisely zero plans to step outside her wards, no matter how much the people waiting in the sedan were no doubt hoping she would. Julian had texted that Analisa was "sending someone" to pick up the necklace. He'd failed to specify who, but as soon as the car doors opened and its two occupants stepped out, she had a pretty good idea who—or what—they were.

Thralls.

A man and a woman in identical garb, loose black pants and black tunic-like shirts, walked toward her. At first glance, and if they weren't moving, they might seem perfectly normal. But one look in their eyes and she knew something was off. Their eyes were dead, like there wasn't a mind behind them. They turned to the gate and walked up to it in perfect unison, their movements at once both fluid and unnatural.

"You have something for me?" the woman asked. Something

about the way she said it hit wrong. The voice matched the body, but the tone and cadence didn't, as if someone else spoke through her mouth.

Meredith's Aspect was an itch beneath her skin in the same way it had been when she'd first seen Jensen hiding behind his glamour. What stood before her wasn't the truth. But it wasn't exactly a lie, either.

An image of the circlet from the repository slipped into her mind, and she was struck with the certainty that if she had it, she could identify the thing that wasn't quite right about the people. That whatever made them Analisa's thralls would be revealed to her.

Jensen nudged her. She shook the image away, pulled the necklace from her pocket and tossed it through the gate. The man caught it and held it up for inspection before nodding. "I look forward to meeting you in person."

Which would be a strange thing for someone she was literally standing in front of to say except that, like the other thrall, this one's voice matched him, but the rhythms of his speech were the same as the woman's had been. As if someone spoke through them like they were mere extensions of something else.

Meredith inclined her head. "I'm sure the pleasure will be all mine, Analisa."

The man's lips split in a wide grin. "Oh, indeed." He turned, the female thrall moving in sync as they climbed into the car and drove away.

"Well, this is going to be creepier than I thought."

Jensen yipped in agreement. Overhead a raven let out a sharp call before diving toward the house.

Hel was back.

❧

They planned for hours, dissecting Hel's information and going through every possible scenario. Sunset had come and gone, and Val was doing a final run-through.

"Meredith, we'll be monitoring your phone's GPS. Once we lose contact with it, we'll know you've entered the bounds of the disorientation spell. From that point, you'll have two hours to locate the Shifters before we arrive. Try not to move on it earlier than that unless you have to, otherwise we won't be there to help you.

"We'll begin moving into the zone at one-point-five hours after your entrance, estimating a half hour travel time for us to be in a usable position. We'll have four teams moving in, starting from a different compass position at the perimeter, each team with a Shifter to guide us past the disorientation spell's range of influence."

Hel's reconnaissance mission had proved the Shifters could pass through the disorientation spell in their animal forms without ill effect. She'd felt the brush of its magic, which had dissipated once the forest gave way to an interior clearing where a manor rested. It meant the spell was likely dome-shaped, allowing it to keep the entirety of the area hidden, but only had ground cover on the exterior, leaving the clearing free of its influence. Necessary, if Analisa intended to host Aspecters who would have clear enough minds to open their wallets at her auction.

"Each of the four teams is a beefed up standard, twenty total. Fourteen Battle Aspecters, four Elementals with combat training, and two specialty Aspecters varying by group. Once we hit the clearing, if we can take down the disorientation spell once we're already in position, it could be a significant drain on the power Analisa's using to fuel it, as well as misdirect her attention. We won't know how feasible that is until we're on the inside."

Hel had counted twenty-six thralls on the grounds. The looks she'd managed through the manor's windows had shown more inside, but trying to get an actual count would have made it all too obvious she wasn't an ordinary bird. She'd also noted two outbuildings on the property, livestock-style windowless barns she'd described as "really big" and "super long." What was inside them was anyone's guess.

"Our priorities are getting the captive Shifters to safety and securing Analisa. The auction attendees will no doubt make a break for it at the first sign of trouble. We apprehend if possible but not at the expense of our first two priorities. Any final questions or concerns? Is everyone clear on their part?" Valkyrie waited, making eye contact with everyone around the table. "Good. Then get some sleep and wake up tomorrow with your heads on straight."

Get some sleep. Sure, like that was going to be happening. The anxiety of tomorrow didn't lend itself well to an insomniac finding sleep.

Meredith left Jensen talking to Hel and Rebekah and went up to her room. It seemed unfair that if she had to infiltrate a home and rescue people within it, she was not a Hollywood super spy. She didn't have a skillset for every situation, she couldn't beat the crap out of anyone, and she didn't have a convenient blueprint of the home or an equally convenient person good at reading blueprints who could look at them and tell her the likeliest place to hold a bunch of strong Shifters.

She wasn't the best person for this job. She was just the one that could get into the auction. *That* does *make you the best person for the job, dumbass. You are good at handling people. No one else can play this part.*

Didn't mean she had to like that once she'd done the schmoozing and misdirection, it would all be on Jensen's shoulders to handle the brute force part of their plan. If anything happened to him... She shook her head. She had her Aspect—it might not be very useful in a fight, but she knew how to be inventive.

Even so, she found herself wandering into one of her large walk-in closets, opening the bottom drawer of her jewelry box. A custom-made lock pick set waited, dripping with diamonds and orange sapphires. If she wore her hair up, the picks could be incorporated into the style, the pick ends hidden in her hair, the half showing looking like nothing more than an expensive hair pin.

She hadn't worn them in over seven years. Not since she'd convinced her mother she was so ditzy there was no use in draining her Aspect dry and locking her away during important events. But as she picked the pins up, held them in her hands and felt the familiar weight and grip, they were a comfort. A reminder of her adaptability.

She placed them on top of the box and went to the side of her closet that held her evening gowns. Dress after dress slid through her fingers as she looked and discarded, hardly seeing them. The soft fabrics against her skin were another comfort. She might not have liked being her mother's little dress-up doll, but she did like nice clothes.

Something about the weight of a quality dress, the way the right cut and design could speak louder than words, was its own kind of armor, but it no longer felt like enough.

Warmth enclosed her and strong arms settled around her waist. Jensen nuzzled the side of her neck, breathing her in like she was something intoxicating instead of just a woman.

"It will be fine," he rumbled in her ear. "I'll be with you the whole time."

"That's not what I'm worried about." She ran her hands over his forearms, feeling the strength of the muscles beneath his skin.

"Then what are you worried about?" His breath grazed the shell of her ear before he nipped it lightly. A tremor ran through her, heightened when his hands slid up her waist, over her stomach. "And don't even try to say you're not."

"I'm afraid you won't come back."

"I will. And so will you, and so will everyone else. What else?"

But she couldn't voice the rest. *I'm afraid that if you do come back, you won't be coming back to me. I'm afraid I'll lose you either way.* He would lead his enclave someday. Would he really want *her* beside him for that?

She didn't want to ask or hear his answer, didn't want to know if the words he spoke would be true or not. He could promise her anything right now. He could even mean it. But meaning it now didn't mean he would mean it later, once the dust had settled.

She was so sick of the myriad ways words could be true and not true. True now, and not true later. How truth was as mutable as the world and, for all her Aspect, she didn't seem to have a firm grasp on either.

She didn't want his pretty words. The only truth she wanted right now was the graze of his lips, the slide of his tongue against hers. She wanted to feel him on top of her, inside her, to feel him be *hers* one last time.

She arched back and tilted her head up, teasing his lips with hers. His hands closed on her hips, pulling her hard against him as his mouth answered her demand, his tongue meeting hers stroke for stroke.

She ground back, rolling her hips, loving the groan she dragged out of his throat.

"You drive me crazy." His hands slid to the insides of her thighs and squeezed. Heat zinged through her, pooling low in her belly.

Yes. If she had to walk straight into Julian's arms tomorrow, she was doing it with Jensen's scent on her skin, the hot brand of his lips on hers, the feel of him inside her.

She lifted her shirt over her head, then unclasped her bra and tossed it aside. Jensen inhaled sharply, his hands closing over her breasts, kneading her flesh. She bit her lips against the pleasure that spilled through her. She'd never wanted anyone like she wanted him, had never felt as right, as easy, as safe, as she did when he touched her.

"You're so beautiful," he whispered. "So perfect." His right hand flicked open the button on her jeans, slid the zipper down and delved inside. "It's no wonder that in that basement, I almost thought I made you up."

His fingers glided through the wetness that soaked her, teasing her entrance before gliding back up to circle her clit. "Tell me you're not a dream, darlin'. Tell me you're real." He moved back down and thrust two fingers inside her.

She arched into his hand. "I'm real," she panted. She tilted her head back, biting his neck and sucking. "Show me you are. Fuck me, Jensen. I want to feel you. I want to still be feeling you tomorrow."

He grabbed the waistband of her jeans, yanked them and her underwear over her hips, down, crouching to pull them off over her high heels. Goosebumps broke out over her skin, something delicious about being naked when he'd yet to take off a stitch of clothing.

He grasped her ankles, running his hands lightly up over her calves, the backs of her thighs. "Jensen..." She didn't know exactly what she was begging for, just that she was.

He pressed a kiss to her low back. Then he dropped and slid beneath her, pulling her down to straddle his face. His hands on her ass held her down as his tongue delved into her, and she cried out. He licked and sucked, driving her higher and higher up that peak until he sent her hurtling off the other side.

He brought her down with gentle kisses, but she didn't want gentle. She sat back and rolled, pulling him on top of her, his hands landing to either side of her face. She fumbled at the clasp on his jeans until she had them open, shoving them down just enough to draw him free.

He groaned, pumping against her hand as he showered her face and neck in kisses. She didn't want to wait, couldn't wait. She guided him to her entrance, locked her legs around his thighs and pulled him into her.

"*Fuck.*" His voice was low and rough and perfect.

Meredith gasped at the sharp hurt of going too fast, of not

easing into it, but she didn't care. It passed soon enough, and when she relaxed, Jensen withdrew and slowly eased back in, filling her. His slow, deep thrusts were torture, the material of his jeans against her thighs a rough contrast to the smooth hardness of his body.

It was *so* good. She just needed more—everything. She arched up and took his lips, her tongue thrusting into his mouth before she turned aside to whisper in his ear. "Make me feel it, baby. Make me feel all of it."

He dropped to his forearms and gave her a quick, hard kiss. He withdrew and thrust back in, hard and deep.

She moaned. "Just like that." She hitched her legs higher around his waist, urging him on. "Harder." He pulled out and slammed home, her hips swiveling up to meet him. "Harder," she repeated, the word almost a mantra as he built a fast, furious rhythm, giving her what she demanded.

Pressure built inside her as they moved together, the slide of his t-shirt against her breasts bringing her nipples to rough peaks. His body tensed, his thrusts growing faster, erratic. He held himself up on one arm and moved his other hand between them. His thumb grazed her clit. Once, twice, and she exploded, convulsing around him as a guttural sound left his throat and he buried himself in her a final time.

He kissed her face, her neck, her collarbone as he came, and when he moved to roll off her she wrapped her arms around his back and held him, inside her, on top of her, loving the heavy weight of him.

I love you. The words pounded through her head in time with the rise and fall of her chest, fast and insistent and ridiculous. She couldn't love him. She didn't *want* to love him. Everything would hurt more, if she did.

But she couldn't shake the thought, the feeling, as they stumbled their way to bed and she fell asleep tucked against his side. And when they both woke in the middle of the night, thrashing from nightmares, those three words were the ones coursing through her veins as they kissed each others' fears away.

I love you, I love you, I love you. Three words she wouldn't say, so she tried to make him feel them instead. In the brush of her lips against his, in the touch of her hands, in the way their bodies moved together. Because that was all she knew how to give him.

TWENTY-EIGHT

Waiting was hell. Meredith had spent the entire day waiting. Waiting to finalize plans, waiting to see if anything went wrong at the last minute, waiting for the evening to come. About the only part she hadn't spent waiting was the two hours Val had dragged her outside for self-defense basics, during which Meredith learned she was naturally adept at only one self-defense move: driving the heel of her palm into someone's nose with great enthusiasm.

Now she sat in her car at Winter Forest Park, Jensen a white wolf in the seat beside her, and waited for Julian to arrive, contemplating how useless a well-placed heel-to-nose strike was likely to be if she found herself in actual trouble.

She shifted in her seat, convinced that something had gone wrong and Julian wouldn't show, when an SUV pulled into the lot and parked one space down from her car. The back passenger-side door opened and Julian stepped out, wearing a black suit with a light blue dress shirt. Thank the goddess she'd gone with the silver dress. The possibility they might match had been upsetting on an oddly visceral level.

She got out, a quick glance through the SUV's front windows showing the same two thralls who'd come to the house yesterday to collect the necklace. She held her door open and Jensen leaped across the console to land on the worn asphalt. Julian's gaze dipped to the wolf, snagging on the black and silver fabric tied around Jensen's throat.

"What is that?"

Meredith beamed at him. "A bowtie. You did say evening wear. I thought it would be a shame if he didn't match the dress code."

The bowtie had actually been Jensen's idea because, as he'd put it, "What says 'whipped' more than a Shifter in a tie?"

Julian's lips curled in distaste. "Your mutt goes in the back."

She walked to the back with Jensen and kept a smile on her face by promising herself that this was the last time she would ever fake what she felt or who she was. One way or another, for better or worse, she was done after tonight.

The SUV was a compact model, with one row of back passenger seats and a small cargo area behind that. She opened the back hatch and Jensen jumped inside. He barely fit. The space wasn't wide enough in the back for him to lie down, and not tall enough for him to fully sit up. He had to half crouch, the tips of his ears folding over where they squished against the roof.

She had a million reasons to want to break Julian Astor's nose. But somehow Jensen's discomfort was the one currently coaxing her blood to an angry simmer. She closed him in carefully and took her place in the backseat. When Julian slid in next to her and his hand settled proprietarily on her thigh, that simmer turned into a boiling rage.

His words from the cafe came back to her. *You're mine.*

She wasn't his. She would *never* be his.

No one else touches what's mine.

Oh, but Jensen had. He'd touched every inch of her last night, kissed every inch of her. The memory of it let her smile when instinct told her to cringe, let her relax beneath Julian's hand. He might make her uncomfortable, but he wouldn't do anything to her here. Not in a car. Not with witnesses, even if those witnesses were a Shifter and two thralls.

Julian liked control too much. He would want her in a room, in a bed, away from anyone who might be persuaded to help her.

She looked out the window, watching the street signs pass by until they came to the edge of the disorientation spell, its magic licking over her. The car drove on, and the spell took her fully in its grasp.

MEREDITH STARTLED when something licked her hand. Jensen, trying to comfort her. Something was wrong. She sat in the backseat of a car, driving through dense forest, the road unfamiliar. She had no idea where she was.

Even as she realized it, the thought tried to slip away from her, the soft magic that blanketed the forest like a mist shushing the thoughts in her mind. She relaxed and leaned her head back against the seat. Her eyes fluttered shut.

There was no need to worry about where she was.

Where she was. Where *was* she?

Her eyes slammed wide open, panic arcing through her even as the soporific effect of the magic saturating the forest tried to lull her back into complacency. Disorientation had her full in its grasp, and she struggled to summon her Aspect through the sleepy fog in her brain.

"There's no point in fighting it," Julian said in a bored tone. "You won't remember anything." He didn't sound sleepy or confused, and she realized the magic affecting her was not affecting him.

She focused on her Aspect, on the need to...do something with it. What did she need to do?

Julian gave a soft laugh as the magic all around fought to lull her back to sleep. Jensen growled in response and licked at her neck, her face.

"Keep that thing in the back or I'll do it for you." The bite in Julian's voice brought her fully awake. She turned her head, registering his disgust. She'd seen an expression just like it on his face at one of her mother's parties years ago, when another guest had bumped into a waitress, causing her to bobble her tray and spill champagne on Julian's shoes.

He'd told the terrified waitress she needed to learn poise, and he'd immobilized her in a ramrod stiff posture, the tray held aloft above her shoulders. The thing about Julian's Aspect? It forced your body into the position he desired—it didn't hold it for you. Your body, your muscles, did the work, and would continue to do so long past the point where you could have forced yourself to maintain the position on your own.

The tray the waitress had been holding, laden with drinks, had probably weighed between seven and ten pounds. Though it might not sound like a lot, she'd held it up for the remaining six hours of the party. Julian hadn't even remembered to release her at the end. She'd been released when he'd left and she was no longer in the range of his magic. Then she'd collapsed. The tray had fallen first and she'd landed on broken glass and spilled champagne.

Meredith's mother had fired her and told the rest of the staff to get her out of her house. Meredith had caught her on the way out, given her all the cash she'd had in the house and told her she was sorry. The woman had told her to piss off, but she was smart—she'd taken the money.

Just like Meredith was smart enough to know she didn't want Julian handling Jensen's unwanted presence right now. She rubbed behind his ears and said, "I'm fine, Monster." Better to get used to calling him by that name again than risk anyone knowing she viewed him as a real person.

Jensen retreated. The SUV broke through the forest into a man-made clearing. Magic dropped its weight from her and she could breathe again, remember again. Remember that this had all been expected, that nothing was wrong.

Softly flickering lanterns lined the drive to either side, seeming to float in the darkness. She squinted out the passenger side window, trying to see what held the lanterns aloft and nearly jumped out of her skin. A pair of vacant, hollow eyes stared back at her.

Thralls. The lanterns were held by thralls, evenly spaced apart and standing perfectly still, their arms holding the lanterns out before them with the same kind of unnatural stillness and lack of trembling the frozen waitress had shown all those years ago.

For one horrible moment, Meredith considered the possibility that there was no Analisa. That all of this was Julian. He hadn't been affected by the disorientation spell, and the lantern holders were as rigid and unmoving as a person caught in his Aspect.

But Julian's power didn't leave this deadness in a person's eyes. For all the waitress's stillness at that party, she had looked every bit as terrified as she'd been. And though Julian could make a person move, someone under his control reacted jerkily, like a doll being forced into various positions. Julian also couldn't make people speak—certainly not like the thralls at her home had spoken to her.

Which made her wonder. "The thralls. Can you immobilize them?"

"Yes."

Thank the goddess. At least Aspect worked on them.

Julian smoothed a nonexistent wrinkle from his pants. "Though it is irrelevant."

"Why?"

"Because they are legion."

A shiver of apprehension crawled down her spine. They *must* be legion, to waste them so frivolously lining a driveway as human lampposts. How did Analisa hold so many? Was she what Jace had theorized—a Life Aspecter corrupted into something different?

How many thralls had they passed on the long drive? Forty? Fifty? Certainly far more than had been present outside when Hel had done her scouting flight. Meredith's stomach knotted. People could die tonight. Her friends could die tonight.

The car rounded a bend and a manor home came into view, lit brightly enough to be seen even from afar at this time of night. It looked like something worthy of the best of gothic horror novels, the dark stone and sharp architectural angles adding to the surreal, phantasmagoric ambience.

The SUV stopped at the walk that led up to the entryway. Three new thralls approached the vehicle. Watching them, Meredith finally realized what they reminded her of, why they seemed so alien to her. They had more in common with drones that answered to a hive queen than with people who kept their own thoughts.

Meredith had every intention of exiting the vehicle before a thrall could prompt her out of it. She opened the door, but Julian stopped her from getting out with a painful squeeze on her thigh.

"Aren't you forgetting something?"

If he thought he was getting the repository location before she had whatever meager protection the presence of other people could provide, he was very wrong. "I'll give the location to Analisa. I'm eager to meet her."

"And I am eager to meet you," the thrall at her door said. "Do come inside."

She didn't want to take the hand the thrall offered her, but her mother's voice in her head kept her from hesitating.

If you show fear, or disgust, or horror, it should be calculated. If you do not desire the reaction an emotion will cause, do not show that emotion. People will treat you in the manner you present yourself.

She stopped wondering precisely what caused the deadness in the thralls' eyes. She stopped thinking of them as people at all, because that was the only way to treat them as if they didn't matter. She fixed an aloof expression on her face and took the thrall's hand. It wasn't cold, precisely, but it wasn't the warmth of a typical person's skin, either.

She dropped the hand as soon as possible, and when Jensen's growl alerted her to the fact that the thrall who had opened his door was now trying to grab him, she stepped protectively in front of Jensen and met the person's hollow eyes.

"My apologies," she said lightly, "but I'm afraid he doesn't do well being handled by anyone but me." *This is* my *one-woman werewolf, bitch.*

The thrall nodded and stepped back. The SUV that had brought them drove away, and Meredith swallowed her panic at the effective removal of any speedy means of retreat. If something kept Siren and the others from coming for them…but then a car wouldn't be much use in that situation. She would just get lost in the woods while she drove.

She rested her hand on Jensen's shoulder as they followed the thrall to the front door. The gesture looked casually possessive and was one-hundred percent for her own emotional support. A good thing, since she otherwise would have stumbled at the sudden absence of her Aspect as they crossed the manor's threshold.

Oh, her power hadn't *gone* anywhere. But she couldn't feel it, couldn't reach for it, couldn't use it.

A nullifying spell. She looked down at her wrists, as if Julian could have cuffed her with a set of nullifiers when she wasn't looking. But her wrists were bare, and flicking back the door rug revealed no hidden spell beneath.

"The house," Julian drawled, amused. "The house is the nullifying spell."

She blinked. Nullifying spells were one of the few Aspect spells that had to be physically drawn in runes and lines, the way movies about witches often had people drawing arcane circles on the ground in chalk.

Because a nullifying spell was meant to negate Aspect, it couldn't be made wholly of it, but had to be drawn in something non-magical and then sparked with Aspect to activate. Several structural variations of the spell existed, so the fact that a house could be made into one was not unbelievable.

The hard part to swallow was that a nullifying spell had to be created with the same amount or more of Aspect as it was meant to contain. Should the Aspect of the person—or persons—held by the spell exceed the Aspect used to create it, those within could access their power and bring down the spell.

She'd never seen one hold more than three Aspecters at once.

"How?" No single person save Siren had enough power to fuel a nullifying spell this large.

Julian shrugged. "Many of her thralls were Aspecters once. Enough to fuel the spell on auction night and keep the attendees from getting overly exuberant."

A brilliant move on Analisa's part, since the nullifying spell didn't affect her, as the thralls were as blank-eyed as ever within the walls. The spell was designed specifically for Aspect, so either Analisa had never been Aspect, or her power was twisted enough that the nullifying spell no longer worked on her.

Their guiding thrall led them up a stairwell, then around several turns until they arrived on a level that overlooked a ballroom. Below, people dressed in tuxes and elaborate evening gowns sipped champagne and strolled between tables that contained artful displays not unlike the ones in her mother's repository.

She scanned the room, half-expecting to see a metal cage with a Shifter inside, on display. She didn't.

"You don't think it's a risk?" she asked casually. "Letting them wander your priceless auction goods?"

"A thing is only a risk if you do not have full control over the outcome," a female voice said. A woman approached, her carriage regal, two thralls to either side of her. Thick black hair cascaded over her shoulders in lush waves, the dark color in soft contrast to her pale skin. Her dress was the exact shade of her hair, a simple silk design that clung to her frame.

"And you have full control?"

"Of course. I have my lovelies, after all." The thrall to either side leaned into her, as if drawn by her mention of them. "And those *are* the items of lesser importance."

Her age was impossible to guess. She could have been twenty or sixty. Every time Meredith blinked she looked slightly different, younger or older, though her physical appearance wasn't actually changing.

Instinctively, Meredith reached for her Aspect, only to remember it was beyond her.

"Are all of the…lovelies yours?"

The woman smiled, revealing unnaturally white teeth. "Everything here is mine."

"You're Analisa?"

"It is the name I use, these days. Now, I believe you have something that belongs to me."

Meredith told her the repository location. Analisa's eyes misted white for a moment before clearing, and Meredith would bet every one of her cars that somewhere in the manor, thralls were now rushing to get to Savannah Townsend's mausoleum. Meredith itched to know how Analisa's connection to the thralls worked. Was there any independence left in the minds of the people? Did they fight against Ana's control, or had she obliterated any individuality, until all that was left was an empty husk?

"A delight to have that matter resolved. But when I said you had something of mine, I meant him." Analisa pointed at Jensen.

Meredith's heart kicked behind her chest. "I was under the impression you had your own Shifters for the auction. This one is mine."

"I have several, but they have all been so disappointing. They refused to change shape after the first weeks in captivity, remaining in their animal skins. Pain is supposed to trigger the change in them, but they grew resistant to that method, and their savagery in response grew tiresome.

"I lost over four dozen of my lovelies in attempts to train them. I haven't lost *that* many in the last hundred years. It tempted me to put the beasts down—they won't turn much profit in their wild state, but I thought something was better than nothing at this point. And then I saw that one." She pointed at Jensen "Elijah was training it for me. He clearly did an excellent job. It's so *docile*."

Meredith didn't need her Aspect to peg that lie. "Elijah wasn't training him for you. He was taking him apart to see how he worked. I put in the effort. I brought him to heel."

Analisa laughed. "You Truthfinders are all the same. So unwilling to let a lie stand even when you would be better off shutting your mouth. The only truth that matters is the truth you make. The truth you can take. And here, now, I say that *that* was meant for me. That is a truth I can make and take."

Meredith's fingers curled into Jensen's fur. The nearby thralls all focused their attention on her as if they—as if Analisa—were preparing for an attack. If she showed herself to be weak and submissive, Analisa would take Jensen from her. He was large. He was strong. Maybe he could fight through the thralls on this level. But the rest of them in the house? On the grounds?

No. She couldn't afford to get into a pissing contest with Analisa. She would lose.

Meredith ran through everything she'd gleaned from the whole five minutes since she'd met her. Analisa had convinced no small number of Aspect heavyweights to voluntarily enter a building where their power meant nothing and her power meant everything. She had enough thralls to form a personal army.

She was rich and powerful and beautiful. By her own admission she had lived for at least a century. In short, she was the god Julian had labeled her.

Gods, if mythology could be trusted, were often bored. They had lived it all, seen it all, and they desperately wanted someone to surprise or entertain them, frequently to their detriment. Here was to hoping Analisa ranked among them.

Meredith tilted her head back and laughed. Analisa blinked.

"Here is a truth I can make for you," Meredith said. "You can take my little Monster from me. You obviously have the manpower to do so. But I regret to tell you his…docility isn't training. I rescued him, and now he's mine."

"Is that so?"

"Monster—" she leaned toward Jensen, as if the two were in on an elaborate secret "—do you like the pretty lady?"

Jensen bared his teeth and snarled.

"Do you like me?"

Jensen quit snarling and bumped his face against her stomach. Meredith rubbed behind his ears, her gaze fixed on Analisa. "As I've said, I have no doubt you can take him. But you will lose quite a few more of your 'lovelies,' and I suspect he'll make you kill him before he lets you have him." Meredith shrugged, as if it didn't much matter. "But you can try."

Analisa's eyes narrowed. "What makes you think I can't simply *make* him one of my lovelies?"

Meredith's chest tightened. The thought of Jensen, vacant and hollow-eyed like the thralls, made her want to vomit. Her brain caught up to her gut reaction, and her smile never wavered. "If you could do that, you would have already enthralled every Shifter in your possession. And I truly doubt you would be selling them at this auction."

Tense silence stretched between them. Julian was looking at Meredith like he'd never seen her before. *That's right, Julian. You aren't the important one here.*

"Or," Meredith said, when the tension had grown so taut it was in danger of snapping, "you can accept that Monster is mine, and we can come to an arrangement."

"An arrangement?" She sounded amused. "As in, I get him on the weekends?"

"As in, point us toward what you want and we'll get it for you. Monster stays with me and, in return, if you call, we jump."

"An interesting proposal." Analisa's eyes roved over the two of them. She wanted Jensen, that much was obvious, and he'd hardly snarled enough to be truly terrifying earlier, but— "What do you get out of it?"

"Respect. You have it. I want it. I'm tired of being tolerated like I'm a silly little girl."

Analisa narrowed her eyes. "I'll consider it. Go circulate among the guests and show them how desirable a tame Shifter can be. I don't want to see a single specimen go for less than a million. I'd like to make my money back on them."

It was too easy a capitulation. Meredith didn't hold out a single iota of hope that Analisa had even the smallest trust in her. But for now, Ana was letting her play the game.

CHAPTER

TWENTY-NINE

If Meredith had thought she hated playing the pretty, vapid socialite at her mother's parties, it was nothing compared to how she felt circulating a room showing Jensen off like he was a well-trained German Shepherd. Everyone wanted to touch him or pet him or look at his teeth. They wanted him to roll over or shake hands, derisive laughter in their eyes at seeing the two-hundred pound wolf act like a puppy.

"He's so *pretty*," squealed a brunette with big doe eyes and the alluring blush of youth. She turned said doe eyes on the man she was hanging off of. "Baby, I want one. Can I have one?"

The girl was nineteen if she was a day, too young and too pretty to be on the arm of a man more than twice her age. Aldrich Weston was an Elemental Aspecter Meredith knew by reputation if not by personal association. He specialized in earth ores, and his mining operations were worth billions.

Billions easily bought too young and too pretty, and Meredith thought the girl ought to be careful. Aldrich had the irritated expression on his face that indicated he might have forgotten how tiresome the exuberance of youth could be, and was considering upgrading to a mid-twenties model.

"We do have one wolf shifter in the auction," Julian said silk-ily, "though its coat is black, not white."

The girl—what had her name been? Trixie? Trudy? *Trina*—widened her eyes like a five-year-old in a candy store. "They come in black?"

They're people, you vapid little brat, not sports cars.

"Can I have the black one, baby?" *Baby* was Trina's favorite word. It made an appearance in every sentence she spoke, some-times twice.

Aldrich looked like he was calculating which would be less detrimental to his hearing: Trina's whining over wanting a Shifter, or her excitement at getting one.

"Perhaps. Why don't you be a good little girl and fetch me a scotch?"

A good little girl? Ugh.

"Okay." Trina bounded away. Considering the number of thralls in this room whose sole purpose was to provide guests with any and every drink they could possibly want, Trina's retrieval of one wasn't even a badly disguised attempt to get rid of her for a minute. Not that she seemed to have picked up on the fact.

"You disapprove," Aldrich said.

Meredith snapped her eyes from Trina back to Aldrich. "Your personal taste is just that—personal."

"You know, your mother offered *you* to me once."

Meredith's brain screeched to a halt. Her mother had *what*?

Aldrich smiled. "You were seventeen or eighteen at the time, I think? I'd expressed an interest before then, but—" he shrugged "—she had better uses for you then. The later offer was a clear attempt to salvage the situation with the Winters, and I dislike other men's castoffs."

Fury coiled in her gut. So when she'd broken things off with Jace, dear old mum had tried to sell her off to a man twice her age. She shouldn't be surprised. But it irked her that Savannah Townsend could still cut her from beyond the grave.

Outwardly, she telegraphed bored indifference. "Devastated though I am by your lack of interest, I'll manage to go on somehow." She looked over his shoulder to where Trina was coming back, drink in hand. "Your date's returning. Be a good sugar daddy and buy her a puppy tonight, won't you?"

Meredith turned on her heel and walked away. She circulated the room for another ten minutes, keeping her smile on her face by sheer force of will. The energy radiating off Jensen told her he worked just as hard to control himself.

When a woman whose name she'd already forgotten pinned Julian down with questions about one of the displayed items, Meredith broke for the exit. Three steps outside the room two thralls moved in, blocking her path. She stepped sideways. They moved with her.

Meredith threw her shoulders back. "Ana?"

"A moment of your time, Ms. Townsend." The thrall turned and Meredith followed them down the hall to a sitting room. Analisa stood by the room's far window, the curtain held back with her index finger. She let the fabric fall and faced Meredith. "I must admit, you work a room well. Truthfully, I didn't expect much out of you. From the way your mother used to talk about you, I thought you'd be an empty-headed thing with too much Aspect and no idea how to use it."

"Then why did you bring me here?"

"For the wolf, and for Julian. As tedious as Julian can be, he walks where I cannot anymore." Her gaze dropped to Jensen. "And he does have a knack for finding me the most interesting things. Do you know how long I've been searching for a Shifter?"

Not long enough. "No."

"One-hundred and twenty-three years." Analisa waited for the number to sink in. "You don't seem surprised. Or skeptical."

Meredith shrugged. "Julian spoke of your thralls a couple days ago. I went looking and found a mention of the term in some old book. I'm not sure I believe you used to be Life, though. You're nothing like Siren."

Darkness flashed in Analisa's eyes. "That is because your pet Life Aspecter has had a charmed existence so far."

Charmed? Parents murdered at birth, Aspect experimented on, nearly killed in an attempt to make her into the magical equivalent of an atom bomb, but yes. Charmed.

"This century has its flaws, but at least on paper there are rules. We didn't have many of those when I was born. Such a *rare* gift, Life. So special." She sneered. "So special I never had one of my own. By the time I was eight my father was selling me to heal every cut, cold, and disease in the village, all for a pittance so he could drink himself into the ditch.

"But of course, such things draw attention. One day a man came to the village. He offered to buy me. My father refused. The man killed him and I became the property of a wealthy merchant who liked to whore himself into every disease under the sun.

"He was smarter than my father and tried to keep me a secret. But healing is a compulsion for those born to Life. I couldn't *not* do it, and one man can only require so much work. And why was it fair that he became whole over and over again, when the women he used and discarded were left to be ravaged by the bodies men used them for? So I started healing them.

"A bit of advice? Never show kindness to a whore. They'll turn around and sell you to the highest bidder with no remorse. I ended up a prince's property. He used my abilities to curry political favor. I was fifteen when he decided I was pretty enough to fuck.

"I was nineteen when I realized it was never going to end. I would never have anything more, never *be* anything more. All I did was give and give, pouring my power into rotting old men and letting them pour themselves into me whenever *he* decided it would be useful.

"And then one day I was cleaning up the excesses of his alcoholism, feeling the faint flutter of his heartbeat in his chest, and I realized I could simply take it. I drank his life down like water and when he rested on that pivotal threshold between life and death, I held him, and he obeyed."

Triumph flashed in her eyes at the memory. "He was my very first lovely. Thralls, as I later learned the term. I did a great deal with him until some enterprising chit snuck into his bedchamber and realized he had no heartbeat.

"I've been called many things since that day. Vampire. Necromancer. I've been chased out of town by mobs with pitchforks and torches. Almost died several times. I can't turn someone into a thrall at the drop of a hat. It does require a certain connection." She lifted her hand to the cheek of the thrall next to her and he leaned into the touch.

Meredith's stomach turned and she tightened her fingers in Jensen's fur.

"I was somewhat of a magical urban legend by the time I made my way to this continent. I came here around the same time as the Shifter enclaves made a mass exodus from the European shores, hoping for acceptance here, or at least anonymity." Her fingernails dug into the thrall's skin, blood trickling down his cheek. "I had no quarrel with them. I never caused them any harm. I thought we were alike in so many ways. Thought as of less than human, as things that shouldn't exist.

"I thought we could be allies. But apparently *I* was too much of an abomination for *them*. People always feel better about their own inferiority as long as there's someone on the rung beneath them." Her hand fell away from the thrall. "Would you like to see what they did to me?"

No. No, Meredith wouldn't. But her throat stayed closed, and Analisa's features shifted. Lines—claw marks—opened up on her skin, blood pouring from the wounds.

It wasn't illusion. It was whatever was left of her Aspect, and she was using it to recreate a moment when she'd almost died.

The thrall she'd been touching dropped and Meredith stared, horrified, at the ruin of a woman before her.

"Pretty, aren't I?" The words came out slurred through the chunk of her bottom lip that was missing. As quickly as they'd come on, the wounds closed over, turning to scars that faded and left unblemished skin in their wake. The bits of her that were missing regrew. The second thrall in the room dropped.

Meredith forced herself to think through the horror. Analisa could still heal herself, but it cost her in thralls to do it.

Analisa bent down, her eyes level with Jensen. "And that's why I hate your kind. That's why I don't care if Elijah pulled you apart over and over, or how much your sister screamed when I ripped her claws out."

Fear gripped Meredith—not for herself, but for Jensen. But though he tensed beneath her hand, he remained rigidly still.

Analisa laughed. "I suppose he must have something of a man left inside him. Because only a man can be broken so completely to a woman." She straightened, smiling at Meredith. "It's a rush, isn't it? Your first conquest? That first time having another life wrapped so completely in your own power.

"I thought that's what I wanted from the Shifters. If I couldn't enthrall them, I wanted to break them. But breaking takes a patience and finesse I don't have where they're concerned. I thought of wiping them out, next, but eradication goes so quickly.

"But selling them?" Her smile widened. "Letting those of them that remain free wonder when the thief in the night will come for them? Letting that misery trickle down the bloodlines? That is a vengeance worth enacting."

"Why are you telling me all of this?"

Analisa fished in the first dead thrall's pockets for a handkerchief and proceeded to wipe at the blood on her face. "Because I like you. But I've learned that little good comes from liking people. A business arrangement is always more suitable, so long as one honors it. And I'm afraid I have a business arrangement with Julian."

The door behind Meredith opened and six thralls stepped into the room. Meredith's blood turned to ice. "I see," she said softly. "And what price did I go for?"

"Oh, all of this has been about you, right from the beginning. The man truly is obsessed. I dislike obsessions, so I gave him an impossible task. Find the Shifters, find your mother's missing repository, and I would help deliver you to him. But then he went and succeeded, and I owed him. Although, you do have yourself to blame a little. I don't think he would ever have found your mother's repository without you."

Analisa stepped closer. "I always honor my debts. The wolf goes to the holding cages. You go to a room upstairs. Julian will come for you soon. He won't be able to wait. But my obligation to him ends there.

"Were he to meet a tragic end? Well, I would need a replacement for him. Another individual adept at moving through the higher rungs of Aspect Society."

Right. "Let me make sure I have this straight. If my wolf walks pliantly into a cage, and if I manage to kill Julian instead of enduring the no doubt many unpleasant things he wants to do to me, then I get his job and my dog back?"

"That is the gist of it, yes."

Meredith's gaze darted to the thralls. Jensen could take them. But not the dozens that would pour in after him.

Meredith arched an eyebrow at Analisa. "If you've no objection to Julian's death, I don't suppose you feel like providing me with a weapon?"

"We *are* weapons. If you haven't figured that out by now, perhaps you *won't* be as useful to me as Julian. So if you don't want to live the rest of your life as his plaything, I suggest you figure it out."

For a moment, Meredith couldn't move, frozen on the edge of fight or flight. No small part of her thought it might be better to die here. To pick a battle here that she couldn't win, but which would at least be of her own choosing.

Jensen would fight for her. She had no doubt of that. Even knowing they would lose, knowing he would never reach his sister, she knew he would fight for her. So she wouldn't do anything less for him.

She knelt and took his face in her hands. "Be a good boy and do what you're told." He growled and shook his head. "I'll miss you too," she said, willing him not to make an issue of it. He had to know if they made a move right now they were dead. "Everything will be fine, and I'll see you soon enough." She rose and locked Analisa's gaze. "Touch him, and when I'm through taking out your trash I will make you regret it. It might take me a year, or ten, or twenty, but I will see it done."

She was at the door when Analisa laughed. "You're in love with it, aren't you? Does it feel the same way about you? Is that the secret to truly breaking something? Love?"

"I guess you'll never know." Meredith walked out and she didn't look back. She refused to think as the thralls led her to the staircase, herding her up to the second floor while they led Jensen down a hallway on the first. He stopped and swiveled his head back, his eyes boring into hers.

"Go on," she said softly, knowing he would hear. "I'll be fine."

The thrall to her left stopped, opening a door and gesturing her in. She gave running another brief thought, but she had nowhere to run to. She would be dragged back to this room and Jensen would still be in a cage somewhere in this house.

There was one solution, one way out: she had to kill Julian.

CHAPTER

THIRTY

Killing a man without use of her Aspect was nowhere in Meredith's repertoire of life skills.

She tossed her clutch on the bed and set about searching the room for murder weapons anyway, because doing something kept the panic clawing at her throat at bay.

The room contained a four poster bed, an empty dresser, and an empty nightstand. Not even a lamp to use as a bludgeoning object. Val had tried to convince her to wear a knife in a thigh-sheath under her dress, but none of Valkyrie's weaponry was actually designed to hide beneath an evening gown.

She'd strapped it on just long enough to show Valkyrie that, no, it wouldn't work—to not be seen it had to be strapped to the inside of her thigh, where it knocked against the opposite thigh each time she walked, and the hilt poked her in the crotch when she sat down.

Besides which, all she knew about proper knife work was that the pointy end went into the other person. Was she capable of doing that? In the heat of the moment, if it was kill or be killed? Yes. She didn't think she would hesitate. But offensively? She wasn't sure. Her Aspect was a better bet for defense, and none of them could have seen a mass nullifying spell coming.

Would it have killed Analisa to give her *some* kind of weapon out of a sense of feminine solidarity?

We are the weapon.

Meredith snorted. *Aspect* was a weapon. One she didn't have access to.

A thorough examination of the bathroom proved it didn't have any loose bludgeoning objects either. She checked the room over again, but even the curtain rod for the draperies was bolted to the supporting hooks.

She twitched the material back, wondering if she could do something with the cloth, and realized the curtains had hidden the entrance to a balcony. She threw the doors open and stepped out. The balcony railing was low, barely to her waist. Easy enough to climb over, but if she did there was nothing on the walls to hold onto.

Even if there had been, she wasn't delusional enough to think she could scale a wall in heels and an evening dress when she had precisely zero experience climbing. She would fall, and the best case scenario left her with some broken bits that prevented her from getting to Jensen.

Her chest tightened and her heart rate picked up, sweat slicking down her palms. Goddess, she was useless.

"*Such a waste.*" Her mother's voice, the one she'd gotten good at blocking out, reared its head in her mind, dragging her back in time. "*All my raw power but you came out a Truthfinder like your father. And you ruined my womb on the way out so I couldn't even make a more useful alternative.*"

The sharp pain of her mother's Aspect gripped Meredith, spreading through her like rotating blades had sprouted in her veins, intent on carving their way out. "*All you have is a pretty face and nice tits. And you're too dumb to use them well.*"

Another spasm as the invisible blades churned through her. It's not real, it's not real, it's not real. *The mantra that let her survive. Except the pain was real, even if the blades and the physical damage weren't.*

"What am I supposed to do with you? What good are you to me now?"

"I'm s-sorry."

"You're **sorry?**" Her mother sneered. "Three years of work on that boy and not only did you fail to convince him to crawl back to his father, you bungled it so badly he dropped you."

One of the blades inside her grew and slowed, slicing through her midsection. She panted, trying to breathe through the pain. Then she wondered why she was trying. All she had to do was tell her mother the truth—that she'd left Jace. That she'd ruined it on purpose, been so cruel and hurt him so thoroughly he would never take her back. So that what she experienced now, the pain driving her to the brink of insanity, would never be his experience.

If she revealed that, her mother might finally spin one of those invisible blades into Meredith's heart. What was that old quote? Something about the truth setting you free? Death was a kind of freedom, she supposed.

"You don't even understand how good you had it. The Winters boy was so nice. So polite. So **caring.**" She listed the traits like they were personal defects. "I bet he was the same way when he took you to bed. Most men aren't like that, you know? And since men are all you're good for, I hope you remember this little lesson, and how it all could have been different if you hadn't been so useless."

The pain ebbed to a low, dull throbbing. A person could only handle so much pain before the mind blacked out, and Savannah Townsend was a master of making a person ride that edge. Of taking them to the limits of what they could endure and then granting them enough relief to keep them conscious.

"I'm not," Meredith panted, "U-useless."

The blade in her stomach whirred to life, spinning from her stomach straight into her throat. Meredith choked and coughed, her throat closing over the spiked edges.

"I could give you to Julian," her mother mused, as if Meredith hadn't spoken. As if her daughter wasn't coughing out blood on the floor because sometimes when the pain was real enough, Meredith's *body overloaded.* "He's *wanted you for years. It's a weakness, this obsession of his, and I don't like to indulge weaknesses. But I do believe in punishment, and I don't think you would enjoy his hands on you.*"

A click jolted Meredith back to the present—the room's doorknob turned. She wiped her palms on her dress, feeling now like she had then: helpless. She heard the door close.

Think. The morning after Meredith's mother had threatened to "give her" to Julian, she'd re-tested for her Truthfinder affinity, careful to score just well enough to be at the very bottom range of high aptitude. An hour later she had signed an agreement to contract as a Truthfinder for the Council, giving Savannah a foothold back into two things she was interested in: the Council, and Elijah Winters who was on the Council.

Meredith had thought her way out of the situation then. She could do the same thing now.

Think, damn it. Back then, Meredith had given her mother something she wanted. Meredith couldn't—wouldn't—give Julian what he wanted. She couldn't run away because she would fall off this balcony to her probable death and—

Oh. She didn't have to be the one falling off the balcony. So long as she distracted Julian—by giving the appearance that she was going to give him what he wanted—she might even manage it.

Meredith leaned against the balcony and rested her hands on the railing, shoulders back and relaxed. A soft breeze blew, ruffling her hair, and she knew the picture she painted, the picture Julian would see.

His footsteps approached. "What are you doing out here?"

She looked over her shoulder and smiled. "Waiting for you."

"Were you?" His fingers closed on her chin in a bruising grip and he turned her to face him. "I find that difficult to believe."

"Why? Because I took control when we spoke to Analisa?"

A muscle beneath his eye twitched. He hadn't appreciated the idea that she was capable of controlling anything. But if she let him turn this into a contest of physical dominance, she would lose. He wanted her under his control, and she needed to give him that fantasy.

"I thought she needed to see that we could both be useful to her." She smiled at him and stepped in closer. "Was I wrong?"

He let go of her chin and trailed his fingers down her neck to the hollow between her breasts. "In the future, you will discuss what you say to our associates with me first."

Oh, of course.

"You need to learn your place."

"And where is my place? Is it—" She dropped to her knees and looked up at him through her lashes "—on my knees?"

Lowering herself into this position came with the risk that it would put Julian on his guard. That he would realize what she planned. Because after reliving the memory of her mother's threat, she'd remembered she did, in fact, know one other self-defense move. One she'd looked up before discovering another way out of that situation. One that didn't require practice, because even if it did, no one was going to let you practice it on them.

Please let this work. He might be suspicious of her, but it was more likely he would expect her to humiliate him than to do what she was going to do. After all, her weapons of choice had always been words and emotional manipulation prior to this moment.

You said I belonged to you. Get on with the using what's yours part so I can block this from my memory for all eternity.

He let her kneel there, the beading on her dress digging into her knees, for a full minute before he reached for the buckle on his pants.

Nerves threatened to make her hands tremble but she broke everything down into steps in her mind, focusing on her objective to the extent that it drowned out what was actually happening. What she was actually doing.

Be quick. Don't overthink it. Don't lose your damn nerve.

He unzipped his pants. She slipped her hand inside...and

closed it in a fist around his balls. She twisted viciously and pulled. Julian screamed, hunching over. She shot up, driving the heel of her palm into his nose, just like she'd practice with Valkyrie.

Bone crunched. Julian staggered and his back hit the railing. She lunged, putting the full force of her momentum into her drive, and struck him in the chest. He toppled over the railing. As he fell his hand lashed out, grabbed her right arm and dragged her over the side with him.

She scrabbled, caught the top of the railing with her left hand, the muscles in her shoulder wrenching as Julian's weight pulled on her. Her fingers slipped. But so did his. She kicked out, the sharp stiletto of her heel catching him in the throat, and his weakening grip gave.

She wrenched her right arm up, grabbing on to a vertical balcony bar just as she lost her original hold. She latched back on with her left hand and hung there, shuddering as the breeze caught the heavy skirt of her gown and swayed her slightly back and forth.

She squeezed her eyes shut. She hated heights. Sweat slicked her palms, making her already precarious grip more so. She forced her eyes open and looked up. Her hands were locked on to the iron bars at the very bottom of the three-foot-high railing. A horizontal bar crossed the vertical ones about a foot up from the bottom. She just had to pull herself up enough to reach it.

Her heart pounded in her chest. What if she missed the bar? What if she fell?

Then you'll die, you idiot, because no one is coming to rescue you. She was the bloody rescue party and if she didn't get off this balcony not only was she going to die, but Jensen probably would too.

Her recent love affair with working out meant she could do a pull-up. On a good day she could do three. She'd never done one hanging from two stories up so scared she could barely think.

"Fuck." She was not going out like this. No way. Not after what had just happened.

She took a deep breath, engaged her core, and exhaled as she pulled. Her muscles screamed and she drew her shoulders up to level with her wrists. She held there for a fraction of a second and lunged for the horizontal bar with her left hand. Her right arm almost gave out before her left caught.

But it caught. It *fucking caught.* She forced herself to keep moving, her right hand coming up to join the left on the horizontal bar. The ache in her muscles, the shakiness of her grip, told her she couldn't do it again. But with the higher position, she didn't have to. She kicked her right leg through the side slit in her gown, freeing it from the skirts and began to swing side to side. It took two tries to hook her right foot between two of the vertical bars, but once she did she had the leverage to pull the rest of her up, to crawl over the top and land on her back, safe on the balcony floor.

Her whole body shook, the relief so intense tears leaked out the corners of her eyes. How did Val do this shit all the time? Meredith wanted to curl into a ball and kiss the solid ground beneath her. But she had a feeling if she did that she might not get up for an hour.

She rolled onto her stomach and peered over the side. Julian lay on the ground. No thralls came to investigate and she didn't know if that meant he was dead, or if Analisa simply didn't care enough to check it out. Meredith pushed herself up and started walking.

Inside, she caught sight of herself in the dresser mirror. Her hair was a mess from where Julian had wrenched it and the wind had blown through it. She reached up, checking the pins were still in. Dirt streaked her dress, the right strap had almost given way, and the skin of her hands was torn and bloody. A bruise already blossomed on her wrist from Julian's grip.

She looked like some feral pageant queen. That was fine. Feral things were deadly when cornered, and pageant queens knew how to take a lot of shit and keep going. Besides, a queen needed a crown—like the one that rested on the white satin pillow on the dresser.

Had Julian known it called to her? Had her mother held it in that repository for Meredith all these years? Was it meant to be worn by a Truthfinder?

Inside the house, with the nullifying spell in full force, she couldn't feel the circlet's call. Not like she had in the repository, but more like the faint call she'd felt every time she'd gone to her mother's mausoleum. It wasn't the place that had pulled her there—it had been the faint pull of the circlet.

She hesitated a moment before placing it on her head. Without access to her Aspect, the all-consuming need that had overtaken her in the repository didn't come. Until the magic came back, her crown was only a crown.

She stepped out into the hallway. Two thralls waited, one to either side of the door. She picked one at random. "I'm alive. Julian's not. I want my wolf."

The thrall inclined his head. Meredith followed him to the first level, then to a large steel door that opened into—what else? —a basement.

"If you go in," the thrall said, "you stay until the auction is over."

Meredith smiled. "Not a problem."

CHAPTER

THIRTY-ONE

She stepped into the basement, the door clanging shut behind her. Dim electric lighting followed her down the stairs, growing stronger when she reached the bottom. The basement itself occupied a rectangular space, cages lining both sides of the walls. Soft, rhythmic breathing filled the air.

The Shifters that occupied the cages, from the great tiger nearest her to the bear at the opposite end, were asleep. Muzzles covered their faces and blood stained the fur between their paws.

She remembered Analisa saying she'd ripped Natalie's claws out. Had she done that to all of them?

Dread filled her and she hurried down the cage row until she found Jensen. Like the others, he was asleep.

"Jensen?" His paw twitched. Hopeful, she reached through the bars and shook him. He gave a loud, wolf snore. Perfect. Her big, bad werewolf was off in dreamland.

Magically induced sleep or medical? And how was she going to wake him up? How was she going to wake *all* of them up?

If Analisa had sedatives to knock them out, maybe she had stimulants to wake them up. She looked around and found the basement had another door at this end of the room. A try of the handle found it unlocked. In the small room on the other side, four refrigerators lined the walls. The first three were stuffed full of ground hamburger meat. The fourth one held vial upon vial of clear liquid. She looked at the label but the name didn't mean anything to her. She was reaching for the phone in her clutch to look up the name when she remembered she didn't have cell reception here. But the vials were all the same, so it was likely the sedative, with no stimulant in sight.

Still, signs pointed to medical sedation, which was...good. If it was medical then their super Shifter metabolisms could kick through it quickly, right? Except they *weren't*. Maybe they just needed a little incentive.

She took a hamburger package, ripped it open and placed it by Jensen's nose. His paws twitched. A low growl started in his throat and he woke without warning, snapping and snarling until his eyes lit on her with recognition.

"Hey, handsome."

He shook himself, downed the hamburger meat, and shifted. He'd barely regained human form before he was talking. "Are you okay?"

"What? You don't like my grunge look?" She pulled the lock picks from her hair, looking over the lock before making her selection. Before she could set to work, Jensen's hands slid through the bars, closing over her wrists. "What happened? Are you hurt?"

"I'm fine."

He didn't let go. "Where is Julian? Did he touch you?"

Apparently she wasn't allowed to rescue her husband until after she talked to him. "Look, it wasn't exactly fun but nothing happened. He thought I was going to suck his dick, I nearly tore his balls off, punched him in the nose, and tossed him off a balcony."

Jensen blinked.

"Unfortunately I nearly went off the balcony with him. But I didn't, so everything's fine. May I please pick the lock on your cage now?" He let go of her wrists, but his hand came up to cup her cheek.

"I'm sorry," he said roughly. "I shouldn't have let you go without me."

"I'm the one who told you to go. If you hadn't, we'd both be dead." She focused her attention on the lock. After a minute, she said, "It matters. That you trusted I could handle it. Thank you."

She didn't look up, but she could feel his attention on her. "I do trust you, but Meredith? Please don't ever ask me to leave you like that again."

She let out a shaky laugh. "Deal."

He crouched down, watching her work. "Are those your hair pins?"

"Technically, they are lock picks disguised as hair pins."

"And you…know how to use them?"

"Mmm-hmm."

"Why do you know how to use them? And why did you conveniently have diamond-encrusted lock picks?"

She worked the pins, feeling out the tumblers. "When I was younger, my mother used to waltz me through parties having me lie detect for public amusement. I'm still not sure if it was because she wanted to humiliate me, because she actually wanted the information I got for her, or if she just wanted to exhaust all my Aspect.

"Once I was tapped out, she'd lock me in my room. The thing about Aspecters is they tend to forget there are mundane solutions to anything. They're so used to relying on Aspect to solve all their problems, they think that if someone runs out of it for the time being, that person is helpless. I didn't want to be helpless."

She felt the lock click and relief flooded her. *Still got it.*

"Your mother was a piece of work."

Meredith laughed. "I'm fully aware of that." She swung the

door open. Jensen stepped out, took her face in his hands, and kissed her. "I'm glad you're okay."

"Back at you."

His fingers brushed the circlet. "Do I even want to ask?"

"I think it's made for Truth. For me."

"I don't think it's safe."

"It's no harm to me inside the house. If we make it out okay, I'll take it off before my magic comes back. But if the world's still in chaos when we get outside? I may need it. Don't ask me to throw away the one weapon I have."

He exhaled, long and slow. "Okay."

"Okay. Is Natalie here?"

He nodded and walked down the row of cages, stopping at the one three down from his own. A snow leopard slept on the floor. Her fur, though it looked freshly bathed for the auction, couldn't hide that she was too skinny. Not as skinny as Jensen had been when he'd come out of Elijah's basement, but enough to weaken her.

She wore one of the black muzzles all the Shifters did and her paws…up close, it was too easy to see the mutilation.

Meredith had no doubt the Shifters could regrow the digits, or Analisa wouldn't have done it on something she intended to sell as a predatory weapon. But she'd clearly wanted to remove those natural weapons until they were transferred to their new owners, so she'd sedated and starved them enough that they wouldn't have the natural resources to heal until the auction was over.

"Open it." Jensen's voice was ragged.

Meredith went to work. She moved faster this time, fresh off her experience with the previous lock, and this one soon popped open. Jensen went in and gently unbuckled the muzzle. He stroked Natalie's fur and spoke in low, soothing tones, but she didn't stir.

He looked up. "She needs food. Where did you get the hamburger?"

"Refrigerators, I'll get it." She grabbed as many packages as she could carry and brought them back to Jensen.

The snow leopard came awake like—well, like a cat scenting prey. The food disappeared in a matter of seconds. As soon as it was gone she scuttled backwards to the far side of the cage. As if she feared attack. She was still half asleep, her eyes unfocused.

"Nat?" Jensen's voice was low, soft, soothing.

The snow leopard's head jerked up. She shuddered, and Meredith felt the magic burning through the girl—burning off the sedative. Another wave of magic pulsed through her and claws sprouted from her forepaws. Her eyes snapped into focus, locking on Jensen.

"Hey, kid."

Her whiskers trembled. A low, hurt sound escaped her throat and she launched herself across the cage. For one terrible moment Meredith thought the girl was so traumatized she hadn't recognized Jensen, and Meredith braced for teeth and claws and blood.

Jensen caught the snow leopard, who threw her forelegs around Jensen's neck in an awkward feline embrace, buried her face in his neck, and cried. Strangled meows and those low, hurt sounds so particular to the various feline species, the kind that could cut right through to the heart and tear it to shreds.

Natalie shivered and poured out her pain while Jensen held her tight, murmuring so softly Meredith couldn't make out what he said. Tears streamed down his own face.

Meredith felt like a voyeur, intruding on a private moment that wasn't meant for her. Her heart hurt, and she'd never wished for Valkyrie's abilities so much in that moment, because the desire to leave this room and rip Analisa's head off was overpowering.

Beneath that, she felt like an asshole for the urge to tell them they needed to get up and go. Go before someone came in, before something happened. Five minutes. She could give them five minutes while she worked on the rest of the locks.

She took a step back, her heel scuffing on the floor. The snow leopard stilled, her eyes fixing on Meredith. A snarl emanated from her throat and she lunged.

Jensen held onto her. "It's okay, Nat. She's with us. She's… my wife."

That knocked the snow leopard into stunned stillness, her gaze traveling down to where a decorative cuff covered Meredith's infinity tattoo. Meredith took the cuff off and held the tattoo out. Jensen gave her an encouraging look.

Er, right. Would it be polite to crouch, or would Natalie consider that condescending? In the end, she stayed where she was. "Hi. I'm Meredith. I know you don't have a good track record with my kind, but I promise I'm here to help."

Natalie gave Jensen a look that telegraphed incredulity even via snow leopard facial expressions. Magic roiled through the cage again and Natalie's skin began to writhe, her features shifting.

"Nat, *stop*." Jensen's hand clamped on her shoulder. "You don't have the strength to shift back to cat and we don't have an easy escape route. You're going to need claws."

Nat paused.

"I promise, I'll explain everything later. But right now I need you to trust me."

The changes in Natalie's body reversed, leaving her full snow leopard again, and Jensen relaxed.

To Meredith he said, "How fast can you get the remaining cages open?"

"Probably faster than you can convince them not to kill me. Jensen…we don't have time to talk to them all one by one." Given how things had gone with Natalie, she didn't think opening every cage and having Jensen go inside to talk to the Shifter was a viable plan.

"We wake them up," Jensen said, "then we let them out."

That was how Meredith found herself opening packages of

ground beef and shoving them through cell bars, divvying up everything the refrigerators had to offer.

The Shifters woke as if by magic. As Jensen explained it, scent would filter through to them even in sleep, at which point their magic, sensing the promise of food, did a cost-benefit analysis and decided it was worth burning the energy to shake off the sedative for the reward of fresh caloric intake.

Soon they had a room full of alert, wary-eyed, but curiously quiet Shifters. More than one eye darted to the door—or rather to the wall beside the door, where a tactical stun baton hung on the wall. She supposed if you came awake snarling and got shocked for your trouble, you'd start waking up quiet.

"I'm Jensen King." His voice was quiet to avoid alerting any thralls who might be outside, but judging by the way ears pricked from all the way down the line, everyone heard him just fine. "Some of you I've met, some I haven't. But you know who I am. I'm here to get you out, but we're in less than ideal circumstances. Analisa is preparing to sell you at auction to the highest bidder.

"I don't know how long we have until they come to bring you out. She can open your cages." Jensen gestured at Meredith and a few soft growls spread through the room. "Yeah, I know she's Aspect. She's also the only reason we found you. So deal with it."

A grumbling assent went through the room.

"Odds are good that we're going to have to fight our way out. We don't have the numbers to take everyone in this building, so we need to clear a path to the door and run for it. If nothing has gone wrong, reinforcements will be coming from outside. Some of them will be ours, and some of them will be Aspect. You'll know our Aspecters from the Aspecters attending the auction, because they will be the ones in tactical gear instead of evening wear.

"They won't attack you if you don't attack them. Once we're clear of the house, I won't blame anyone who wants to run for the hills. You want to stay, we can offer food and shelter and get you back to your enclave.

"If anyone has a violent objection to this plan, make some noise." The room stayed quiet. "Good. One last thing. That woman right there?" He pointed at Meredith. "She's my wife. You touch her, you hurt her, and I'll end you. Am I clear?"

Furry heads around the room nodded. Meredith wasn't sure if it was appropriate in this day and age to have a panty-melting response to a guy threatening to kill anyone who touched you, but she was having one and didn't have time to examine it.

Jensen shifted back to his wolf form as Meredith went to work on the cages. The first held a bengal tiger, who watched her warily as she jimmied the door open. His eyes kept flicking to the tattoo on her wrist.

Once the lock popped Jensen stepped in, planting himself between her and the tiger. He caught the straps of the muzzle in his teeth and tore it off, leaving the tiger free to descend on the hamburger. Meredith moved on to the next cage.

They fell into a rhythm. Unlock cage, remove muzzle, move on. She was two cages from having them all out when she heard the unmistakable sound of the stairwell door opening. The thrall didn't even get the door fully open before the Shifters were on him.

The tiger clamped his jaws over the thrall's wrist and bit down. Once, twice, and the hand came off. A black wolf latched onto the thrall's leg and dragged him inside. Bile crept up Meredith's throat and she turned away. She understood the rage. She understood this had to be done. But she couldn't watch it.

She forced herself to focus on the last two locks, to ignore the sounds of tearing flesh and breaking bones. She wasn't sure if it was better or worse that the thralls never screamed.

Finally they had every cage open and she had no choice but to turn back to the door. The bodies on the floor were in too many pieces for her to know how many people they added up to. Seven? Maybe eight?

The tiger, still closest to the door, looked back and saw the cages all open. He looked to Jensen, who nodded. Then he opened his mouth and *roared*. The sound was deafening. The tiger pawed the door fully open and bounded out, a flurry of Shifters on his tail.

CHAPTER

THIRTY-TWO

The hallways of the house were a battlefield. One Meredith was ill-equipped to navigate. She'd grabbed the stun baton from the cage room on her way out. While it packed a strong enough electric charge to send the thralls into temporary muscles spasms this did little to deter them from her, as they didn't appear to feel pain.

It also wasn't a viable weapon for mass defense, so she mostly tried to stay out of the way as more and more thralls poured into the already packed halls. Powerful though the Shifters were, they were half-starved, and there were thirteen of them to the unending masses of the thralls. If it weren't for the natural bottleneck provided by the halls, it would have been a slaughterhouse.

Her phone chimed. She'd thrown her clutch away earlier, stuffing her cellphone into the top of her dress, just in case. It shouldn't work inside the disorientation spell's influence. So if it *was*, then maybe Val and the others had brought the spell down.

"Jensen, I need two minutes of cover." He herded her into a corner and put himself between her and everything else.

She dug out her phone.

Val: *You alive in there?*

She typed back. *So far. We could use some help in here.*

Ellipses appeared on the screen. Meredith chewed at her bottom lip.

That's a problem. We're knee-deep in thralls plus every asshole Aspecter at this auction.

The attendees must have fled outside as soon as they'd heard the Shifters start tearing into the thralls.

Can you hold out another fifteen minutes?

Meredith looked at the chaos around her. They weren't going to last fifteen minutes. She needed her Aspect.

No. Do you have enough wind Elementals to rip the roof off the house?

Yes? Why?

Just do it as soon as you can. If the roof came off it would destroy enough of the physical makeup of the nullifying spell to render it useless.

Give me three minutes.

Meredith stuffed the phone back in her dress, tapped Jensen to let him know she was alert to her own safety again, and counted the seconds in her head.

Meredith's Aspect didn't lend itself well to martial endeavors, but her shields were good. Not good enough to protect all the Shifters at once, but if she built a thick enough shield around herself she could barrel through the thrall-blocked hallway. At worst, it would provide a distraction. At best, she might open a path the Shifters could follow through.

One-hundred and seventy-three seconds from Val's last text, the building rattled. It shook and groaned, and Meredith felt it as the roof tore free.

Her Aspect inundated her. She reached for it, the shielding spell at her fingertips, but froze before it could blossom. Power flowed into the circlet and the crown caught it like a person might catch their partner in a dance. Catch. Spin. Toss.

Her Aspect, amplified, shot out from the diamond between her brows, blanketing the room like a mist. It saturated every surface, every person, and through its lens she saw truth. Every thing, every person, held truths. Their very existence was a type of truth—the truth of what they were, of *how* they were.

The Shifters were vibrant dualities, their human side and their animal side each as real as the other. But the thralls were empty and distorted, vacant shells twisted from what they had been born to be and changed to living batteries to be drained at will. They were no longer alive in the typical sense, but mere extensions of Analisa. Meredith didn't think necromancer had been a half bad description.

She gripped the nearest thralls in the fist of her power. *Show them*, she whispered to her Aspect. Like a Truthfinder's Telling but different, more potent. Where the Telling made a person confront the things they already knew but hid from, this showed the thralls a truth they were unaware of, one Analisa's tie kept from them. In every way that mattered, they were already dead.

Her Aspect both revealed the fact and imposed it upon them. Faced with a reality that could not be denied, could not be hidden from or ignored, the thralls had no choice but to accept it.

The ties that bound them to Analisa unraveled and they dropped like stones to the ground, their bodies disintegrating to ash. Deep in the house she heard Analisa's anguished cry, half pain, half fury. The remaining thralls surged forward, ignoring the Shifters, ignoring everything in their frenzy to get to Meredith.

So she showed them, too, what they were, and they too fell. Not all of these disintegrated. Only the ones the circlet showed her were the oldest.

Wave after wave of thralls crashed upon her, and wave after wave fell, until bodies and dust lined the halls. Meredith picked her way through them.

By the time she emerged into the home's main foyer, the Shifters at her back, the blood-stained hem of her dress had acquired a six-inch deep coating of ash. Analisa stood in the center of the room, her posture rigid, a deep, mutinous fire in her eyes. A ring of twenty thralls encircled her. All that remained.

"I should have killed you," Analisa said. She sounded tired. "But I just wanted one person to understand."

"I do." Meredith understood how easily she might have become someone like her. Someone twisted by pain and helplessness, who finally found a way out and didn't care who paid the cost of that freedom, so long as it wasn't her. "I don't blame you for your origins. But I blame you for them." She gestured to the Shifters. "And for everyone like them. And I will tell you the truth in your heart, and give it to you. You want this to be over. You've wanted it all to be over for a long time now, but you didn't know how to let go."

The feelings were there, burning in Analisa's eyes. The need to be done, and the opposite need to cling to life. Meredith saw the truth she'd whispered to Jensen on that first night now written in Analisa's soul: *All I know is we have to keep going... Because otherwise, what the fuck was it all for?*

Analisa didn't know how to stop. Meredith's power reached for the remaining thralls, and they dropped. These were her oldest, and they spun to ash before they even hit the ground. Meredith looked at Jensen. "Maybe she doesn't deserve it, but make it quick. For me."

She turned away as the Shifters shot forward, burying Analisa beneath a mound of furry bodies. She reached for the circlet, but as her fingers brushed the cool metal she couldn't bring herself to take it off. Not yet.

The world was so wondrous through its gaze. Hypnotic. Here was every truth she'd ever wanted. Physical, objective truths that weren't mutable based on what people believed. She just wanted to see a little more, to *know* a little more.

Jensen snapped Analisa's neck in one powerful bite. He would never excuse the things she had done, what she had become, but he understood why Meredith had asked what she had of him. And he'd seen too much of pain to want more of it, to think that causing it in kind could do anything but darken the stains on a person's soul.

He left the Shifters to vent their own pain and fury on a dead woman, and searched for Meredith. She stood by the front door, her hands clutching the circlet, but she didn't lift it off. A faraway light burned in her eyes. With the hem of her dress coated in blood and the circlet on her head blazing power, she looked like some ancient goddess come to dispense vengeance.

She was beautiful, as a goddess. But he thought she was more beautiful as just Meredith.

Take it off, darlin'.

But her hands fell to her sides, empty. She turned and walked out. He tore after her. If she noticed when he reached her side, she gave no indication.

Outside, the conflict was winding down. The lawn to his left was filled with handcuffed men and women, and he scented the same magic on the metal restraints that had kept Meredith from accessing her Aspect inside the house.

She paused, turning in a slow circle and froze, her gaze fixed on a figure coming slowly but determinedly toward them.

Julian.

The bastard had survived his trip off the balcony, then. He had a hitch in his step and his right arm hung at an awkward angle.

Jensen's hackles rose. He stepped forward, growling, and found himself seized in that same fist of power that had held him the night Julian had taken him.

Meredith shook her head. "I've been meaning to tell you, Julian, your holds have a weak spot." Her Aspect wrapped around Jensen. Pressure built, her power struggling against

Julian, and then the hold on Jensen vanished. He gathered himself to leap but Meredith said, "He's mine."

Power snaked from her like a whip and coiled around Julian. He jerked, his eyes bulging. Meredith spoke a single word. "Confess."

Her voice rolled like thunder, magic booming with the word, and Julian began to speak. The words tumbled out of his mouth one atop the other, as if he couldn't get them out fast enough, like he was trying to excise some horror from deep within him. But the more he spoke, the more panicked he became, babbling faster and faster, his face twisted in a rictus mask of pain. The things he said made Jensen's stomach turn.

Aspect poured from Meredith, like an endless fountain seeking to flood the world. And it did. As it brushed over Jensen, he found himself thinking on things he did his best not to. Defining moments in his life, times when he'd made choices that had been difficult to live with. Times when he'd made the wrong choices. The hard moments that had made him who he was.

Guilt rose up, threatening to crush him. He shook his head, growling. That wasn't *all* he was—the failures, the wrongs. He was his successes, too. He was the good choices, and the striving to be better than he was. He was the desire to help rather than hurt, to protect but not smother.

He was both sides of himself, and he could accept that.

The magic let him go and he inhaled sharply. Freed from his internal struggle, he found the night alive with voices. With confession. The full assault of Meredith's power had struck Julian, but what he couldn't absorb had filtered out, affecting everyone else. And Meredith's power wasn't stopping.

He reached beyond the exhaustion of the battle and the two shifts he'd already done, and forced himself to change. Human again, he struggled past the lethargy weighing him down—he'd done too much, and his body badly wanted to shut him down so it could recover.

"Meredith? Darlin' you need to stop."

She blinked. The Aspect spilling from her ebbed but didn't stop. Not fully.

The circlet. *That* was where the problem lay. He just needed to rip it off her head and everything would be fine.

He reached for it. A hand grabbed him. He ripped his arm free, swung on instinct, and stopped just shy of punching Jace. It was a damn good thing he'd recognized him in time to pull the punch, because while his fist might have stopped five inches from Jace's face, that was only one inch from the wall of solid ice that had sprung up between them.

Hitting that would have hurt like a bitch. He dropped his hand and the ice wall melted into water that streamed off to splash on the ground a few feet away.

"She has to take the circlet off," Jace said.

"What do you think I was going for when you came up?"

"No, *she* has to take it off. She's wearing the damn crown of Solomon. It's amplifying her power and her Aspect's in a feed-back loop with it. If anyone but her tries to remove it, they will interrupt that loop. In all likelihood, the backlash will kill whoever that is. Think of it like trying to shut off electricity by grabbing onto a power line with your bare hands. You die, and the electricity's still on."

"So what do you suggest?"

"Get her to remove it voluntarily."

"How?"

"Get through to her," was Jace's oh-so-helpful advice.

"Again, how?"

"You could try kissing me." The trickle of Aspect still spilling from Meredith shut off.

Jace and Jensen spun toward her. She'd crossed her arms beneath her chest and she looked amused.

"It always works in the movies. Whenever the power-crazy person is on the brink of destroying everything she loves, the hot guy kisses her and it fixes everything."

Jace gaped at her. "You're wearing the crown of Solomon. He

wore it once and couldn't take it off. Drove half of his constituents insane."

"Solomon was a lightweight. Historians estimate him as a high-mid-level Truthfinder at best. If I hadn't bungled my test on purpose, you'd know I rank high-high, and my control is off the charts." She lifted the crown off her head and held it out to Jace, who took it like it was an adder that might bite. Despite her calm words, she watched it go with something like longing on her face. "But just in case, maybe lock it up somewhere I don't know about."

She turned to Jensen. "It won't save the world from me, but I could use that kiss."

CHAPTER

THIRTY-THREE

Meredith was dead on her feet. She wanted a shower, food, sleep, and Jensen. Not necessarily in that order. She figured if she was lucky, she might get two of those things. Her home had become Shifter central.

Of the eleven Shifters they'd liberated from Analisa, two had died—the great tiger who'd led the charge, and one of the cougars—and two had, by best guest, taken Jensen's offer to disappear into the night and find their own way home.

That had left them with seven injured Shifters in need of food and shelter. Meredith figured she already had four Shifters staying with her, so what was another seven? Random and Jace had gotten stuck with the grocery store runs while Siren and Valkyrie sorted out the apprehended criminals back at council headquarters. Rebekah contacted the other enclave leaders, and Meredith and Jensen got the Shifters sorted.

About half of them had managed to go human after devouring the first food delivery. The others had sustained enough damage in the fight that, combined with months of being fed just enough to keep them alive, Jensen said it would take them a few more hours to recuperate enough to shift.

The ones that were still furry were sleeping off food comas in her living room, while the ones who'd shifted had all disappeared upstairs with a stack of clothes and hygiene products. Random and Jace's first shopping spree had hit Walmart, from which they'd returned with the store's entire stock of meat cuts, dozens of shirts and sweatpants in every size, and enough hygiene products to shower and pamper six times as many Shifters as they had.

Her kitchen door opened and the two of them hauled in another mountain of supplies, making four more trips back out to Jace's truck before they got it all in.

"That's it for the night." Random deposited four bags of takeout on the counter while Jace methodically organized meat into her refrigerator. Fortunately the fridge had been mostly empty, otherwise it wouldn't have all fit.

Random shoved a takeout box and a fork at her. "Sit. Eat."

She accepted the items on reflex, then set them down and picked up two of the bags of takeout boxes. "I need to take these upstairs." The Shifters who were in human form and awake were probably already hungry again. And after what they'd been through, they deserved to eat something that wasn't raw meat.

"You need to sit down before you fall down." Jensen's arms came around her and he gently removed the bags from her grip.

"I'm fine, I—"

"Need a shower and clothes that aren't using blood as a fashion statement," he growled.

She looked down at the ruined evening dress. She'd sort of forgotten she was still wearing it and now felt vaguely ridiculous. It *did* explain why she was so uncomfortable. "But—"

"No buts." He handed her the takeout box she'd rejected moments before. "Go upstairs. Eat. Shower. Go to sleep. You need it."

Covert glances at Random and Jace revealed they were in

total agreement, so she wouldn't be getting any help from that corner. She turned back to Jensen and lifted her chin. "I could tell you the same thing." He hadn't slowed down any more than she had, barely pausing long enough to put on clothes. If he stood still for any length of time he inevitably swayed, like he was about to topple over at any moment.

"I'll be up soon," he said softly. "I just need to check on Nat."

MEREDITH FELL ASLEEP LEANING against the shower wall with conditioner still in her hair. She jerked awake when the water ran cold and nearly died an ignominious death as her feet slid out from under her and she landed on her ass on the tile floor.

She'd survived an energy vampire, her thrall army, *and* a magic circlet to nearly become a statistic in American bathroom fatalities. Brilliant.

She rinsed out the conditioner as the water got progressively colder. She was in full-body shivers by the time she finished, and decided she was upgrading to a point-of-use water heater that could deliver an endless supply of hot water. Provided, of course, she didn't end up torching the house as some sort of final, cathartic *fuck you* to her mother.

The thought of Savannah Townsend didn't inspire its usual round of unwanted memories, helplessness, and rage. People said revenge didn't help but...Meredith kind of thought it had. Maybe not the revenge itself, but the taking charge of a situation. She'd wanted to do something—to help Jensen and the Shifters, to deal with Julian—and she had.

The voice in her head, the one constantly telling her she was weak and stupid and useless had finally shut up. With it gone, the need to *do* something with the house—to either make it hers or destroy it—was gone too. It was just a building. Terrible things had happened in it, but that didn't make it a bad place. It wasn't a place she wanted to live in, anymore, but it could be a home for someone else.

She could sell it and buy a new one. No—she could *build* a new one. Maybe not with her own hands, but she could design it. A house that would be *hers*. A place she could never feel like she didn't belong because she had chosen every single thing about it. A *home*.

Her father's gardens would be hard to let go but she could rebuild those, too. Plant new ones in his honor, a kind of living memorial to the man her mother had never let her properly grieve.

She would contact a realtor and get it on the market as soon as she could. Rent somewhere in town until she found the perfect place to build what she wanted. Until she figured out *what* she wanted.

The decision made, it felt like a physical weight dropped from her shoulders. She put on a pair of warm sweats and a t-shirt, wishing she had one of Jensen's instead. She slowly ate her now-cold takeout and tried not to feel too disappointed that Jensen hadn't come up. Between her shower nap and her intentionally slow meal time, it had been over an hour since she'd left him downstairs.

She fought sleep, waiting even though some part of her knew if he was going to come up, he would have done it by now. His sister had been through hell. Natalie needed him.

I need him too. She shoved the thought away. She didn't want to need him. She didn't want the bed to feel empty without him.

I would have asked you to be mine. She'd known better than to hold onto those words. He was Natalie's guardian. His sister was going to need him and her life—his life—wasn't in Seclusion. He would want to take her home, where she would be surrounded by familiar places and people and things.

Maybe, once he'd done that, once Natalie was back on her feet...maybe then he'd have space in his life for Meredith. If he still *wanted* to have space for her, then. If all of this between them hadn't just been situational proximity and emotion and post-traumatic stress.

She hugged a pillow to her chest and told herself that letting him go couldn't hurt more than all the hell her mother had put her through.

She fell asleep to the gentle hum of her magic calling her a liar.

CHAPTER

THIRTY-FOUR

A week and a half after the events of the auction night, Meredith's house had turned into a full-on Shifter hotel. In addition to housing those rescued from the auction, the protectors from the other five Shifter enclaves—Vayne, Archer, Silver, Temple, and River—had arrived six days ago with entourages in tow. Meredith, being a gracious sort setting the example for Shifter/Aspect relations, had offered them all the hospitality of her home.

If said home was now a hotel, its guests seemed to view Meredith as the manager with whom all complaints were to be filed. So far, she had rearranged no less than five room assignments, arbitrated a dispute between members of the Vayne and Archer enclaves involving who should be allowed first right to the shared shower in the morning, tracked down a hard-to-find brand of licorice tea for a Silver enclaver who frequently got an upset stomach, and purchased an alarming number of refrigerators to ensure that each enclave didn't have to share food space with another. She now had an entire room dedicated to refrigerators.

It was six-thirty in the morning, half an hour before she was expected in the formal dining room for day five of the peace talks. She'd hoped to steal that half an hour to drink her coffee on the porch and think fondly of the depressed silence the house used to exude.

Instead, Lacey from the River enclave had pinned her down at the kitchen island and launched into a detailed rant about how her mother wanted Lacey to follow in her footsteps and become the enclave archivist when she graduated high school in the spring, but Lacey didn't think it was for her. She wanted to go to college for marine biology, and her mother sending her on this trip to chronicle Aspect/Shifter relations wasn't changing her mind on her life's aspirations, and did Meredith think it was selfish of Lacey to tell her mother no?

Meredith wasn't an idiot. She understood she was being tested. She even understood why. She was the surprise wife of the next King enclave protector, and none of the Shifters save Rebekah and Serenity knew that marriage wasn't a permanent situation.

The other Shifters wanted to know if they could respect her. If people came to her with what seemed like trivial problems, would she blow them off or do something about it anyway? Was she easily frustrated? When she did get frustrated, did she take it out on other people?

That, or they were just trying to drive her to the brink of insanity to figure out when she would break. Meredith was determined not to, if for no other reason than that Serenity always managed to be nearby whenever one of these interactions occurred. Currently, she sat at the end of the kitchen island filing her nails and looking bored.

Meredith still wasn't sure where the two of them stood. The hostility between them had lessened, and they'd even had a few interactions that might be termed marginally cordial, but Meredith didn't think they would ever like each other.

Lacey wrapped up her long list of reasons why being a marine biologist was preferable to being an archivist, and stared at Meredith with overly-earnest eyes waiting for her response.

Right. "Is the archivist position important within your enclave?"

"Yes, which Mom is keen to go on and on and on about every time she wants to badger me into training for it."

"Is the position typically inherited?"

"Also yes, but it's not unheard of for it to pass to someone new. She just won't consider it because she doesn't think I'm taking the responsibility seriously. She thinks my head is full of 'college ideas' and I just need to 'grow up and stop being rebellious.' So what should I do?"

Meredith couldn't figure out what Lacey—and the Shifters diligently eavesdropping on the conversation while pretending not to—could be getting out of her advice on this matter. This was the kind of discussion you had with your friends, not with a stranger you'd just met. Even if you thought said stranger was your next leader's main squeeze. But there *were* all of those listening Shifter ears, one pair of which belonged to Serenity, so she sucked it up and gave it her best go.

"Have you sat down and really tried to explain to her why you don't want to do it, or have you just said that you don't want to?"

Lacey ducked her head. "What's the point in explaining? She won't listen to me."

"I don't know your mom. Maybe she won't listen to you, but maybe she will. Sit down, use your college ideas and write out a coherent argument for why you aren't the right person for the job. If it's an important position that should be treated with respect, and you believe you won't ever be able to do the job justice because it's not where your heart is, lay it all out there for her.

"Show her that you're not just blowing her off and that you've actually given it thought. If you do all that and she ignores you? Maybe you need some space from her until she recognizes you're an adult and not a child. But maybe she'll understand that you feel strongly about it. She might not give up on the idea immediately, but it should open the door to actual discussion instead of the two of you simply butting heads."

Lacey brightened. "That's not a bad idea. Maybe I'll write her an essay." She turned, looking like she was off to find a laptop right then to begin composing her magnum opus. Halfway to the stairs, where she was in prime hearing range of every Shifter who'd pretended not to be paying attention, she stopped and said, "Meredith? Your hair looks really pretty today."

Serenity got a pinched expression on her face. The compliment was another part of this bizarre testing ritual. Every time Meredith was asked to give advice, arbitrate a dispute, or otherwise express her opinion on a matter, afterwards someone would inevitably complement her or otherwise try to be pleasant or helpful.

You look so nice today, Meredith. Where did you find that stunning blouse, Meredith? Delicious coffee, Meredith, what blend is it? I picked these flowers for you, Meredith, I hope you like them. Can I carry that for you, Meredith?

These displays were always done very publicly and the speaker always made a point to use her name, as if there might be some confusion about who was being complemented or catered to. All of it made her feel like a fraud, because once a Shifter made a decision about her, they were so damned genuine about it. They made her feel like she was being accepted into a family, and they had no idea she was planning on abandoning them.

Jensen should be the one explaining all of this to her but he hadn't been around for more than five seconds to ask. Which hurt her more than she cared to admit.

Now that the Lacey crowd had dispersed, Meredith refilled her coffee and made her escape to the porch. She had a whole fifteen minutes left before she had to be in the dining room. If only she could bang her head against the outdoor coffee table and moan, *Why me?*, maybe she would feel better.

Or maybe yell it at the top of her lungs. She could put a

silencing spell on the porch so no one could hear her scream, but anyone watching would still *see* her screaming, and then she would just look crazy.

Twelve minutes of blissful pretend-solitude left.

The sliding glass doors opened and Serenity came out, taking the seat across from her. Meredith restrained a groan. What now?

"Could I speak with you for a moment in private?"

Why me?

"Of course." Meredith silenced the porch area and waited.

Serenity drew her legs up, tucking her bare feet beneath her and staring off at the gardens. She looked effortlessly pretty and vulnerable, the kind of woman a man would instinctively feel the need to protect. Meredith kept waiting for Jensen to come to his senses and realize he did want to marry Serenity and give her three children and a white picket fence.

"They like you," Serenity finally said. "They never even bothered to test me. I was with him for two years, and no one ever asked me for so much as my opinion on pizza toppings." She picked at her fingernails. "They knew he'd never marry me. I was the only one who didn't."

Her words were laced with a raw hurt that went farther back than a failed relationship. Suddenly, Meredith wasn't looking at Jensen's ex anymore. She was looking at a woman who had wanted to matter—to be respected by the people she belonged to —and felt like she didn't. Maybe that was why Serenity had spoken up for Hel when the younger woman had wanted to be trusted for the reconnaissance mission.

"I just keep thinking, why couldn't it have been me, you know? What is so wrong with me that no one wants me? I'm pretty enough to fuck but not good enough to marry, because I never behaved quite right. I knew what I was supposed to do. I was supposed to grow up, smile, and keep my thoughts to myself so someone would marry me to keep as his pretty little arm candy.

"But I always managed to sabotage it somehow. I didn't want

to be a trophy wife, but I wasn't smart enough to be respected for my intellect. Just opinionated enough to make men tire of me in a few months and too pretty for women to want me around their men." She laughed, soft and bitter. "I'll be a pariah in the King enclave by the time word of you gets around. Why do you get to be strong and beautiful and everyone loves you for it, but I'm just difficult cheat-bait?"

"Because people are stupid."

Serenity's head snapped up. Tears shimmered in her eyes, ones she refused to let fall.

"People are stupid," Meredith repeated. "They form opinions of us when we're young, based on what we're taught to show them, and they never allow for the fact that what they see might not be the real us. They never allow for the fact that people grow.

"Most people in Aspect Society think I'm a clueless nitwit. Even my friends, who love me, still think of me as the flighty socialite I had to act like to survive. You heard them—they were shocked I could do math." She leaned forward, resting her elbows on her knees. "Do you want to know why your people like me? It's not because I'm so great. It's because they like Jensen, and Jensen, who has been vocal about his desire to never marry, married me.

"I am unknown and mysterious, and they think I attained the unattainable. Therefore, one of two things must be true. Either I am special and brilliant and one in a million, and therefore worthy of their respect, or I'm a great lay and Jensen's head has been so turned by my magical orgasmic powers that there's no use reasoning with him."

Serenity snorted.

"The people predisposed to be reasonable toward a random new addition to their lives need very little convincing to decide to like and respect me. The people who are going to look at me and see a blonde with boobs are never going to be convinced I'm anything but a bunny in the sack. And you know what? Fuck all of them.

"None of this is about me, or you. It's all about Jensen. Do I still want them to like me? Of course I do. It's human nature. No one wants to be disliked. And I will feel bad when all of this is over and it comes out that our marriage is a joke, because so many of them welcomed me when they didn't have to.

"It would be easy to just stay married to him. Given the givens, he probably wouldn't fight me on it. But the only power I've ever had in my life has been based on what other people have deigned to give me, and I'm not going down that route again. I don't want people to like me because I'm Jensen King's wife. I want them to like me—or not—because of who I am. And I'm still figuring out who I am."

Silence followed for long enough that Meredith wondered if she'd been an idiot to say everything she had. Serenity had been raw and honest with her, and she'd wanted to be the same in return. Maybe they didn't like each other. Maybe they never would. But Meredith couldn't stand seeing her look so broken.

"Maybe I need to figure out who I am, somewhere no one knows me." Serenity sounded more like she was talking to herself than to Meredith. Louder, she said, "You've never been anything but honest with me, so I'll try to return that. You may think he married you to protect you. It might even be true. But he wouldn't have cared enough to do that for another woman, and the only people in this house confused about what that means are you and him. Get a divorce, if it will make you both happy. But in every way that functionally matters, you'll still be the wife of the King enclave's next protector."

Meredith's heart squeezed. She wanted that to be true. But the truth was, she'd hardly seen Jensen since the protectors from the other enclaves had arrived. He sat next to her during the official meetings. Outside of official meetings…well, he had responsibilities. He had Natalie to take care of, he had his life to put back together. She understood it, which was why she'd told him, after that first night he hadn't come up to her room when he'd said he would, that she didn't expect him to.

She figured he needed time and space to regroup and process, so she'd given it to him before he could feel like she was an obligation. She just hadn't expected him to take quite so *much* space. He'd hardly spoken to her in the last four days. He wasn't rude or hostile, he was just…distant.

He'd never promised her anything. She hadn't promised *him* anything. And this, right here, was exactly why. Because some part of her had guessed that at the end of all of this he'd come to his senses and realize she'd been a crutch. Someone to lean on when he hadn't had anyone else, and now that he had his friends and family back, he didn't need her anymore.

She wouldn't blame him, if it were true. It would hurt, but she wouldn't blame him. Either way, she deserved to hear it from his lips. They needed to talk, but she wasn't going to force the issue until Aspect and Shifter had reached an official agreement one way or the other.

Across from her, Serenity nodded to herself, as if she'd come to a decision. She stood. "Could you drop the silencing spell?"

Wary, Meredith did.

Serenity smiled at her, the first genuine one Meredith thought she'd given her. "Your home has the loveliest gardens, Meredith." The compliment—and her support—given, she rose and disappeared inside the house.

Something that felt suspiciously like warm fuzzy feelings sprouted in Meredith's chest. It annoyed her. Her heart was supposed to be a cold, dead thing, and the chest it resided in was therefore supposed to be a barren landscape in which warm fuzzies were incapable of flourishing.

She looked at the time. Two minutes left.

CHAPTER

THIRTY-FIVE

Meredith took her place in the dining room next to Jensen. He nodded at her. She nodded back. Great. Their non-relationship had deteriorated to the level of *people who nodded at each other*.

Three hours later her back was stiff, her butt was going numb, and her ears hurt from listening to people argue. So. Many. People.

Twenty-four didn't sound like a large number, but once you'd listened to them all bicker until they were blue in the face you realized it was about twenty-three more people than you wanted to be around.

The numbers were split evenly, twelve on each side. The Shifters had their six enclave protectors, each of whom had brought their seconds, and Siren had brought her advisory committee. Meredith was on it, along with Jace, Random, and Valkyrie. The remaining members she'd chosen might not make sense to most people at first glance. They weren't politicians or people who'd ever been involved in Council business before. But they were people who were deeply rooted in the Aspect community.

Hank Trembley and Betty Lou Walker-Trembley both owned stores in Seclusion's downtown area and had seen three generations of Aspect Society come and go. Shane and Derek Anders were well-known by their extensive volunteer work, and Derek was a therapist who now worked at The Refuge. Siren had also included two of the Aspect Academy teachers, one of whom was Mr. Struthers, to whom Meredith had given the civil-war-could-be-avoided-by-facials response.

Charles Jackson finished out the group. As an Oracle, Charles wasn't technically Aspect Society, but when Siren had submitted her list of committee candidates for approval, he'd passed the affirmation vote. He was also here by video chat, because the simplest randomly-asked question had the potential to throw Oracles out of the here-and-now. Questions tossed around through a technological interface had a lessened affect.

While Random's thorough examination of the laws that had propelled Siren to interim Head Councilor had proved beyond all doubt that she had the authority to make this decision, having the full approval of the advisory committee would be invaluable toward getting Aspecters at large to accept and respect it.

At least, it *would* do that, if a decision could ever be reached. At the opposite end of the table from Meredith, the Silver enclave's protector, Kait, wrapped up a five-minute speech that used a lot of ten dollar words and essentially boiled down to, *I'm pissy I've been asked to consider this alliance.*

Meredith geared up for another round of reassurances from the Aspect side when Clyde Bell's irritated voice said, "Are we boring you, Ms. Townsend?"

He was present as the second to the Temple enclave's protector, and he was decidedly not Team Meredith. She'd been doodling random geometric shapes in her notebook, and apparently he couldn't miss the opportunity to point it out to the rest of the room. She knew the right pretty words to say, the ones designed to make her appear chastened and contrite, that would satisfy the room and do it smoothly enough that no one would even remember the incident later.

She should probably use them. But the glazed look on faces around the room told her everyone was as fed up with the pointless back-and-forth as she was. They'd been in here for four days, eight hours a day, and they had nothing to show for it. At the rate things were going, they wouldn't have anything to show for today, either.

"You aren't boring me, you're wasting my time." Clyde's face flushed red with outrage, and she suddenly had the undivided attention of every single person present. "Everyone in here is wasting everyone else's time. We have spent the last four days arguing the minutiae of theoretical infractions and what-if this and what-if that.

"Our purpose in being here is not actually that complicated. We want an agreement that Aspect Society has no quarrel with Shifter Society and vice-versa. That we both want to peacefully coexist without the need for either society to hide from or live in fear of the other."

Clyde sneered. "Spoken like a naive, foolish girl."

Spoken like a bitter old man. She bit back the retort because right now, he was the one who looked like an asshole. She might not care about burning the bridge that was Clyde Bell—he was never going to like her, and his enclave's protector, Carsten Temple, was the one who would be voting in this matter—but alienating the enclave protectors by saying something petty would be foolish.

Rebekah shot Clyde a sharp look. "I'd like to hear what she has to say."

He gave a derisive laugh. "I have no intention of listening to some chit who's only here because she crawled into your grandson's bed."

Siren's irritation crackled across the room with tangible force.

"Meredith is here because she is a member of my advisory committee. Her thoughts hold the same weight as anyone else's, and have nothing to do with whose bed she is in, a matter which is none of your concern and is not open for public discussion. If you can't keep a professional, civil tongue in your mouth I will adjourn this session until Carsten has replaced you with someone who can."

Clyde's face shaded from red to purple. He opened his mouth but Carsten cut him off. "Take a five minute walk and calm down. If you can't be neutral by the end of it, send Elizabeth here in your stead."

Clyde shoved his chair back and stalked out. Carsten nodded at Meredith. "You have the Temple enclave's sincerest apologies. I, too, would be interested in hearing what you have to say once my second has returned or been replaced."

Three minutes later Elizabeth walked in and took the seat next to Carsten. "I heard a new idea was up for discussion?" she said brightly.

All eyes turned to Meredith. Well, she had their attention. "So far, we've been approaching this as if an entirely new set of laws needs to be made. But we aren't here to discuss a merger of our societies. We aren't even here to discuss a peace treaty in the typical sense, because we are not at war. Neither of us has attempted to take possession of the other's territory or resources, and neither is attempting to do so now.

"At the root, *all* we are here to do is establish a formal recognition of the fact that we all wish to peacefully coexist." She looked at the Shifter half of the room. "You have concerns. Given what you've dealt with in the past, and the recent capture of several of your people, those concerns are more than understandable. Those in our community involved in these crimes have been stripped of their Aspect." It was the first time in over a century that that particular punishment had been enacted. "We have also agreed to reparations that will be made regardless of what outcome these discussions have.

"So the way I see it, there are two simple options. One, we have closed borders. Aspecters do not enter Shifter territory, and Shifters do not enter Aspect territory. Failure to observe this is grounds for retaliation. Two, we have open borders. Our people are free to intermingle, with the expectation that they are respectful of the territory they are in."

Silence reigned. The protector of the Vayne enclave, a tall, lean woman with muscle definition to rival Valkyrie's, broke it. "I appreciate your intentions," Moira Vayne said. The hum of Meredith's Aspect told her she even meant it. "But you make a complex thing sound simple. We are two very different peoples. Our societies are structured on different laws and mores."

As if no two different societies had ever managed to have a working relationship before. "When we interact in the Null world, outside our territories, do we not manage to abide by their laws and mores?"

"Yes. But we are all also citizens of this country. We are already also bound by those laws."

"And none of us have ever visited another country, of which we are not citizens, and managed to behave accordingly?"

"One *is* required to have a passport to enter a foreign country."

"Then let's get passports."

"And how far do you propose we allow this countries analogy to run?" Kait Silver asked. "Are we to consider allowing permanent residence? Dual citizenship?"

Elizabeth, her voice amused, said, "What horrifies you more? An Aspecter wanting to live in your territory, or the opposite? Or," she continued before Kait could respond, "is your true fear that?" She pointed at Meredith and Jensen.

"If you have something to say, spit it out."

"I'm saying that your bigotry drove my parents from the Silver enclave to Temple. If you can't even handle a white man marrying a Black woman with the objectivity a leader should have, how are we to expect you to have *any* objectivity when it comes to the possibility of a Shifter marrying an Aspecter?"

"Of course. Cry racial discrimination at the first available opportunity. Am I supposed to trip all over myself to make amends for your perceived slight?"

Elizabeth arched an eyebrow. It was a good arched eyebrow, conveying the perfect amount of bored disdain. Someone had taught her well. "This isn't about me."

"No, it isn't. But since you brought it up, let's consider the issue marriage poses. What happens when we have half-breed children littering the landscape? Is an Aspecter to understand what a Shifter child needs? Is a Shifter parent to nurture the foul development of Aspect in their child?"

"Enough." Darren Archer's deep voice said he'd had it. "People raise children from two different backgrounds all the time. How you feel about it is your personal issue. Shifters don't have laws about who you can and can't marry. Do Aspecters?"

"No," Siren answered.

"Good. Then let's not get bogged back down in the squabbles Ms. Townsend is valiantly trying to drag us out of. I propose a two-hour recess. The Shifters will put together a set of rules we feel are necessary to maintain successful open borders, and Aspect will do the same. We meet and come to an agreement on a combined set. Then we vote to accept it or go with closed borders. Objections?"

Kait opened her mouth, but the combined displeasure emanating at her from the rest of the room caused her to shut it.

"Excellent." Darren swiped up his notepad—which looked suspiciously as if it might also contain doodles. "Two hours."

THE VOTE FOR ALLIANCE PASSED, with Kait as the single holdout. Fortunately, Shifter society only required a majority vote to pass new measures. They agreed to establish outposts in each Shifter or Aspect controlled territory. Anyone visiting was required to check in at the outpost to announce their presence, and be briefed on local laws. The outposts would also serve as short-term lodging to any visitors who might feel more comfortable there than seeking accommodations elsewhere, and would be staffed with a Liaison from the territory in which the outpost resided.

Any confrontation between Aspecters and Shifters that required legal arbitration or punishment would be overseen by a joint committee between the two societies. Children born to an Aspect/Shifter union would indeed have "dual citizenship." There were a handful of other agreed-upon rules, but those were the important ones as far as Meredith was concerned.

She had offered her house as the Seclusion outpost. It was something useful to do with a property she didn't want, and she'd already bought enough supplies for the Shifters currently staying in it now that it was practically set up as a hotel already. It would need staffing, and someone to serve as the Aspect Liaison, but those were decisions for Siren to make.

They'd gotten the best outcome they could have hoped for. So why didn't she feel relieved?

Because Jensen disappeared as soon as the ink was dry.

The enclave protectors were already packing up to take their people back home. Was Jensen doing the same? Was he even planning on saying goodbye, or was she just going to wake up to an empty house tomorrow?

I would have asked you to be mine. Sure he would have. Was he here right now, asking her?

You know what? Screw it. He didn't get to just disappear on her. If nothing else, he still owed her a damn divorce.

Unfortunately, her plan to corner him and demand he speak actual words to her was thwarted when Siren and Val stepped into her path. She tried her diplomatic smile. "I would love to talk, but at the moment—"

"Porch," Valkyrie ordered. "Now."

Ugh. That was Valkyrie's I-will-pick-you-up-and-carry-you-if-I-have-to voice. Since being picked up and hauled somewhere by her best friend was undignified, she gave the stairs to the Shifter floor a longing look before walking outside.

CHAPTER

THIRTY-SIX

Meredith glared at the porch's concrete foundation.

"Has the porch offended you in some way?" Val asked.

"I think it's cursed. Way too many important conversations happen on this porch." She stabbed a finger at Valkyrie. "It's your fault." Valkyrie had come to her months ago needing date-wear advice. Somehow they'd both ended up talking about their parents, and their friendship had had its first tentative rekindling. "You started the trend of important conversations on this porch and now it won't stop."

Siren patted her hand. She was looking much better these days. She was indeed carrying a Death child, and given the antithesis between Life and Death, just needed someone else to feed the kid non-Life Aspect on a daily basis. Aunt Ella was over the moon.

Now that she was feeling better, Meredith felt fine about snapping at her over the hand-patting. "If you say, *There there, it will all be fine,* I'll wait until you're no longer pregnant and punch you."

Valkyrie leaned into Siren and faux-whispered. "No cause for concern. She can't throw a punch for shit."

Meredith threw her hands up and tossed out the silencing spell that was now second nature to her. "Is there something I can help the two of you with? In case you haven't noticed, I have a house full of Shifters who require an alarming amount of catering-to, and a man to divorce."

Siren and Valkyrie shared a look. "How are you and Jensen?" Siren asked casually.

Meredith narrowed her eyes. "That depends. Why do you ask?"

"I want to offer you the Seclusion Liaison position."

"Come again?"

"You donated the house to the Shifter/Aspect relations cause. I was hoping you might come with it."

Meredith chewed on it even as her pulse beat with something that felt suspiciously like excitement. "Why me?" If Siren was only offering it because Meredith was married to a Shifter...

"You're adept at handling social situations. You know what the right thing to say in most situations is, and you know when and how to say it. We'll flush out the full details of the position later, but the primary purpose is to give any Shifters visiting this outpost an initial contact with an Aspecter, someone who can bridge any law variations between us, and prove that not all Aspecters are psychopaths.

"The last week has already proved you're more than capable of doing the job. You've been asked some exceptionally bizarre shit and handled it with a level head. You're calm, able to solve problems as they arise without needing someone to hold your hand, and all of the Shifters who aren't assholes like you. You haven't punched any of the ones who *are* assholes, which is something I've had to restrain Val from doing an average of five times a day."

Gainful employment had never actually sounded interesting before. "You know they only like me because they think Jensen actually married me, right? All of this 'problem solving' I've been doing is because they think I'm going to be their next Mrs. Protector, and they want to know I won't be a tyrant."

"They don't *only* like you because of Jensen. If anything, having an outsider thrown into an almost-leadership role should make them like you less. I've been listening all week. Every problem and complaint they've thrown at you? It's all the kind of bullshit stuff meant to make you lose your cool and explode so everyone can point and say, 'Oh my god, a hysterical woman.' You haven't exploded. I'd understand if you didn't want the job—"

"I do," Meredith said quickly. "I just...want to make sure you're not offering it to me because I'm your friend."

"I'm offering it to you because I think you're the best person for the job."

Meredith blew out a breath. She could say no. Maybe she *should* say no. What experience did she have with jobs anyway? Her Truthfinding work for the Council hadn't exactly been nine-to-five. More like consulting on an as-needed basis if she felt like it.

"Hours? Benefits? Do I get vacation time?"

"We'll work out hours. Standard Council benefits package. Is that a yes?"

"It's a probably yes. I want to talk to Jensen and make sure he doesn't think it'll be an issue when our divorce goes public. There's no point in me taking it if all of the Shifters who might come here will hate me because I dumped their werewolf prince.

"Speaking of, I'm going to go find my husband before he manages to skate out of here without divorcing me first. I'll let you know on the job by tomorrow."

"Okay," Siren said. She hesitated, then added, "Listen, about Jensen—if it matters at all, we like him. All of us like him."

Meredith sighed. "Yeah, I like him too."

"So are you going to keep him?" Valkyrie asked. "After you divorce him, I mean."

Oh, what the hell. Visualize what you want and all that, right? "If he'll have me? Yes, I'm going to keep him."

∽

Jensen had been staying in the room next to Natalie's. Meredith found it empty so she tried Hel's room next, then Dom's. She didn't actually expect to find him in Serenity's room, but she tried it too. Serenity's clothes were gone, the bed made, and a folded note lay on the bedspread with Meredith's name on the front.

Starting over somewhere new. Tell Hel I'm sorry I didn't say good-bye. I still don't like you. But I wish you nothing but the best.

"You too," she whispered. She tucked the note into her pocket and pulled out her phone. Jensen still hadn't answered her texts, and he didn't pick up when she called. After a moment's hesitation, she knocked on Natalie's door.

"Who is it?" a small voice called.

"It's Meredith."

She heard the shuffling of feet and then the door opened six inches and Natalie peered out. Shifter magic and all the food money could buy had filled out some of her body's gauntness, though not to the level Meredith would have expected. And it would take more than food to lift the haunted look from her eyes.

Meredith hadn't spoken to her much. The girl hardly left her room, and Meredith hadn't wanted to pry. She didn't know Natalie, didn't know if Jensen wanted her to know his sister. If he had, surely he would have officially introduced them.

Natalie waited for her to speak. Meredith cleared her throat. "Is your brother here?"

"He said he was going for a walk."

Which meant he could be anywhere. Now she had to decide if it was worth the risk to walk the grounds in search of him when doing so came with the potential of getting run through the testing mill by every Shifter she ran into.

"Thank you." Something stopped her from just walking away. Maybe it was the way Natalie lingered in the doorway instead of shutting it. "Do you need anything?"

"No." But as Meredith turned, Natalie blurted out, "Jensen said you've been through shit. Really bad shit. Like us, but worse."

"I don't know how to gauge what's worse, but...yes. I've 'been through shit.'"

"Could you...do you want to come in?"

Oh boy. Meredith stepped inside. Natalie closed the door behind them and started to pace, her skinny arms hugged around herself.

Meredith was so not cut out for this. Whatever Natalie needed from her right now, what if she couldn't give it? What if she said the wrong thing and she screwed the girl up even worse? And yes, Meredith had a laundry list of issues a mile long but she hadn't been through what Natalie had. Hadn't been stolen away from her home and everything she'd ever known. Shouldn't Natalie be talking to the other Shifters who'd been taken?

"The others blame me," Natalie said, so quiet Meredith almost didn't hear it. She wondered if the girl had plucked Meredith's thoughts right out of her head, but then she realized that this was what she'd wanted to talk about.

"Blame you for what?"

She stared at her feet. "For getting the others captured. For the auction. For everything."

"Natalie, look at me." Meredith waited until she did, rage simmering under her skin. Natalie was a sixteen-year-old kid. She needed support, not blame. "That is bullshit. What happened is not your fault, and anyone who says otherwise can go to hell."

Natalie's eyes widened. "They'll *hear you*."

"Good. I'll say it again." She raised her voice. "Anyone who blames you for what happened is the same sort of short-sighted asshole who wants to let rapists off because the victim 'asked for it' or 'didn't object strenuously enough.'"

Natalie shook her head. "But it *is* my fault. I knew Julian was Aspect and I didn't tell anyone."

"And did you meet him, and immediately tell him you were a Shifter, and then write him out a long list and say, 'Here, here are some other Shifters, please go kidnap them?' "

"No! It wasn't like that. I didn't tell him what I was, he already knew." She slumped down on the bed and wrapped her arms tighter around herself.

"How?"

Natalie shrugged. "I don't know. I worked at this coffee shop and he used to come in on weekdays when it super slow. He seemed nice and I was bored and we'd end up talking, you know? Then one day we were talking about cats and he asked if I had the urge to groom when I was in my snow leopard form.

"I answered without thinking. He asked it so natural, and I was so comfortable with him I forgot that he wasn't supposed to know. When I realized what I'd said I tried to take it back, but he said it was okay. He said it would be our secret. That he had a secret too. And then he did magic." her face took on a wondrous expression. "He made this ball of light. Right there in the shop, like it didn't matter."

Meredith sat on the bed next to Natalie and lifted her hand, palm up. "Like this?" She summoned a ball of witchlight.

"Yeah." Natalie looked at it longingly. "I always wanted to be able to do magic."

Meredith let the witchlight fade. "You shift into a snow leopard. That's pretty damn magical."

"It's magic. But it's not *doing* magic. It's not making things happen. Other kids were afraid of the stories everyone told about Aspecters. About them summoning storms and being able to punch through rock and stuff. But I liked them.

"When I was little, I used to think I could hear the wind talk. I wanted it to be true so bad I even thought I made a dust devil in the back yard once. But Grams told me I imagined it and I needed to stop playing make-believe before someone got the wrong idea." Natalie sighed. "She was right. I already didn't fit in. I wasn't a very good Shifter."

Uneasiness settled in Meredith's gut. Jace, who had a secondary affinity for air, used to say that it was like talking to the wind.

Jensen's mother had just dropped Natalie in his arms. No mention of who her father was. And she'd told him to protect her—not to take care of her, which should have been the more natural word choice.

"Anyway, I know I should have told someone but they would have killed him, and Julian was—I *thought* he was—my friend. He didn't bring the leopard stuff up again for weeks. Nothing bad happened. Then one day he asked another question about what it was like. Shifting. It seemed harmless, so I answered. It was nice, having someone to talk to about every-thing, and he listened to me."

Her face hardened. "He was just using me as an information bag. The questions started getting too detailed, almost technical. And then one day he asked if he could meet another Shifter, and he got angry when I said no. Then he tried to smooth it over, so I pretended to go along with him.

"I knew I had to get home and tell Jensen everything. But Julian must have figured out it wasn't safe to let me go. His magic pinned me and I couldn't move. It was like I was para-lyzed." She squeezed her eyes shut, a tear trickling out the corner of her eye. "I told him I'd never tell him anything else. That I'd never tell him where to find another Shifter.

"He said I didn't have to. He said he'd already found everyone he needed to by watching me." The tears were spilling down her cheeks now. "So it *is* my fault. If I'd told Jensen about him the first day, none of this would have happened."

Meredith took her shoulders gently. "Even if it were true that Jensen could have stopped this, it still wouldn't be your fault. But Natalie, Julian *already* knew you were a Shifter. He'd probably been following you for months by that point. He already knew where to find the rest of you.

"If you hadn't answered his question that first day, if you'd blown him off, he'd have known that you'd go home and tell someone. He would have taken you that first day and everything else would have happened the same way. Just a little sooner."

"Why me? How did he find me?"

"I don't know." Oh, but she had an idea.

"Jensen said he's in jail. I want to see him."

"That's up to Jensen and Rebekah. But if they okay it, you should know Julian probably won't recognize you."

"What do you mean?"

Meredith hesitated. "Did Jensen tell you what I did to Julian?"

"He said you made him tell the truth."

Meredith laughed. "He gave you the G-rated version. I'm a Truthfinder. If a Truthfinder is strong enough, they can do what's called a Truthfinder's Telling. It makes a person confront the truth about themself. Every facet of themself that they've hidden from, they can't anymore. It usually screws people up for a few days, unless they've always been very honest with themselves. I hit Julian with a Telling, but I was kind of hopped up on a magic power crown at the time."

She thought maybe she should feel guilty about that but she just…couldn't.

Natalie gave her a look full of teenage skepticism. "Really?"

"Really. It warped the Telling. Julian didn't just confront his own truth as he saw himself. He confronted it as everyone else saw it, too. As I saw him. And then he confessed it.

"There isn't a gentle way to say this. I fried his brain and I can't undo it. If Jensen says you can see him, then someone will take you. But if you're hoping for some kind of explanation from him, there isn't enough left of him to give one. I'm sorry."

Natalie shook her head. "It's fine." Two words that meant next to nothing. "Thanks for talking to me, but I think I'd like to be alone for a bit."

"Okay. If you need anything, you can come to me."

Her hand was on the doorknob when Natalie blurted out, "Can I stay here? In Seclusion, with you?"

Meredith's heart constricted.

"Please? I don't wanna go back home. I already didn't belong there and now everyone hates me. Don't you need people to stay here? Shifters? That's the point of this outpost? To show everyone we don't have to be afraid of each other? And if I can do that, it should mean something, right?"

"Natalie…it isn't my choice to make. I'm not your guardian."

"But Jensen is, and you're his wife. Under Shifter law that makes me as much yours as his. Please let me stay, I can't go back there."

Natalie burst into sobs, the full-on, wrecking ball kind. Meredith crossed the room and wrapped her in a hug, her heart breaking. Probably the adult thing to do was to tell her that running away from her problems wouldn't make them disappear, and she should go back home and face them.

But honestly, Meredith thought it was shit advice. Going back into a toxic environment where she didn't fit in might prove Natalie was tough enough to endure it, but it wouldn't make her happy.

Meredith squeezed her eyes shut. Jensen was going to kill her. "I can't make you any promises. But if Jensen agrees, of course you can stay."

THIRTY-SEVEN

J ensen stood down the hall from Natalie's room, listening to his sister cry and beg Meredith to let her stay. Every time he'd tried to get Natalie to open up about anything, she'd shut him down. Meredith met her for two seconds and his sister dumped all of her fears and worries in the woman's lap. And Meredith had taken it and told her all the things Jensen had, except her words seemed to get through where his hadn't.

He wished Nat hadn't asked Meredith to let her stay. He wished he'd known just how isolated she'd felt. She'd always been a quiet kid, and getting her to talk was like pulling teeth. Unless, apparently, you were Meredith, and then she opened right up.

Had he gone wrong somewhere, that she hadn't been able to tell *him* she didn't want to go back? He'd thought she would want to go home, would want familiarity. He'd thought *he* was the selfish one for wanting to stay. And here she was, begging Meredith to be her knight in shining armor and knock him down.

He heard Meredith's answer and winced. She wouldn't

realize Nat was going to take that as *Meredith and Jensen are going to live happily ever after and I just have to convince them to do it here.*

A few minutes later the door opened. Meredith stepped out, the sadness on her face shifting to cold fury in a blink. She didn't see him, turning away and striding to his grandmother's room. She knocked on it like she'd bust the door down if Rebekah didn't let her in.

The door opened, Meredith disappeared, and all sound from within shut off. She was pissed and wanted to talk to his grandmother, and she didn't want anyone to hear.

Rebekah King looked resigned, and that pissed Meredith off even more.

"You heard everything?"

Rebekah nodded.

"I need you to answer something for me. If you lie to me, I will know. She said she thought she made a dust devil once. Did she?"

Rebekah's eyes closed briefly. "Yes."

Meredith had guessed. But part of her had thought she was making connections where there weren't any. "Her father was an Aspecter."

"Yes." Rebekah sighed and sat down on the bed. "My Amelia —Jensen and Natalie's mother—she was always a wild thing. Never any use trying to hold onto her. She had Jensen when she was nineteen. Dumped him with me he was five and I let her do it because his daddy was a drunk. A few years later the man ended up setting the house on fire in a drunken stupor. Amelia made it out. Jensen's father didn't.

"She came home then, wanting Jensen back and I told her no. She got mad and took off and I didn't see her again. Not until she came back with Natalie."

Meredith frowned. "Jensen said she brought Natalie to him. That you were gone."

Rebekah laughed. "Oh, she brought her to him alright. Brought her to him because I told her no. She came to me with a sob story about what Natalie's father was. Got all teary-eyed and told me how he'd freaked out when she told him she was pregnant and then she went on the run, and how I needed to take Nat because I was the protector, and I could keep her safe.

"Damn fool didn't realize I can't make decisions that go against the good of the enclave. So I told her no, and then I didn't go home. Took her a week to recognize her second option. So I stayed away on some bullshit business until my neighbor called to tell me that Amelia had dumped a baby with Jensen.

"And then I stayed away for a month so that when I came back, she'd already be his by law." Rebekah's face softened. "He's a good kid. I knew he'd do it. Lord knows making him a parent at eighteen wasn't fair. But as long as she was his and not mine then she was a part of the enclave and protecting her was my duty."

Meredith tried to understand, but it was hard. "You made her think she was crazy. Do you know what it does to us to try to deny what we are? To not use Aspect?" Of course she'd felt like she never belonged. She hadn't understood who she was. "What would it be like if you told a Shifter not to shift? It's like only being half of what you are."

"Better being half of what she is than being dead," Rebekah snapped. "You heard Kait going on about half-breed children. What do you think would have happened to Natalie if she started making dust devils and windstorms every time she got in a temper?"

"That's why you wanted this alliance so bad. That's why you jumped on the first flight down here and pretended to like me."

Rebekah nodded. "I wanted her to be safe. Legally safe. To not have to hide anymore. And now she doesn't." A small smile tilted up the corner of Rebekah's mouth. "And for the record, I do actually like you."

Truth could be annoying sometimes. "Did Jensen know? About Natalie?"

Rebekah shook her head. "Amelia was smart enough not to mention it after she struck out with me."

"I'm going to tell him."

"Yes, I imagine you will."

"She needs to be trained. To understand there's nothing wrong with her."

"Then do it."

Maybe I will. "Am I to take it that means you have no objection to her remaining in Seclusion?"

"None. But I'm not the person you need to be asking. I love her. I helped raise her. But legally, she's Jensen's."

Then I'll go talk to him.

She didn't have to look far to find him. He was leaned back against the wall opposite the door when she walked out, his arms crossed and a question on his face.

"Let's go for a drive," she said.

Jensen watched the miles pass by out the passenger window. He'd spoken once, but Meredith had just shaken her head at him and said, "Not yet."

So he waited. He figured out where she was going once she drove into Fayetteville, so he wasn't surprised when she pulled into the hotel he'd stayed at when he'd been looking for Nat. He knew she'd wanted to be away from the house to discuss whatever she and Rebekah had talked about, but he couldn't help but wonder if she'd brought him back here, where they'd had their beginning, to end things.

He hadn't known where they stood the past few days. That first night he'd had Natalie back, he'd been so exhausted he'd passed out on her floor and never made it up to Meredith's room. The next day, Meredith had gone on about how she understood he had responsibilities, and must want to spend time with his family, and how he didn't need to worry about her. She'd made the room up next to Natalie's for him if he wanted.

She'd said it all without ever looking him in the eye, and he'd gotten the message just fine. She didn't want him in her bed, and she wanted space. So he'd given it to her. With Natalie back, she must have realized he came with more baggage than she'd anticipated. Seeing where things went was all fun and games until you realized that where things were going involved high levels of political bullshit and your potential boyfriend's traumatized teenage ward.

He followed Meredith as she bypassed the front desk, leading them straight to room 413. The same room that had been his home the month he'd spent here looking for Natalie. Meredith pulled a keycard from her purse.

"I think they disable those when you don't turn them in at checkout," he pointed out.

She slid the card in. The door light turned green and the locking mechanism clicked open. She gave him a half smile. "I rented it a week or so after you disappeared. It was a good place to think."

She'd rented it, as in, she'd had it since he disappeared? He followed her inside. She dropped her purse and keys on the little table just inside the door, like she always had when she'd come back with him. Little touches of her were everywhere. Her cosmetics on the bathroom vanity. Her robe on the door hanger. A stack of books by the bed. One of those scent-warmer things that made the room smell like baked apple pie.

How often had she come here?

She strode to the far end of the room and twitched the window curtains closed, no doubt remembering Julian's comment about watching the two of them. "I don't know how to say this, so I'll just say it."

Here it comes. For the love of God, just don't say, It's not you, it's me.

"Natalie's only half Shifter. The other half is Aspect." She let the window curtain fall back and looked at him. "She has wind Aspect."

Jensen hadn't expected that. He replayed Natalie and Meredith's conversation, trying to figure out where she'd gotten the idea. "If this is because of what Nat said about making a dust devil in the yard, she didn't actually do that."

"She did. Your grandmother confirmed it."

That…couldn't be right.

"Your mother—she brought Natalie to your grandmother first. She told her that Natalie's father was an Aspecter. She thought Rebekah could protect Natalie."

He shook his head. "Rebekah's the last person she would have gone to if the father was an Aspecter."

"The last person she *should* have gone to. Which is why Rebekah told her no. And waited for her to go to you."

Jensen's entire world tilted sideways and slid off its axis. He'd been scared out of his mind when his mother dropped Natalie with him. He'd been eighteen, he hadn't had a clue what to do with a baby. So he'd taken Natalie to his neighbor, Eileen, because she had a baby and he figured she could tell him what to do with one.

Eileen had offered to keep Natalie until Grams came home. He still didn't know why he hadn't taken her up on it. Except that his mother had given her to *him*, had told *him* to take care of her, and Grams had called that morning to tell him she'd be gone for the next month and unreachable by phone. If he'd let Eileen take Natalie, then by the time Grams got home, Eileen would have had legal guardianship rights, if she wanted them.

He knew what it was like to be dropped off by their mother like an unwanted package. He'd looked into Natalie's eyes and known he didn't want to explain to her, when she was old enough, how their mother had dumped her on him and he'd turned around and dumped her on someone else.

So he'd kept her. And now he knew Grams had orchestrated all of it.

"Fuck." He dropped down on the bed and ran his hand over his face. "Fuck."

He understood why. He even understood why she hadn't told him Natalie's father was Aspect. Because if it had come to light before this alliance had been signed, and the Shifters learned he'd known about it…that wouldn't have been pretty.

Meredith sat down next to him.

"I yelled at her. Natalie," he whispered hoarsely. "I was twenty-three and working twelve hour days in construction, so Grams watched her during the day. I came to pick her up and Grams came out all pissed off. Told me Natalie was too old to be making shit like wind powers up, and if I couldn't get her to stop maybe I shouldn't have her.

"I was stressed out. If I didn't have Natalie, who would? Grams had already said she wouldn't do it. Then I felt guilty because part of me wanted it to happen. I felt like I was in over my head and having the decision made for me might be a relief.

"So when Nat started telling me how she really had made the wind move I went off on her. I told her she needed to grow up. She cried. It's not like I hadn't seen her cry before. But it was the first time she'd done it because I was a complete asshole to her. She just quietly told me it really had happened and then went to her room. She never talked about it again."

"Your grandmother's very smart," Meredith said. "She handled the situation in a way guaranteed to get you to act exactly like you did. So you *would* hurt Natalie, so she wouldn't bring it up again. So she wouldn't do it again. It wasn't your fault."

He'd like to believe that. "If I'd listened to her, if she'd felt like she could talk to me, maybe none of this would have happened."

"If Rebekah had been honest with either of you, maybe this wouldn't have happened. How do you think Julian found her in the first place?"

"I have no idea."

"Well, I do. Her father's an Aspecter. He must have talked about his affair with a Shifter at some point, and that story got back to Julian, who tracked him down. Nat's father knew your mother was pregnant when she left him. So Julian realized all he had to do to find a Shifter, was find the daughter.

"Aspecters can track a person by blood if that person doesn't know how to Shield against it. And Julian had Natalie's father's to Track her by. You couldn't have stopped this."

Meredith wanted to wrap her arms around Jensen. To kiss away the pain on his face until he stopped blaming himself for things that were out of his control. But she didn't know if he would want her to.

"She'll need to be trained," she made herself say. "She must have found subconscious outlets for her Aspect, or it would have built up and exploded out of her in spectacular fashion. But she deserves to know that half of herself. To be able to control it."

"I'll take care of it." He gathered himself. She watched him do it, watched him pack up the hurt and the grief and the doubt and shove it down so he could keep going. Because that's what you did when people were counting on you and you felt like you didn't have anyone to help you through it. He was used to doing everything on his own.

He ran his hand over the tattoo on his wrist. "Guess we have a marriage to dissolve," he said abruptly.

"Yeah." She had more to say, but it could wait until this was done. She held out her hand and he took it. "What do we do?"

But even as she asked she felt the tug of magic, and watched as the tattoos faded.

"We both agreed," he said, "so it's done."

So simple. *It's done.* Did he mean the marriage, or them?

She ran her hand over the bare expanse of her skin. "I have something I need to say."

"It's okay." His face took on a carefully neutral expression. "You don't have to explain. I get it."

"You get what, exactly?"

"That this is more than you bargained for. I come with a teenager. She's got two years until she can live on her own, and I'm not going to kick her to the curb the second she turns eighteen. And if Rebekah has her way, I'll be running the enclave some day. You've gotten an up front taste of what being in the middle of our politics is like.

"It's a lot to put on a person. We barely know each other. You don't have to explain to me how it was fun while it lasted, but it was the emotion of the moment or whatever, and how it's not me, it's you. It's me. It's fine."

She couldn't decide whether to smile, because she was pretty sure he wanted her to stay, or throttle him for having already decided she was leaving. She kept her tone light. "How nice of you to lay my words out for me so I don't even have to say them."

He looked at her sharply. "I was trying to spare us both the guilt and regret and drama. Haven't we been through enough in the last week without it?"

"I see. And by your logic, am I supposed to thank you for putting it all so succinctly and drive you back home in silence, where we will amicably part without any *drama*?"

"What do you want? Do you want to yell at me?" He stood, facing her and opening his arms wide in invitation. "Fine. If it's what you need, get it out. What did you want to say?"

"I love you."

His hands dropped to his sides. "Come again?"

"I love you. *That's* what I was going to say before your little speech. I was then going to follow it with how I know Natalie is very important to you, and I don't have any qualifications to recommend me as a parental figure, but she is going to need someone with Aspect to look to for advice and I was hoping you might trust me enough for that person to be me.

"If you were on board with what I was saying by that point, I was going to ask to discuss living arrangements. However, since apparently what I want is to break up with you without any drama, I suppose we can just go get that silent car ride started."

Jensen looked stunned. She stood and turned for the door. She'd taken five steps toward it when she started to worry he was actually going to let her walk through it. Maybe she had read the room wrong. Maybe what he did want was a drama-less end to their non-relationship. Maybe—

His arms wrapped around her waist and hauled her back, flush against him. "Pretty sure I heard somewhere that if you love someone, you're not supposed to just walk away without a fight."

Her pulse raced. "Pretty sure I heard somewhere that if you love someone, you're not supposed to let them go without a fight." She regretted the words as soon as she said them. Had she *had* to push for the sentiment to be returned? He'd come after her. Wasn't that enough?

"Do you want me to tell you I love you, darlin'?" he whispered. "Because I do." He nipped gently at the sensitive skin just below her ear. "I love you, Meredith. We have a lot to learn about each other. I can't promise you that everything will work out like a fairy tale and it will be perfect between us just because we want it to be.

"But I can promise you that I'll try. I need to know if that's good enough."

"It's good enough." It was more than good enough. She tilted her head back and kissed him. "I'm not perfect either. I have a lot of issues. You're probably going to regret this in a month."

"Doubtful." He kissed her again, his hands grazing over her stomach.

Her body wanted to give itself over to his mouth and his hands while her brain was still clinging desperately to logistics. "I'm going to accept the Aspect Liaison position. I have to stay in Seclusion and your enclave is—I don't even know where your enclave is."

"Pennsylvania." His lips trailed down her neck, hands slipping under her shirt.

With the way he drawled *darlin'* all the time, she'd been expecting Texas. "Pennsylvania isn't exactly weekend driving distance."

"We'll figure it out."

He stopped kissing and spun her around to face him. "There's just one more thing I need to be clear on. I'm never having kids. I love Natalie. I don't regret raising her, and if I could make the choice over knowing what I know now, I would make the same one. I'm not bitter about what I've given up for her. But I don't want to do it again. I *won't* do it again."

Relief hit her square in the chest. Even knowing he'd broken things off with Serenity because she wanted marriage and children and he didn't, after seeing him with Natalie there'd been a part of her that feared he might change his mind and decide he wanted one of his own after all.

"Jensen, I have no interest in having children. It might be more accurate to say I live in mortal fear of ever having children. It's never been something I wanted. You don't have to worry about me changing my mind on that."

"Good. Are we done talking?"

"You're the one doing most of the talking."

He just waited. She blew out a breath. "Yes, we're done talking. Are you happy now?"

"Ecstatic."

His hands slid down her back, over her ass and down to grip the backs of her thighs. He hauled her up and tumbled them both onto the bed.

They didn't do much talking after that.

EPILOGUE

One Year Later

"Become the Aspect Liaison, I said to myself, it will give your life purpose, I said to myself." Meredith typed the final word in her report, slumped back in her desk chair, and declared the work day officially over.

"Rough day, darlin'?" The low drawl made her heart skip a beat. Jensen stood in her office doorway in faded jeans and dusty boots, his shirt wrinkled from travel. Nothing and no one had ever looked so good.

A strangled noise escaped her throat. *Back. He was back.* She ran across the room and launched herself into his arms. He caught her and kissed her with the kind of enthusiasm that would have had her dragging him inside and locking the door were it not for the fact that this was now her place of employment instead of her home, and the Shifters currently in residence at the outpost would know exactly what she and Jensen were doing.

She reluctantly slid down, bare toes kissing the soft carpet. He noticed.

"Still enjoying your new feet?" he asked.

"You have no idea." After Siren's kid had popped out and the redhead had gone back to being their indestructible spitfire, Meredith had let her fix the years of damage done by her footwear. She'd wanted to have a ceremonial bonfire for every pair of heels she owned, but Siren had gotten that pained expression on her face that meant she was calculating the potential harm to the environment, so Meredith had donated them instead.

Jensen laughed. "Oh, I have some idea. Every time I call you now you're out for a run."

"Who knew running was so fun? That runner's high thing is totally real. And I have to do something to distract me from missing you when you're gone." He'd split his time in the last year between his enclave in Pennsylvania and Seclusion. Rebekah wanted to step down, but she didn't want to hand the reins off to anyone but Jensen.

He wouldn't commit to taking them because Meredith was in Seclusion. She wasn't leaving, and if he actually took over the enclave he couldn't spend half his time here. They'd both agreed he shouldn't refuse the position outright. Relations between Shifter and Aspect Societies were going fairly well, given the givens, but Rebekah handing the King Enclave to an unknown could create complications.

And though she hadn't said it, Meredith hadn't wanted Jensen to give it up for her. What if they didn't work out? What if he resented her for it later? But it had been clear within a couple months that they *were* working out. More than. Every time he left, it hurt a little bit more.

"Nothing distracts me from missing you while I'm gone," he said. "It's the only thing I do."

I wish you didn't have to go. She didn't want to make him feel guilty, so she didn't say it. "You're back early."

"I missed you." He kissed her. "And I heard there was a shindig tonight."

Meredith rolled her eyes. "There's a shindig every night for the next five days. Siren somehow managed to make an entire week out of Christmas." She looked at the clock. "And if you want to go, we should get home and change. We need to pick up Natalie, and Siren's been on a punctuality kick."

"Home" was currently a condo near downtown. She hadn't wanted to live at the outpost anymore, even though she could have, and she'd been holding off making any permanent decisions. She'd collaborated with Hel—who worked for Jensen's construction company—to draw up designs for a new house. She'd picked out everything she wanted down to the countertops and the baseboard height and then she'd just...stalled.

If she'd been by herself, she would have moved forward in a heartbeat. When Hel had pushed her to get started with the building, and asked if she didn't like something about the design, Meredith had blurted out, "What does Jensen want in a house?" Then she'd been mortified, said "Never mind," and refused to ever discuss this lapse of her tongue again.

She and Jensen hadn't talked about *the next step*. He had clothes and things in her apartment, and he stayed here when he was in town. But it was still *her* condo, not theirs. And that was the hangup with building a house. She didn't want to build her home. She wanted to build theirs.

"Everything okay?" Jensen asked. An understandable question if your girlfriend had been standing in the bathroom holding her lipstick for the last five minutes while she stared into space.

"I'm just thinking."

"About what?"

She gave him a wicked smile. "Everything I'm going to do to you later."

He plucked the lipstick out of her hand, tossed it away and

drew her in. "You know what? Shindigs are overrated. Let's stay in."

He kissed her, the warmth of his body pressing against hers, and staying in sounded very, very good. She groaned and broke away. "We can't. I promised Natalie I'd take her tonight."

Given Natalie's firm desire not to go back to the enclave, and the necessity of her learning about the Aspect half of her abilities, Jensen had agreed to let her stay in Seclusion. But since he was gone for weeks at a time, he couldn't exactly just get an apartment and leave her alone in it. And while Meredith would have let Natalie live with her if they'd asked, she didn't know anything about raising kids. Teenagers were pretty self-sufficient, she imagined, but they still scared the living daylights out of her.

When Siren suggested The Refuge, it had been the perfect solution. It was essentially a boarding school with round-the-clock supervision, kids Natalie's age, Aspect tutors, and therapists to help her deal with what she'd been through. When they'd taken her to tour it, she'd been hesitant but she'd agreed to give it a try.

The first three weeks of enrollment, Natalie had spent the weekends at Meredith's. But as time went by she acclimated more, and now she didn't come over on weekends unless she was having a tough time or Jensen was in town.

Jensen sighed against Meredith's lips. "If we're not staying in then you'd better get your ass out the door or I'm getting it out of those jeans."

She walked more slowly toward the door than necessary, and with more sway in her hips than was perhaps natural. Outside, Jensen raised his eyebrows when she unlocked the Escalade.

"Not feeling the need for speed tonight?"

"Of course I am. But this is the mom vehicle." Her condo came with two garage spaces, so she'd only kept the Escalade and her Porsche. "When I said I promised Natalie I'd take her tonight, I meant she conned me into taking her and her friends, so she could be the cool kid who gets to take her friends to a bonfire party."

He laughed. "Pushover."

He wasn't wrong. Meredith had Dying to Be the Cool Stepmom Syndrome. If Natalie mentioned wanting, needing, or even vaguely being interested in something, be it clothes, technology, or hobbies, Meredith bought it for her. There was probably a bad precedent being set somewhere in there, but Natalie hadn't suddenly turned into a materialistic bitch overnight, so maybe it was fine.

Twenty minutes later Natalie, Rath, and Ruin piled into the backseat. The two telepaths—was telepath even the right word, if they could only talk mentally to each other?—were so in tune with non-verbal communication they frequently forgot to speak out loud with each other when they weren't alone.

Add in their self-given names and the fact they both considered themselves adults after having basically parented all the kids in their group for six months, and they were just odd enough in a school full of odd children that they hadn't fit in. Natalie gravitated to them because they were quiet—at least on the outside—and she was somewhat of an oddity too.

Hearing them all at turns bickering and laughing hysterically in the backseat, Meredith couldn't help but smile. The front gates to Siren and Jace's estate was wide open. Technically, the kids probably could have walked here—The Refuge was the old Winters' estate, which was sandwiched directly between Siren and Jace's property, and Random and Valkyrie's—except no one trusted them to not "accidentally get lost" on the way over.

A pang of longing hit her as she drove down to the house. Her condo was fine, but she missed the quiet and open space of having some acreage between her and everyone else. And she was a little jealous that her friends got to live on the same road. It was like they had their own little community, one she wanted to be a part of, and so did they.

They'd both casually mentioned about a dozen times that the

lot next to Siren's had been abandoned for a slew of years, and maybe someone should track down who owned it and see if they wanted to sell. Meredith had, and the owners did.

But she'd hesitated to pull the trigger because she wanted to ask Jensen if he could see himself living there. With her. Then she'd been terrified to ask him, so she kept putting off the actual purchase. She should have just bought it—she could afford to even if she never used it—but she'd put it off for months. When she'd finally made the decision to go for it, the owner had already sold.

Apparently her interest had made someone else realize they wanted what she did. The ramshackle structure on it had been torn down, and a new home had started going up in record time. She'd stopped letting herself drive by and look at the progress once the frame went up, because it made her sad.

She parked and twisted around in the seat to address the kids. "The most important thing to remember tonight is that, no matter what wild stories Hel tells you of her childhood, setting things on fire is never the way to go." Jensen's cousin and a handful of Shifters from his enclave had moved to Seclusion soon after the agreement was signed. It had made her hopeful that maybe the whole enclave would decide to relocate. Unlikely, but a girl could have dreams. "I need you all back at the car at midnight on the dot. Have fun and behave."

Natalie rolled her eyes. "Yes, *Mom*." She jumped out with Rath and Ruin, leaving a stunned Meredith in her wake.

"You alright there, darlin'?"

"That was an affectionate *Mom*, right? Like, it was sarcastic, and I get she's not actually calling me her mom, but it was like, sarcastic-affectionate, right?"

Jensen pressed the back of his hand to her forehead.

"What are you doing?"

"Checking for a fever," he murmured. "Are you having any other symptoms? Feelings of being unfulfilled? The random sense that a clock somewhere is ticking?"

She slapped his hand away. "No. My feelings of being *unful-filled* lie in another direction."

His eyes heated. "Is that so?"

"And while that act might have a biological purpose, if you put a kid in me, I will murder you."

"That's a relief. I was worried your one year of part-time parenting might have made you realize you wanted one or five of your own." Meredith shuddered and Jensen chuckled. "You should see the look on your face."

"My year of part-time parenting has made me glad I'm not actually a parent. Let's go join everyone before they think we're fogging up the windows."

He leaned across the console and skated his fingers down her arm. "Or, we could fog up the windows and take care of those fulfillment issues." He kissed the sensitive skin of her neck and her breathing quickened.

"I'm not having sex with you in a car in my friend's drive-way." Afraid she would do just that, she opened the door and jumped out into the frigid December air.

"Tease," he called, following her.

"You started it."

He rushed her from behind, gripped her in a bear hug and spun her in a circle. "I'm going to finish it, too. Keep that in mind for the next four hours."

"Now who's the tease?" she grumbled.

Her mind was fixated on wholly inappropriate things by the time they reached the bonfire. The ground around the blazing tower had been cleared down to the dirt in that smooth, not-a-blade-of-grass-in-sight way that could only be achieved by professional landscapers or an Elemental Aspecter with an earth affinity. No random lawn fires were getting started tonight.

The backyard buzzed with people. Swarms and swarms of people. No less than three grills were going, despite the fact that reasonable people found it too cold to grill. Also, it was a Christmas week gathering, not a backyard barbecue. She blamed

Random for the grills. Apparently, he'd had the suburban dream of being a married man holding a beer in one hand and flipping things on a grill with the other. Now that he'd attained the missing wife element, he flocked to grills at all outdoor occasions.

"You two get lost on the way down?" Random called from—you guessed it—a grill.

Ha, ha.

He flipped the four burgers on the grill.

"Isn't it against the vegetarian code of ethics to cook meat even if it's not for you?"

He leaned in and whispered conspiratorially. "It's not meat." It certainly *looked* like hamburger. "Don't tell anyone, trust me, they aren't going to know the difference."

Jensen gave the scent coming off the "burgers" a skeptical sniff.

"Okay, the Shifters will probably know," Random amended. "But they taste good, you should try one."

The gears in Jensen's brain were obviously trying to figure out how to decline without giving offense when Jace walked up, his son Ethan in his arms and a frazzled expression on his face.

"Siren needs you inside," he told Random. "Something about the chili tasting bland? Apparently it's a matter of national emergency."

"Right." He handed his spatula off to Jensen. "You're in charge here, two more minutes and take them off." He headed for the house, muttering something about liquid smoke and smoked paprika. How many things with smoke in the title needed to go into a chili anyway?

Meredith gave Jace a hard appraisal. The man looked dead on his feet, and she wasn't the only one who noticed. The Queen of Death marched their way, steely determination in her eyes.

"Hand over my grandchild before you fall asleep on your feet." Ella considered Random and Jace the sons of her heart, if not her biological sons, and she was determined that Ethan would grow up calling her Grandma.

Jace handed his son to her with a look of gratitude followed by immediate anxiety. "Make sure to—"

"I'll return him in the same condition, never you worry."

Jace watched her tote his son off with bloodshot eyes.

"Hanging in there?" Jensen asked.

"Babies are exhausting. I love him and he is wonderful, and I would have him again, but he is exhausting."

"I remember." Jensen's tone, while it held a certain level of fondness, also held a strong degree of *glad that's over*.

"Where's yours at?" Jace asked.

Jensen looked at Meredith, like she would magically know. "Oh," she said innocently, "I think Valkyrie's showing the kids how to throw knives."

"What?" Jensen rapidly scanned the area for flying daggers.

"Relax, joking." Valkyrie had done Introduction to Knife Throwing last week. Rath and Ruin were obsessed and in it for the long haul, but since Natalie could grow claws at will, she'd gotten bored once the initial thrill wore off.

Where *were* the kids, anyway? Oh—there, roasting marshmallows on the bonfire. It had been difficult to see them through the throngs of people.

"Did Siren invite everyone in Seclusion?"

Jace winced. "You remember how you had to leave last month's Council session early to go to The Refuge?"

She remembered. Jensen had been in Pennsylvania, so Meredith had gotten the call that Natalie had punched another girl at school. The other girl had called her a "dirty animal." Natalie had replied that if she was going to call her that, Natalie might as well act like one. Hence the punching.

The counselor in charge of the situation had made it very clear that Meredith was supposed to explain to Natalie that violence was never the answer and force her to apologize. Meredith had responded that if violence was *never* the answer,

Elijah Winters would still be alive, and all of the children in the school would be locked up in various illegal research institutions. She'd then explained that she was taking Natalie out of school for the rest of the day, because self-care was important and they needed to go to the movies and have ice cream.

Privately, Meredith had told Nat that punching people didn't always solve your problems, and usually people who publicly belittled others had personal issues they were having difficulty dealing with. Every kid at that school had personal issues they were having difficulty dealing with. Knowing this didn't make it Natalie's responsibility to fix those problems or put up with abuse, but if she could avoid punching people unless physically threatened, her life would probably go a lot smoother.

The counselor had recommended to Siren that Meredith's right to respond to disciplinary issues regarding Natalie be revoked. Siren had suggested the counselor find a new job, or Siren would do it for her. All in all, Meredith thought it had gone pretty well. And she'd gotten out of the monthly Council session.

"Well, after you left," Jace continued, "Marietta Jordan submitted a petition to have the vacant lot off Decatur turned into a community garden. She quoted an outlandishly large number for funding and clearly expected it to be approved."

Meredith frowned. "Don't we have a community garden two blocks from that lot?"

"Yes, which is exactly what Siren told her when she denied the request. Three guesses who started the other community garden."

"Tabitha Jordan?" Marietta and her sister feuded over anything that could be feuded over.

Jace nodded. "Marietta wasn't happy and accused Siren of not wanting to help those in need."

"Siren then accused Marietta of attempting to manipulate Council funds to win a pissing contest with Tabitha—she'd gotten about an hour of sleep the night before. Anyway, Marietta took offense to that and suggested that maybe Siren had gotten too comfortable in her nice house behind her fancy gates and didn't interact with her constituents enough to be in touch with the needs of the common people.

"Siren took it personally and so, yeah, basically everyone she has ever met and more that she hasn't have been in and out all week. She broke them all up into themed categories. Tonight is security teams night."

Ah. That explained why Valkyrie was standing in a group of people, speaking actual words and not looking like she wanted to kill anyone. Really, the only time she didn't look like she wanted to kill someone was when she was discussing the finer points of *ways* to kill people.

"What's Christmas Eve night?" Meredith asked warily. Siren had informed her that the other shindig nights were optional, but she and Jensen and Natalie were expected to be here on Christmas Eve, *or else*.

"Family night." Siren's tired voice came from behind Meredith as she trudged up to the grill. "The only people allowed in my home that day are the people I give all the fucks about." Her eyes lit on Jace's empty arms. "Where is Ethan?"

"Aunt Ella took him."

Siren's shoulders relaxed as Jace pulled her into his side. "Oh good. That's good." She stumbled over the last word as a yawn split her face. "Random kicked me out of the kitchen. I almost poured sugar in the chili and he called me a menace to society."

"He was just looking for an excuse to kick you out. He thinks every kitchen belongs to him."

"Some advice?" Jensen offered. "Someone you trust is currently in possession of your kid. Go inside and sleep for fifteen minutes."

"But there are people here."

"Uh-huh. Lots and lots of people. The more people at a party, the less important the host. Random has the kitchen, we've got things handled out here. Go."

Wisely, Siren and Jace didn't require any more coaxing.

"You know," Meredith said, "you're pretty good at this whole sage advice thing."

"If you tell me it's because I'm old, you'll regret it later."

"Oh, I don't know, the last time I called you old, it worked out pretty well for me."

He let out a frustrated breath. "Remind me why we're hanging around so many people, in public, where I can't rip your clothes off?"

"Because we are being good friends?"

"Right. That."

A man approached. Meredith recognized him in that vague way that meant she'd seen him before, but she couldn't place him. "Mr. King? Could I speak with you for a moment? I was hoping to get your opinion on how the integration is going. Just a quote or two."

Ah, that's right, he was a reporter for the Aspect Times. Jensen's face took on that patient, polite expression she expected Natalie had seen often growing up. She could tell he'd hoped not to be approached in any official capacity tonight, but wouldn't risk bad publicity by saying no. "Of course." He handed Meredith the spatula. "I'm afraid you'll have to take over here, darlin'."

Take over what? Jensen had diligently flipped the burgers, but he certainly hadn't taken them off after two minutes like Random had ordered, and they'd now developed a crispy black exterior crust. She suspected Jensen had been deeply offended by the non-meat nature of them and "forgotten" the instructions.

Meredith turned the grill off, dutifully transferred the burnt patties onto a plate, and carried it inside. Between people approaching either her or Jensen, she hardly saw him for the next two hours, and the evening started to feel a lot more like work than fun.

She had just escaped around the corner of the house to steal a few minutes of solitude when she heard footsteps approaching. Rapidly.

Jensen came around the corner at a jog, grabbed her hand and dragged her with him.

"What are you doing?"

"*We.* What are *we* doing? We are escaping. Right now, before anyone else tries to talk to us."

"We can't escape, we have kids to take home in an hour."

"Nope, I pawned them off on Valkyrie and Random. We are free, and we are going." He palmed the keys from her pocket and she let him have them. She figured it was only fair he was allowed to drive *some* of the time.

He turned quiet once they pulled out of Siren's drive, and he turned in the wrong direction to head back to the condo.

"Where are we going?"

"I want to give you your Christmas present."

"It's not Christmas yet."

"I know. I don't want to wait."

"Okay." She dragged the word out into two syllables, but it failed to have the desired result of getting him to explain further. He pulled into the driveway of the plot next to Siren's house, the one Meredith should have bought. "This is private property," she pointed out.

"I'm aware."

Oh, well, as long as he was aware... "I'm not having car sex with you on someone else's property if that's what you couldn't wait for."

He gave her a roguish grin. "Don't worry. I was never dumb enough to think car sex counted as an actual Christmas present."

Then what were they doing here? He was driving right up to the house. The one she had diligently avoided driving by to look at once the framing had gone up, because she hadn't wanted to see someone else's house on this land.

Except the finished building she found herself looking at

wasn't someone else's house. It was *her* house—a little different, but it had the bones of the one she'd designed with Hel.

The exterior was the stone siding she'd picked out, a gray that was almost silver. Black shingles covered the gabled roof and the wraparound porch beneath was supported by black iron columns to match.

This house was larger than the one she'd planned, two stories instead of one, with a balcony room on the second floor that overlooked—

Her father's gardens.

She had the car door open before she could stop herself. Her feet moved on autopilot, picking up speed until she hit the cobblestone path. It was wintertime, so there wasn't actually anything planted, but the walkways, the arbors, the benches... She could see what it would become

Footsteps crunched on the ground behind her. "Do you like it?"

She turned. Jensen stood with his hands in his pockets.

"I don't understand," she said finally.

"Come here." He took her hand and let her to the front door, past the deep cushioned porch swing that was definitely the exact one she'd selected from the catalog. He pulled out a key and unlocked the door.

Why did he have a key?

Don't be dumb, Meredith, you know why people have keys to houses.

But that didn't make it make any sense. He pushed the door open. Warmth drifted out. Jensen flipped the light switch just inside the door and pulled her in. She just stared. At the light hardwood floors. The cherrywood kitchen cabinets and granite countertops. Every appliance she'd picked out with Hel, down to the coffeemaker.

She walked further in, feeling like she was caught in a spell. Jensen followed her, quiet, like a shadow.

The first floor was almost exactly like she'd designed with

Hel, the kitchen, living room, and dining area all in an open floor plan, the hallway that led back to the bright, windowed room she'd planned as the home gym on one side, and what had been the master suite in her plans on the other. The room was a little smaller now, but with its own attached bath.

Her plans hadn't included a second floor but she went up to it now, the landing letting out onto a small secondary living area. Off the right were two smaller rooms likely meant for home offices. Off the left was the master bedroom. The master bathroom was exactly as she'd planned it with soft gray tile, rain shower, and sunken tub. The bedroom had built-in bookshelves on two of the sidewalls.

On the wall next to the bed, French doors let out onto the balcony. She opened them and walked out, looking down at where the gardens would grow come spring. Jensen appeared beside her. He didn't touch her, almost as if he was afraid to.

He repeated the question he'd asked when they'd been standing on that cobblestone path. "Do you like it?"

"It's yours?"

He hesitated. "It's ours. If you want it to be. I was hoping you'd want it to be ours."

Ours. The word burrowed under her skin and warmed her.

He continued. "This trip to Pennsylvania—it was my last one. The King Enclave is splitting. A lot of people have built their lives there and they don't want to move. They'll stay with Grams and she'll find someone else to take over.

"Anyone who wants to relocate here will become part of the New King Enclave." He swallowed. "Say something."

"You aren't leaving anymore?"

"No."

"You're relocating to Seclusion? Permanently?"

"Yes."

"And you want to live in this house with me? You and Natalie?"

"If you'll have us."

She tried to speak but words wouldn't form around the lump in her throat. Tears slid down her cheeks and the damn things wouldn't stop. The more she *tried* to stop them, the worse they got.

"Shit," he said, "please don't cry. I misunderstood. Hel said you were ready to go on the plans, but you asked about me and backed out and I thought you wanted—I misunderstood." His hands cupped her face, concern in his eyes. "You don't have to want this, darlin'. It doesn't have to change anything, I—"

"I want it." There. She made words.

He tilted his head. "Now I'm the one who doesn't understand. You're crying like I broke your heart."

"I'll quit eventually." But he *had* broken her heart—broken the shell she'd built up around it wide open, and it hurt in the best way possible.

"But you…want the house?"

"The house, you, and Natalie."

"And that's the truth?"

She smiled, thinking back to how all of this had started with truth and promises. "It's the truth. I promise."

He claimed her mouth with his, kissing her until the tears stopped and she was lost in the taste and feel of him. And when the last trace of them was gone, when her body hummed with awareness of his, he picked her up and carried her into their home.

ABOUT THE AUTHOR

Michelle lives in a desolate land with a dark wizard, a unicorn, and a feline overlord. Despite certain stereotypes you may be familiar with, the dark wizard is not holding her captive, nor does the unicorn require virgin riders. The feline overlord, however, may well be evil.

You can find Michelle on her website: Michellemanus.com or join her newsletter (michellemanus.com/newsletter) for updates on new releases, and to receive exclusive bonus content.

ALSO BY MICHELLE MANUS

The Aspect Society Trilogy

Siren's Song

Valkyrie's Call

Truthfinder's Promise

The Nyx Fortuna Series

Guardian of Chaos

Guardian of Shadows

Guardian of Madness